MENNONITE
SOLDIER

MENNONITE SOLDIER

Kenneth Reed

HERALD PRESS
Scottdale, Pennsylvania
Kitchener, Ontario
1974

Library of Congress Cataloging in Publication Data

Reed, Kenneth, 1944-
   Mennonite Soldier.
   I. Title.
PZ4.R3243Me   [PS3568.E3667]   813'.5'4   74-1355
ISBN 0-8361-1734-4

While many of the events in this novel are based on actual happenings, the characters are the creation of the author.

MENNONITE SOLDIER

Copyright © 1974 by Herald Press, Scottdale, Pa. 15683
Library of Congress Catalog Card Number: 74-1355
International Standard Book Number: 0-8361-1734-4
Printed in the United States of America

Design by Alice B. Shetler

Dedicated to five beautiful women:
Aunt Sarah, Martha Y. of Scottdale,
Sumiko Y. of Asahikawa, Helen A. of Scottdale,
and my mom, the most beautiful of them all.

Though I speak with the tongues of men and of angels, and have not charity, I am become as sounding brass, or a tinkling cymbal. And though I have the gift of prophecy, and understand all mysteries, and all knowledge; and though I have all faith, so that I could remove mountains . . . and though I give my body to be burned, and have not charity, it profiteth me nothing. 1 Corinthians 13:1-3.

And he would fain have filled his belly with the husks that the swine did eat: and no man gave unto him. And when he came to himself, he said, 'How many hired servants of my father's have bread enough and to spare and I perish with hunger! Luke 15:16, 17.

I. Susquehannock, 1917

1

The story of a prodigal, that's what it is. What makes a boy go bad and leave the way of his fathers? Or can a boy go good and leave the way of his fathers? Sometimes it's hypocrisy — the fathers say many beautiful words but not one of them do they mean. Sometimes a boy is tricked away by a sweet-talking stranger, and sometimes a boy just gets tired of the way things are and wants a change.

Or is it true as some people say, that we boys are all numbered dice which the devil and God are rolling back and forth in the golden gutters of heaven, and some He wins and some He loses? One thing sure, there aren't any boys that are born prodigals, just as there aren't any apples rotten from the blossom.

Mastie Stoltzfus was perhaps a prodigal.

He'd been watching the bishop's son all evening with blood on his mind. The bishop's son was dancing with his girl.

He sat almost in the dark with one hand supporting his chin, in the other a good bottle of beer, although he had lost count which one it was. The dancers on the barn floor had just begun to swim a little before his eyes and it looked like there were twice as many as there were before, foursomes instead of twosomes. Two lanterns in the center of the barn grew into each other like Siamese twins and cast a double set of shadows on the barn walls. The boy with the strange double-sized fiddle was playing his instrument with two bows. There were two of *him* out there dancing with two of Annie. They wheeled around and he saw two boy's hands tight against the point of Annie's triangular cape where it touched her waist behind. Only there seemed to be two capes as well. He hated that boy all of a sudden.

Music, glorious music! On the barn floor between the haylofts, which were full to the eaves with hay since it was already July, fifty Mennonite boys swung fifty Mennonite girls to the old tune of "Turkey in the Straw." It was a sort of square dance. The lantern on the overhead beam jiggled and quivered a few inches with the floor of the barn and that in turn made the shadows of cobwebs and barn beams jump two or three feet. Did the dancers even hear the music though? The noise of their feet and laughter and shouting at friends whom they hadn't seen for a whole week nearly overpowered the fiddle. Truthfully, the party was illegal by church rules — at least frowned on. Next week they would all be at a singing with German or English hymnals, singing the songs of the church, but not tonight.

The music stopped and everyone stood around puffing and smiling. Several boys took off their vests and their plain black hats, too, in order to wipe the sweat from their foreheads. They immediately put their hats back on. None of them would have thought to take off his hat and hang it on a nail, because it was the custom not to, just as none of the girls would have thought to untie the neck ribbons of her large white prayer covering, pull it off, and hang it on a nail while a friend undid the pins of her bun for her and let the long hair fall to her waist. It was unthinkable.

"Hey!" one of the boys said. He looked around at the others. "Who's the wise guy?" He spoke in the German dialect, as all of them did. He brushed his shoulders. There was a rattle of corn falling on the hard black hats. "Hey!" the tall boy, the bishop's son, said again. "Who's throwing corn?" He took off his hat and shook the corn from it. "Did you see who did it?" he said to Annie.

"No," she said.

A shower of corn fell the third time and everybody standing around the tall boy was hit by some of it. They began to laugh and the girls picked the corn out of their hair while they looked up at the rafters, as if that were the direction the corn had come from.

"Was that you, Ira?" the tall boy said.

"What?" said Ira. He was standing in the line of boys around the open barn doors, the boys who were acting nonchalant and talking about the wheat crop this year, but none of them was nearly as interested in the wheat crop as he was in the line of girls standing against the haymow, the eligibles, so to speak.

"The corn. Who's throwing the corn?"

Ira didn't have time to answer. The music began again and couples enthusiastically re-formed. Ira left his place in the line and walked to the far side of the barn. There was a hay hole there in the dark, with a rung ladder leading down to the first floor. The hay hole was covered by a trapdoor, and Mastie was

13

sitting on it, shelling an ear of corn with one hand and steadying his bottle with the other.

"You're here!" Ira said, surprised. "I thought you weren't coming. Did you throw the corn?"

"Hmm?" Mastie said, without looking up.

"I said, did you throw the corn?"

"What corn?" Mastie looked up. Ira laughed, in spite of himself. There was something funny about Mastie, about the expression on his face, or maybe it was his head, which appeared a tiny fraction too big for his body.

"What are you laughing at?" Mastie said. His voice was thick.

"Nothing."

"Yes you are. You're laughing at something."

"You're drunk," Ira said. "Give me the bottle."

"Hmm?" Mastie said, holding up the bottle as if to offer its contents to Ira. Ira shook his head. He didn't drink, not anymore. Maybe it was because he took his baptismal vows and the church discipline seriously, which forbade drunkenness even if it didn't forbid drinking, but Ira took everything seriously. More likely it was because he put great stock in thinking clearly, and beer was always a little hard on thoughts and logic.

"Put it away now," Ira said severely. "You know what Pop will say." They were brothers.

"Do me a favor," Mastie said to his brother.

"What?"

"See that little bastard out there with my girl?"

"Benjie?"

"Go punch him in the mouth for me."

"You don't have to talk like that," Ira said.

"Look how he holds her," Mastie said.

"He's only touching her natural," Ira said.

"Natural? Natural nothing," Mastie said. "Look how tight he holds her." Without moving his seat he mimicked the couple on the floor and held his arm around an imaginary girl's back. "Doota doota doota doota. He likes his hand on my girl's middle, does he?"

"If you're so mad at him," Ira said, "why didn't you bring her to the dance yourself? Then he wouldn't be dancing with her. I don't see what you have to complain about."

"Hmm," Mastie said. "Mennonite girls. They're all the same."

"Tell me something," Ira said earnestly. He crouched down to talk with Mastie more easily. His face had a serious, studied look, he wore steel glasses, and he was still wearing his Mennonite coat because he hadn't gotten hot enough yet this evening to take it off. "How do you ask them?" he said. "What do you say first?"

"Hmm?" Mastie said. "Ask who?" He went on shelling corn into a pile on the trapdoor. His movements were languorous, like a man who has had too much to drink and is so relaxed he hardly wants to move.

"Girls," Ira said.

"Girls?" said Mastie, looking up with amazement.

"I was thinking about asking one of them over at the other haymow."

"Which one? Which one?" Mastie said. He got up partway and looked.

"The dark-haired one. She's talking now. There! There! She's raising her hand."

"Susanna," Mastie said, and he sat down again

15

with a *whoosh.* "She's okay."

"Susanna who?"

"Susanna Beiler."

"Susanna Beiler? Is she a sister to your Annie?"

"My Annie?" Mastie said. "Hmm? *My* Annie? I'd like to punch that smart bishop's boy — "

"How do you ask them?" Ira said again.

"You just ask 'em," Mastie said. He yawned enormously. "You just walk up to 'em and say, 'Hi, Susanna. How are ya? You want to dance with me?' "

"It's not that easy," Ira said.

"Hmm? This is dumb," Mastie said. He wasn't exactly sure what was stupid, but he felt a headache coming on.

"Every time I'm about to go up to her I lose my nerve," Ira said. "I can't."

Mastie was silent. Ira had turned around to look at the dancers because the song had ended again. "You gonna do me that favor?" Mastie said. Ira shook his head. "Come on!" He slapped Ira's back savagely.

Ira stood up. "That hurt!" he said.

At that moment the bishop's boy and Annie crossed the barn floor to Ira. From his place in the hay hole Mastie saw them coming.

"You're funny," the bishop's son said to Ira. "That was you that was throwing the corn, not?"

"Do you know where Mastie is?" Annie said.

They were standing only a few feet away from him. *I could throw him,* Mastie was thinking. *With one hand on each ankle at the same time I could throw him flat on his back.* What happened after that was questionable though. Mastie was wired together like a barn swallow, light and swift. Benjie, on the other

16

hand, had powerful arm and back muscles from a spring of tobacco work, irrigation ditches, and haying. Benjie leaned back against the barn crosspiece beside Ira.

"Oh, that's fun," Benjie said. "I'd be good for a few more, huh?" Apparently he was talking to Annie. Mastie reached up and pinched the seat of Benjie's pants.

Benjie yelled loudly, "You bugger!" He turned around and looked down at Mastie. "You bugger!" He laughed this time. "Whew, I thought a wasp got me. How are you, Mastie?" He stretched out his hand and Mastie let the bishop's son shake his hand. "She dances nice," Benjie said to Mastie, and he leaned forward on the crosspiece to see him better.

Mastie didn't look back. He was wondering about Annie, but he couldn't see her face from where he was sitting, only her long white gingham dress.

"So, how are you?" Benjie said again, biting a stalk of hay.

Mastie stood up. "What's it to you?" he said. "Why so chummy all of a sudden? It ain't enough you dance with my girl. You want me to be chummy yet?"

"Look at that hat," Benjie said, pointing at Mastie's white, President Wilson style hat. "He got a President Wilson!" Other than that, Mastie was dressed plain, but the hat was very conspicuous.

"Get away," Mastie said, motioning Benjie aside with his hand.

Benjie put one hand on Mastie's chest. "All that's left for you tonight is bed, that's what," he said, and laughed. "What's that I smell?"

Mastie passed Annie. He knew she was looking

at him but he went right on by, across the barn floor. He stopped to put his arm around a girl's shoulder and pull her against him.

"How you doing, Ruthie?" he said. The girl turned around.

"Mastie!" she said. "I didn't know you was coming." She clucked. "Look at that hat!"

"Having fun?" said Mastie. He went on. He could hear Annie coming behind him. He went out the big open barn doors and started down the barn hill, zigzagging back and forth between the parked buggies. The light through the open barn door lit up and cast strange shadows among the buggies. Annie tried to catch up with him but she bumped into a couple and then she couldn't see him after she got out onto the barn hill.

"Wait for me!" she said, not so loudly that anyone in the barn could hear. "Wait for me, Mastie." He went off into the dark toward the big cherry tree, and his horse whinnied when it smelled him.

"Hey boy," he said, "You been waiting for me?"

She bumped into him in the dark. "Mastie, I didn't want to," she said, touching his shoulders, "but he asked me, so what was I supposed to — "

"Shhhh — "

"I'd of much rather it was you, Mastie — "

"Shh!" he said, turning around slowly. "What was that? Ah, it's just a kitty cat. Here kitty kitty," he said, reaching down and picking up the kitten. "Nice kitty."

"You didn't tell me you were coming," she said. "When did you come?"

"She's purring!" he said, holding the cat up against his face.

18

"Mastie!" she said. "I waited and waited for a letter, then I thought I might meet you here, so Susie and I came together tonight, and then when I didn't see you I — "

"Now you go catch yourself a big fat mouse," he said, putting the kitten down. "Go on."

"Are you listening?" she said. He turned back and looked at her. His mind was clearing quickly in the cool outside air. "Was it fun?" he said. "Was the bishop's boy fun?"

"No!" she said. Her voice was full of suffering.

He looked at her. It was dark but he could still see her face. It was round and not beautiful at all like her sister Susanna's. Her hair was combed both ways from the part in the middle and that made it seem rounder still. Her eyes were like two round pennies and her mouth was a round half dollar, freshly minted. She had very warm eyes. Whenever she looked at him like that his stomach turned. He didn't know how to explain it. It never turned when he was with any other girls but with her it did. It just felt like a plow was crossing his stomach and turning up deep fresh feelings. He wanted to grab her and kiss and kiss.

"Kith me," he said, lisping deliberately. She threw her arms around his neck and kissed him. She was warm from dancing. Immediately she backed away. "You smell terrible," she said.

"I smell terrible, huh?" he said. "I smell terrible and the bishop's boy has such nice breath. Look!" He pointed at the barn. "He's sticking out his head and gawking around for you. You better go. He's looking for you."

"I don't want to go," she said. "I want to stay

with you, Mastie."

"My breath smells terrible," he said. "Go on. Go!"
She hesitated. He turned back to the horse. "How's
Apple Boy?" he said. "Hmm?" He petted the
horse's nose. "Give me a smooch. Come on, a big
smooch. That a boy. How about one on this cheek?"
He heard her going, the grass brushing against her
long skirts. "You don't even care if I smell bad,
do you?

"I'll tell you something, Apple Boy. They put me to
sleep. Don't everybody all do something interesting
at once. I might get a heart attack. Know what?"
he said, stroking the horse's soft fine nose, "We ought
to take a trip. You and me. You're a stinker. Now
you want to know where, don't you? But I ain't
telling. Just a trip. We'll start going once and just
keep going until either you or me gets tired of it.
How do you like that? Someplace where people
have fun, see? Haha, sure you do. Smart so and so.
You want a *Schnoogling,* don't you?" he said, and he
rubbed his face against the horse's nose. "Why don't
people do interesting things? Uh-uh, I know
what you're thinking. No, not that, you old horny.
I mean *interesting things,* things that ain't religious.
That's all anybody does around here, religious things.
They wear religious things, they act religious, and if
you don't they wonder what's wrong with you. Ain't
you converted? That's what they start wondering,
and they watch you and watch you to see, and shall
I tell you what? The most of them's hypocrites.

"How about a big long ride? And we keep driving
until there aren't any more of *them.* No more Mennonites. Some place where they ain't even heard
of them. I wonder if there's a place like that. Where

20

you can start all over, fresh, and there's not a one of them around to tell you what you're doin's not right. What you think of that, Apple Boy? Huh?'' He went back and got a bagful of grain from under the buggy seat and let the horse stick his nose down into it. The horse began to eat noisily. "You got it pretty good," Mastie said. "Yeah you do, you old horse.''

He unhooked his horse from the cherry tree. "Awfully quiet, out here, huh? What do you say we give that bishop's boy a surprise?" He took his mouth organ from his pocket. "Throw a little of the devil at him.''

Back in the barn it was exactly as Mastie had predicted. The bishop's son saw Annie coming back up the hill and met her at the barn doors.

"Everything okay?" he said. She didn't look happy. "You need some music to cheer you up." He took hold of her hand and tugged her in the direction of the dancers.

"No, I don't want to," she said.

"Why not?" he said. "Next week's the hymn sing. You better dance while you can." He grinned. He was a diplomat, like his father. "Mastie's not in a good mood, huh? He's got something on his mind, I can see that, and it's never good when Mastie has something on his mind. I bet he's going to do something really wild.''

"What do you mean, 'wild'? she said, looking intently at him.

"Like run away," he said.

"Run away!''

"Oh, I don't know," he said. "I have no idea what he's going to do." She left him and crossed to the line of girls against the mow, but he followed her in a few minutes with a glass of cold tea. "Like some tea?" he said. Refreshments had been served while she was gone and during the break Ira had taken the opportunity to talk to Susanna. Actually, he probably wouldn't have worked up enough nerve, but his friends assisted him. They grabbed him by both arms and pushed him right up to Susanna, all the while he was acting like he had been brought against his will. Several of her friends joined the fun by grabbing her to keep her from leaving in embarrassment. But Susanna wasn't embarrassed.

"This is Ira Stoltzfus, the schoolteacher," one of the boys said to her. "He wants to talk to you." Then the boys abandoned Ira and ran. He turned around and saw them go. When he turned back she was still there, smiling good-naturedly. He blushed.

"They're funny," she said.

"You're Susanna, aren't you?" he said. He grinned. From there it was only a small step to ask her to dance, the words just seemed to fall out of his mouth. Pretty soon they were doing "Arkansas Traveller" and then "Shoot the Buffalo."

The fiddler was standing on a wagon positioned crossways at the back of the barn, but from his elevation he could look out over the heads of the dancers toward the open barn doors. He stopped playing his fiddle abruptly in "Shoot the Buffalo" and pointed toward the door with his bow. "Look out!" he said.

The dancers looked around. Mastie's horse and buggy came up out of the dark, up over the ledge into the barn. Mastie was standing up in the buggy, one hand on the reins and with his other holding the mouth organ to his mouth. He was still wearing his President Wilson hat. The buggy tilted dangerously as it came over the ledge. Mastie took the mouth organ from his mouth and held it at arm's length. "Charge!" he shouted. Dancers scattered both ways to the haymow and the center divider. He blew on the mouth organ and turned his horse the only possible way it could go at the far end of the barn, to the right through the opening in the large log skeleton dividing the barn in half. It looked as though he was going to lose his head on an overhead beam but at the last moment, he dodged. The buggy came around the other side of the divider. "Charge!" he shouted again, holding up the mouth organ like a cavalry sword.

Then he stopped the horse abruptly and jumped down with the momentum of the buggy. The dancers laughed, mainly with relief. Everyone immediately began to talk. "That Mastie, something crazy every time," somebody said.

Mastie put his mouth organ back into his pocket and walked over to Benjie and Annie, who were standing together against the haymow. "She dances pretty nice, huh?" he said. He smiled. "Son of a bitch!" He hit Benjie twice with his fists, once in the stomach and once on the nose. Benjie fell right down against the hay. The dancers began to push to see. The boys cheered.

"Come on, Benjie! Don't let him get away with it."

"Hit him again, Mastie. Hit him again."

Ira came running up and put one hand on his brother's chest. "Okay," he said, "that's enough."

The bishop's son opened his eyes and licked his lips. His nose was bleeding a little. "Something to drink," he said.

"You take your horse and go home right now,"
Ira said.

"I guess I'll go when I want to go," Mastie
said.

"They'll make a soldier out of you, that's what,"
Ira said.

Mastie got up onto the buggy. He turned around
and looked back. Then he drove out of the barn.
Before he was more than a mile down the hard road
he was alseep. Apple Boy, however, being a horse
rather than one of those newfangled Fords, knew the
way home.

2

Red Isaac rose from his rocking chair to greet his two guests. "Brother Paul," he said, reaching for Paul's hand and at the same time leaning forward to give him the holy kiss. "God bless," he said.

Paul smiled. "Hope we aren't interfering with your harvesting. A nice day like this with sun, perfect harvesting weather, not?" Isaac ran his fingers through his smooth black hair. It contrasted brightly with the red beard for which he had been nicknamed *Red* Isaac. In obedience to a regulation, his moustache was shaved. "The boys are at it."

"Oh, yes, the boys," said Paul. Unlike Isaac and the bishop, Mose Brubaker, Paul was clean-shaven. In that sense, he represented the new crop of church leaders being ordained. Isaac turned to the bishop. They shook hands and automatically leaned forward for the kiss.

"God bless," said the bishop.

"Have seats," said Isaac. The bishop crossed the room to a high-backed rocker and sat down. Isaac unconsciously took a handkerchief from his pocket and wiped away the bishop's kiss of peace. It didn't pass the bishop's eye. He was just taking off his large black hat. Without the hat, he was Leonardo da Vinci, perfectly bald on top with his gray beard

25

going down to the third button of his shirt. All three men wore long black frock coats with a high collar at the throat. Split in the back, the coats had first been designed that way to make it easier to ride a horse. But none of the three rode horseback, at least not with their good clothes on. It was just that this type of coat had now become standard garb for a lot of the eastern Mennonites. In fact, it was required for ministers.

Isaac Stoltzfus returned to his own chair and sat down. "Well —" Paul said, "Shall we open with prayer? I believe you have another meeting yet today, Brother Mose —" He looked at the bishop, who was feeling in his pocket for a throat lozenge. The bishop didn't reply, so Paul went ahead and said a short prayer. "Now, I believe you were going to make a recommendation to us on the bonnet," Paul said, looking at the bishop again.

"Right," the bishop said, looking up finally. He glanced at both of them. "A number of our conferences have already passed resolutions on the bonnet. We've talked about it and talked about it and ended up doing nothing, so we see our ladies appearing on the streets in all sorts of headdress. Some of them, I think, would make the Apostle Paul weep. I see hats with frills, hats with feathers, and in a word, anything that Paris is dumb enough to come up with, our sisters are willing to buy. When they put on the hat, it smashes the prayer veiling and so I've gotten reports of several sisters not wearing the veiling at all when they wear their fancy hats. Such things ought not to be."

"What do you recommend?" said Isaac. It was an unnecessary question. It was common knowledge that the bishop wanted to require the bonnet for women, a position Isaac opposed.

"The plain bonnet," said the bishop.

"Most of our older sisters are wearing the bonnet already," Paul said.

"*Most,*" said the bishop, "but not all. What about the younger sisters? Why does the church tolerate what no other group would tolerate? The Army, for example, has a uniform. The policeman has a uniform. The nurse has a uniform. The world recognizes what the church don't — there's a kind of power in our looking alike. Why can't we get to the place where people point and say, 'That person's a Christian,' even if they don't know him. His simplicity gives him away."

Isaac cleared his throat. He had sinus problems, and they always came during harvesttime when he was working with his threshing crew for several weeks in a row.

"Did you have something?" Paul said.

"Yes," Isaac said.

"I'd like to say one more thing first," said the bishop.

"It's the *principle* of not living like the world we're after," said Isaac, speaking as soon as his throat cleared, without waiting for Mose to finish. "And the comparison to Army uniforms isn't at all helpful. Not a bit. Maybe the Army boys all look alike. Maybe they do, but that don't mean they all want to fight. I want to see people who believe in the unworldly life. Not people drafted into it like soldiers."

"All right," said the bishop, "All right. But how do we learn the principle of the unworldly life? Just like a baby learns about clothes. A baby don't care about clothes. He'd just as soon lie there like he is, naked. A baby don't have a sense of shame or modesty. He learns it."

"You're saying that by wearing the clothes the church asks us to we learn modesty?" said Paul, interpreting for Mose.

"How we love the flesh," the bishop said, leaning back on his rocker. "Oh how we love it. Ask folks not to do something and say 'Please don't' and we'll do it anyway. Put a penalty on something and we think twice before we do it. I'll tell you what, brethren. If we don't say to the sisters, 'Either wear the plain bonnet or no communion,' we're not going to have any obedience on this. It'll be as it was in the Book of *Judges* when everyone did that which was right in his own eyes."

"You'd make it a test of membership then?" said Paul. Isaac looked at the bishop steadily. He didn't say anything.

"You talk about principles, Isaac," said the bishop. "I'll tell you what principle we're dealing with here. *Drift,* that's what. Today it's the bonnet, tomorrow it's the prayer covering, the next day it's long hair — snip, snip — and the day after that, what? Clothes maybe. Bare limbs like the people who go to the beaches or — what do they call them — 'can-can girls'?" When a woman's lost her respect of church standards, she just drifts from one thing to the next. I ain't saying it's all the woman. Your men too. One thing, then the next, then the next until *boom,* they're out in the world with no beliefs. Let me illustrate that."

The bishop began to rock slowly, leaning his head back against the chair to look at the ceiling. His

Adam's apple bobbed up and down unseen behind his beard.

"When I was a boy, just a little guy, ten maybe, my daddy set me to notching logs. You know how it's done. You nick a good big piece out of each end with your ax so you can set another one down on top. Well, we had a hundred-and-some of these logs to notch, so my daddy put me to work while he was off digging out a foundation. I notched away all morning and afternoon and about milking time I only had five or ten to go — I had blisters by this time — and here comes my daddy. He takes one look at those logs and goes and cuts himself a willow switch. You know why?" Paul smiled and nodded. He knew. "Every one of them logs was wrong except the first two because instead of modeling my logs after the first one each time, I modeled after the last one I had cut, and I got further and further away from the right pattern. We had to recut every one of them logs." The bishop slapped his leg and laughed.

"I heard of stories like that before," said Isaac dryly. He didn't laugh.

"You see what I mean — unless we follow the master pattern we'll all be worthless."

"What's the Master Pattern?" said Isaac.

"The Bible," said Mose.

"What's that have to do with bonnets?"

"The woman's head shall be covered," said Mose. "First Corinthians Eleven."

"With a bonnet?"

"There's a certain attitude in your questions I don't like," said Mose. "Do you love the church or don't you? Jesus gave His power to the church and

29

told her to remain righteous. That's what we're trying to do. We're trying to get our people to live righteous and do the right things, and I know you're going to come back and say you can't force that on people. Granted. But if people get in the habit of doing modest and right, the right attitude will develop inside."

"That's not true!" said Isaac, and he sat forward on his chair loudly. "We have boys who look right and they hardly know the name of Jesus."

"I doubt it," the bishop said.

"It's true," said Isaac. His sinuses began to act up again and Mose looked at him, waiting patiently. Isaac cleared his throat into his handkerchief. "Bonnets!" said Isaac. "Bonnets! What are we talking about headgear for when we have things five times as big to talk about."

"What are you referring to?" said the bishop.

"There was a party last night," said Isaac. "I mean a *party*. A couple of boys were drinking like frogs and two or three of them got into a fight and a boy's nose got busted. That's what I'm referring to. That's what we should be talking about."

The bishop nodded. "It's no sense. You're right," he said. "We don't approve of getting drunk. Our boys know that. We don't believe in fighting either."

Isaac seemed to be getting worked up. He scowled and worked his jaws. As soon as Mose was finished speaking he jumped up. "This country is at war, do you know that?" he said. Mose and Paul looked back at him, puzzled. Neither of them said anything for a bit.

Paul smiled finally and said,

"No, we don't," said Isaac. "This country is at

war and the government is reaching out like this — "
he stretched out his hand and begun to pluck at
the air, " — to get this boy and this boy and that
boy over there, and don't fool yourself, they're after
our boys too."

"They won't go," said Mose. "Absolutely not!" He
brought his open hand down against the cold stove
so hard that the door rattled. Red Isaac was beginning to irritate him. "Our boys are nonresistant,
they've all been told fighting's wrong, and they're
going to go conscientious objector."

Isaac smiled and nodded his head a very little. He
was still standing in front of his chair. "We hope," he
said. "We hope." He sat down again.

It didn't quite seem right to go back to the bonnet
question without clearing up this one first, and
Paul, an unofficial moderator of the meeting, recognized it. "I'm not sure what you're driving at," Paul
said. "We were talking about the bonnet question
and then you brought up this about the party the
other night. Then you mention the war. I'm not sure
I see the connection."

"Why there's all the connection in the world,"
said Isaac. He smiled mysteriously. "The government
ain't the least bit impressed by what we told our
boys. They believe what they want to believe about
us. They got people investigating us right now because
we speak the German, and who do you think they're
going to believe? Us when we tell them our boys
don't fight and they're going to go conscientious
objector? Or their informers and our townspeople who
tell them some of our boys don't know what they
believe, they just do it because they have to, some
of them are wild — "

"One time," said Mose, "and one or two boys — not the whole group. It ain't right to imply this is how they all act, and I'll be frank, I think you're making a big sensation out of one incident. Like I said, our boys have been told about this. They all know fighting ain't right."

"This is where your bonnets get you," said Red Isaac. "Go ahead. Make some rules about bonnets. I don't care. Make a rule about fighting. We'll get a generation of hypocrites. Some day the sheep are going to be judged from the goats. Then we'll see who were real and who were just looking right."

"I think we're getting bonnets and the war pretty mixed up here," said Mose. "Where were we, Paul?"

"That's it!" said Isaac. "That's it! We got bonnets and the war all mixed up, just tangled all up." He knotted his fingers together. "And," he said, raising one finger dramatically, "way out of kilter. Here we are. We've been here an hour already, talking about bonnets and what we should be talking about is the immortal souls of our boys. My goodness! Where are they going? Are their hearts right? Do they love the Lord? If they don't, what are we going to do about it?"

"I think I see our brother's point," said Paul, wrinkling his forehead. The bishop took another lozenge.

"Bonnets!" said Red Isaac. "No, no, let's talk about excommunication."

"Excommunication?" Mose and Paul looked at Red Isaac in astonishment.

"Excommunication," said Red Isaac. At that moment his sinuses got the best of him. Two large tears fell out of his eyes and ran down his cheeks. "My son, Mastie," he said, and he fumbled in his pocket for his handkerchief. The door connecting the living room to the kitchen banged a little against its frame and a muffled cry came from the other side. "For drunkenness and fighting," said Isaac. "Not once, many times." He got up out of his chair and walked to the kitchen. He opened the door, went into the kitchen, and closed the door again.

His wife was standing against the wall with her face buried in one of his large winter coats hanging there. She was crying.

"Emma," he said. "I told you not to listen." He didn't say it harshly though. "Emma." He put his arms on her shoulders and patted her face. "Sit down, Emma," he said. She turned around swiftly and sat down at the table, hardly hiding her crying.

"He'll spite you for it," she said.

"I had to do it," said Isaac. "You know that."

He pulled up another chair and sat down beside her. Her back was partly turned to him though. "I didn't want to do it," said Isaac. "God knows. My favorite son. He always was, you know that. Ira was always yours."

"Don't say that," she said.

"It's true. He likes reading like you do, but Mastie takes after me. He's a fighter. But he's got to learn, Mom. He's got to see that temper of his and those bad habits have got to change. As long as we let him get away with it he's not going to know he's done wrong. Maybe this will bring him around."

"He needs to meet Jesus," said Emma.

"I don't know what all he needs," said Isaac.

"But he'll hate you for it when he finds out," said Emma.

Isaac stood up. He put his hands on his wife's shoulders and massaged them a little. "Now calm yourself," he said. She nodded, but she continued to catch her breath in sharp gasps. "I'm going back in," he said. He went into the other room again and closed the door behind him.

"I don't know about this," said the bishop, "When your own helpmeet — "

"We're agreed on it," said Isaac, sitting down again in his chair. "Train up a child in the way he should go and when he is old he will not depart."

"A child, yes," said the bishop. "He's no child anymore. He's a brother in the church and that's more important than the fact you're his earthly father."

"Excommunication," said Red Isaac, and he pursed his lips and began to nod his head, as though he were agreeing with himself.

Paul looked at Red Isaac and then at the bishop. "There's a serious side to this," he said, "with the army drafting now — "

"You better think about that," said the bishop, looking at Isaac. He had two draft-age boys of his own. "We excommunicate him now and he's going to have no claim on church membership or conscientious objection. If he gets drafted, the Army will snap him up."

"Well?" said Red Isaac, again looking at his lap as if he were talking to himself rather than to them. "What is the end? The end isn't to stay out of the Army. The end isn't to look righteous. The end — " He stopped. There was a long silence.

"Go ahead, Isaac," said Paul.

"The end is — " Isaac stopped again. He covered

his mouth with his hand. "I don't know," he said.

Bishop Mose began to rock again in his rocker. "Well — " said Mose, as if he were about to expound.

"The end is to love God and keep his commandments. That's what!" said Isaac all at once.

"So said, we'll proceed to counsel the boy ourselves and if he is in-cal-ci-trant, let him be to us as the Gentiles and tax collectors."

Paul nodded. He made a little note on a piece of paper. "Now," he said, "On the matter of bonnets — "

3

As the men on church council had said, it was a lovely day for threshing. The sun blasted the wheat fields and made the grasshoppers sing continuously. The men all sweated through their shirts. Red Isaac's threshing crew was in its third week now. How long would the weather hold? It seemed too hot to go on much longer. Secretly, some of the men were wishing for rain, although they didn't mention it around Isaac.

The threshers had shut down for dinner and the men were lining up in front of Jonas Beiler's house for the high point of each threshing day, the noon meal. Beiler's wife had prepared an enormous feast and it was now spread out bowl by bowl and plate by plate on a little picnic table under the maple tree. A boiler full of ham and another one full of fried chicken, bowls of sweet potatoes, corn, and lima beans bumped against plates of pickled eggs, homemade pickles, baked beans, and pickled cantaloupe which led to a row of pies, a letter pricked on the top crust of each one with a fork either to show what kind of pie it was or to let the hot air escape as it was baking. Who knew? That was one of Mary Beiler's secrets.

She stood behind the table with an eighty-pound

milk can full of meadow tea, picked it up, and dumped three pitchers full. Her Jonas was standing alongside grinning at the thresherman. Why they'd been moving from the moment they got awake to get everything ready in time.

"Ach you," she said to one fly that kept returning to the mince pie. "Catch him, Pop, will you. He keeps coming back." Jonas caught him with one swoop of his hand.

"We needed another rack wagon this morning, didn't we, Mastie? Maybe if I catch another fly we can harness the two of them to my extra wagon."

"Ha! Oh, and I *love* ham," said Mastie as he picked three big pieces out of the boiler.

"Take lots," said Jonas. "We have more on the hoof." Then he laughed. There was a good possibility Mastie would be his son-in-law, and one always treated a possible son-in-law with an extra measure of respect. "Come on, men. Eat it up! Eat it up! Mom, what are we going to do with all this food if they don't eat it?"

"I don't know," she said, and straightened up. "Maybe we'll have to feed it to the pigs."

"Well, if that's the case — " said the man who ran the threshing engine, and he took an extra helping of sweet potatoes, which was exactly what Jonas wanted him to do. The farmers who belonged to the threshing ring actually competed to see who could give the threshing crew the best feed. It would seem after two or three weeks of such eating all the men would be too well larded to do any work but that wasn't the case at all. They burned it all up in the wheat field.

"Okay, *Junge*," said a farmer, and he threw the

dirty towel to Ira. Ira pumped himself a pail full of water and took off his shirt. He shook it and coughed. A cloud of chaff came out of his shirt. The water was cold, especially when he dipped his whole head in, but was there any other way to get the stuffed-up feeling out? He poured the rest of the bucket over his back and gasped. It was really cold!

"Hurry up before these guys eat it all," said Jonas. Ira looked up and grinned from under the towel. That was when he first noticed Susanna.

She was shooing flies from the table with a home-made swatter with long paper strips attached. She looked up as he got in line. She smiled.

"Do you know this man?" said Jonas. Beilers were from a different church district and Jonas was new in the threshing ring this year.

"Ira Stoltzfus," said Susanna.

"Not Mastie's brother?" said Jonas.

Ira nodded.

"Well, who would have guessed it? Your daddy was a courting friend of ours. Give him an extra helping of pie, Mom. We like Mastie around here."

He sat under a pear tree in the lawn. Some of the men were already finished eating and were lying with their heads propped up in the shade and flat straw hats over their eyes. The sun was warming their full bellies. In a few minutes they were going to be asleep.

Ira sat so he could watch the table as he ate. It was the second time he had talked to her but there was something about her that drew his eyes. She was barefoot and dressed in a long traditional skirt. She had dark, strong hair. There was something noble about the way she held herself and moved about the table. It reminded him of Natasha in *War and Peace*.

The next thing he knew the pear tree behind him was jiggling and he opened his eyes and yawned.

"Hi," she said, "Was it good?" She was hanging wash on a line that ran over his head.

"What?"

"Your sleep. "I'm sorry. I didn't want to wake you, but I bumped the line."

"That's okay." He looked around. The lawn was perfectly quiet but the men were still scattered around under various trees. The thresher and his water monkey had gone back to the barn to get ready for the afternoon run. She seemed different in the afternoon than she had at midnight. She seemed more self-confident.

"Is it hard work?" she said.

"Not so bad." Should he tell her how he amused himself by singing songs, every song he knew in fact, and recited poems to himself while he was driving the rack wagon?

"But it's hot, isn't it. Pop says it will probably rain tonight."

"I wish it would hold off another day."

Her basket was empty and the next line stretched between two trees on the other side of the lawn. Would she go?

She stood with the wash basket against her hip. She smiled.

"You're not like your brother Mastie at all, are you?"

"I don't know."

"No, he's very — he's always moving around doing things and one day he's mad and you can't talk to him and the next day he's happy. But you're more serious — like a schoolteacher," she said and laughed. He had told her the other night that he was teaching winters.

"Why don't you rest?" he said, and he surprised himself by saying it. It was what he had wanted to say but he didn't think he was going to be able to say it.

"Why, maybe I'll do that," she said and sat down not more than three feet from him. She stretched out her feet and wiggled her toes. "I like threshing season," she said. "It's the best time of the year, don't you think? Well, it's hot, too, for one thing, but everything's happening at once. There's so much work to be done — but this washing and cooking — that's when I wish I were a man sometimes so I could help with the threshing. I can drive a rack wagon, you know." It wasn't a small feat. Rack wagons were tricky to drive. "I used to drive one before Pop joined the threshing ring.

"But then the men have to go to war. I know I wouldn't like that. I'm sorry. I'm doing all the talking. What does your horse look like? Is he a good one?"

"I don't like to talk about horses and buggies," he said. "It's transportation, that's all."

"Well, that's another thing about Mastie. He's crazy about his horse, you know. So what do you like to talk about?"

He liked her frankness. It made him want to uncork himself, but he thought, no, she'd be bored by his things.

"Oh, books. Books and geometry, history. Especially history."

"Do you know what? When you were just a boy

your parents once came to our church and you told me the story of Ali Baba. Do you remember that?"

"No, is that right?" He laughed. "That's a good story. I tell that to my students sometimes. I'm also interested in the war, what will happen to us. Do you know," he said, and adjusted his glasses, "1917 is going to be a year remembered in history. It will be like the Continental Divide, and people in the future will talk about everything as either, 'It happened before 1917' or 'It happened after 1917.'"

"Why is it so important?" she said. She smiled. She wasn't bored and she wasn't afraid of him.

"Because it's the beginning of a worldwide war," he said. "Up until now it was only Europe but now America is jumping in and who knows who will be next? Russia is flying apart, did you know that? But this is a different war, don't you see? It's not an ordinary one. Men are digging trenches and lying in them for months and shooting at other men who aren't any further away than from here to the barn, but they never ever see their faces. And everybody is a part of it, even the women back home because they run the factories that send weapons to the men. Before this an army would prepare itself in one country and stock up in weapons and then go over in the other country and chase their enemy around for a while until they came to a big open field and then one army would capture the other one. But now it's a war between whole countries — every healthy man is being drafted and every woman back home is making supplies for the men. Do you see how different it is? Now, what about the church? That is the big question. What will the church do? In the Civil War we paid three hundred dollars to have a substi-

tute fight for us, but is that right? If you don't believe in fighting, is it right to hire someone else to
do it for you? We must think about these things
for the first time in fifty years, but really for the
first time since the French and Indian War, because
this is the first time that the government requires us
to fight."

"So what will you do?" said Susanna.

"Me? I think — " he stopped. "I won't fight. But
sometimes I don't know. What will become of us?
What will the government do if we say *no*? If we
say 'no,' I think they will become terribly angry. But
if we say 'yes,' then what will become of us? If they
force me to go I will fire my rifle into the air, that's
what I'll do. Maybe I'll aim at a bird. How can I
fire it at a man, even a German? Why, we came from
Germany once upon a tin.e. Maybe I'd be killing
one of my cousins, huh? Maybe I'd be killing a Christian from over there who didn't want to go to war
either."

He coughed. Maybe she wasn't interested in what
he was saying. "I'm sorry, I didn't mean to do all the
talking," he said.

"No, I'm not bored," she said. She didn't look
bored. Between her fingers she twiddled a stalk of
wheat that had fallen from his pant cuffs. "Do I look
bored?" She readjusted herself on the lawn. "Aren't
you interested in girls?" she said. "I mean, are you
interested in people, too, or mainly in the war? Me,
I love people, all kinds of people. I think I'll be a
schoolteacher someday so I can talk to them all the
time and get paid for it besides. Do you like to talk
about people or are they like horses?"

"They're better than horses."

"But not as good as the war?"

"I wouldn't say that."

"I think it's funny how different you and your brother are."

"Do you think so? He'd better start thinking about the war," said Ira.

"Why?"

"Because it's here and Uncle Sam will be around to all of us sooner or later. So what's he going to do? I don't think he's thought about it yet."

"Don't be too sure."

"I don't think he has. Those camps aren't easy, I hear. The officers are doing all they can to make soldiers out of everyone. If you're straddling the fence, they pull you over to their side. You've got to think about what you're going to do before you get in the hot spots, not after you get there."

He looked around.

"It's about time to go," he said, but he made no move to get up. He wanted to know more about her, but what should he ask? She looked at him easily. She wasn't afraid of him, and he liked that.

"Tell me about yourself," she said and her hand bumped his foot and then began to twirl the wheat stalk again. "Are you really always serious-minded like they say?"

He really should be going. There was threshing to do and it was best to get it done while it was hot, but thinking of the heat reminded him of the meeting in Indiana and he wanted to tell her about that yet.

"Did they tell you about Clinton Frame?" he said.

"Clinton Frame? No, what's that?"

"You haven't heard about it?" he said. "I was

there." He looked at his feet and at her straw because he didn't want to stare into her eyes. She was good to talk to. He could tell she was listening. "I was visiting my uncles and aunts in Indiana when word came to us at night that they were holding a meeting the next day to decide what the church should do about the draft, so I went with my cousin. Well, when we got there the church was already full and people were standing up in the aisles, Amish and Mennonites of all sorts and varieties — I never knew there were so many kinds — but there they were gathered in this church house. It was quiet and I started wondering what was going on, but about that time a whole party of ministers opened the double doors at the back. They were shocked to see us, I guess, because they thought they were alone in the building, downstairs. That's how quietly it filled up. The moderator, he was a great big red-faced man with a voice like this — " he demonstrated and she laughed. He smiled, "Came up front and said he was pleased to see the turnout and he asked that the draft laws be read. A deacon from Michigan read them and the moderator asked for questions. Then he said since the young men were the ones most affected, how did they feel? And one by one they said, come what may, whatever persecution or government laws, they vowed to be true to God and the church *first* and after that, as much as possible they would obey the leaders of our country. When it came my turn I said I agreed with the brothers and as far as I was concerned I would say 'no' to taking part in this war."

He was caught up in the story and waving his hands. "Young men no older than myself were talking

44

and the whole church and all the leaders sat in
silence and listened and when the young men were
done, the moderator said 'Amen, so let it be. Let us
pray for them.' It was a tearful moment."

"Hey!" It was Mastie. "Get your ass out here. If
you have to court, wait until the work's done."

Ira jumped up.

"The pitchers are waiting out there in the field
for a wagon, getting paid for it, and where are you?
What do you think this is, huh? A party? How's
come you always put the work on me? Pop's going to
hear about this."

He ran out to the barn, wishing he had watched
the time, embarrassed that it had happened in front
of her. But no sooner had he jumped on the rack
wagon than he forgot all about Mastie and remembered her hand on his arm and he felt a strange
warm feeling. Did she really like him or was she
only being polite?

4

Mom had made a big batch of pork and sauerkraut. It smelled up the whole house and as soon as Mastie and Ira came home from threshing they smelled it.

"Sauerkraut!" said Mastie. "Mmm, mmm, I love you, Mama," and he patted her gently on the cheek and sat down.

Ira was right behind him coming into the kitchen. He hung up his hat but he was hardly thinking of sauerkraut. His eyes were still back under the pear tree looking up into Susanna's smiling face.

"And cherry pie!" said Mastie, catching sight of it. He looked slyly at Pop and pulled a cherry out of the pie and ate it.

Red Isaac's mind was not on sauerkraut either. The difficult task of telling Mastie he faced excommunication was on his mind. It should be done tonight — tomorrow was Sunday and it wasn't right for him to learn the news by way of some snide rumor by someone. Pop didn't believe in that sort of discipline. A boy deserves to hear it straight and plain and hard, he felt, and he had no sympathy for other men of his own age who pretended to be cordial to the boys but began to complain about them as soon as they went out the door. It is the duty of old men to be truthful, he thought. He had come to the table with his mind made up. They would go into the spare room and talk about the excommunication as soon as supper was over, just the two of them. But now his courage began to flag. Mastie was in an excellent mood, as soon as the prayer ended he began to devour the sauerkraut as if he had not eaten lunch, telling Mom again and again how good it was. It would have been much easier to tell him if he had been in a bad mood already. The news was sure to make him angry.

"The wheat this year is something else, Pop," said Mastie. "Those heads are that long, I'll bet." He measured off three inches with his fingers. "And big kernels. I couldn't believe it when I saw them coming out. How about it, Ira? Fifty bushel to the acre, maybe? What's wrong? What's everybody so quiet for?" He looked around slyly. "I think Ira met someone unforgettable."

"He did?" said Mom. "Who?"

"Ohh — " and Ira grinned in spite of his decision to keep it a secret.

"Well, this is news," said Mom.

"Nothing much," said Ira.

"What does that mean?" said Mastie. "Nothing much!"

"Tell us about Clinton Frame," said Pop to Ira.

"Oh, it was a wonderful meeting," said Ira, and no sooner had he begun to explain it than Mastie became silent and absorbed in his sauerkraut. Ira looked at him. "I predict the war will last long enough to take you — and you better listen, Mastie. Things are rough for the objector in the army camps, they're saying."

Mastie burped. "Who said I'm an objector?"

"Mastie!" It was Mom.

"What makes you so sure this war is wrong? The Germans have done a lot of terrible things over there, I hear. No, I guess I'm an objector, Mom."

"Go ahead with your story," said Pop.

"Well, there we were in the church house on a Tuesday afternoon — it was a Mennonite church, I think."

"Everybody was notified the night before that there was to be a meeting of the boys who were up before the draft and the ministry didn't know if anyone would come or not, but they wanted to think and pray through this whole thing themselves, so they were down in the basement consulting and praying. I mean, it was an important moment. The churches were about to decide where we stood on the draft and that was the first time our people have had to think about that since the Civil War."

He looked at Mastie. Mastie was not listening, though. He had closed his eyes and began to hum a little tune. Ira looked at him hard.

"Go ahead," said Mastie loudly and went back to his humming. Pop looked at Mastie.

"Are you that tired?" said Mom. Then she looked back at Ira and smiled.

"Go ahead," said Pop. He was listening carefully and now and then taking one hand out of his beard and flicking a fly away from the sauerkraut with it.

"Are you really interested?" said Ira.

"Sure. Sure."

"Well, all of sudden the ministers opened the doors in back and they saw the upstairs was solid from window to window with men, a good half of them young men like me from the Mennonites, from the

48

Amish, from the River Brethren. Six or so different groups of plain people were represented. Well, one question in particular seemed to stand out. 'Shall we go into the noncombatant corps that the government provides (we were all opposed to outright military participation — carrying the gun, digging trenches, and the like) or shall we choose not to cooperate with the army at all, even if it means prison?"

"Prison!" said Mom.

"A resident at the bar," said Mastie without opening his eyes.

"The bar?" said Mom. "You mean a saloon?"

"No, bars," said Mastie. "Like the monkey looks through." He held his fists up on both sides of his eyes and looked through them as though he were a monkey in a cage.

Pop began to laugh and couldn't stop.

"Crazy flies," he said and got up and reached for a flyswatter. He leaned over the table and began to swat them.

"Pop!" said Mom, "now stop that. Next thing one will fall in the sauerkraut."

"There." Pop sat down and laid the swatter beside his dish. "Now go ahead, Ira. I'm sorry for the interruption."

Mastie began to hum again.

"Would you stop humming?" said Ira.

"Oh," said Mastie, and stopped, but he closed his eyes again anyway.

"I don't know what's wrong with you, Mastie," said Mom. "Are you that sleepy?" He didn't answer.

"Go ahead," said Pop.

"That's about it," said Ira.

"Now, what did you resolve? How did it all come

out?" said Pop. He looked at Ira and blinked his eyes, serious.

"Well — I don't know. Does anybody care?"

"Yes," said Mom. "I really wondered while you were out there. I kept wondering what you were learning," She smiled. "I don't know what's wrong with Mastie," she said.

"He's still thinking of the residents at the bar," said Pop, and he began to laugh. "Excuse me." He stopped laughing. He tried to look serious as if he regretted laughing at Mastie. "Go ahead," he said to Ira.

"Well, the leader asked the young boys if they had anything to say then. After all, they are the ones who are facing the draft, or prison, or whatever. And I said, 'Come what may, I want to be faithful to what I believe God is telling me and if I were to go right now I would not cooperate with the army at all."

" 'Faithful to what I believe God is telling me — ' " said Mom. "That's wonderful, Ira."

"It's a historic moment," said Pop. "There's no doubt about it. In years to come Ira will look back on this as a great moment of his life — maybe the greatest. I wish I could have been there, but with the threshing — " he picked up the flyswatter and brought it down on a fly that was sitting on the edge of the sauerkraut dish.

"Pop!"

The fly flew up in the air and disappeared.

"Did I get him?"

"I think he's in the sauerkraut," said Ira. He looked. "Yes, there he is."

"Oh, no," said Pop, and he bent over the bowl

with his beard almost brushing it and reached in. He fumbled several times. (He needed new glasses.) The fly was still alive and trying to escape but it was drenched. It buzzed. Finally Pop got hold of the fly and pulled it out between his thumb and forefinger, along with a hunk of sauerkraut.

"Now that's enough," said Mom. "These boys will never eat sauerkraut again."

"I'm going to find out where they're coming into the house at," said Pop. He got up. "Thanks for your story, Ira. Mastie, before you get away, I want to talk with you a few minutes in the spare room." Mastie followed him out of the room.

Ira began to clean the table.

"He's disgusting," said Ira. "He'll be drafted — then what will he do if he hasn't thought about how he believes?"

"I'm so glad you got to go to Indiana," said Mom, placing her hand on Ira's.

In the spare room, Pop motioned a chair to Mastie and sat down in the rocker himself.

"I have to go shortly," said Mastie. "Crazy flies, huh?" The old man looked at Mastie and laughed until he had to wipe his eyes. That was the way Mastie was. There was something wry and intriguing about his face. In spite of himself, Pop laughed at his son. He immediately regretted it. It was no time to laugh. He cleared his throat.

"Seriously though, Mastie, on this matter of the draft, you should listen to your brother. That's what I want to talk to you about. Not the draft, your attitudes. . . ."

Mastie looked disinterested.

"Listen carefully, son. I believe a father should

talk seriously to his son. One thing I have noticed is that parents and leaders in the church often let the young men slop along and find their own way through things without even telling them. And that's wrong. The older people have a responsibility to give the young people a foundation to stand on. *In love.* I don't want you to doubt my love, Mastie. Do you understand? I've always had a special interest in you. A father is sometimes more attached to one of his children than the others. Your mother loves Ira, but you are the apple of my eye, as the Bible puts it. You're intelligent, you're good-looking — yes, you are — and you're easy to get along with, Mastie. That's something your brother has yet to learn."

"Pop, what is it?"

"What is what?"

"What do you want to tell me?"

"All right, I'm getting to that. But I want you to know first of all that I do love you. Do you hear me?"

"Fifteen minutes, Pop. I have to go change clothes in fifteen minutes."

"Mastie, I'm not here to tell you what to do. You're old enough to know, but if you can't control that temper, people are going to dislike you and steer clear of you. I'm speaking from experience, Mastie. They won't tell you what they think for fear you'll explode. You may even end up in prison because you'll do something ram-bang that you will regret forever. That fight the other night — "

"There were two sides."

"Of course there were two sides. There are always two sides. There might be three sides, four sides, five sides, ten sides, but that doesn't excuse you if you're one of them." He stopped. "Mastie, the council decided this afternoon to excommunicate you, unless — "

"I knew it! I knew it! I knew that's what you were going to say."

"For drunkenness, fighting, a negative attitude toward the church." Pop's voice choked and he got up from his chair. He was bent and getting old. "But if you're sorry — "

"For what?"

"Mastie." The old man put one hand on Mastie's shoulder and covered his own mouth with the other. He couldn't speak.

"So if that's all you have to say, I'm going. . . . Rules, rules, rules, rules. Rules! I'm sick of rules. Heaven, huh? Who cares about heaven anyway? I want to live good down here and I don't care what happens after I die."

Pop sat down beside Mastie on the bench by the window. "It was for your sake, for your good, Mastie," said Pop. "I asked for it."

"You asked for it? You want me to thank you?"

"I asked for it, but understand me, son, it was the hardest thing I ever did. Don't you think I wanted to do it, because it's not true. But I prayed. . . . I prayed. . . . It's for your good, son. I want you to know how far away from the church and your promises to God you've gone. How can we let you slide along thinking that you're still a part of us . . . so I asked them to cut you off. Now you know where you stand. It's not forever, son. It's only for as long as you choose. When you choose to come back, then I want to be the first to forgive you and welcome

you in. No, God's the first, but I want to be second."
He sobbed.

"Can I go?"

"Don't look at me like that," said Pop. His life,
it seemed, was a beautiful quilt sewn carefully together, year by year, piece by piece, and now one
corner was being torn off violently. "Come in, Mom,"
he said. She was at the door. He was sitting beside
Mastie on the bench yet, his hand covering his forehead.

"Is that all?" said Mastie. "I'm out."

"No. It's up to you, Son."

Mastie sat down and looked at Mom. She held
a handkerchief to her mouth.

"It's not your fault, Mom. It's his."

"Mastie. Mastie."

"I want you to listen to me, Mastie," said Pop.

"I'm listening."

"I don't think you are."

"My sinuses ain't stuffed up."

"Mastie!" His mother said sharply.

"Okay. I'm sorry."

"Mastie. I don't want you to ride along in the
church just to escape the army, and when you're no
longer a member, the army might take you just like
that." He slapped his hands. "You knew what you
were getting into when you joined the Mennonite
Church. You were nineteen, that's old enough to tell a
mule from a horse, isn't it? We don't go down on our
knees before God for the fun of it. And that's what
you did when you were baptized, you went down
on your knees before God and confessed His name
and promised to be faithful. You weren't saying
that to the church. You were saying it to God. A

54

long time ago your mother and I got married and we went down on our knees and promised to be faithful, just like you may do some day, but I wasn't just telling your mother I would be faithful to her. I was telling God. I was promising Him. God has been good to us. We were faithful. You're old enough to know what it means to keep a promise, and you promised to obey the Mennonite discipline.

"What is the discipline?" the old man went on."
"Is it a bunch of rules? Maybe. What is a marriage? Perhaps a bunch of rules. We're talking man-to-man, Mastie. Girls are as attractive to me as they are to you but I have fastened blinders on my mind. I see the girls but I don't see them as mates for me. Because I belong to your mother and she belongs to me. Oh, it's not easy. But when I am away from home and meet new girls I fill my mind with thoughts of your mother. I'm being frank with you because I love you, Mastie.

"And what of the church discipline?" he continued. "Well, that too is like blinders that we of our own choosing screw fast to our minds to keep us faithful to the church. 'How I love thy law, O Lord. It is my meditation all the day.'" The old man rolled back his head and closed his eyes and began to recite in a singsong fashion.

"*How can a young man keep his way pure? By guarding it according to thy word.*

"*With my whole heart I seek thee; let me not wander from thy commandments.*

"*I have laid up thy word in my heart, that I might not sin against thee.*

"*Turn my eyes from looking at vanities.*

"*The godless besmear me with lies, but with my*

whole heart I keep thy precepts. Their heart is gross like fat, but I delight in thy law.

"How sweet are thy words to my taste, sweeter than honey to my mouth.

"Great peace have those who love thy law: nothing can make them stumble."

He opened his eyes.

"You make me sick," said Mastie."

"Why?"

"Anyone knows Mennonite rules aren't God's law. They're hangovers from our great-great-grand-fathers or someone back there. Menno Simons maybe. I know a Christian who is going to the army. That's just a Mennonite rule about not going."

"Thou shalt not kill," said Pop.

"Murder, that's what that means."

"The Mennonites ain't the only true church," Pop said. He looked into his son's eyes. "They try to be faithful to the commandments though. I want you to think about that promise you made to be faithful when we baptized you. Are you listening?"

Mom rocked back and forth on her rocker, nursing the sorrow inside of her. "I'm getting old," she said, "I've served God for a long time. I don't regret it."

"Let's pray," the old man said.

Mastie pushed back the bench and got up. "I've got to check on the cows before I go," he said. He went out.

The old man put his head between his hands, and Emma got up and came over behind him and put her hands on his shoulders. She began to massage them. He pulled her hand down and rubbed it.

"Why are your hands cold on a warm night like this?" he said.

"Are they cold?"

"Sure they are."

"I must be getting old."

"Don't say that."

"Well, we are, Isaac. You're sixty already."

"I'm not going to get old. There are too many things that need to be done. Look how much work there is to do in the church. How many boys like Mastie are there and how many — I shouldn't say it — blockheads like our bishop brother this afternoon. There's too much work to get old. I'm not going to get old!" he said and hit his fist on the table. "I mean that. My body, yes, my cells will deteriorate but I will not get old. Get me the Bible." He leafed through it. "I don't want to get old — *here*," he said, and touched his hands to the top of his head.

"Well, I hope not, as long as you're physically strong, but there are always the young to carry on."

"So foolish!" said the old man. He closed the Bible and said his name. "Mastie! But this may be a turning point. He needed to run his head into the barn wall once."

"Ira's not that way," said Emma. "Why couldn't he be like Ira, sensible and interested in the deeper things of life? Courteous."

"Nonsense!" said Pop. "Ira's tame. Mastie is the young colt with blood in his legs. He'll be frisky and unmanageable until he's broken, but then you watch. He'll be a better horse than Ira. Ira's tame on the outside, but who knows what he's like inside? It might do him good to get drunk once."

"Pop! How can you say that?"

"What?" Pop said. "Getting drunk? All right. Something to loosen him up, anyway."

5

It was no secret where Mastie went Friday nights. Everybody knew he met his girl at the Red Dragon Market and walked around with her, unless there was a special party of some sort.

Mastie spent a half hour in the tub, washing the barley husks out of his hair and anointing his eyes with an eyedropper. Working in the thresher chaff had made them sore. The harvest was over. Let it rain. It hadn't rained for weeks. The sun had gone on getting hotter and hotter until it was almost a sentence to have to work out in it. About three o'clock clouds began to pile up in the west. Was that the rain? On his way out to the horse stable Mastie checked the hives. Even the bees were silent.

Richmond's Apple Boy had his head up, snorting when he saw Mastie.

"You're a good boy," said Mastie, even though 'boy' didn't quite apply anymore to a horse who had had *that* operation, "but you're getting fat, you know. Yeah, you're getting fat. Too much of the good life." That was one of the few bad things about automobiles in Mastie's mind. They didn't have personality. They didn't stick their heads up to greet you and smack their big lips on your ear like a horse did. They just chugged mechanically. But one thing wonderful about them, they never got tired. They just ran on and on forever and carried you right out of your suffocating little community into another world. *I'd like that,* he thought.

Oh, it wasn't that he hated the community, but sometimes he needed to get out for a breath of fresh air and check up on the Lutheran girls. He had a weakness for sandy hair and blue eyes, that was the problem. When they kissed you, they held on for dear life as if you were the last sweet candy on earth and they were relishing you, but a Mennonite girl — well, she had a way of kissing and looking up into your eyes at the same time to say, "When are you coming again?" as if that kiss wasn't enough. She wanted another one on some other day, and that one surely wouldn't be enough either and the next thing you knew, you'd be eating wedding cake with her.

"Just like a chigger, that's what they are," said Mastie. "Yeah, just like a chigger." He tickled the horse's soft nose. She snorted. "Okay, we ready to go?" He led her out and hitched up the carriage.

Mastie wasn't sure how he felt about the war. For one thing he thought it was a lot of ballyhoo that would soon blow over without affecting him. He was sure how he felt about Annie though. He felt an urge to put his arm around her and protect her whenever she was with him — well, she didn't need any protection really, but it was an excuse to put his arm around her. "Let me protect you," he would whisper in her ear when his head was on her shoulder, and she laughed out, but when she turned to look at him, her face held something like the face of a new flower that again made his stomach turn over, and he wanted to kiss her. But tonight as he drove to the Market there was a new feeling in him — an urge to hurt her. She had danced with the bishop's son and let him hold her, hadn't she? He licked Apple Boy with the whip.

But what was this? A crowd had gathered on the street at the edge of town and completely blocked the corner where he usually turned to reach the Market. If he had been in a hurry, he would have wheeled around right there, but he wasn't. It was a warm evening and crowds interested Mastie. They said excitement, maybe a snake medicine woman, or a politician, or an accident. He reined the buggy over to the curb and got out.

A platform had been temporarily erected in front of the Immanuel Bible Church on the corner. Flags were flying over the platform and at that moment a tall man in black clerical robes climbed up the steps to the top of the platform. The people began to clap — they were dressed up, most of them.

"Friends," he said, and smiled, "friends, we're glad to be back. Europe has good wine and good bread, as they said, but there's nothing like a bit of shoofly pie." The crowd laughed and some winked at each other. He was their pastor, apparently.

"But friends, we didn't come here to talk about shoofly pie. We came here to talk about the war and the horrible crimes this nation of thieves and murderers is perpetrating on the rest of civilization. We're going to be plain. I'm going to tell you the truth about the war and if you have tender ears you'd better leave because it isn't nice, this story."

Mastie lit a cigar.

"I have here in my pocket a little silver medallion — can you see that, folks? Now this little medallion is carried by every German soldier. It's given to him by his commander or officer before he goes into combat, and this is what the medallion says. Listen carefully." He held the medallion up and turned it sideways so the sunlight would strike it and read slowly and dramatically.

" 'I, the Kaiser of Germany, declare herewith on the authority committed to me by God Almighty, that the bearer of this token is permitted to commit any crime he may desire, and I, the Kaiser of Germany, will take upon myself the responsibility to God for the same.' "

He stopped and the audience stopped with him.

"My God," he said in a whisper, "what a license." Suddenly he roared. "What crimes have they done? These Germans? Can you picture any human being drinking blood from an empty skull? I couldn't. I couldn't imagine any human being stooping to *drink blood*, but I was told by a young English soldier who had been to the front that he stumbled upon a group of German soldiers having lunch one day in a woods and while he was hiding there, loading his gun to blow them all to their eternal reward he heard horrible laughter and when he looked they were drinking from a human skull and trickles of blood ran down their chins and onto their uniforms!"

A woman gasped.

"I met a young Belgian one morning after church who came up to me with tears in his eyes. He was looking this way and that, as if afraid that he might be followed and spied upon by someone. We were near the war zone, and that town had been tossed back and forth, first in the hands of one army, then in the hands of the other. That young Belgian said, 'Pastor from America, I want to tell you what they did in my town. They took my wife and stripped her and made a crucifix for her like the one they used for Jesus Christ and they nailed her fast and held our little baby before her eyes as she died. Pastor, tell your people this and tell them we need help now. Help us! We need soldiers and money to fight these men.' Dare we even call them men — dare we call a man who behaves like a beast a man?''

"No! No!" the crowd was heating up.

"Friends, there are other stories too horrible to tell. They should be whispered, not named, by men when they are alone. When men tell each other these stories they should fall down on their knees and pray Almighty God that he will give us a *will* to stop these savages. What else can you call them? Men who will cut the breasts off women they have used, who force polygamy on all the young girls of their own country including their own daughters, who spray prisoners with burning oil — are these men? Or beasts? No! A hundred years from now all people will look back at the word 'German' as we look back on the dinosaur now — an extinct monster."

The crowd roared again.

"So what are we going to do?" said the pastor. "How are we going to respond to this call to come into Macedonia and help? I, for one, will have nothing to do with anything that represents this nation of barbarians in the future. I like sauerkraut, my wife cooks me a bit sometimes, but I told her last night, 'Ruth, no more sauerkraut! No more pretzels! No more Beethoven!' "

"No more German in the high schools," somebody called, and he was applauded.

"What shall we do with this *Kaiser*?"

"We should hang him by his thumbs," said an old man in a coat and cravat. The banker, perhaps? The pastor held up his hand for silence.

"If we could only see the world as God does, in the light of eternity, not through a glass darkly, we would see who the Kaiser actually is. None other than the Antichrist himself! What will happen to the Antichrist according to Revelation? Why he will be tied up back and front and cast into the bottomless pit for a thousand years. That's what will happen to him. We are living in the end times — don't deceive yourselves — and prophecy is being fulfilled right in front of us. The question to you and me is, "Will we stand by? Will we stand by and watch prophecy being fulfilled or will we join in fulfilling it?

"You might ask me, friends, how it is that we Christians might be called upon to fight? Didn't Christ command us to love one another?" He looked at them in silence.

"Not the Germans," said someone.

"Ah, there is the crux of the matter. We fight him because we love him. Does that sound strange? But aren't we showing love if we stop a madman from doing some act of madness? If he could think, wouldn't he beg us to stop him?

"We are on the edge of a new world, brothers and sisters, a new world run by Christian principles and great men of God — the Bible calls it the Millennium — but I like to think of it as the age of peace and light. What could be more pleasing in God's eyes than a world run according to Christian principles, a world where each man has a voice and the voices of all the people speak together. Like the wind! We are the people, brothers! Democracy for all,

63

sisters! We are fighting to bring democracy to the dark corners of the world and we fight — not in spite of the fact that we are Christians — we fight *because* we are Christians!"

The boy on the platform behind Pastor Rydell jiggled the Christian flag up and down.

"Now I know," said the pastor, "that many of you will ask about our own town. We have lawbreakers here, not many, but a few. We have sin among our own people! Marriages fail, children turn sour, men that you and I would call good occasionally lose purpose and turn to graft. Why? If our land is a Christian land and we live as Christians by Christian principles, why do these things persist? I have an answer for that.

"While I was in Europe I met many boys. Some of those boys were still wet with mud and blood from the trenches. But I noticed a strange thing about those boys. There was a light in their tired eyes as if — as if like Paul on the road to Damascus they had suddenly seen something none of the rest of us can see. A blinding light, perhaps, like Francis Scott Key says about the rockets' red glare and bombs bursting in air.

"They had come through fire and fire purifies! 'Sprinkle me with hyssop, Lord, and I shall be cleansed, wash me, and I shall be whiter than snow!' War has a purifying effect. It is giving our boys purpose that will last them a lifetime. You know, we lose track of purpose sometimes in bearing children and watching them grow up, and listening to our wives grouse about the broken door, and doing our jobs from the time the sun comes up until it goes down. I'm not against babies, you know that," and he smiled at a mother and her baby. "I'm not against wives. I love my wife. I'm not against jobs because I have a job. But there's got to be more. Men will go on having children and marrying, or marrying and having children and working until the stars fall out of the sky, but we are no longer content with that alone."

Yes, yes, Mastie thought. *That's exactly how it is.*

"We have seen the light! Democracy! Progress! We have a purpose! Spread democracy to the seven continents and five oceans! And I don't want to end on a downhill note, but as long as you keep your sons at home and your pocketbooks buttoned up, the Antichrist will run across Europe and democracy will lie in spider webs right where it started, on the big white page of the Constitution."

He sat down, and the audience began to clap. They clapped and the boys whistled. Then they clapped and whistled some more. Finally Pastor Rydell smiled and nodded. A burly little man got up.

"It's good to have our pastor back," he said, "but when he returns with a fire in his bones and such a vision, what can we say? I want to pledge $500 in Liberty Bonds."

"Two hundred," said someone else.

"Fifty dollars."

"We're going the wrong way, but keep them coming," said the burly little man. He was writing down their names. "That's fifty dollars for Mrs. Douglas."

Rydell got to his feet. "If it will put the Kaiser where he belongs, I'm willing to pledge my entire savings of one thousand dollars.

The crowd clapped loudly, and people began to move toward the base of the platform to make their commitments to the burly little man.

"Wonderful, he's wonderful, huh?" said a man with a pipe, turning to look at Mastie. "Oh — " He noticed the plain black hat and homemade clothes. "You're a conchie, aren't you?"

Mastie shook his head.

The crowd was disbanding. It was time to go.

"Hey," the man said loudly. "Look what we have here — one of those German sympathizers. You even speak German, don't you, and your preachers are telling folks not to give to the Liberty Bond drive. Come on, say something. Is it true?"

Mastie's muscles tensed. He threw his cigar into the ditch.

"I don't know what you're talking about." He turned and began to walk back to the buggy, one hand in his pocket. But several of the men were following him, three or four of them, and when he got into the carriage they surrounded the horse. He picked up his whip. He had no intentions of hitting them, but the uneasy feeling was right there inside him.

"Wait a minute," said the one man. "Don't lift that buggy whip yet. We're just asking you nice, Are you a yellowbelly or ain't you? Are you a conchie who won't fight or — "

"God damn it!" said Mastie. "No!" He lifted the buggy whip and brought it down smartly on Apple Boy's back.

"Just wondered," said the man and he let go of the bridle and stepped aside, smiling. The buggy wheeled around them smartly and turned the corner.

Well, I'm not, thought Mastie. *I wouldn't say I'm going to fight, but I'm no conchie either. That's Ira's department.*

6

The Red Dragon Market was a riot of food stalls, people from a dozen local towns, and auctioneers bawling in competition with the calves that had been brought for sale. The electric lights were on and hanging in clusters over the stalls although it was still light enough to see without them. It was the lights that fascinated Mastie. All week long he ate supper under a gas lamp because Pop couldn't afford a generator yet, but here there was magic. On any normal occasion he would have stopped at the soft pretzel stand before he even tied up and bought himself several, but today he had an appointment and he was late. No time for pretzels or bright lights. He drove straight up to the hitching shed and tied up alongside the hundred or so other rigs. He gave the stableboy a couple coins to feed his horse some hay. Then he reached under the buggy seat again and produced a small sweet-smelling bottle. He rubbed a bit of it on his face and hands.

She wasn't here! He walked around the ice cream stand twice to be sure. He was late. Had she gone with some friends? He frowned and turned to ask the out-of-town woman in the fashionable long white dress and pompadour hair under a flowery hat.

"Excuse me, was there a Mennonite girl — " the

woman turned toward him and puckered her lips. "Annie!" Her eyes couldn't fool him, "What in the world?" She had transformed herself into a fashionable lady. "What are you doing with those things on?"

"You're late, darling," she said in English.

"Take those clothes off. Where are your right clothes?"

"Mastie," she spoke in Dutch this time. "Don't get mad. But I was waiting and waiting. I had to find something to do. Everyone was going by and asking me to come along with him but I was waiting for you. So I walked around the whole market once and I found a little photographer's shop on the other side of the auction barn where they let you dress up and they take your picture for twenty-five cents. So I asked them if I could borrow one of their extra dresses and hats just for a while and I left my regular clothes there so they'd know I was bringing these back. Wasn't that clever? No one recognized me." She lowered her voice. "You're the only one."

"You couldn't fool me."

"Do you like it? They have men's clothes too," She laughed and tugged at his arm. "Let's go."

"I'm not walking with you. What if someone saw me?"

"Okay, then, I'll lead the way."

"You're funny," he said, and looked at her. "You're not mad at me?"

"Where's this photographer's shop?"

They slipped up a dark alley behind the stalls to a large tent that glowed like a yellow pumpkin from the electric lights inside.

The photographer was sitting in the shopwindow under a big sign that read "Your Picture — Only

68

Twenty-five Cents." Behind him a black camera mounted on a tripod looked into a room and an assistant was scurrying in and out of the room.

"Oh, it's you again," the photographer said.

"We'd like to have the men's outfit, too," said Mastie. The photographer nodded silently and motioned them in.

"Wilson, where's that extra men's outfit we have? You look great in that," he said, eyeing Annie again. "Why don't you just go into town and buy yourself one at Watt and Shand's? A girl with a face like yours shouldn't be wearing solid colors like those you had on. You should be wearing piles of bright colors. A hat to set off the face. What do you think of your girl in that outfit, son?" He turned to Mastie.

Mastie shrugged his shoulders.

"Ah, come on. Don't be so closemouthed, son. She's pretty. Compliment a girl. It makes her feel good. Right?" He tweaked Annie's ear. "Wilson!"

Wilson came struggling through the door with a mannequin. "This is the only extra."

"Well, give it to him. Yes, sir. Can I help you?" A young couple had come to the front of the tent, smiling and laughing. They looked as if they might be honeymooning.

"We'd like something to remember our trip to Pennsylvania by and my wife — this is my wife of two days, Rosie. . . ."

"Congratulations, sir, congratulations!" The photographer shook the man's hand.

"Thank you. Thank you. My wife says, 'Let's go get our pictures taken.'" He squeezed her and she giggled. "Still want to go through with it, Honey?"

"Twenty-five cents, sir. Your choice of backgrounds. An outdoor gazebo with roses, a Roman courtyard, or a wilderness landscape."

The attendant was struggling to get the coat off the mannequin. It was dusty on the shoulders, but it was a well-made coat with a double-breasted front and golden buttons. "And here are the matching trousers. Go ahead. Put them on. Just go back of the back of the wagon to change. No one will see

Mastie looked at Annie in the white lacy dress that fell to the floor. He didn't think he liked it. There was something good about her in her plain clothes. Something simple and familiar and her smile stood out of her simple clothes like a flag. Her white cap was like a crown.

"Come on," she said in Dutch. "No one will see you." The attendant, who was from out-of-state, looked up a little startled. He didn't understand Dutch.

Mastie took the clothes and went up into the photographer's van. He pulled the mannequin's stylish white coat on. The photographer looked up when Mastie came back and clapped his hands.

"Big artillery!" he said. "Here, we can't have that hat though. Where'd you get that black thing?" He took off his own white, President Wilson-style hat and set it on Mastie's head. "Yes sir, you're a good-looking boy. What do you think?" he said to his attendant. "A little like making a Christian out of the Congo nigger? Huh?" He laughed loudly. "Let's take the picture just like that. Step inside, would you?"

"What do you think?" Mastie said in Dutch. Annie was looking at him curiously. She laughed when she saw him looking.

They posed in front of a painted wall with painted roses and a low wall running to a summer gazebo. Mastie sat on a great wooden chair with curved arms and Annie stood behind him, her one hand on his shoulder and a rose curling up over her shoulder on the painted wall behind. The photographer snapped. When he came out, he smiled.

"I want a copy of that photo for my collection," he said. "A beautiful couple! Yes, you are. No, no thanks, you don't have to pay anything."

But Mastie insisted with his twenty-five cents. It wasn't right to have your picture taken and not pay. They changed back into their street clothes and walked down the alley between the stalls. It was warm. A strong breeze was blowing. He put his arm around her and pulled her against him so she could hardly walk without tramping on his feet.

"Somone will see us."

"Don't worry about it."

Each stall was a temporary table or two standing at the back of a wagon or van loaded with more fruit, vegetables, or whatever was being offered for sale. The horse was tied at the front of each wagon to a permanent hitching post. The alley formed between the two rows of stalls was wide, but on a hot summer night like this one, it was crowded with farmers and their families from all over Lancaster County. The children were licking ice-cream cones and holding onto their parents' hands. Here and there a soldier boy on leave from the barracks in Lancaster was walking with his arm around some farmer's daughter. The plain people and the "English folks" mixed freely. Amish women with simple smiling faces and a baby on the hip plus two or three toddlers were passing "English" women in stylish hats with baby carriages.

It was twilight and a kind of magic hung over the market area. Bright lights shone on fat green watermelons. "Hey, get your watermelon here. We'll plug it for you!"

"Po-TAY-toes! Po-TAY-toes! Ninety cents a bushel! Po-TAY-toes!"

"Hi, would you like some fudge? No, we don't have any mint. Vanilla, yes, chocolate, yes, but no mint. A pound, you say? Okay. That'll be eleven cents, ma'am. Beautiful evening, ain't it? Think it's gonna rain?"

"Hey, young lady. How would you like to eat fresh fish for once again? What's that? Sure, they're fresh. Fresh from the Chesapeake Bay by the evening train. Sea bass, trout, and porkies. Sea bass, trout, and porkies, I said. Here, smell 'em. An old fish smells fishy but we keep ours on ice. Good fish. Ah, come on, lady — stuff it in your ear."

"That's right, a genuine boa constrictor. We caught him in South America and he's a cousin to the big boas who can swallow a pig or a man whole. I'm going to let him wrap around my neck. Can you all see? I'm going to let him wrap around my neck but before I do — before I do, I want to tell you something, especially you folks out there who are visiting the doctor. You're being swindled — did you know that? Did you know that scientists have shown that there's no one that needs to go to the hospital? My grandfather was a full-blooded Indian of the Iroquois tribe and he never had a sick day in his life. That's right. Why? Because he ate only natural foods and ate natural herbs to protect himself. Sassafras, ginseng, arrowroot. . . ."

"Get your soft pretzel here. Soooooft pretzels. Sooooft pretzels. Get your soft pretzels here." It thundered.

They bought a couple soft pretzels and walked into the sales barn. It was closed down for the night. One or two cows were lying there yet, waiting for their new owners to come for them. Behind the stalls there was a pile of hay, half-hidden in the dark. "Let's sit down."

They sank into the pile of hay and once again Mastie felt the urge to hurt her, but it was mixed with a desire to know if she was his or not. Did she love him? He put his arm around her.

"Annie, marry me."

She drew a sharp breath, but said nothing. After a bit he said, "Annie, will you marry me?"

She shook her head.

"Why not? Did I surprise you?"

She shook her head again.

"Mmmm," he said, and began to kiss her. He stopped. "Don't you love me? No, you don't, do you? Is that why you danced with the bishop's son so long? You love him? Well, he's not as good-looking as he used to be."

She didn't look at him, not even when he tugged gently at her chin with his fingers. "Why won't you marry me? We could have a fine house and a new Ford someday and drive around together day and night, no more of this weekend stuff . . . and children . . ." he said. "I love children . . . lots of children. . . ."

Oh, and she was crying.

"What's wrong?"

"It's not that I don't want to," she said.

"Then what?"

"You're the one, Mastie. Remember when you took me to the Atglen Singing? I was just sixteen. And you stayed late at our house to talk. Do you remember? That's when I first knew you were the one."

"Then it's the bishop's boy."

She shook her head. "He's a mouse." She began to laugh in spite of herself, sniffing at the same time.

"Then marry me!" he said and wrapped himself around her. Her face was so close that it was out of focus but he could tell her eyes were following him because they kept flickering with light. They were running back and forth over his face. Her breath was warm and smelled faintly like a good soft pretzel. Her mouth was salty.

"I'm too young," she whispered. "Pop wouldn't let me." It was true, she was only eighteen, but was that so young?

"You don't love me?" he said.

"Yes, yes," she said.

"Then love me," he said, and slowly ran his hand down over her neck and into her dress.

"Don't," she said, and caught his hand.

He caressed her.

"Don't," she whispered, but it was more faint this time, like a thirsty, fasting pilgrim refusing water when his body is pleading for it, his conscience failing under the powerful thirst of his body. He kissed her again and again. "Don't," she said, but she had given up.

It began to rain on the tin roof overhead.

7

Mastie held Apple Boy with one hand and reached
out with his other hand to help Annie into the buggy. What took her so long? Then he heard her
splashing through the puddles on the other side of
the buggy and crawling in unassisted. He got in and
whistled to the horse.

"Are you cold?" he said. Annie was sitting, rigid,
looking out into the rain. "Is something wrong?" That
was another thing about her. Every feeling she had
flickered once in her eyes before she said it with her
mouth, if she said it at all. It was never a surprise
when she said it, if he watched her eyes he knew
it already. He pulled out a blanket and spread it
over their legs. It was chilly, and occasional rain-
drops and mist flew inside the buggy.

"There, how's that?" He reached over and put
his arm around her.

"No. No." She shook her head. "No." He took his
arm away.

"What's wrong? What did I do?"

"Everything!" she said, and burst out crying, bury-
ing her face in the blanket on her knees. They rode
in silence for five or ten minutes, the carriage wheels
splashing through the puddles that were beginning
to form by the side of the road. What could he say?

He brushed the hair back from her ear with one hand and ran his fingers lightly along her neck. That was another good thing about Apple Boy, you could think about the girl with you while he took you where you wanted to go.

"Could you tell me what's wrong?" he said. "Or shall I take you home?"

She shook her head "no." Another fifteen minutes and they were at the lane where he had planned to turn, but there was no point in going in. Neither of them was ready to go home yet. He whipped the horse and they went straight ahead.

"Where are we going?" she said, without looking.

"I don't know," he said. "Nowhere until we get things straightened out."

"Everything's wrong," she whispered. "Everything."

"Me?" he said.

She nodded.

"You don't love me anymore, you think I'm easy —"

"Annie!"

"It's true. You think I'm an easy girl."

Guilt ran down over him like a dipper of cold water. He dismissed it immediately. Of course he was in love with her. He wanted her again, to tell the truth, but she wouldn't let him touch her.

"You know I love you," he said. "Come, let me keep you warm." He put his arm around her.

She shook her head. "Don't. You don't love me, you think I'm easy — just like a town girl."

"That's not true. There's nobody else like you."

"You're just saying it."

"No." He was getting angry. What sort of a reflection on his honor was this? Did she think he loved every girl he met like that? "No, you're the only one I ever — " he began, and was embarrassed. "No, you're not easy, you're very — " He was going to say 'hard to get' but that didn't sound right. Did he have her then? No, because here she was defying him, telling him that he was lying to her.

"What am I?" she said, and covered her face. "Go ahead and say it, 'I'm an easy girl!' "

He jerked the reins hard and the jolt almost threw them out of the carriage. They were stopped on the edge of the road. He took hold of her shoulders and lifted her up, but her eyes wouldn't open to him. They were red and swollen and directed toward the carriage floor. "Annie, don't say that again," he said. "Never. I love you. Believe me. How long have we been seeing each other? Two years? You think I would go with you for two years if I thought you were that kind? No, I would have known it the first time I saw you. Why do you keep saying that stuff? I'm sorry. But bygones are bygones. Are you listening to me?"

She nodded.

"There's something different about you. You're spiritual. Yeah, you are. You make me think God must love us because you believe in Him and when you believe in something — well, you don't make mistakes. I mean if you believe something then it must be real. That's how you are. Didn't you know that? You're not easy. Don't let anyone say that. I've known you for two years and I still don't understand you. Well, almost. But not quite."

She laughed a little and opened her eyes to look at him. She hung in his hands like a rag doll and would have fallen right out of the buggy into the rain if he had let go.

"You still don't understand me?" she said. "You know me much better than Mom and Pop do."

"And do I love you?"

"If you say you do."

"Okay, we have that straight," he said and positioned her back in the buggy seat and pulled up the blanket again. "Are you comfortable? Where shall we go?"

"It's still not all right," she said.

"What now?"

She laughed at the look on his face. "No, it's not. I mean, you're out of the church, Mastie."

"So what?"

"That's one reason I can't marry you, I guess."

"You were there, weren't you? What was it like?"

"Your father read that Scripture about 'If your brother sins against you, go and tell him his fault . . . and if he refuses to listen even to the church let him be to you as a Gentile and a tax collector.' You know, and there was no comment otherwise from the congregation so he said, 'Then, let him be to us as a Gentile and a tax collector.' Your mother went out."

"How did my father act?"

"He didn't show anything."

"Hardhearted old bastard."

"I don't think so," she said. "You're the hardhearted one."

"What is this? You're really down on me tonight, eh? Why don't I just take you home." He cracked his whip and the buggy wheeled around on the road.

"Well, aren't you? I don't mean it nasty. No, I

don't, Mastie. The only reason I tell you is I love you. I wouldn't tell you if I didn't love you."

"You love me. Okay. So?"

"But everybody says it behind your back. They say your name and then they shake their heads. After church someone came up and said, 'And he won't come back either. You mark my word.' I told her it wasn't true."

"Who was it? That owl-face Mattie Hartzler? Or her little bat turd sister with eyes that follow you around, watching you, and as soon as you're out of sight she is a cow in heat that's bawling to all the church that *she thinks* she saw you doing so-and-so? Or Hannah Kratzflats who is too fat to reach her toes to clean them so she sits around knitting stuff and thinking what will become of everyone she knows and how the world is going to the dogs? Which one? Did I miss?"

"I wouldn't tell you if you did have it right."

"I think I'll take a long trip and not come back until the old cows die off. I think I'll join the Army. Things must be better there. At least they don't have old women in the Army. Here's the lane again. Shall we go in? No? Okay, so we look at cornfields a while." It was raining harder than ever and they passed one cornfield after the other in the dark.

"Even my father — " said Annie.

"What about your father?"

"I don't want you to be mad at him."

"Mad? Who's mad?"

"He says you're not to come back. You're not to come for me anymore, and if he sees you at our house he'll ask you to leave and if you keep coming he'll lock me in and watch the door himself.

It's just he wants to obey the church, Mastie. He likes
you, but as long as — "

"So he'd chase me off, huh?"

"He didn't say 'chase,' he said he'd ask you to
leave."

"I hope his barn burns down some night. No, I
don't. But he's a bastard, too. They all are."

They rode in silence for a long time, over the
covered bridge they passed every time they left her
place, past a creek that was high with water, past a
dozen little farms back in lanes, where mothers
were undoubtedly tucking their children in bed just
now and singing them good-night songs, fathers were
counting the costs and profits of their wheat harvests,
pigs were chewing on some old corncob that had just
turned up under a foot of mud, rainwater was pouring
into the cistern and grandmothers were washing their
hair with a basinful of it while grandfathers read to
themselves out of some great Bible printed in beautiful German script, young people were singing in
someone's house the same songs they had sung last
Saturday night and the Saturday night before that and
the Saturday night before that.

He yawned and yawned. There had to be
something more than this, somewhere out there.
Somewhere people must be doing exciting things
that were changing the world and great forces
were crashing together like stars out of orbit to
change lives. He was even tired of her and the
way her mind, too, was molded exactly like everyone
else's and the same thoughts and answers came
out of her head like the Chocolate Kisses up at
Hershey — each one exactly like all the one thousand
before it. What was happening over there? Was it

true it gave the boys a new excitement that could last them a lifetime?

"Mastie. . . ." Annie moved over against him and wrapped her arm around his. "Maybe you think they're all against you, but I'm not. I love you." She buried her face in his shoulder, and he could *hear* her smiling in the dark. "Let's pray," she said suddenly, and looked up at him. "He knows the way home." She meant the horse.

"Go ahead," he said.

"No, together. Close your eyes."

" . . . and for Mastie, dear Father," she said, "because You love him like I do . . ." she was holding fast to his arm, " . . . that someday he will believe You. We'll believe You together. . . ."

It was the last straw.

8

Mastie was picking stones out of the old wheat field. It was one of those jobs that came around every September, after the wheat was all harvested and the fields plowed up. Pop hooked the team to one of their old spring wagons and they went back and forth across the field, picking out any stones bigger than a child's fist that the plow had turned up.

"The Lord blessed Lancaster County," Pop said as he held a big one against his chest with both hands and brought it over to the wagon. "So much so he had to throw a few stones around to remind us it's still a world of troubles and care."

"It ain't paradise, that's for sure," said Mastie.

Ira was working on the far side of the wagon, silently.

"But it's as close to paradise as you'll ever find a place," said Pop. "Think about that."

"Hey, an airplane." Mastie shielded his eyes to look at it coming in out of the morning sun, buzzing, with its wings reflecting the sun. It came straight overhead, so low he could see the pilot. "Hey!" He threw up his arms. The man didn't hear him, of course, not above the roar. He went right on over to the mountains.

"Probably on his way to France," said Ira.

"He'll take care of himself. We have a lot of stones to pick," said Pop.

"That's it," said Mastie, taking his eyes off the plane. "Stones to pick, stones to pick. All we think about is stones to pick, and there's a war going on."

"So what do you want us to do?" said Pop.

"I don't know. Something."

"We can pray," said Pop.

"Pray? So how does praying beat the Germans? Tell me that?"

"We're German, too, Mastie. Think about it. Maybe God doesn't want the Germans to get beat. Maybe he doesn't want the English to get beat. Maybe he just wants everybody to stop fighting. I don't know, but the Bible says, 'Pray for your rulers.' Now what does that mean? That means —"

Mastie had already boarded up his mind, and he was with the pilot overhead, flying along over the open country and looking down on the county. The fields ran by below like a moving checkerboard and the houses were no bigger than the checkers themselves. Maybe there were some people in a field. What would people look like from the air? They must be tiny, possibly so tiny that you couldn't see them, so who would ever know from the air how many people were looking up and shouting at you? The air whistled around your head like it did in an open-top car — he'd had a ride in one — and you were on your way to — to France!

He had no idea what France was like, but surely they didn't pick stones out of the fields over there. There were vineyards, he had heard, and pretty girls to pick the grapes. More wonderful than Annie? Well, who knew, but at least they weren't dressed plain. France, that was where Paris was, wasn't it, and all the new styles of clothes came from there. No one was walking around in clothes that some bishop had said they must wear. France was where the fighting was, too. What was that like?

"Prayer," said Pop, and he was still standing at the edge of the wagon with the big stone clutched against his chest. "Listen, Mastie." He looked at him and his sharp eyes seemed to examine Mastie's soul like a doctor gazing down his patient's throat. "Are you listening? Don't you ever underestimate prayer. It's the most powerful weapon there is."

"Then why don't the Germans use it instead of zeppelins?"

"This is ridiculous," said Ira and he threw a handful of stones into the wagon. "We're all going to be drafted shortly and then what are we going to do? Talk about whether we should pray or not? Of course not. We're going to think about what we should do. Should we fight or shouldn't we fight?"

"What makes you so sure the war is wrong?" said Mastie. "The Germans have done a lot of terrible things over there. Newspapermen aren't allowed to tell half the stories, they're that terrible. I heard those soldiers carry around little medals from the Kaiser in their pockets that say they can do any crime they want to and the Kaiser takes the responsibility...."

"I don't believe it," said Ira. "Where'd you hear that story? From that Rydell preacher? I thought so."

"Well, he was over to Europe, and you weren't. He should know what he's talking about. If we don't stop the Germans from killing, who will?"

" 'He that taketh the sword shall perish by the sword,' " said Ira. "Now what does that mean? Historically, our church. . . ."

Mastie was back in France. . . . He had been hearing the bugles and watching the boys drill on the town square every time he went in and it was a glorious sight. When the bugle played they all marched one way. When it played another tune they all marched back. Then they lay down on the curb of the street, shoulder to shoulder, and aimed rifles out across the park. Not real rifles, because they didn't have any, but stocks or something. All at once the bugle sounded and they leaped up and went jumping over the hedge into the park with their rifles up in the air. It was a high hedge and half of the boys fell into it the time he watched, but he was sure he could jump it. In fact, he tried it one evening late at night on his way back from Annie's and sure enough, he cleared it with inches to spare. In France did they actually have hedges like that one? They were using horses over there, in what way he wasn't sure, but could their horsemen swim a river? Could their horsemen keep a horse's mouth as beautiful and scarless as a girl's? Did their horses run with their tails and necks high and good chest muscles like his did? What about planes, how were they using them?

"Boys," said Pop, and at last he dropped the rock into the wagon and looked at a thumb that he had skinned. "Let me just tell you this story yet, and then we must get back to work. When you were a baby, Mastie, and Ira was four or five, we took a trip to the Susquehanna one Sunday." He had told the story to them a hundred times before. "Seven of us there were — you boys, your Aunt Lena who was living with us at the time, and of course Grandpa and Grandma — that's your mother's father and mother. You know how the water comes down over the Prince George Falls. It sails so smooth right up to within ten feet of the falls that you'd never guess there was a falls ahead, and suddenly it hits those rocks and boom . . . boom . . .boom — " he waved his hand as if it were waves of water " — the water goes through the rocks and down over those falls. If anything ever went over those falls, it wouldn't have much of a chance. There's rocks below the falls the size of our shed. It was a pretty day, you know. The leaves were turning and Mom thought we'd go out to see the leaves, so she packed a picnic and I was talking to Grandpop and you boys were chasing leaves, I guess, and the next thing I knew, Mom screamed and I jumped up and there you were, out in the stream — in the smooth part. You said you were chasing a leaf, Ira, and you didn't think about your little brother and he went toddling right on in after you. You were at least 500 yards from us and I mean my heart stopped when I saw that." He breathed in sharply and held his breath, just as he did that afternoon. "And I just prayed right there. I couldn't tell you what I prayed — it wasn't long — and the next second the current caught Mastie here and he was so fat he just floated. And it pushed him right down the stream to a rock on the edge of the falls. I ran, I mean *I ran,* and I expected any moment the water would take you on over. But it didn't. I picked you up from those slippery rocks — "

"What about me, Pop?" said Ira.

"I think you were out by that time because you saw — It was a miracle, that's all. It was a miracle, boys, and I could only conclude that God had some reason for saving you, Mastie."

"No, the miracle was you got there in time," said Mastie. "You were a good runner and — "

"No. No. I could never have made it if you hadn't stuck on that rock for a moment."

"Okay, so we were fortunate there was a rock there."

"No. It was a miracle of God," said Pop, and he opened his eyes wide and gestured powerfully with his hands.

"What does that have to do with what we were talking about?" said Ira.

"Airplanes," said Mastie.

"Prayer," said the old man. "God hears the prayers of the righteous man. If God could save a boy from the falls, is it any problem for Him to solve a war?"

"Prayer!" said Mastie, and he threw a rock onto the wagon. One thing prayer didn't do was pick the rocks out of the field. It didn't solve wars either. Men did that.

"Mastie, you can go. We'll finish up here."

It was a routine run into town for a can of grease and a new plowshare so he could get back to plowing the other wheat field this afternoon.

Mastie ran into the house for his money, and suddenly, there it was again — another buzzing overhead. This time there were three planes in a triangle, like a group of cabbage butterflies. Something buzzed at the same time in his brain, and without hesitating, he turned and took a large box from the closet and be-

gan to stuff his clothes in. Not all of his clothes
— he could buy a few — but his shoes, yes. He put
in his toothbrush and the bottle of sweet cologne that
he used sometimes, and his razor, and the picture
of Annie and himself they had taken at the Red
Dragon Market.

He went downstairs and passed his mother on the
way out. She was baking bread and the whole
house smelled of it.

"Going to town?" she said, as he went by.

"Yeah."

"Get me a couple cantaloupe, would you? Do you
have money?"

"Yes."

"Well, here take a dollar anyway."

He went out the door and hooked up the wagon.
He put in his box and came back to the kitchen.

"Mom, can I take one of these loaves along?"

"You're that hungry? Why, you'll be back in time
for dinner."

"Not if there's a holdup in town. Everyone's starting the fall plowing, I may have to wait at the hardware."

"You don't just want bread. Why don't you wait
until you come back? I'm making stew."

"Bread's fine." He picked up a loaf and it was
still so hot it burned his fingers.

"Here, wrap it in this." She wrapped it for him,
and then he put his arm around her shoulder. He
dropped her dollar onto the windowsill behind her.
"Be good, Mom." He went out the door, and his
mother stood, startled, in the kitchen door.

"Mastie! Mastie!" He was up on the wagon now,
clucking to the horse. The wheels rolled.

"Mastie!"

"What?" He looked up.

"Where are you going?"

"Town."

"When are you coming back?"

Should he tell her the truth?

"Later," he shouted, and the horse headed out the lane.

He drove out the long lane and up the hard road past cornfield after cornfield. The roads were dusty. He came into Susquehannock and passed the hardware and the fruit market and the parade grounds. He drove straight up to the town hall and walked in past several beautiful posters of brave young men.

"I want to enlist," he said.

From there he went to the Acey's Clothes Emporium and bought himself a set of fashionable clothes, which he put on right here in the store, and then he went to the barbershop. He sat down in the chair.

"Don't you usually get yours cut at home?" the barber said.

"I want it short," said Mastie.

"Short? How short?"

"An Army cut." His friends and family would hardly recognize him now.

From there he went to the hotel. He put his money on the counter.

"Just passing through, are you?" said the clerk.

"No, on my way to France."

"You are? What a fine young man," she said and reached over the counter to shake his hand. "Jake. Jake." A sleepy head poked out through the kitchen door.

"What?"

"This young fellow's on his way to France."

"And he's staying here tonight?"

"Right."

"Why then, we put him up free!" said Jake, and he grinned. "You hear that, Mildred? We're not taking any money from this young fellow. He's on his way to get a job done." Jake's head disappeared.

It was evening. Mastie went back to the barbershop for his horse and hitched him in front of the hotel and went up to the room. He opened the window and sat on the windowsill with both legs hanging out, eating his loaf of bread.

"Hey!" someone yelled.

"Hey what?"

"You'll fall out of there."

"Nonsense. I'm in the Army!"

"Oh, you are. Well, bless your heart."

He took another bite of his bread and exhilaration ran through him. He felt like a new man. The air was sweeter; the people on the street below seemed like friends. Why, they were all in this together. France, here we come. He ate another bite.

"Nice evening, eh?" said someone below. It was the paper boy.

"Yes, but I'd rather be in France. Flying a plane maybe." He ducked his head and spread his arms as if he were a plane.

"Look out! You'll fall!"

Mastie stopped and grinned.

"Are you a pilot?" said the boy.

"Not yet."

"You're going to be?"

"I don't know. How much are your papers?"

"Two cents."

"Here." He dropped a nickel to the boy. "See if you can hit me."

The boy pitched the paper perfectly past Mastie's outstretched arm and into the room behind. He retrieved it. France needed horses and men to handle them. It was the first article at the top of the page, right under the news of a French victory. Horsemen? Why he could outhorse them all.

There were too few people in the street. He wanted to tell everyone his momentous decision. He ate the last of his bread and got down out of the window, and was just about to close it when he saw two friends on the street.

"Glick! Benjie!"

They looked up strangely.

"How do you know me?" said Benjie. His nose was bandaged.

"You don't recognize me?" said Mastie. He grinned. "Well, how do you like my girl now? She dances good, huh?" he said in Dutch.

"Mastie! Good God! What did you do to yourself?" said Glick. Benjie only looked at him strangely.

"Come on up," he said, and closed the window.

It was midnight before they finally broke up. Mastie drove them down to their buggies, which were parked on the outskirts of town, and from there he headed toward Annie's house.

9

Exactly at midnight Mastie tied his buggy to a tree in the Beiler apple orchard and ran to the house. The lights were out. He threw a handful of fine pebbles against the screen of Annie's second-floor window. It was a lovely night, perfectly dark and warm. The moon hadn't come up yet. He threw another handful.

"Who's there?" Annie said in a low voice. She had opened the window and removed the screen.

"It's me, Mastie."

"I'm coming," she said, and replaced the screen.

He went up on the porch to wait for her. The door opened and she was standing there in a white robe, tied modestly around the middle. She was barefoot and her hair hung loose down her back — it was the first time he had ever seen her with her hair loose. She smiled.

"What do you want, Mastie?"

"To talk," he said. Even in the dark he could hardly take his eyes off her. Her face shone as pure as a martyr's and her hair was incredibly long, combed tight against her head to the back and from there it fell down well below her waist. She smelled faintly of soap. She must have just come from the bath. "Were you sleeping?" he said.

"Yes," she said, and smiled again, and then her

92

smile vanished, as if she felt guilty for smiling.

"Let's sit down," he said, indicating the porch swing. "Does it squeak?"

"No, we just oiled it."

She smiled again and he felt sick. They sat down. He didn't want to tell her all of a sudden. She seemed to be expecting some good news, what he couldn't imagine. *We're not on those terms,* he thought, *if she could see into me. . . .*

Do you still love me? Her eyes said. *Is that why you came to see me?* She didn't smile; she only looked into his eyes in the dark as if she were trying to plumb them.

"You're wearing English clothes," she said.

"So are you." Had anybody ever heard of a *plain* bathrobe?

"What do you want to talk about?" she said, and smiled but almost instantly the smile vanished again. Then she *saw.* "Mastie!" she said.

"Shh. . . ."

"Mastie, you cut your hair."

"Not so loud. You'll wake your pop and mom." He took off his hat and turned sideways so she could see. It was cut short, just like an army boy's. "It was too hot in the summer," he said.

"You look terrible. Mastie, why did you do it?"

"Who's to keep me from it? I'm not part of the church anymore."

"You've done something," she said, and looked at him, "I know you have."

"I got a haircut, yes."

"You've done something. That's why you came."

He didn't want to tell her, but he was rapidly losing patience with all this fuss. He had planned to tell her straight out and then go back to the hotel, but here he was, dawdling and looking at her.

"Who says I did anything?"

But you did, her eyes said. *And it was because of me, wasn't it? You've come to tell me you don't love me anymore.*

"I enlisted," he said. "That's all. I'm going to France."

She smiled and suddenly burst into tears.

"No, no," she said.

He put his arm around her and pulled her against him. Her hair was still wet.

"You can't leave me," she said. "You don't love me anymore." She started to stand up and tears were running down her round face one after the other. He caught her arms and pulled her down. "You don't want me anymore. You're done with me."

"Annie. I'm not going through that again. It has nothing to do with you. I just have to get out of here." *It has lots to do with you,* he was thinking, *because you're the one person who could still keep me here and I don't want to stay. So, it's painful now but we'll both get over it. There are lots of girls out in the world.* He wasn't sure where all he meant when he thought of the world, but France, for one place. "Well, I should be going," he said. "The train leaves tomorrow. I need some sleep."

"Not yet, Mastie," she said. She dried her eyes on her sleeve. "I won't cry again." She tried to smile. "It's not too late to change your mind, is it?"

He nodded.

"But you never told me," she said.

"That's why I came tonight. So, it's only a few years until the war ends and then I come back. What's so terrible about that? Look, Annie, I am so sick of my father's preaching I could croak. And Ira's no better, only he preaches about the war. Okay, so I go see what the war's like once and for all. Then we can discuss."

"You'll get killed," said Annie. "That's what happens in the war."

"Don't be silly. How many people get killed? Maybe one out of a hundred or so, and maybe twice that many get wounded. So my chances are pretty small. I could fall off a horse here at home and be kicked to death." He wasn't quite sure of his reasoning. It made sense, but then he thought, *Somebody has to be killed. That's the purpose of fighting. If nobody got killed the war would go on forever.*

"But falling off a horse is different. You're not killing anyone else."

"I'm not going to kill anyone else. I'll be with the horses or flying a plane. That's the kind of job I'm getting."

"Promise me you won't kill anybody, Mastie. It would be terrible if you shot someone."

"Shot somebody!"

"The Bible says it's wrong, you know. I don't want you to shoot anybody."

It hadn't even occurred to him that he might shoot somebody. He was going to see France, maybe to ride the horses and pull a few artillery guns, or go jumping over hedges. There was the possibility he would make friends with some mademoiselle — nothing permanent, just a cup of coffee together, maybe. And there was still the possibility of flying a plane. They needed pilots, the posters in the enlistment office had said — pilots for those cabbage butterflies to fly over the country and, of course, they would fire at enemy planes. If it should happen that he got sent to the front, of course he would fire his rifle in the direction of the enemy. They would fire back. If luck was with him, he wouldn't get hit. If luck was with them, they wouldn't get hit.

But shoot somebody point-blank? Never!

"Okay, I won't."

Annie began to push the porch swing a little with her legs.

"I knew you were going to go," she said.

"How did you know?"

"I just knew, even before you told me about it."

"You're funny. You're a wonderful girl," he said and wrapped his arms around her and the stiffness between them was gone. "You're just like a good cigar," he said. "You make me good again."

"A cigar!"

"Shh. . . ." She was more than a good cigar. She was like a narcotic, and when he was with her he wanted the sun to stop right where it was on the other side of the planet while he had his arms around her, one arm covered by that cascade of hair. His arms felt heavy and sleepy. He couldn't leave. It was a pure embrace. "Schnoogli — boogli," he whispered and blew into her ear. It was his other name for her. She smiled to herself, like the last smile of a sunflower before it is cut down at the end of the summer.

"When are you coming back?" said Annie after a bit.

"I don't know. When the war's over, I guess."

"Mastie, promise me you'll come back," she said. He felt her face turning. She was trying to see his eyes.

"Promises, promises. Don't you take my word for anything?" The spell was over. She had broken the spell. He leaned back against the swing.

"But you didn't say you will come back."

"How do I know? Maybe I'll like France and decide to stay and farm over there."

"What about me?"

"I could send for you."

"What about the church, Mastie?"

"Are you going to preach?" he said. "They have churches in France."

"But not our Mennonite Church," she said. They're the ones that excommunicated you and you should ask forgiveness from them. It's not the same in France."

"Don't get me mad," he said.

"But tell me," she said. "Tell me if you're coming back."

"How do I know? Nobody here wants me to. Why should I? Do you want me to?"

"You know I do."

"Okay, so I'll come back."

"Promise me," she said.

"Okay, I promise." If that made her happy, all right. It didn't change his mind. At the bottom of him someplace he knew he was never coming back. He knew he was never going to see her again.

"So, I must go," he said, and stood up.

She stood up and the porch swing began to creak

wildly behind them. Immediately the guinea hens roosting on the other edge of the porch began to cackle.

"*Donnerwetter!* I thought it didn't screech." The window on the other side of the house opened and they could hear someone talking.

"If it's that fox after the guineas again, Pop, I think you better go down."

"Look if Annie's in bed."

"She's not."

"Well, maybe it's her. Annie!"

"Yes."

"Is that you?"

"Yes."

"What are you doing?"

"Just getting a breath of air, Pop."

"Well, come to bed or you won't be fit for anything tomorrow."

"Okay."

He walked her to the edge of the porch.

"Well. . . ."

She threw her arms around him again.

"Mastie . . ." she said.

"Now, you be a tough girl," he said. "You take care of yourself so when I come back you're in good health." *So this is it*, he thought. He kissed her once and put on his new white straw hat, the flat kind that everybody was wearing in town. Then he turned around and walked right out of the lawn, out the lane to the apple orchard, and got into his buggy without looking back once.

10

Mom's eyes were red and swollen, and every few minutes she would reach into her cape for her handkerchief and wipe her eyes again. That would prompt Pop to say, "Now Mom. . . ."

To Mastie, though, it seemed like the longest meal he had ever eaten. He shouldn't have come, he told himself. It would have been much less painful that way, but Glick and the bishop's son, Benjie, had persuaded him to. "You never can tell what will happen. You ought to go say good-bye." He picked at his food. Things seemed different already after three days away. It hardly seemed like his home anymore. He was on his way to France and these people here clutching at him — they'd get over their feelings. He wished Mom would at least stop crying. It made him feel criminal.

"Look, Mom — "

"I don't know what we did wrong," she said.

"What's the sense of bawling? You didn't do anything wrong."

"Train up a child in the way he shall go and when he is old he will not depart — depart — " said Mom, and she couldn't finish it.

"Now, Mom . . ." Pop put his hand on her shoulder. "So, what did Annie have to say?"

"I don't think that's anybody else's business."

"Listen, Mastie. It's our business. You are our business. We brought you into this world. We raised you and you're our boy."

"I didn't come to argue. You said, 'Come for dinner,' so here I am. Now can I eat? Pass the potatoes." There was a long silence.

"Your hair used to look so nice the other way," said Mom. "I don't know why you suddenly want to throw everything away. It just doesn't make sense to me. No, it doesn't."

"This is the way I like it, that's why," said Mastie. He went back to his potatoes.

"The Army — " said Mom. "When I think of the awful things that are happening in France that we hear so much about, and then think that my boy might kill some other mother's boy — "

"I'm not going to kill anyone. Anyway, they're not just 'mothers' boys.' They're German soldiers."

"We're German," said Pop.

"We're not German. We're American!"

"Well, we were once German — and Swiss. We speak Pennsylvania German. They're no different than we are, except for one thing. They've caught a disease and now they're sick, and if we don't watch out we're going to catch the disease too, because it's contagious. Do you know what that disease is?"

"No."

"Why *war,* of course. War is a disease, just like tuberculosis, and it's catching. Now does it make sense to get sick yourself in order to help a sick man?"

Mastie yawned. He hadn't had much sleep.

"I have a plan," said Pop. "I'm going to write

100

to your Uncle Joe's in Indiana and see if he can scrape up some work for you. Joe's in carpentering and he makes some of the best tables and chairs in the Midwest. There's a chance for you to apprentice yourself to a real master and learn something you could take with you for a lifetime. Having a trade is a gift of God. You can always use it. I was thinking of this a while already but I wasn't going to suggest it for another year or so, but since you're set on leaving — "

"I've enlisted, Pop," said Mastie, "and there's a law against quitting once you're in."

"You leave that to me," said Pop. "I'm going into town in the morning and I'll call on those people and explain how things are. I know the officer there in town — Sholley. We used to be just like that in school." He twined his fingers. "He's a man who listens to reason. There's a difference between being drafted and enlisting. You're not twenty-one yet."

"You're not going to take me out."

"Sure I am. You're not going to the Army, son."

"Do you think you can stand up to the United States government? You can't — they'll squash you — and secondly, I'm going to France and you and the whole church can't stop me. You may be able to keep Ira out if you're lucky, but you're not keeping me. I want to go."

"Mastie, I understand. I understand," said Pop. "Believe me, I know why you want to leave home. I can understand. I wasn't born yesterday. You take what we have for granted — you were born in it — but I don't. I'm going to tell you a story."

"I don't have time," said Mastie.

"What time does your train leave?"

"Six, but I have to go back to the hotel first."

"Are you packed?"

"Yes."

"Then you have plenty of time. Okay," he said, crossing his legs. "You made a foolish decision but you'll live with it. Just like I lived with somebody's foolish decision. I was born a bastard."

"A . . ." Mastie opened his mouth.

"Illegitimate," said Pop. "That's right." Mom didn't seem the least bit surprised. She was calmly peeling an orange.

"But Grandpop Stoltzfus —"

"A bastard," said Pop. "That's not a kind word to use, but I was called that many a time when I was in country school. We always told you Grandpop Stoltzfus, that would be my father — your grandfather — wasn't around anymore and you may have thought he died long ago. The truth is, he only died a year or two ago. We found that out in the papers, but I never met him."

"He only died that recent?"

"Yes. You always liked your Grandmom, didn't you? Everybody did, because she had a personality just like that." He snapped his fingers. "All sunshine and flowers. But, you see, that was her downfall. She didn't use her head. She wasn't more than eighteen when her father — that would be my grandfather — first began to let her work outside the home, mainly cleaning houses for rich people in town. Well, she got work with a man in town whose name was Pierce, and the next thing she was in love with him, but he was already married. But love — well, it's a hot item. The next thing she knew she was in the family way with me. You didn't know this story, did you? Because I didn't tell you — that history of my birth has dogged me from the day I was born. Shall I continue?" His audience was silent, so he went on.

"But I was happy, don't misunderstand. I was happy and I played around my grandfather's farm because I was just like any other child, as far as I knew. I never wondered who my father was. Mother never talked about any other man, so I just assumed it was Grandpa. In my child's mind that made sense. He was a good man who taught me how to fish and ride horse and occasionally he cut a willow switch and whipped me, so I thought he was my father. Very shortly I started to go to school and the other little children — some of them were plain and some of them weren't — would giggle when my back was turned. I began to wonder. I asked them why they were giggling and none of them would tell me. One day I had a fight with the neighbor boy and he called me a bastard. I didn't know what that meant but I was sure it wasn't good, so I really scrubbed his head in the dirt, you can be sure."

"When I got home I asked my mother, 'What's a bastard?' and she got a terrible look on her face and said, 'Don't ever say that word again. "That's a bad word.' But I wanted to know what it meant, so I went to Grandpa and asked him and he looked surprised, but he told me. Then I said, 'You're my papa, aren't you, Grandpa?' and he said, yes, he was my papa.

"But that didn't settle it, because about a year later the same boy called me a bastard again and this time I told him it wasn't true. I had a father only I called him 'Grandpa' instead of 'Father' like most of them called their fathers. That smart little cookie just laughed. I can still remember him laughing and saying, 'So your Grandpa has two wives, does he?' Word got around — why do people like to tell such things? — and the other children teased me mercilessly. I don't even want to repeat the things they said, but one thing I remember. The boys had a club that sometimes walked around together at the farmer's market or went fishing together or something like that and I wanted to become a member but they said, 'No, you can only become a member if you have a father.'

"So I began to wonder if Grandpa really was my father. Maybe it was Uncle Aaron, I thought, because he didn't have a wife, although as I got older that didn't make sense either because all the fathers of the boys lived with their mothers. There was much less divorce in the county in those days than now, you see. I wasn't really close to Uncle Aaron, but I decided to ask him just to make sure, and he said, 'No!' That's all he said, 'No,' and he turned away and went back to whatever he was doing, pounding a shoe on his horse, I believe, so you see how things piled up. First it was the schoolchildren telling me I didn't have a father and then it was my own family refusing to answer the question straight for me. Well, about the time I reached ten — Oh, yes, there was one other incident from my earlier school years.

"There wasn't enough work to do on Grandpa's farm over the winter, so my mother started to go again to the homes of rich people who lived in town and help them with their cleaning and take care of their children for a day or two. Then in the evening, around the supper table, she'd tell us all about the place where she'd been. She was good at telling stories and describing things, and she'd get so caught up in the story she'd forget to eat her potatoes and Grandmom — that's my grandmom — would say, 'Mattie, eat your potatoes before they get cold.' But my mother went on with her story. How she loved to tell stories." He picked up his cigar and lit it, which was a sign that something important was coming in his own story.

A change had come over the dinner table as well. Pop had relaxed into the story. He spoke forcefully, with a minimum of work, moving his hands to make a point. Mastie forgot the clock.

"Anyway, she came home one evening to me and she had hardly unbuttoned her winter coat when she came over to me and rubbed her hands on my cheeks and said, 'Guess what, Isaac. The folks where I worked today have a little boy and he's in the third grade, too, at a private school. And his name is Isaac, too!' That excited me because I didn't know any other Isaacs at the time, although I've met a lot since, so I said, 'And did you tell them you have a little boy named Isaac, too?' I'll never forget it, Mastie. She got red all over and then she began to cry and I had never seen her cry before. She ran into another room and didn't come out for supper. She never did answer my question, but I'm sure she didn't tell that family about me.

"As I said earlier, by the time I was ten, I didn't care much who my father was though. I was busy, here and there, learning all kinds of good things on the farm and after a while I got interested in girls, although your mother was still far off the picture. When I was about fourteen, though, two important things happened that brought back the whole subject of my birth again. I had never really forgotten it, of course. In fact, it affected my personality because I never wanted to tell people about my family. If I did, there was that *question* again. But when I was fourteen, I found out how babies were born because Grandpa told me. I always knew how calves and puppies were born, but I never knew it was the same for humans.

"Suddenly I was terribly curious. Oh, I was burning with curiosity to know who my father was, because — pardon me for saying it, Mom, but I should give Mastie the whole picture — because I imagined all sorts of men in bed with my mother. I was miserable. I stood at the mirror and looked at myself for hours to see who I looked like. I knew my father had to be white, and I thought my ears looked like Grandpop's, but that was as far as I got. I started to pester my mother to tell me who my father was, but she wouldn't tell me. One day when we were at market, though, she went out and bought a newspaper and stood right there in the street looking through the paper and all of a sudden she stopped at a picture and said, 'There, that's him.' It was the mayor of Ephrata!"

"The mayor!" said Mastie.

"I found out afterward it was true. She had worked at his home for a year or so around the time I was born. Maybe you think I was happy to have such a well-known man as my father, even if he didn't know me, his little Dutch farm boy. I wasn't though. I was afraid. Yes, I was afraid if I met him in town I might hurt him, or even kill him, and in the second place I was angry because I was sure he'd tricked her. One good thing came out of the whole experience. I resolved to have a good family and to bring them up in a community of God's people. I thank my grandfather for that." The old man stopped, put out his cigar on the sole of his shoe and looked up at Mastie.

"I didn't know that," said Mastie, spellbound.

"No, I didn't suppose you did."

"Why are you telling me now?"

The old man shrugged his shoulders and smiled. "Who knows? Does it have anything to do with who we are today and who you are?"

"What do you mean?"

"Does it have anything to do with your wanting to leave home?"

"No," said Mastie, and slapped his mind shut like a buggy box. It was, after all, going to be a sermon.

"Get me another one," said Pop, pointing to the drawer where the cigars were kept. "I think it does."

"I have to go," said Mastie. He stood up.

"One minute. Sit down." The old man gestured toward the drawer.

"You shouldn't," said Mom. "It's bad for your health."

"Okay, then, a cup of tea. Meadow tea. Are you still thinking?" he said, turning to Mastie. Partly out of fear, partly out of respect, Mastie didn't walk out, but no, truthfully, he was not thinking of the question anymore. *The mayor of Ephrata was my grandfather!* he was thinking.

"Mastie, you want to leave God's people and I want you to know what you'll find over there. You'll find women, just like the mayor, who want to trick you. You'll find out what it is like to be lonely and cut off. It's only your own good and protection I'm looking for when I tell you to stay and go into carpentering."

"I'm done thinking," said Mastie. He went to the nail for his jacket. "Thanks for the story."

"Sit down," said Pop.

"I'm going," said Mastie. "What our country needs is soldiers, not *carpenters*. What good is it to build fancy tables if they end up in the kitchen of a German? That sounds crazy, but they want our country. I'm for protecting ourselves and having a little progress once in a while."

"That makes sense to you, because you are young," said Mom, "but when you are old like Poppy and I, then you will see that we leave things up to God. . ."

"You've been influenced by Pop," said Mastie, "You even think like he does. You can't see because you have blinders on your eyes just like a horse to keep him from seeing left or right, only straight ahead."

"What's this about blinders?" said Pop.

"Nothing, nothing."

"Come on. I want to hear it."

"I said your eyes are blinded like a horse's. You only see straight ahead, never left and right. All you see is the church and Jesus, Jesus, Jesus, and nothing on the left or right of you."

"Mastie, you don't know how right you are," said Pop, shaking a knife at him, with which he was about to peel an orange. "But finish it."

"Finish what?"

"Finish your story."

108

"That's all."

"No, it's not. You've told us how we are. Now how are you?"

"What do you mean?"

"If we have horse blinders and can't see sideways, what about you?"

"Me? Why I see everything. I see left and right and all around."

"Everywhere," said Pop. "Right? Everywhere but straight ahead. Your blinders are down across the fronts of your eyes so you can see everywhere but straight ahead. And what will you have if you throw this life on the manure pile?" said Pop. "Yes, you can do that. But let me warn you what the Bible says. It says the devil walks about looking for vacant spots. And if you throw away everything you've ever had, and I mean the things you grew up with, the traditions, and God too, that's what you will be. A vacant spot. The very sort of a place the devil will walk into smiling."

"Are you telling me I'm going to hell?" said Mastie.

"No," said Pop, "I didn't say that. But that's where you may end up. . . ."

"Pop." It was Mom.

"I'm going," said Mastie. He put on the jacket.

"Sit down," Pop said. "We're not going to part like this, Mom, sit down and we'll have a prayer together."

Mastie kissed Mom on the forehead abruptly and walked right past Pop on his way to the door.

"Mastie!"

His father stood up, and that was the way he remembered him — standing at the table, his eyes piercing and attempting to hook Mastie with one last futile try, his fists on the table and his long red beard for which he was named Red Isaac failing to conceal his trembling mouth.

II. Mastie, 1918

1

Morning came very slowly into the bay where the big troopship lay. It was foggy and the fog had collected in icicles on the ship's railing. After all, it was January.

"Quiet as a viewing," said the fat soldier, looking out at the water.

"You think we're near France?" said the skinny soldier. He wore glasses and after two weeks below deck his face looked about the same color as a pile of old newspapers.

"Hey, I don't hear the motor."

The skinny soldier's eyes got bigger. He listened carefully. Sure enough, there wasn't a sound from the bottom of the ship.

"Maybe we ran out of fuel," he said. "What if we ran out of fuel? We're helpless. The submarines can come up and pop us off — just like that."

"We're not out of fuel."

"What's that?" said the skinny soldier.

"What's what?"

"Over there. That black thing."

"I don't see anything."

"Right over there. It's getting bigger. It's a sub!"

The fat soldier grabbed the skinny soldier's arm.

"Just a minute before you go yelling that. I don't

see anything."

"Look at it, Froggie. It's black. It's bigger than a sub. It must be a ship."

All of a sudden, Froggie saw it, right there where he had been looking all the time. The fog had eliminated perspective. It was impossible to tell if it was five hundred feet away or two miles away. But it ran both ways as far as he could see.

"That?" he said. "That's France."

"France?" said the skinny soldier Caloway. "We're here?"

Froggie turned around and leaned his back on the railing. He filled up with air and suddenly blew a long mournful note. It was exactly like a trumpet, but he did it with his big, vibrating lips.

"Hey, France!"

Soldiers jumped out of bunks below the decks.

"No more bean soup, Caloway!" said Froggie, and he suddenly grabbed Caloway and hugged him tremendously. "You want to know what I'm having when we make shore? Meat. Meat, Caloway. Real meat. In a big stew with onions and garlic and peppers, cooked with tomatoes, and all together in a puddle on a plate of rice that big! How do you like that, huh? Real meat, Caloway!"

Caloway took a deep breath.

"They don't eat meat in France. They eat snails."

"Snails?"

"Yes, snails."

"You mean raw? Raw snails?"

"No, they cook them."

"Cooked snails. No."

The first soldiers came running up, still buttoning themselves.

114

"Where is it?"

"Over there."

"Where?"

"There!"

Sure enough, it was getting bigger and clearer all the time as the fog lifted.

"Who's whistling?" said Froggie.

"It's that college boy."

He was whistling as he came up the steps from the lower deck. It wasn't an ordinary whistle either, but a beautiful whistle that trilled and twittered.

"Tell that guy to shut up," a navy man said.

The soldier went on whistling though. He was wearing a perfectly starched and ironed uniform, in contrast to Froggie and Caloway who wore damp, rumpled clothes that they had pulled on while they were still half asleep.

"Shut up," the navy man said again.

"Okay, you don't appreciate good music," said the soldier. "That's not my fault."

"Good music. Ha!"

"Mozart."

"Ha!"

"So, that big black thing is France?" the college boy said, joining the line along the rail.

"You better hope it ain't Germany," said Froggie.

"Shall we tell them we're here," said the soldier. "Good morning, France!" He grinned at Caloway and Froggie. "Who knows? That may be the shore from which William the Conqueror launched his ships on a trip that would forever change England. And the English language. And here we are, paying back the compliment, so to speak. A hundred years from now, five hundred maybe, people will say that the day

Woodrow sent his men to France was the day that changed France forever. The French language, the French people, the French food — "

"Churchill, tell me the truth," said the fat soldier. "Do they eat snails in France?"

"Of course they do," said Churchill. "And stinky cheese."

"Cheese?" said Froggie.

"Cheese. Camembert, it was Bonaparte's favorite. They make it here."

"Cheese and snails. Pass the bean soup again, boys."

"How about wine?" said Churchill. "How about that?"

"They make wine?"

"Sure they make wine."

"Where's the farmer?" said Froggie. "I thought farmers were such early risers. Where is he now?"

"The new guy? The one who transferred from Camp Meade?"

"Yeah. Where is he?"

"I'll get him," said Caloway. He ran downstairs and came back in about ten minutes with Mastie.

"Hey, farmer, I thought you guys all get up at three to milk the cows."

Mastie didn't say anything. His bones were sore from two weeks in the bottom of the ship and he had lost all of last summer's tan. He had also lost a good twenty pounds in camp training. If he had good muscles before, his muscles were like grapevines now. He went to the rail.

"Wake up, farmer." Froggie clapped his shoulder.

"Mmm." He shrugged off the hand.

"That's it over there," said Churchill, pointing

at the black land.

"France?" said Mastie.

"France!" said Churchill in a magnificent voice.

"Why didn't anybody tell me? We're here."

"We're here is right," said Churchill. " 'And we won't come home till it's over, over here.' You like that song, France? But you know, war isn't what it used to be."

"Oh?" said Froggie.

"No, it's not. War used to be something glorious. The flower of England's youth would go forth against the flower of France — "

"Flowers?"

"It's an expression. The best, so to speak. England's best took up arms against France's finest, and maybe they fought for a whole day, like they did at Hastings, with longbows and swords and shields. Or Troy, when the Greeks came up in ships against the Trojans and each man prayed his god would help him, and they went at each other with their swords. You looked your enemy right in the eyes and you could see if he was afraid or not. But who sees an enemy's face in this war? You know they have guns now that shoot twenty miles? No heroes in a war like that. The day of heroes is over."

"All I want to do," said Froggie, "is get out of this alive. That's all."

"Well, progress," said Churchill. "Progress in weapons has taken away the glory of battles and heroes. It's a new kind of war, not for honor and bravery but for democracy!"

Froggie belched loudly.

Churchill looked at him with disgust. "How uncouth," he said.

"I could swim from here to the shore," said Mastie. "If it wasn't for the fishnets."

"You'd freeze."

"I meant if it was summer."

"We're moving!" said Caloway. "Hey, we're moving!"

Without their noticing, the motors had started. The coastline began to move closer. Why, there was a city on the banks. A boat or two appeared, still a long way off, and then factories on the waterfront began to throw up smoke. A group of smaller boats passed them on the way out to sea. Fishing boats, maybe. The men aboard waved up at the big convoy ship.

"Look at those houses, would you?" said Mastie. "Aren't they pretty with red roofs?" He wasn't in the least bored, and that was a change from the way he had felt back home.

"What's so great about a house? A house is a house," said Froggie.

"But they're French houses," said Mastie. He was getting excited. "French people live here."

"Of course. It would be a lot more wonderful if there were Africans living in them."

"Smells like rotten fish," said Mastie.

"Harbors always smell that way," said Churchill. "I hope the Heinies, wherever they are, hear us coming, because as sure as my two feet are pointing at the shore, I plan to make a few think about the crimes they've perpetrated."

"They've what?" said Froggie.

"Perpetrated. Committed. Done."

"Well, say 'done' then. I hate people who use big words."

"There's people down on the docks. See them."
Mastie pointed them out. At first only their hats were
discernible, but as the ship moved closer, they could
also see waving arms, then faces. "Looks like the
whole town." A raw cold wind was blowing. On the
walls of the warehouses along the waterfront there
were signs with strange words.

"*Café, café!*" I know that one," said Froggie.

"Okay, what's it mean?"

"To eat. A place to eat. In other words, honey,
a restaurant!"

"They're waving at us. Isn't this fun?" said
Mastie. "Hello, hello." The people on shore began to wave their hats now too. The soldiers on the
ship waved back but as the ship moved closer and
they saw strange clothes and faces, the cheering
gradually died down on both sides. The ship was
actually tilting left because of the weight of the
thousands of men on that side. The people on the
dock looked up with curiosity. The cheering stopped.

"Isn't this great?" Mastie said, and he pounded
Caloway on the back. "Don't it just make you glad
to be alive? We'll be landing in a few minutes,
and after that who knows what?"

Caloway nodded. "Who knows what?" he said. "I
don't want to die."

"Die? Who said anything about dying?"

"That's what happens in France. Read the papers."

"You won't die unless you're supposed to," said
Churchill.

"Well? We just going to look into each other's
eyes?" said Froggie. The ship was less than three
hundred yards away now, drifting under a tugboat's
push. "Well, anybody?" said Froggie. He held up his

119

hands as if to clap, and at the same moment he blew a trumpet note out of his fat cheeks. The soldiers hurrahed on his signal and began to clap. They took off their hats and waved them.

"They're clapping back," said Mastie, pointing at the dock. "Hey, hey. . . ." A girl on the dock caught his eye. Her hands were in a muff, but she was smiling at him, he was sure of that. Something about the way she stood there with a smile in her round penny face reminded him of Annie. He crossed his arms in an X.

"What's that?" said Froggie. He was still waving his hat. Down on the dock, the girl took one hand out of her muff and crossed her arms in an X. "Hey, Pennsylvania has himself a French girl!"

The ship trembled against the dock and now they were looking down on the crowd from several stories up. They cheered and cheered. Some men tried out a few French words on the crowd and a man in the crowd shouted up in English to the soldiers. In a little while they all got tired of that, though. Still, there was no order to leave the ship. Lunchtime came and nobody ate at the cafes on shore. They all had biscuits and bologna gravy on the ship. After dinner, there wasn't anyone left on the dock except for a few boys who walked on their hands and danced for money. What were they waiting for? This was France, wasn't it?

They stayed on ship all through the night as well. The rumor was that the ship had docked on the wrong river and rather than go back out to sea and risk the submarines again, they were going to unload right here and march cross-country to the town where they would train. The walk would be good for them and besides, things weren't ready in the town where they were going. They would be billeted in citizens' houses and the citizens hadn't been asked permission yet. After all, the French were friendlies. The army couldn't just walk in and take over. Not without a day or two's advance notice.

2

It was dark and snowing. The big flakes landed on the shoulders and hats of the soldiers as they marched. At first they melted. But shortly they began to stick.

French snow! Mastie thought. It didn't bother him at all that his ears were getting wet. It didn't bother him that he had been marching since sunrise and had a fat blister on each of his big toes. It was all part of the adventure. Why, even the words had a magical ring to them. *French* food, and over there, wasn't that a *French* cow? her head sticking through an open barn door and looking at them in the dark. Tomorrow maybe a *French* girl would set a stool under her and milk her.

"Is this that French town we were looking for?" someone yelled out up ahead. Sure enough, they were coming into a town. On all sides of the broad street the buildings were dark and picturesque. They certainly didn't look like the buildings in Susquehannock, but more like the buildings you might see on a picture postcard that someone sent you.

Up ahead the regiment commander was sitting on his horse under the one elegant iron streetlight in the town square. His horse kept twitching its ears to dump the snow out. The commander suddenly pointed his riding crop and began to shout. Like the

122

foot of a tall rooster planting itself on the heart of the town, the marching column broke into three around him, one part to his right, one part straight ahead, and the third to his left.

A window shutter creaked and opened a crack. Then a man wearing a nightcap and dressed in a nightgown thrust his head out and looked right at Mastie. Mastie saluted cheerfully. The man's head immediately disappeared, then reappeared with an American flag. He began to shout and wave his flag.

"*Venez vite! Les Yankees sont là!*" (The Yankees are here!), he shouted. His mouth steamed. The town woke up and two or three heads appeared in every window. The snow went on falling gently, crossing the lighted windows like swarms of mosquitoes in summertime. The marching men did not look left or right at first. Only their eyes acknowledged the welcome Lyoncourt was giving them. The snow was collecting on the brims of their hats.

"Left, right, left, right, left, right, left, right. . . ."

Perhaps it was the first group of Americans this town had seen. The citizens were shouting as if it was. Every window along the street was lit by now and several boys even came out in the snow to cheer, and throw snowballs at each other. Then the American band in the rear started playing.

"*Over there, over there, send the word, send the word over there. . . .*"

The whole regiment, a half mile long with their horses, sang along.

"*Over there, over there. Send the word, send the word over there,*

That the Yanks are coming, the Yanks are coming,

the drums rumtumming everywhere.
So prepare, say a prayer. Send the word, send the
word to beware,
We'll be over, we're coming over, and we won't be
back 'til it's over, over there."

The melody broke. Once more the only sound was of boots with cold feet inside and once more the townspeople cheered. Once more the band struck up the tune and they sang the song again. Mastie's column turned right under the streetlamp.

"Hello! Hello!" said Churchill. He waved at someone.

"Do you know them or something?"

"Of course I do — they're the people we came to defend."

"Oo-la-la," said the fat soldier.

"I'll bet she's a war widow, that's what I'll bet," said Caloway.

"Then she needs a little friendship, don't you say?"

"I guess this is where we stop."

Up ahead, the lieutenant was standing at a doorway under a weak houselight, the snow still falling on his hat. He was talking with a lot of gestures to a man with a moustache that took up a large part of his face. The lieutenant turned.

"Okay. Fall in here. Brush the snow off before you go in."

"You mean this is where we sleep?"

"What's wrong with you? You want to spend another night in a tent?"

"No, sir."

"Looks like they have cows," said Mastie.

"Gawd!" the fat soldier said, looking at the manure pile that they had to pass to get into the house.

124

"So, we get fresh milk."

"Fresh, all right," said the fat soldier. "It smells fresh."

"Fall in, fall in," the lieutenant said. "Get that snow off your hats before you get here. And I don't want to hear anything except boots. You think this is Christmas or something? Gawd, you're a bunch of turkeys."

The line was slow, however, not because of their talking but because the man with the moustache wanted to greet each soldier personally as he came in. The lieutenant could not communicate that he wanted the welcome time cut down. He gave up. The Frenchman stretched out his arms to Mastie and planted his moustache first on one cheek, then on the other, at the same time mumbling something in French.

"Thank you. And the same to you," said Mastie. He nodded to the man's family behind him in the kitchen and without noticing cracked the butt of his training rifle against a large crock on the floor, set there to prop the door open. The woman shrieked and jumped up. Juice was already running around his boots.

"Clumsy!" The lieutenant yelled.

"Antoinette!" The Frenchman yelled, waving his hands.

"They lend us their barn and then you break their pot," said the lieutenant. "Why?" A big pickle floated out of the crock and onto the floor and the woman got down on her haunches with both hands to the side of the crock, holding back the pickles and calling something to her daughter, who came running with a plate on which she dropped the pickles, one by one, while another daughter came with a mop.

"I'm sorry," Mastie said to the Frenchman. "I didn't see it and when I turned my back — my gun — you know, my gun — my gun hit — "and he slipped his fist into his palm. The Frenchman nodded.

"Move along," said the lieutenant.

It occurred to Mastie to offer to pay for the crock and he pulled out a handful of French money and offered it to the man with the moustache. The Frenchman shook his head and waved his hands in front of his face.

"Move!" the lieutenant said. "I'll take care of it. And no smoking in the barn. Tell those men. All we need yet is to have someone burn the barn down."

On the other side of the room, the door opened out into the dark. It smelled of cows and fresh hay. He could hear noises. "Where are you?"

"Up here," someone said. A tuft of hay fell on his neck. He was standing under the hay hole. The man overhead lit a match and held it so Mastie could see him.

"Put out that match. You want to burn us up?"

"Well, I'd like to know how we're going to see up here." The man hauled him over the top into the loose hay. He took the shoulder straps of his pack off and rolled sideways to get out of it.

"You can't sleep here."

"Why not?"

"You'll fall down the hay hole." There were voices all over the loft in the dark. He took his pack by one strap and stood up.

"Hey, watch where you're going. Don't step on my glasses."

"Where are they?"

"In my boots."

"Well, hold onto your boots. then." He stepped into a depression and dropped his pack to keep his balance.

"Ohhh. . . " someone sneezed and sneezed again.

"Is somebody there?"

"Get your pack off my head or I die of suffocation." The man had a Spanish accent.

He lifted the pack and went down on his hands and knees to feel the area.

"Now you have your hand on my leg. What's wrong with you? You homosexual or something?" The men around him cackled.

"Sorry."

"Sure you're sorry. So am I. How about looking before you move."

"Looking?"

"If you can't see, wait till your eyes get used to it."

His eyes were beginning to pick out shapes here and there. It looked like the whole loft was full.

"First I have to smell this barnyard and I'm sure I won't be able to sleep with that, then this guy comes along and breaks my nose, and now I can't smell a thing." The soldier sneezed again.

"Aren't you the fat soldier?" said Mastie.

"You trying to insult me? I have a name. Hector. Hector Chavez. Okay, so you can't pronounce it, but you'll admit it's more interesting than John or Bill. How many Johns have I met since I got in the army? I don't know. Now I find out this place is one big john. Smell it. If he hasn't busted your nose like he did mine."

Mastie began to unroll his things.

"What are you doing?" said the fat soldier.

"Unrolling."

"You sleeping here?"

"Look! I'm tired. I can't spend all night hunting around."

"Okay, okay. I just wondered. How about putting your sack between so you don't roll on me." Mastie got into his blankets.

"There's pigeons in here," someone said.

"Where?"

"Over here. Hey, he crapped on me."

"Chase 'em over to Froggie."

"You chase them over here and I'll wring their necks," said Froggie.

"What did you say your name is?" said Mastie. He was settled now.

"They all call me Froggie."

"Froggie."

"Froggie. It's a nickname. Hector Chavez from New York, really. Manhattan. You ever been to New York? No? You never been to New York? Well, you ain't missing nothing. Except the trolley cars. You ever ride on a trolley car? You never rode on a trolley car? Where you from? The Ozarks or something?"

"Lancaster," said Mastie.

"Lancaster? Where's that?"

"Pennsylvania."

"Oh, that's right. That's not so far from New York. Come up. I'll give you a ride on my trolley car. I'm a conductor, see. 'Next stop, Battery Park. To your right the Statue of Liberty built by the French sculptor Bartholdi and presented by the French government to the government of our United

128

States of America in the year of our Lord 1886.'
It don't cost you much. Five cents a ride."

"I thought you said I'm not missing anything if I
don't come."

"You ain't. It's dirty. We have rats. We have
Potato-Eaters. You a Potato-Eater?"

"Me? I eat potatoes, sure."

"Sure, sure, you eat potatoes, but are you a Potato-
Eater? An Irish."

"No."

"What are you, then?"

"I'm Mennonite."

"Mennonite? What's that? Mennonite? I never
heard of Mennonite."

"Oh, it's a group."

"Oh, a group, huh. But you're not a Potato-Eater. Well, then we're friends. Because I hate them
Potato-Eaters. They think they own New York. Like
the Heinies. They think they can just walk in and
take over a place. Well, we're going to go show the
Heinies first, then we're coming back to show the
Irish. What kind of a group?"

"Oh, a religious group."

"Religious, huh? That's okay. My Maria is religious. She goes to the priest every Saturday and
confesses her sins. 'Bless me Father, for I have
sinned. . . .' You know what I mean? Only she ain't
sinned. That girl is the purest thing since Mary. She
prays regular. And when she prays, my eyes get
wet. It's that beautiful."

"Well, I'm not religious myself anymore," said
Mastie. "It's garbage, that's what I say."

"What do you mean it's garbage?"

"It's garbage, done just because they have to."

129

"You making fun of Maria or something? Don't do that. Make fun of me if you want to. Go ahead. Call me a fat soldier. I know I ain't skinny. But don't you make fun of Maria."

"I wasn't. I just said — "

"I heard you!"

Mastie rolled over on his sack and closed his eyes.

"But you want to know something about the trolley cars that most people don't know?"

"Will you shut up and let me sleep?" said someone across the loft. "We're here to win a war, not to hear about your old trolley cars."

"I'm telling you what I'm fighting for, Potato-Eater. You have to have a reason to fight or you won't fight, right? I'm fighting for New York, even if it is dirty and full of people like you. Nice people like you. I'm fighting for the trolley car conductors."

"I'd rather not hear about it."

"I'm not telling you. I'm telling him. What's your name, buddy?"

Silence.

"You probably put him to sleep."

Sure enough, Mastie was asleep.

3

Dear Mastie,

Greetings in the name of our Lord. I was so glad to get your postcard. Even if it only said, "Somewhere in France," that's better than out at sea. One hears so many stories about the submarines these days. Now that we're not as close as we were when you were in camp, we can just hope that the mail service is good.

It's awful quiet around here since you've gone. I went to one or two singings but it just wasn't the same. Some of our friends are gone, but the one I was missing most was you. I missed your fine bass when we sang "This Is My Father's World." I know you liked that one. So I'm staying home in the evenings, and there's always tobacco to strip on my day off. We have a third of ours to go.

There was something I wanted to write earlier but I guess I just didn't. It's about the bad things we did in our courtship. More and more I feel I should go talk to your father. There have been rumors among some of the folks and some people told my mom all kinds of things that weren't true. It seems people whisper things around more these days. Maybe I would be able to be a better Christian if I told your father. What do you think, Mastie? I don't want to make things bad between you and him, though. Lately I have not been able to pray at all.

Now a little about myself.

I will be working five days a week for the Federoffs and going to market for my pop Saturdays, as always. I don't know what kind of people they are yet, but they seem rich. They're about to have a baby. The first night he took me on a tour of the house and it seemed to go on and on. I have my own room at the top of the stairway, and it's the east room. Do you know what that means? Every morning when I get up I can look out the window — to France! Then I will think how just a few hours ago that same sun was over you.

I miss you very much.
    Annie

Somewhere in France
February 3, 1918

Dear Annie,

Well, we're here. I just got done watering the horses, which is my job right now until we get organized. They have about two hundred horses — that's our regiment — and most of them aren't much. Bony old nags, that's all. Somebody said they used to be nice but it was coming across the ocean that made them so skinny. They lost a lot of weight, as did we all. The food was pretty terrible and they served it on a big tray hanging from the ceiling. Well, everytime a wave hit us, you can guess what happened. The worst was during a storm once. I declare there was soup three inches deep on the floor of the eating room. We had to wade into the room.

But things are better here. They have regular cooks.

Oh, there are one or two really nice horses, though. One's a pretty bay with a high tail. She almost looks like one of our New Holland horses. Maybe that's where they got her. I don't know. I wouldn't mind taking her for a ride around the countryside, exploring a bit, but you can't do that in the Army. Everything's orders and bugle calls. There's a bugle call to get up, one to get dressed, one for roll call, one for breakfast, and one after breakfast for cleaning up the grounds. Now that's just the first hour and a half. Rising time is 5:45, which doesn't bother me, and you should hear some of these city boys. Me, I like to get up and get a breath of that winter air. There's some snow on the ground.

It doesn't look like I'm going to be a pilot. They're not even looking for pilots, which is different than what I heard back there. Mostly it's ground soldiers — that's the infantry — and machine gunners and such like that they're after. Now that basic's over, I'm with machine guns, which I hear go pretty far behind the front lines and out of the danger zone. So I probably won't come near another plane or horse for the rest of the war. That's the breaks.

Well, I must say I'm pretty happy I came. Sure, there's good things in Lancaster County — lots of them — but a man needs a change. Are you enjoying yourself? Write me some letters now and then — I don't see any reason to stop that, do you?

Oh, and I forgot to tell you when I was home yet, but don't shut yourself off. I mean, I hope you keep on going to hoedowns and singings, maybe with some other boys. I won't feel bad about it. Maybe you have another boyfriend already? In other words, you don't need to wait for me, but don't forget about me completely.

Well, I can't think of anything else to write. They're blowing another bugle now, I think it's "taps." That's lights out.

> Yours,
> *Mastie*

4

Early on a Sunday morning Mastie led a group of horses down to water. At the end of their street was a large artificial pond that probably contained lily pads and goldfish in the summer but just now it was covered with a two-inch skin of ice. He didn't have to water the horses — they belonged to the artillery — but he always loved a good horse, and in the middle of a lot of strange things it was nice to have at least one friend who for no reason at all rubbed his nose against you and allowed himself to be petted.

He had to break the ice on the surface with a shovel and even then the horses would only stick their noses in for a moment before they brought them out again, blowing great clouds of steam into the air. The water was cold. Even so, there were women on the other side of the pond washing their clothes in buckets of the water. Strange-looking women in skirts to their ankles, their hair under kerchiefs and talking in a strange babble.

"A chicken, you know what I mean?" said someone. It was Froggie, addressing a woman in her backyard, just up from the edge of the pond. The woman pointed to her mouth and shook her head.

"I don't think you understand. I would like a

chicken. You know, 'Buk-buk-buk-buk-baaku.' It goes
like that." The woman's eyes got big. "I want to
buy a chicken." The chickens were behind her in the
yard, scratching through the snow for seeds. The
woman did not understand, though. She stood at
the gate which led into the farmyard, with both
hands on the pale fence. Her eyes were infinitely blue
and they rolled back and forth, watching Froggie.
"Listen," said Froggie, "I have money, see." He
took a handful of francs from his pocket and jingled
them before the woman's eyes. "And I want to buy
a chicken. "Buk-buk-buk-buk-baaku.' To eat," he
said, holding his hands to his mouth as if he were
eating an imaginary drumstick.

"*Vous êtes acteur?*" (You are an actor?), said the
woman, and her eyes rolled back and forth. She
shouted something at the woman by the pond and in
a moment there were four or five of them standing
outside the gate, watching the fat soldier.

"Buddie, can you help me?" said Froggie. "I am
trying and trying and they don't understand.
What's French for chicken?"

"I don't know. Maybe rooster," said Mastie.

"Maybe rooster, that's it." He ran back to the
fence and faced the woman. "Okay, a rooster. I
want to buy a rooster."

The women looked at each other blankly and one
woman repeated the word. "Rooster."

"Yes, a rooster," said Froggie. "It's the first one up
in the morning and its stretches itself out like this
with its chest out, and puts its head up in the air
and flaps its wings like this and crows, "Err-er-er-
errru!' " He came back into human form again
and looked at the women. They burst out laughing.

He took a handful of francs from his pocket and jingled them in front of the women. "Here, I want to buy one to eat. *Café. Café.*"

"*Est-ce qu'il fait payer pour le voir?*" (Is he charging us to watch him?), said a woman.

"*C'est trop*" (it's too much), said another. "*Un franc, encore?*" (A franc, maybe?) She reached into her pocket and laid a franc on his palm.

"No, no, I'm going to pay you. You have it backwards," said the soldier. "Damn it, I don't have all night. I want to cook it yet." Suddenly he jumped over the fence into the lady's garden and began to chase the chickens and with a flying leap he caught one and somersaulted. The front of his uniform came up wet and dirty. "Now, I'll kill it and then there's no more argument." He wrung the chicken's neck.

"Ohh . . ." the women gasped. It was one thing if he wanted to be funny but something entirely different when this strange soldier began to kill their animals.

"*Vous avez tué mon seul coq. Comment donc aurai-je des poussins au printemps?*" (You've killed my only rooster. Now how do I get chicks next spring?) said the woman, who owned the house.

Froggie stood there with a strange smile, the dead rooster hanging by one of its legs from under his arm while he fished into his pocket for his money once more. "Now, how much do you charge?" He held out the handful of money for the third time and this time the women erupted in a conversation that sounded like nothing else but a bunch of widowed hens cackling. Froggie pointed at the rooster, at his mouth, and then at his stomach. When he got to his stomach, he grinned. "Ah, delicious."

"Delicious," said one of the women. "*Ah, il veut le manger, Germaine, il veut vous payer le coq pour qu'il puisse le manger.*" (Ah, he wants to eat it. Germaine, he wants to pay you for the rooster so he can eat it.) The woman at the gate smiled and she reached out and took a one franc piece from the soldier. "Thank you," she said.

Froggie was all smiles.

"Even in New York we don't have such wonderful women," he said and he held the rooster up for Mastie to see it. "Now we need bread to stuff it. Ave Maria, I hope I don't have to go through an ordeal like that again. This French, I tell you, it runs out people's noses in streams and there's not a single word of it you can understand. I'm getting myself a dictionary. One never knows in what circumstances he might need it. Maybe next time it's not a chicken I want, but some friendly girl. Then what do I do? Aha, so we buy a dictionary, too."

They went to the grocery store at the corner of the block when Mastie had finished watering the horses. He tied his last horse to the picket line and they went back up the street to the corner store.

"Amazing, huh," said Froggie. "All we see is women around here. No men."

"They're at the front, I guess," said Mastie.

"Even the trolley car operators — women!" he laughed.

"What are the black armbands for that you see? Is that a club?"

"I don't know."

They went into the store. It was a small one and seemed to be operated by two women, one of them a young girl who smiled at Mastie as if she knew him. She was a little pudgy, but her eyes were black and alive. He didn't know her — he was sure of that — but she was pretty. Seventeen, maybe, and still wearing a school uniform. He looked at the older woman.

"Hello. I guess we want some bread," he said. "Bread."

"Yes," said the woman, seeming to understand.

"A dictionary," said Froggie, and then turning to Mastie he said, "No sense in living the monk's life while you're here. For myself, I think of Maria back home each time I hold a new one — that way when she asks me someday how I behaved myself in France I'll tell her, 'Well, I couldn't forget you, Maria. Whenever I saw a girl over there I thought of you. I just couldn't get you out of my head.' "

The girl returned to say she was sorry, but they didn't have dictionaries. After a bit the woman came with a loaf of bread. He sniffed it to see if it was fresh. "Okay." He held out a handful of money and let her pick out how much she wanted. He turned around to hear Froggie say, "You're pretty," to the girl at the counter. Something rattled outside on the sidewalk and the door opened. A man in a dark uniform, apparently an official of some sort walked past them, drew himself up to attention, and said, *"Madame, le capitane Ernest Lefévre a été tué sur le front hier á Verdun"* (Madam, Captain Ernest Lefever was killed in action yesterday at Verdun).

The woman stared and her mouth opened. Then she drew in her breath and began to shake. She covered her face with her hands and wailed. The girl rushed around the counter and took hold of the woman's arm and at the same moment a baby began to cry. The woman picked up the baby and clutched him to her, kissing him first on one cheek and then the other while her tears ran down the baby's face.

"I think we better go," said Mastie. Before they even got to the door, however, it opened in front of them and two children in heavy coats and scarves ran in, one of them chasing the other with a snowball, and the little one squealing with delight.

"*Annette. Jason,*" said the girl by the counter. They looked up with mischievous faces and at the same time the older one noticed her mother.

"Mama!" she said.

The two men went out into the street.

"Someone must have been killed," said Mastie. He looked back as the door closed and saw the girl with her arms still around the woman, loosening the black band from her own arm and slipping it onto the woman's.

"Just when I was getting to know the girl at the counter," said Froggie.

"Her husband, maybe?" said Mastie, thinking of the woman.

"She was pretty, you know," said Froggie, thinking of the girl.

"He was probably a soldier."

"And her eyes. Did you see what big black eyes she had? I wonder how you say 'pretty eyes' in French?"

On the following day when they returned from drills the girl was there in the corner store again, only this time by herself. She smiled at Mastie.

"How's come you know me?

"Yes," she said in schoolgirl English, and bobbed her head. "You broke the pickle jar.

140

"How do you know?"

"It's my father. My father owns the house."

"You mean I'm living at your house?"

"Yes."

"Your English is pretty good. What's your name?"

"No, I don't think so. My name — Madeleine."

"Magdalene! That's an American name, I have an Aunt Magdalena."

"No, it's French, I think."

"I'm sorry about the pickle jar. I don't think your father understood. It was an accident."

"Yes, he understood. An accident. Sure, it's okay." There didn't seem to be anything else to say, so he nosed around the store for a while, thinking up strategies.

"What time do you get finished?" he said. "Can we go for a walk? Maybe to the cafe?"

"Pardon. Don't speak so fast."

"I said, let's go for a walk when you finish."

"Oh," She thought about it a while and pretended to look at the supply of candy. "Tomorrow," she said. "Come back tomorrow, maybe eight o'clock."

"Seven? I'm free at seven."

The next night he showed up at seven in a fresh uniform, shaved, and with a bit of cologne sprinkled on. Why, she was transformed. She no longer wore her school uniform, but a dark red outfit and a ribbon in her hair behind.

"You lead the way," he said. "I don't know this town." His blood was running faster. He wanted to put his arm around her, but no, it was too early yet. Maybe a little later. She didn't walk close to him, but several feet away.

She pointed at a tall tower across town.

"That," she said, "is a cathedral — maybe 300 years old — and the architect, my — What do you say?" She piled her hands on top of each other. "Father, grandfather — "

"Great-grandfather, great-great-grandfather, great-great-great-grandfather — " It was a grandfather with ten greats in the front. They both laughed. "He must have been famous," said Mastie.

"Very famous. Do you want to see the church?"

"Sure."

"And that house is the house of the mayor. He's a nice man, big moustache."

"Everyone has moustaches. Hey, tell me. Why did that woman cry in the store the other day?"

"Pardon. More slowly, please. Cry?" she said.

"Your friend — why did she cry in the store? You know what crying is?" He demonstrated.

"Oh, Anna-Marie. Her husband was killed by a bullet." She tapped her neck to show him where it had hit. "My brother was killed so," she said, "and my uncle, my three school friends, so many, many men — too many men. The church," she announced. It was a large cathedral, unlike the tiny chapel by the watering pond, which he had already investigated.

Mastie had never seen anything like it before. The building seemed to rise like a balloon over his head, up, up, and up to peaks where he imagined there were probably pigeons or bats. There were always pigeons and bats in the silos back home. But this was twice or three times the height of a silo. The winter sun had set but its light still cast strange reflections through the glass windows and lit their faces in blue and red. He looked at her. She was transformed by the light into a red angel. The building was empty, except for a few old women in black kneeling before a row of flickering candles near the front and mumbling to themselves, and a priest who walked in and out of the doors. His voice echoed when he spoke.

"Hey, neat!" He said. "Think they care if we sit down?"

They sat down and he looked at her. She was pretty in the little store, but she was truly beautiful in the cathedral. She seemed a part of a great, strange tradition that he knew nothing about, almost like one of the saints cut in glass and soldered into the background on the window scene above. She reached into her pocket and put a lacy handkerchief on her head. It reminded him of his mother and the white prayer veil she wore all the time. Why, even here in France women wore veils. The veil covered her eyes from him. He reached over to pull it back and saw that her eyes were closed and her lips were moving. She made the sign of the cross and opened her eyes, and looked at him. Yes, as Froggie had said, they were large and black. She smiled. He reached over and put his arm around her shoulder.

"No, no," she said and suddenly got up and began to walk out.

He caught up with her at the door.

"I'm sorry, Magdalene," he said.

"We must hurry. That over there — " They were on the steps of the cathedral. "That is the market-place, where you buy vegetables in the summertime, or fish. Do you like fish?"

"Yes." He was puzzled by her.

"Do you like chicken? You do, I know. Your friend kills the chicken."

"Haha, Froggie. Yes, but he didn't eat it yet. It's still frozen up in some ice. We don't have a stove."

"Froggie." she said. "A strange name, isn't it?"

"I guess. He's from New York. New York City."

"Here we are," she said. Then she looked at him. "I learned that from the lieutenant. Every night when he come back he says, 'Well, here we are.' "

Goodness, she was observant.

He went into the house and there was the whole family, waiting. Two children with forks in their hands were sitting on chairs at the table, Mama was cutting bread against her stomach with a long iron knife, and Papa was at the fireplace at the far end of the room, looking down at the fire — which was now reduced to coals — and a fat young rooster that turned itself slowly over the coals by means of a clockwork affair and dropped hot fat into the fire, filling the room with a tremendous aroma.

"My family," said Madeleine.

Mastie nodded and smiled. He went over and shook hands with Papa.

"Chicken!" he said, "Mmmm!"

The mother said something and Madeleine interpreted and held up a plate.

"Also pickles." Mastie laughed and that seemed to be the cue to the whole family to laugh. Papa got up from the fireplace and put his hand on Mastie's shoulder. He said something through his nose.

"He says he will not forget the pickles."

Mastie laughed again.

"Tell him I'm sorry. I'm sorry, Mister."

"It's okay," said the old man. "Sit down. So how do you like our town?" he asked by way of his translator.

144

"It's nice," said Mastie. "The people are friendly," and he grinned at Madeleine, "the houses are beautiful, but the bedroom is terribly cold."

"Ah, yes," said Papa, "the bedroom is cold. I'm sorry. It's the only place we have for you. But it's good to sleep in the cold, you know. We even kill the stove at night."

"My son was a soldier, too," said Mama. "He gave his life at Verdun for the liberty of France. He was an officer, and a brave one." Madeleine was quietly translating what they said, stumbling for words. She sat at the other end of the table from Mastie.

"Aha!" said Papa. "We have something very good." He got up from his place at the fire and went into another room.

"Chicken," said Mastie and he looked at Madeleine. He laughed. "Chicken and pickles. Too much." He shook his head.

The old man returned with a dark, musty looking bottle and two fine crystal glasses. He removed the cork skillfully and poured a half glass. "It's very old," he said. "Bordeaux, and impossible to get now that the war is on." He handed a glass to Mastie.

"Cheers," he said in English, and grinned from one corner of his moustache to the other. He passed the glass back and forth before his nose and, in a moment, the wine was gone. Mastie swallowed his and it tasted like the cellar under their house in Pennsylvania. Old damp logs, barrels, rusty spikes, and spider webs.

"How is it?" said the old man.

"Very good." It was horrible.

In a moment the chicken was done and the old man pushed it off the spit with a bread knife onto a beautiful white platter. Madeleine pointed to the platter. "This was my great-great — "

"The one who built the church?" said Mastie.

"His grandson."

Once the pedigree of everything was established, they began to eat, and the rooster was the best of all, even if it wasn't old or once possessed by some great man. But who knew, maybe the grandfather of that rooster belonged to Napoleon. The family meal made the army chow seem pale.

When the meal was done, there wasn't much time left. Mastie could already hear soldiers coming into the barn by the back way past the cows and clumping up the ladder into the loft.

"Let's go out," he said to Madeleine.

She shook her head.

"It's not our way," she said.

So they sat together on two wooden chairs and studied her English textbook while Papa read the newspaper and Mama sewed. The children had already gone off to bed.

"Is it difficult?" he said.

"Oh, English is the most difficult language."

"Can you speak any other language?"

"Italian," and she gestured with her fingers, "a little."

"*Kannscht du deitch schvetza?* (Can you speak German?)

"What's that?"

"German."

"You speak German? They'll think you are a — " She looked it up in her dictionary. "A spy. Are you

146

a spy? "My father — " and she looked at the soldier fearfully. "My father is a police," she said.

"Don't worry. I ain't no spy. In Pennsylvania we speak German — the Pennsylvania Dutch." He stopped. "You have pretty eyes. Did you know that?"

"You embarrass me." But she had to look in the dictionary first for "embarrass."

At 9:30, he got up to go and Papa looked up from the paper. He stood up. Mama stood up. Madeleine stood up and she went into the next room. Not more wine, he was thinking. No, it was a pretty bouquet of dried strawflowers. She pinned them on his coat.

"Thank you," said Mastie.

"Good night," said the old man and he grabbed Mastie and buried his moustache in his cheek again, first the one side and then the other. "Good night," said Mama, and she put her hands on his shoulders and touched her lips on both cheeks. "Good night," said Madeleine. A that moment someone knocked at the door that connected the house to the barn and opened it.

"Any of my men in here?" said the lieutenant, just in time to see Mastie greeting the grocery store clerk "good night."

"Well, I'll be," the lieutenant said.

5

January 26, 1918

Dear Mastie,

I can hardly write to you this evening because my heart is so full of questions. Rumors are flying around that you are married to some American nurse over there. I don't know who started them, but Benjie told me. Please tell me if it is true or not.

Sincerely,
Annie

February 10

Dear Annie,

For once I'm not hungry. Tonight I had a yummy chicken for supper, with pickles, potatoes, and some wine. It was horrible, but I had to drink it, really. I was eating supper with the man and lady who own the house where our company is billeted. They also have some children.

The country is really nice here but you wouldn't believe how people farm. I haven't seen it yet in the summertime, but the barns are not very modern. The barns are really connected to the houses, which is why, wherever you go, you smell you know what.

But I don't mind. I like that smell. Smells like home to me.

And I am now practicing with the machine gun. We practiced taking a gun apart and putting it back together in the dark, pitch dark. Then they give you a bagful of gun parts and tell you to put it together in such and such amount of time. I guess I will be seeing some action, because the machine gunners are usually not too far behind the front line. But don't worry. You know that scar I have under my chin where Apple Boy kicked me right after I got him? I figure if he couldn't find the right spot, neither can the Germans. Few people back there have any idea what it's like over here. It's just a different world, that's all. I won't even try to explain, but I will say my mind is changing about things. For one thing, it's pretty clear to me now we have to stop the Huns here or they'll be over to visit us in Pennsylvania. We're not here for the fun of it. So that's about all I've been doing.

What I wanted to ask you, though, was where you are hearing those rumors. They make me mad. How does anybody think I can get married over here when I'm in the Army? They must be crazy. We couldn't get married even if we wanted to. I think a lot of people back there are trying to take advantage of me just because they didn't like what I did, so they run around spreading rumors. Why do you believe Benjie more than me? All I say is Benjie B. and I better never cross paths when I get home, or he'll want more than a bandage this time.

What you were asking about our courting days, though, let me give you an answer. In my opinion, you better not say anything to my pop. Maybe we did some things that weren't so good but they're between you and me and I can keep my mouth closed. Pop never told me about his courting days, so I don't see any reason why I should tell him about mine. I'm sure he did plenty. For one thing, I don't care to read sermons in the mail yet. That's what I came here to get away from.

I haven't forgotten you, don't worry. It seems every evening about this time I think of you. I wish you were here right now so I could reach over and grab you and talk to you. This morning I woke up about an hour before it was time to get up. I was dreaming of Pennsylvania and I dreamt I saw you and me in a carriage with our children going for a ride somewhere. I believe it was Christmas because people were singing Christmas songs. Then I awoke and here I was in France, sleeping in somebody's haymow with a lot of soldiers. Do you believe in dreams? I do.

I really don't know if I love you, though, Annie. Like I said, so much is happening.

Yours,
Mastie

6

The machine gun company was on a night maneuver. The situation, as Mastie's lieutenant put it, was — gas. *A cloud of mustard gas is moving in over our trenches without warning. This is a gas alert. That means you get your mask on, get to your position, assemble your gun and stand ready for the attack to follow.*

It was as dark as their billeting barn and about as spooky. Odd shapes kept rising out of the ground, and it was impossible to guess what they might be. Anyway, the men were all snuffling for air inside their gas masks and looking like big pigs with human legs as they ran for the trench. They jumped into the trench and Mastie pulled the barrel of the gun from a gunnysack.

"Is the gas over?"

"What gas? It's just a game. I'm taking this dumb thing off," said Froggie.

"Leave it on. You want to be gassed?" He assembled the gun by feel, threw it down on the wall of the trench, and pointed it at the imaginary enemy. "Load her up."

"I can't see worth a penny." Froggie ripped off his mask and took a deep gasp of air. "Stay in there if you want to. I'm enjoying the good air."

The barrage started and the belt of bullets began to feed through the gun. It made the eardrums vibrate and tickle, and Froggie was trying to find a way to close one ear with his finger, hug his other ear against a shoulder, and still hold onto the cartridge belt with the free hand.

"Cease-fire!"

"If this is how it's going to be, I'm joining out," said Froggie. A half-dozen guns were still firing after the order. To their right the gun team of Churchill and Caloway was just falling into the ditch, after accidentally having run one trench too far the first time and remaining pinned there during the firing. "Nobody knows what they're doing."

Mastie took off his mask. "Ah, fresh air! And you're dead," he said to Froggie, even though he couldn't see his face. "You've been gassed."

"Funny. Very funny."

"Fresh air! Mmm. I like cold air like that, don't you? It's sort of an adventure, huh? I mean, when you think how you used to spend your nights."

"How am I supposed to know how you used to spend your nights?"

"Well, you know. Parties and girlfriends, and work, mostly. But I like being out like this. What's that?" said Mastie.

"Where?"

"Those white lights — there, see 'em between the trees. That ain't town, is it? I mean, we can't see clear back there from here."

"Railroad station."

"Oh yeah? They're loading up again? Some luckies are going to the front."

"You called them that, not me."

"Well, that's where things are happening, not? Here we play games but there it's the real thing. The action! That's what I want. This really gets me excited though. Don't it you? We're in France, Froggie. Think about that."

Froggie looked at him.

"How could I forget it?"

"No, but don't it just get you by the soles of your feet and shake you up? It does me. Over there the boys are going up to the front, getting their horses and guns together, and getting on the trains, and over here we're down in a trench with our gas masks and guns, sitting out here in the dark like it was the real thing. And the money, isn't this money just the funniest stuff?" He reached into his pocket and brought out a handful of coins. He held a franc up toward the sky but it didn't help a bit; it was too dark to see anything. "It's like play money." He put a coin on his thumbnail and snapped it off into the trees someplace. "I just spend it and spend it because I hardly think of it as money."

"Are you okay?" said Froggie. The trench was silent now, they were waiting for another order to bring them up, out, and running for the next objective but something had gone awry. The lieutenant was standing above the trench conferring with the French officer who was a specialist in trench warfare.

"And meters and kilometers," said Mastie. "Can you make any sense out of that? Like he said the other day, 'We're going for a ten-kilometer hike' — well, I thought we'd be hiking all night so I put on my extra underwear so I wouldn't freeze and here it turned out to be only five miles or so."

"Stupid. Two kilometers to a mile — more or less.

That's how you remember it."

"Is that how much it is? How about the girls," said Mastie. "How about them, huh?" Before Froggie could answer, though, the lieutenant called for an advance. They scrambled up out of the trench and ran for the next one. This one had been newly dug and water was standing in the bottom of it, frozen over. Mastie's foot went through as he jumped down and the water covered his ankle. "Wet foot," he said, pulling it out.

"I don't know why you never wear a coat," said Froggie. "You'll catch pneumonia. Then what will you do?"

Mastie started firing. "Feel the barrel. Is it getting hot?"

"Mmm. Warm. Like me," shouted the fat soldier over the racket. "When I get cold, you know what I do?" He put an arm around Mastie's shoulder. "I just think about that pretty Magdalene — you know which one I mean? The one with the nice *warm* mouth and then I imagine I'm kissing that nice warm mouth like this — *Mmm!*" and he kissed the air. "And then that little white throat like this — *Mmmm!* And then we get down to the shoulders — and by this time I'm warming up, you see, just thinking about her."

"She's a good girl," Mastie shouted.

"Of course, of course. I know she's a good girl. Do you think I'd look a second time at her if she wasn't?

"Cease-fire!"

"Sometime I'll introduce you to my Maria, how's that?" Froggie said. They didn't have to shout any more. "You come to New York and then you'll see.

You know how she walks? Let me show you how she walks."

"Get down."

"I'm not getting out. I'm just going to show you with my hand. She walks like this." And he held the side of his hand against Mastie's shoulder and snaked it gracefully back and forth. "That warms me up, too. But she's a good girl, of course she is."

Mastie played with the gun. It was a new thought. Froggie had his eyes on Madeleine and had hinted . . . . How much could you believe?

"Why so quiet all of a sudden?" said Froggie.

"Problem's over, I guess," said Mastie, looking around in the dark to locate the lieutenant.

"No, you."

"Me?"

"Yes. Why so quiet?"

"I don't have anything to say, that's all."

"A couple minutes ago you were going on and on about how great it is here. Tell me some more. You go to any of their churches or cafés yet? Caloway and I are celebrating at the café Saturday. Come on up."

Mastie didn't say anything. He was remembering a little incident that had happened last night. He had gone to the store where Madeleine worked, hoping to talk with her, and Froggie was there, talking with her and telling her that nobody in New York had eyes like she did. But Froggie said that to everyone, so he dismissed it. When Froggie was gone, he went up and asked her to show him some more of the city on Saturday night and she had said, "No," there was business, or storework or something like that, which kept her busy — just what he couldn't make out from the conversation. Now he wondered if it wasn't Froggie. And he imagined Froggie grabbing her on a back street somewhere and squeezing her and kissing her, just like he had said. . . .

"Everything okay with you?" said Froggie. "You're sure quiet all of a sudden." But Mastie didn't have to answer the question.

"Company, advance," said the lieutenant, and they scrambled up out of the trench again.

7

"Hey, soldier boy!"

It was the fat, smiling face of Froggie, leaning out of a cafe. The cafe was crowded with soldiers with nothing better to do on a Friday night but drink, tell stories of home, and flirt with passersby. Mastie sat down beside Caloway.

"How do you like this?" said Froggie, and he produced a big bottle of champagne from under the table where he was apparently hiding it between his legs, to keep any other thirsty soldiers away. "A glass, waitress! What's wrong with you, pretzel-face? What you been up to?"

"Nothing much," said Mastie. He was feeling low for the first time since they had arrived, and he didn't know how to explain it. He sat with his chin in his hand.

"Hey!" said Caloway to Froggie, looking at a passerby outside the glass. She wore a large frilly hat and a dress that fell to the sidewalk, but as she walked by the light revealed a friendly nose like a tulip bulb and the beginning of a double chin.

"Two," said Froggie, hardly moving his huge neck.

"Two?" said Mastie.

"We have a system," said Caloway, and he began to laugh.

"BROAD — Brotherhood of Reporters Overlooking Anterior Development," said Froggie. "Anterior, anterior. The front, you know. It's Churchill's game. One point, she would have gotten out one loyal soldier to Hastings to fight for her against the English. Ten points. Ten would have gone out."

"Hastings?" said Mastie.

"Sure, don't you know history? The greatest battle in history, Churchill says. One of the old kind of battles when you saw the enemy soldiers' faces and there were heroes — AD 1066, anno domini, in the year of our Lord. See how smart this Churchill is? The French, of course, win in the end because the girls in England are not beautiful enough to put a fire under their soldier boys and get them out there to fight. So if you look at it the other way around, there must have been beautiful girls in France to get William, that's Conqueror William, off his beautiful throne, and out to fight for them. Why else would a man fight if it wasn't for a woman somewhere? Tell me that. Who's your woman, Mastie? Come on, don't play games with us. "There's a ten," he said, turning to stare at a girl walking by. "Not bad, not bad. If they keep up like this, no wonder the French win in 1066."

"You're drunk," said Mastie. He was in a bad mood and he hoped they noticed.

"No."

"Sure, you are."

"Nope, because when I get drunk — when I get drunk, baby, I sing. Ahhh!" He stood up with the bottle in one hand a sausage in the other and began to warble while a few drops of sweat rolled out of his black curls and down across his great cheeks and

158

dropped to his stomach. He sat down.

"That'll attract 'em," said Caloway, laughing almost uncontrollably. He was a simple, good-hearted soldier from back state Virginia, out of one of the hollows there where he had never gone beyond the eighth grade. He cried and laughed easily and he had a heart that easily understood tragedy and pain around him, perhaps because he came from a background full of it. He looked at Mastie. People always warmed up after they had been around Froggie for a few minutes. Why wasn't Mastie warming up?

The girl who rated ten came back up the street while they were drinking their third glass of champagne, and what was left was hardly covering the bottom of the bottle anymore.

"Hi," said Froggie, pushing open the door. A draft of cold air blew in. "Won't you sit down?" She looked at him, *"Ici tootsweet,"* he said and grinned. Caloway began to laugh again and the girl turned away and went on.

"Ici tootsweet!" said Caloway. "What's that?"

"Ici tootsweet. I like you. What's wrong with that one anyway? I take it back — anybody that snotty doesn't get more than two."

"Listen, it's *tooasweet,"* said Caloway. *"Tooasweet Paree.* I like Paris. See, I have it right here in my book." Caloway got out his copy of *English to French, French to English* and thumbed through it until he found the right spot. He pointed it out.

"I don't care," said Froggie. "That's another dialect. In this town, they say *tootsweet."* The waitress passed and he whistled. *"Une bouteille,* waitress. Weee. See that, would you? You just have to pronounce this stuff right. As I was saying, last night

159

this girl said it to me. *You comment ici tootsweet,* which means, Please come again, I like you. That's the trouble with that crazy book, they tell you what to say about Paris or the weather and all about the silver handle of a fork or the fountain pen of my aunt but you can't find such a simple little useful thing like, 'Ain't I seen you somewheres before, babe?' What's wrong with you anyway?" he said, looking at Mastie. "The last three weeks we hear nothing but 'Hey, we're in France! Tra la,' and now all you can do is fume and mope."

"I don't understand them," said Mastie.

"Who?"

"Girls."

"Well, who does. Tell me? *Merci,* waitress. The first toast," said Froggie, "to the Allied Forces. May they bottle the Kaiser up, screw the lid tight, and drop him in the ocean."

"The next toast — " said Caloway, and he began to cough. "I'm hot, oh, I'm so hot." He began to tear his shirt open in the front and fan his throat with a menu card. "Oh, my throat." He stood and went out on the street. They could see him on the street coughing.

"I should go myself," said Froggie. He stood up and squeezed Mastie's shoulder with one of his big hands. "Cheer up," he said. He went out.

Mastie emptied the bottle slowly. He couldn't tell how long he'd been there or what he had thought about, but when he looked up he saw a couple passing. A fat soldier and girl in a dark red outfit. He finished the bottle and as he did, her face seemed to float in the glass. She was looking up at him out of the glass, startled.

160

Mastie stood up. Where were they by now? He went out onto the street. They were not at the house. He saw that by looking in the window. He went up the back street behind the house, then up another street. It would be easy to get lost in this town, he thought. There were lots and lots of streets, and there was no way to track down one man in a city this big, if he were trying to hide. She wasn't safe with him, not if he meant everything he had said on the field last night. She was only a schoolgirl. He imagined her fighting off the fat soldier, calling for help? She was a good girl. Froggie would see that, wouldn't he? She prayed in the church just like his girl Maria. The church! He noticed its light where he hadn't seen it before. He walked toward it. Last week he had been here with her. Where was she tonight?

He went into the cathedral and stood there in the dark. Again it was empty except for a few women at the front who were lighting candles in the corner. Perhaps a dead son, or husband. He liked the dark and silence and was just getting used to it when he heard a giggle from somewhere on his right, and then a white upflung hand appeared over the top of the bench. It was quiet for a few seconds and then he heard a man's low voice saying, "Such beautiful eyes. Yes, you do," in English and a chuckle.

"Oh, Froggie!" followed by a giggle.

Mastie stood still. It became very clear to him in that moment, it wasn't Froggie at all. She was the culprit. All of that nice behavior last week. She was pure and shy. She wouldn't let him put his arm around her. So much rubbish! He would wait right here in the aisle for them and when they got up he would tell her to her face what she was. A bitch!

I can't stay in this unit anymore, he thought. *I can't stay here and listen to him talk like that about her on the practice field. I want a transfer.* That was it. He opened the cathedral door and shut it noisily behind him.

He stood against the outside wall of the cathedral. All of a sudden he wanted to hurt her so he wasn't the only one suffering. His legs wouldn't move though. They felt like they had springs in them. His head rolled around like it had roller bearings. He was hot. He began to sing.

> *"On top of Old Smoky*
> *All covered with snow*
> *I lost my poor lover*
> *By courting too slow."*

It was an old hoedown song.

"*'She'll hug you and kiss you . . .'* But she wouldn't even do that much," he said, looking at the little group that was gathering around him. There were a few old men, several teenage boys. "No, she wouldn't. I'd tell you more, but I'm sleepy, if you know what I mean, and I could stand another bottle of champagne. *Une bouteille de champagne?"*

> *" . . . And tell you more lies,*
> *Than the ties in the railroad,*
> *Or the stars in the skies."*

His stomach was a guitar string about to pop and the wine had gone to his arms and legs. He was sleepy, but his head was wide awake. He turned his back to them and walked home. He came into

162

the cow stable from behind and bumped against the wall in the dark. He felt with his hands along the wall for the loft ladder and then he stopped. A pistol. His right hand was on a pistol hanging from a nail on the wall — a pistol in a Sam Browne belt with bullets. The lieutenant's, undoubtedly. He ran his fingers down the barrel in the dark. It was very cold and solid. He fingered the butt and its fancy carving and then the trigger. Very lightly. Was it loaded? No, it wasn't loaded. He took a shell from the belt. A door opened on the other side of the wall and he heard voices.

"Good evening, Mister. Madame. Ah, it's a great evening, huh. 'It stings the toes and bites the nose' as they say."

"Ah, hello. Yes, Mr. Soldier," and a long line of French, which he didn't understand.

"We had a good walk. What a lovely town. I said, you have a lovely town — translate it for him, would you — and a very bright daughter." More French and then he heard, "Good night, Papa." He could imagine the old man with his arms around Froggie, kissing him, first on one cheek, then the other.

"Just a minute," said a beautiful voice. "I have something." Oh, too beautiful. She was going to get him some of those strawflowers, too. Her shoes tapped across the floor. He took the pistol out of its holster and held the shell in one hand, with the barrel opened.

"Good-night to you, Mama. Your nose — it's just like your daughter's. Haha. Can you translate that?" Mama responded with a babble of words, and then he could hear the tap-tap of shoes again. He stood with one hand on the latch of the door to spring it open and held the loaded gun in the other. Now was the time, just as she reached out to kiss Froggie good-night. He could see their astonished faces.

"Good night, Magdalene."

Something froze. His legs, his arms. The door latch wouldn't move. He couldn't do it. The door opened and Froggie stepped out and closed it behind him. It was black in the stable.

"Who's there?"

"Me." He felt weak now.

"Mastie! What are you doing? What do you have?"

"A pistol."

"A pistol!"

"Yes. Somebody hurt me."

"What are you talking about?"

"The girl I love. . . ."

"The girl you love?" said Froggie.

"Magdalene," said Mastie.

"Magdalene? You love Magdalene? Come on, you're kidding me. Is it true? Are you drunk? You're drunk. Now climb up that ladder and get some sleep. Must I carry you?"

8

February 25

Dear Mastie,

Thank you for your welcome letter. It was waiting for me on my cedar chest when I got home tonight from Federoffs. I am so glad that those rumors weren't true. I don't know what I would do if they were true, but you can't believe I wasn't one of those who believed those rumors anyway. Now I can face them all and tell them it's a big lie about you marrying a nurse. Why do people like rumors so much?

I have dreams lately too, it seems. One night I had a horrible one. I thought someone had put a ladder outside my window and masses and masses of soldiers were coming up it and when each one got to the top he pointed his gun at me. And the very last one was you. Then I woke up and I was so happy it wasn't true. Do you really believe in dreams?

But when things get bad on weekends, I sit down and talk with Uncle Solly. We talk about you and he plays a song on his guitar about you. The words go something like "Mastie is coming home again, home again, home again!" I have to laugh. He really likes you, I don't know why, but I think because you played catch with him that time and you didn't make fun of him like some people, just because he isn't smart. He may not be smart but he is so good. He looks into my eyes sometimes and he can tell exactly how I feel. If I feel bad, he puts his arm around me, and if I feel good, he claps his hands and gets out his guitar.

These days it seems he's the only one I can talk to. Everyone else is too busy with babies, or their tobacco, or something. I don't think I want to talk to them anyway. All some can say, it seems, is that you won't come back. "Now that he's eaten the forbidden fruit like Adam, he won't come back," one lady said. I won't say her name or you'll feel bad toward her. But I know you better. I know you keep your promises.

Sometimes I look at the headlines in the paper and then I wonder if you're at that place. France is really big on the map. I'm glad the people in your town are friendly and ask you for supper. French people must be friendly. I often wonder how we would be if someone from there came to stay in our house.

The ice has been good this year. We skated and skated.

I did not tell your pop about our courtship after all. If you don't want me to, I won't.

Just me,
Annie

9

Mastie's entire division was on a twenty-mile march. *At four miles an hour,* he thought, *we will be there in five hours, and then we turn around and march back. In the mud.* What kind of sense did that make? A whole day of cleaning everything up, polishing everything until it shone, even the hooves of the artillery horses, and after the first ten minutes on the road it looked like no one had cleaned for a month. And for what? For what purpose were they marching forty miles in the mud, in perfect formation the whole way? In order that a big general could look at them for a few minutes and then get down off his horse and ride away in his private car.

Ten hours. What a waste. Think of all the hay you could make in ten hours. He wasn't going to sing — he wasn't in the mood for that — even though a lot of the soldiers were singing because there was nothing else to do with their heads for the next ten hours. As for thinking, what was there to think about?

Well, his muscles maybe. Mastie was rather proud of his muscles and the last two months of training had made him tougher than ever. Winter at home had always been a bad time because he got all out of shape — pulling leaves off tobacco stalks in a nice warm cellar never built muscles. When spring came and the annual spring fence building began, his arms and neck always ached for a few days. He also had a slight stoop. It seemed to run in the family. Was that from being humble? Pop always said, "Humble thyself to walk with the Lord." You could get a stoop from walking around humble too long. At any rate, it wasn't a medical problem because in two months of training he had eliminated his stoop and walked perfectly erect. His face was tanned again — windburned, more likely — from being out on the practice range, and his body was a powerful rubber band, stretching and coming together, pulling back and forth from the muscles in his shoulders to the muscles in his ankles. His stomach was as hard as his jaw from crawling over the frozen ground to the machine gun.

But the one thought that he kept coming back to was this — Why was I so dumb? She was only another girl. Then why get so worked up over her? He had taken a gun and loaded it and pointed it at a door. On the other side of that door was his friend. How stupid could one get? *What if I had shot it? Why, they would have surrounded me in minutes. And what if I had hit? I really wasn't planning to shoot him*, Mastie thought. *It was just to let him know he better take his meat hooks off my girl.* But it wasn't Froggie who was guilty. She was the one who had betrayed him. What did Froggie know about him and Madeleine? He might have guessed there was a little something. *But did he know I loved her? And what if I had shot her? Not to kill, no, just a shot or two to scare her. I wasn't even planning to shoot the gun*, Mastie thought. *I just picked it up because it was handy.*

Good God, what if he had shot? Point-blank!

Meanwhile, they went on marching. Left-squish, right-squish, left-squish, right-squish. A fine drizzle was falling and the division was beginning to wilt.

There was something about Madeleine that — he didn't know how to describe it, but as soon as he thought about her again, her eyes closed and half-blocked by the veil while she said a prayer — as soon as that picture came back to mind his stomach did a somersault. *I believe I love her,* he thought. Then he remembered a dark cathedral hall and one white hand above the bench while someone out of sight whispered, "Even in the dark your eyes. . . ." She had played with him and no one had ever done that to him before. *She's a bitch, that's what she is. A bitch!*

"Keep the line straight. Keep your officer in sight and keep the line straight!" The officer on horseback shouted at the troops.

What was Annie doing these days, he wondered? It must be nine o'clock. Maybe she was washing a big batch of wash. At least she didn't have to get her hands cold by washing in a pond like they did here. She was probably in the washhouse by the wood stove. Maybe she was firing it up. No, it couldn't be that late in the day. It was probably early in the morning — six-thirty maybe. There was a time change between here and there, wasn't there? The sun moved from east to west, so it had to be earlier over there. Maybe she was just getting out of bed.

Her alarm clock had probably just rung and she had jumped up to shut it off. She was wearing the same white robe he had seen that night and her hair was hanging to her waist! Then she pulled it off and

underneath, well, she was wearing something else —
a white slip maybe — but he could see the outline of
her breasts. Ahh . . . How he had hugged her in the
hay barn at the Red Dragon Market! He was about
to enjoy that memory when he remembered her
crying in the buggy later that night. She was in her
Mennonite clothes then, her dark Mennonite clothes,
hanging on his arm, looking into his eyes. There
it was again, that cramped feeling. The church and
his father and her and everything were sitting on his
chest and squeezing the breath out of him.

But they didn't get me. I'm free. I'm in France!
I'm wearing a good brown uniform like all the other
boys and we're about to go to the front. There! At
that moment, he felt such a tremendous relief that
he had escaped Pennsylvania that he enjoyed the
next ten minutes of marching. They were marching
along together, thousands of them. Healthy boys
about to push the Huns into the North Sea. He
threw back his chest and took a deep breath of air.

Things were greening a little. Spring was coming
to France and it was time to spread manure on the
fields. Good, maybe they would get rid of that big
stinking pile at the front of the quarters. Every
morning that pile grew by another steaming wheel-
barrow full and although he liked the smell of cows
and barns, there was something awful about smelling
it while you were eating your soup and ham, wasn't
there? Or when you were just about to drop off to
sleep.

Spring was coming, and there was a Frenchman
plowing his field already. Was the ground dry
enough for that? Apparently. Why didn't he wait for
a dry, sunshiny day? The Frenchman had stopped

plowing to watch the passing troops.

"*Bon voyage, Americains,*" he said every once in a while, but nobody waved back. Ordinarily, yes, but not on the day of a review. All eyes were to be straight ahead.

"Stoltzfus!"

"Yes, sir." It was the lieutenant, motioning him aside.

"Where's Chavez?"

"Who?"

"Chavez. Froggie."

"Froggie? I don't know. Maybe he's marching out of order."

"He's not marching out of order. He never reported to roll call this morning." At that moment a messenger ran up, covered with mud, and stood by the lieutenant, impatiently waving a note. "Well, he's gone," the lieutenant said. "Clean vanished. You guys are a team — did you see him yesterday?"

"Yesterday?"

"Lieutenant," the messenger said. "General Brackside. . . ."

"Get back in line," the lieutenant said to Mastie. "And report to me first thing when we get back. Understand?"

They marched through another town and on the north side of the town circled onto a large open field. It was magnificent to see the troops turning, rain gleaming on the barrels of their guns, perfectly straight, and a half-inch of mud caking their leggings. At the far side of the field an expensive-looking automobile was parked, an American flag was flying alongside a French flag, and a lone figure was sitting on a horse, surrounded by a host of little buzzing figures. The general was waiting for them. The division commander separated from his marching troops and rode ahead to join the general on the far side of the field.

Who was this man who had caused them to march through the mud? At that moment the two generals on horseback met, leaned toward each other's horses, and the French general kissed the American division commander affectionately on both cheeks. They never even noticed Mastie marching by. Forty miles for what? Why, to provide background noise for their kiss. But Mastie was too busy wondering about Froggie and looking at the French general's horse to think about that. The pretty bay bore a striking resemblance to Apple Boy.

And where was Froggie? The truth, Mastie hadn't seen Froggie the day before, which was Sunday. He hadn't been spending any time with him outside of working hours — not since the unforgettable night several weeks ago. On the other hand, he wasn't sure that he didn't know where Froggie was. Froggie had been low for two days after the review before the French general was announced. "It's the last step, you watch," he said. "They march you before the general and if he likes you, bang, they send your whole outfit off to the front. Good-bye, girls. Good-bye, arm or leg. The front's a meat grinder. I ain't going, Mastie."

"They'll make you," Mastie remembered saying.

"Oh no, not me."

"How are you so different?"

"There are ways."

Apparently Froggie had found a way.

Mastie didn't report to the lieutenant right away

when he got back to camp, though. He had to clean up his uniform and shoes before the mud dried on so hard he couldn't get it off.

The regiment officers' headquarters was set up in the second floor of a house several blocks from the barn where Mastie was billeted. Ordinarily he would have walked down the street to get there, but since he was late, Mastie ran up a narrow back alley. Just before he reached the house he heard voices from the second-floor window, which was open a crack for ventilation.

"It was the champagne. I ain't fooling you. It went to my head, sir, and I got happy. I always get happy when I drink. And I missed the road — have you ever been over to Lyon, sir? The streets go every which way — that's all I can say, sir. I missed the road, sir."

Mastie concealed himself against the recessed wall of the house and listened. He could hear another voice, more faintly, and then he could hear Froggie again.

"What would you do, sir? I mean, I was lost. Nobody can tell me where I am — nothing but this French gibberish. And all of a sudden I hear two horses galloping behind me and two men shouting at me. Sure I ran. I didn't know who they were. Maybe they're American-haters. I mean, not everybody here loves us. Then when they catch me I see it's our own officers. Okay, if I'd have known that I wouldn't have ran."

The other man, Mastie presumed it was the lieutenant, said something again that he couldn't hear and then he heard the lieutenant shout angrily.

" . . . deserter! We shoot deserters around here

173

. . . a lot easier for you if you tell me the whole story."

Mastie looked both ways. No one had seen him. He ran back up the side alley and walked down the street and turned the corner. The armed guard in front of the house nodded to him. "Go on up. Lieutenant's waiting for you." Mastie went up the stairs and the talking stopped. The lieutenant met him at the door.

"Come in. Know that man?" He pointed to the corner of the room where a man was sitting hand-cuffed. His clothes were soaked and muddy and cockle-burs were sticking fast to his pant legs.

"Froggie."

Froggie looked up at him. It was the first time he had ever seen Froggie looked scared. Mastie felt his heart beating faster.

"Where were you last night?" the suspicious lieutenant said.

"Me?" Mastie looked at him. He looked at Froggie. "I was at a cafe in Lyon," he said.

"You were?" The lieutenant said, incredulously. "And do you have any idea where this man was?"

"At the same cafe. He was drinking champagne." He noticed Froggie's eyes widen in amazement. The lieutenant walked from him to Froggie and kept his eyes on both of them the whole time.

"How's come you didn't tell me someone was with you?" he said to Froggie. "Okay, what time did the two of you come back?"

"We didn't come back together," Mastie said, and this time he thought he saw Froggie's mouth drop open slightly. "He was about drunk so I just — "

"You say he was drunk?" the lieutenant said.

174

"Yes. So I just got up and left at eight o'clock by myself."

"Well!" the lieutenant said, and he sat down on the table in his office. He looked at the fat soldier. Then he got up and walked over and unlocked the handcuffs.

"You had me fooled," the lieutenant said. Then he burst out laughing. "Thought you ran away. But that ain't the end of the story, Hector. You're still going to pay for carousing. We're here to become soldiers, not winos. You'll be grounded for a month — no passes, and I'm putting you on kitchen duty. That's all."

Froggie didn't say a word on the way back to their quarters. They walked in silence. But shortly after taps Mastie felt a hand on his in the dark.

"Put her there, Mastie," the familiar voice whispered.

They shook hands.

"I didn't want to go to the front, that's all. Is there anything wrong with that?" After a pause, he added, "You're decent, Mastie."

"Decent?"

"I mean, after Magdalene. . . ." He sighed. "If I had another chance, you know what I'd do? No, I won't do it again. You had me scared, Mastie. I was really scared. I didn't know what you'd say. I didn't even know you knew where I was."

"Yeah. Well, we're still friends," Mastie said. He shrugged his shoulders. He liked Froggie again, but he couldn't say why.

"Tell me something now, Mastie. Where were you last night?"

175

10

Dear Annie,

I am getting more and more tied down here. We train and train. Last week we did a march in the rain. But it's all to make us tough, I guess. I'm in pretty good shape.

I don't see how we can ever get back together. Don't misunderstand me. It's not that I don't want to, but my mind is in a blur about the future. I don't think I will come back to the church. For one thing, it all seems like a big crock of crap to me. Excuse me for saying it, but that's what it's like. It has nothing to do with what we are doing right now, which is fighting a war. I don't know how I was blind so long. It's not that I don't like you anymore, Annie. I still think you're the best girl I ever met. But over here I feel free and even though there's some problems, I don't want to go back to that kind of living again. I would suffocate.

I know I promised you once I would come back, but I really don't see how I can fulfill that. I hate people who break promises. Maybe you will hate me for saying this, but it's the way I feel. I don't think we could ever get married because you love the Mennonite way and I don't want to take you away from it. But it's not for me.

Well, it's all my fault.

I sure can't express myself well in letters but right now I don't think I'd do any better if you were here.

Sincerely,
Mastie

March 16

Dear Mastie,

Please write and tell me if you love me or not. I can't be hurt anymore by your answer, no matter what it is, so please tell me. Nobody understands here.

Annie

April 5

Dear Annie,

I can't take time now to think about your letter. Ten minutes ago we were ordered to the front — ready to go in hours. How's that grab you? I don't know in which direction, but "somewhere in France," I guess.

Could you tell my folks? Don't make it sound like too much to them — I don't want them to get all excited. Break it to them gently, in other words.

I probably won't have too much time for letter writing from now on, but I'll try to keep in touch.

Sincerely,
Mastie

It was hardly the front. Not the active front, anyway, but a quiet wooded area called the Vosges where the Germans and their enemy had come to an unwritten truce a long time ago that there would be no shooting. "If you see a German, don't shoot; you'll only start trouble," was the motto there.

But to the boys who had lived the good life in the haymows of a friendly village, it was the front. Why, they even slept in trenches!

III. Ira, Summer of '18

1

The train rested in Lancaster Station like Noah's Ark, full to the roof with boys from a dozen backgrounds and states and waiting to take on more before it set out on its voyage to change the world. The destination was painted on the side in big letters, *"Berlin or Bust,"* and right below it in smaller letters, *"We're out to lick the Kaiser."*

It was like a holiday. Flags were flying all up and down the platform, the band had just come marching up at the far end and they were preparing to play, and the platform itself was thick with relatives and friends wishing their soldier sons well. America had been at war for a year already but there was still nothing like seeing your own son go. No matter how many other boys had gone before, no matter how tired the band was of giving send-offs, for the families of the new boys there on the platform, it was an unforgettable moment.

Pastor Rydell was sending the last of his Sunday school class. "I wish I were young again," he said, and shook his head. They laughed.

"You're not old," said one of the boys.

"But too old for war, they tell me. I wish I could have had the chance to give my life and be transformed in the moment of battle. You're the

181

future of America, boys. You're going to come back with a vision in your heads that will make old men shake our gray heads and wonder. But that is progress, eh? We live just long enough to see the dawning of the next age, and then we go. To me, the automobile and the crystal radio are a wonder. To you, they will be commonplace. To me this new vision of democracy leaping from our nation to other nations is a wonder. To you it will be commonplace. Who knows what kinds of new things you will see in your old age. Progress, huh? I'm getting sentimental. Jeffrey, give me a hand. Take these Bibles with you, boys — do they fit in your pockets? Good. Take the Bible with you and when you get discouraged, read it to each other. I've written some favorite passages in the front of each of them.

"'We wrestle not with flesh and blood but with principalities and powers, with spiritual creatures in high places.' That's one of my favorites. Everybody have a Bible? I've said it before but I'll say it again, You are not going out only to fight for America with an American gun on your back, but you're going out to fight for God and He will stick courage in you. I was in the Spanish-American affair, and I know how it feels when that 'Charge!' is given. You think of home, you think of your girls, and I say that's good. Your officers in camp may tell you differently, but I say it's good to go over the top with memories of the ones you are fighting for, and I don't want to advocate smoking — I'm against it — but if it helps you to just relax at that moment and to remember why you're there, go over the top with a cigarette."

"Is that right, Pastor? I mean, I thought smoking

wasn't good for you. It could become a habit, not? You're not telling us to smoke, are you?"

"Well. . . ."

They laughed at him, scratching his head.

"God forgives us a little vice now and then if in the end it yields a virtue. Ah, I wish I were young, boys, I wish it so bad it hurts me here." He hit himself on the chest. "I remember when your daddy and I were in Cuba, Victor, the camaraderie and that spirit of 'we are brothers, we're in this together' that I felt. He fought like a mother bear your daddy did, and came back from a raid with some thirty prisoners, and was decorated. There was a man who fought with purpose, but I'll tell you honestly that none of us knew what we were fighting for then. I couldn't have hated those Spanish if I'd tried, but it was different then. That's what makes this war an important one and that one an unimportant one. Democracy! And the enemy is a people. . . . Can we call them a people? For want of a better word, a people . . . to whom God and home and freedom mean nothing. What are they but the lackeys of dictators who aim to control the world? If there ever was a holy war with the forces of God lined up against the forces of the devil, it seems to me no exaggeration to call this one a holy war!

"But talk, talk . . it is the privilege of old men, huh, Victor?" He put his arm around Victor's shoulder. "If I were young, I'd be where you are now. 'Berlin or Bust.' I like that. But I wouldn't neglect my girl like this, Victor. What is this, huh? Look at her over there, looking so loving this way. Come on. Have you kissed her good-bye?"

Ira was in love. He was standing at the other

door of the train coach from Rydell and his boys, holding Susanna's hand in his. He felt sort of a nameless joy in standing here with her, even though he hadn't said anything for the last five minutes. What was left to say? He kicked a stone.

"What are you thinking about?" she said.

"Nothing." He was thinking about her, really, but he found it embarrassing to admit. "I just wonder — "

"What?" she said, and smiled. She was outstanding in the crowd because she didn't wear a hat like most of the women who were there to see off their boys, but only a white Mennonite veil on her bare head, tied under the chin by white ribbons. She had a healthy tan, which was more than most of them could say.

"I just wonder if we can remain true."

"There are no girls in the camps," she said, and smiled.

"No," he said. "You're right. But I meant if I can remain true to what I believe. The pressure — oh, there will be pressure." She nodded. He could tell she was disappointed because the conversation had taken a different turn. Did she suppose that all he had to think about was her? *She is a little too full of good Mennonite virtue and love of family life, he* thought. *Maybe she wants me to commit myself to her, but that would be impossible at this point. The greatest decision facing me now isn't whether I love her or not, although I think I do, but whether I can remain true in the army camp.* "I love the *church,*" he said.

"I know you do," she said.

"But did I tell you that I mean to stay true, as we promised at the Clinton Frame meeting?"

184

"Yes, you did," she said, and laughed a little. "I want you to remain true, no matter what," she said, and squeezed his hand. "But what will become of us?" Her voice had some pain in it.

It fascinated him the way she used the word 'us.' She had just started that several weeks ago.

"You know, I often have to think about your brother, Mastie," she said. "What is happening to him in France, I wonder. He writes to Annie, of course — off and on. I know him, I think, because we often used to talk when he brought Annie back from a singing or something, so he's a friend." She laughed. "I used to really like him for a while."

"You talk about him an awful lot," he said suddenly. Had she secretly been interested in him all along? Mastie would come home a war hero. But how would he, a conscientious objector, come home? They were throwing some of the objectors in prison, he heard. One a prisoner, one a war hero. *She is full of love and easily moved by people's stories,* he thought. *Look how she listened to me. What will happen when I leave? Why, she will probably find some other silent one who needs to be brought out like a flower kept in the dark too long. She will forget about me.*

"No, I don't care about him now," she said. "We're just too much like each other, that's it. Besides, I have you." She looked up and smiled. He turned his head away. He couldn't honestly smile just then because he was prickling with jealousy.

"What's wrong?" she said. Susanna was always quick to read people's eyes. He shook his head. "Ira," she said and reached up with both arms to hug him. He was embarrassed. The center of the train station!

He didn't bend his neck and being short, she couldn't reach around his neck. He wanted to bend down, yes, he wanted to bend down and throw his arms around her, but he didn't because he felt like he had been stuck with a thorn and she was going to have to pull that out of him before he would warm up. "What's wrong?" she said. She let go of him and began to cry. "Did I say something wrong?"

"Hey, laddie, don't leave her like that," said an old man coming by. "It ain't so bad. He'll be coming back a hero before you can say '*Schnickelfritz.*' Can I get you something?"

She shook her head and covered her eyes with her handkerchief. Ira was disgusted. The train was filling up and Pop should be here any moment now. It didn't seem right to go like this.

"Look, Susanna," he said. "I'm sorry." He put his arm around her.

"Sometimes you scare me," she said. "Sometimes I don't understand you. At all."

"You're wonderful," he said. "Look, it was just pride, that's all it was. I'm sorry. Really, I am." He bent down as if to kiss her, but stopped short. They had planned to marry in December, even though nobody else knew it yet. And now with the draft, who knew when they would marry?

The train blew a warning blast. Where was Pop? There he was, hurrying down the platform with a basket under his arm. He came up to them.

"Here, take these," he said. "Mom said you need something to eat. Sandwiches." He put them in Ira's hands. "There isn't much time, is there?" He took Ira's hand in his strong, bony ones. "Susanna, give me your hand. Come now, what's the crying? I hardly know what to say — you're a strong man, yes, you are. I wish your brother had some of your strength. 'Fear not those who destroy the body.' " he said with fervor, " 'but fear only him who will destroy body and soul.' "

The old man cleared his throat and began to recite in a low voice, in high German,

> *The Lord is my shepherd; I shall not want,*
> *He maketh me to lie down in green pastures; he*
> *restoreth my soul:*
> *He leadeth me in the paths of righteousness for*
> *his name's sake.*
> *Yea, though I walk through the valley of the*
> *shadow of death,*
> *I will fear no evil: for thou art with me;*
> *Thy rod and thy staff they comfort me. My cup*
> *runneth over with oil.*

He skipped something, Ira thought. His memory's not as good anymore. It was the part about "a table in the presence of mine enemies."

> *"Surely goodness and mercy shall follow me.*
> *And I will dwell in the house of the Lord for ever.*
> *Amen."*

He opened his eyes and embraced Ira. "God bless you," he said. "My son — " He shook his head. "My son — Say good-bye to him Susanna. I think they're ready to go." The conductor was motioning Ira to get on board. The platform was wild with shouting and last-minute embraces through the train windows.

Ira squeezed her shoulder. He picked up his suitcase and got on, looking for a window as he did. Outside, the train conductor raised his arms and turned to look both ways. "Stand back," he shouted. Behind him the band held their trombones and drumsticks in ready position. The conductor dropped his arms and the band behind burst into the "Star Spangled Banner" as the wheels of the train turned slowly. The faces outside began to move. Hundreds and hundreds of faces, but in Ira's eyes there were only two. Why, she was smiling. She looked up and began to smile. He waved and shouted through the window. She waved back. The faces began to blur as the train picked up speed and then the band flashed by, still playing, and after that came wheat fields, ripe with wheat.

BACK ON the platform Pastor Rydell turned in the crowd and walked down to the short, red-bearded man.

"Well, they're gone."

"Yes," said the old man.

"He looked like a brave young chap to me," said Rydell, "his chin up proud and his back straight. Is he yours?" he said to Susanna. "Come on, cheer up. He'll be home on furlough in no time. I know how it feels. Me and my girl were separated during the war in Cuba and it seemed like we'd never see each other again. Now she cooks me a tortilla every once in a while and we sit around and look at pictures of how slender and handsome we used to be. He'll probably come back wanting you to cook him up a snail or two. Isn't that what they eat in France?" He laughed at his own joke. "You have a boy across already, don't you?" he said to Red Isaac.

"Yes, but he's no son," said Isaac. He watched Susanna walk across the platform.

"Oh, I thought he was a son."

"Yes, by the blood, yes. But he's cut himself off as far as we're concerned. He was the apple of my eye, yes, he was, but he rejected everything." He slapped his hands together.

"A prodigal?" said Rydell.

"This one is like his mother, less impulsive and he uses his head. He has real strength, this boy, and he loves the church. But he ain't like the other one. No, he's a tame colt to the other one. I don't like to talk about it."

"The soldier's life might straighten him out," said Rydell. "I know several boys who left home as real — pardon the expression — devils. Hellcats. But the discipline of a soldier's life and fighting for a cause does something for a boy. I've talked to boys in Paris who were fresh out of the trenches who had a light in their eyes like I've never seen before. They speak of the 'baptism of fire,' you know, and I believe it is. I think those boys find their souls in the battle line. God bless them. Maybe it's the ideals they're fighting for that does it. Those ideals take over the boys themselves, even boys who in civilian life were what we might call the bad boys."

Red Isaac's arms were folded. He looked the pastor in the eye and nodded a little from time to time. Finally he cleared his throat.

"That's not the way our church sees it," he said. "If a boy kills another one for whatever reason he has broken God's commandments, 'Thou shalt not kill' and 'Love thy neighbor as thyself.'' If he doesn't repent, God will judge him accordingly. We had to cut him off from the church because he was headed the wrong direction. It was the hardest thing I ever did, Brother Rydell, believe me. To cut off your own son! Perhaps I was too harsh. Perhaps Mom and I didn't love him enough. But there comes promises and baptismal vows and not only as a son. We had to cut him off. As to whether he will find the Lord in France, I doubt it, but I don't want to say that too loud. Who knows what He is capable of." He pointed his finger to the sky and smiled.

"Just a minute," said Rydell. "Do I hear you saying he is wrong *because* he went?"

"It's very complicated," said Isaac. "I don't know where it started, but from here . . . to there . . . to there, he got cold to the faith. If he were warm to the faith, no, I don't think he could have gone."

"Oh," said Rydell, "so you're not in favor of America then. You're not behind our boys."

"I don't want to make any judgment on anyone," said Isaac, "I only know I am sorry about my son. It tears me apart. Both my sons gone and me an old man. But to have a son leave home is nothing compared to losing a son."

"You're a bit hard to understand," said Rydell. He looked at Isaac. "You speak the Dutch, too, don't you? But I wouldn't suppose you have any connection with Germany anymore, do you? You don't have relatives there, do you?" He didn't mean it unkindly — he was just curious — but still there seemed to be something of larger significance here.

"We have brothers in Germany," said Isaac.

"Brothers?" said Rydell. "Your family came over then?"

"No, no. In the Lord. Brothers in the Lord."

"Oh," said Rydell.

"Susanna." Isaac turned and walked toward her. She was still standing on the other side of the platform, looking down the tracks. "Your family will be wondering where you are," he said in English. Rydell watched them go.

Inside the train, the initial commotion of getting started had died and the lights came on as the day faded outside. Ira turned from the window at last, full of mixed feelings.

"Care for a cup?" said his seatmate. Ira shook his head.

The door of the coach opened and two men in brown uniforms with soft felt army hats, boots, and side pistols strode in, stopped, and looked over the trainload of men in civilian clothes. The laughter in the train stopped and several men already deep in a game of pinochle looked up over their hands. A soldier toward the back tossed a cup of whiskey down his throat and said, "What can we do for you?"

"I want to see every whiskey bottle go out that window right now," the small officer said. "Let's go. All right, you're in the Army now, therefore, under military discipline. No one will get off this train until we get to Camp Ethan Allen. Anyone doing so will be arrested by the military police when we get to camp. That's all." The officers walked the length of the coach. Their boots squeaked until they stepped into the next coach. Then Ira's coach was perfectly still.

Suddenly the doors opened again. This time it was three men in uniform, carrying large baskets and grinning.

"Sandwiches!" the lead man said, and he began to pass out sandwiches with both hands. The Army was not only their father. For the next years until the war ended, it was also going to be their mother.

2

Getting off the train is easy when there are only five people ahead of you and the conductor is helping each one with his bags and giving his arm to the old men and women. But getting off the train takes a lifetime, it seems, when there are a thousand men abroad, all of them young and excited. On top of that there was a jam-up at the doors because the officers were issuing folding cots, blankets, a mess kit, a tin bucket for washing, and a bar of soap to each man, and they took each man's name and checked it off in a registration book as he jumped down onto Georgia soil. The night ride had left everybody a little jumpy and excited and the boys were shouting at each other, waving good-bye cheerily as they were taken off to their assigned tents.

Ira jumped out of the train and landed almost at the officer's feet.

"Name."

"Ira Stoltzfus."

"Place of residence."

"Susquehannock, Pennsylvania."

"Draft card." He fumbled in his pocket and got it. Would this be the right man to give his note to? He felt for the note.

"Next."

"This is your folding cot. Number's on the corner. Memorize it. You won't get another one. Tent officer will show you where to place it. Board the truck. Next."

He decided to hold the note until later. Behind him several men, waiting for the truck, were standing around in a circle stretching and yawning.

"I'm starved," said one.

"You guys know we can't go to the camp until they find the man who fell off the train?" said a skinny boy with a floppy woolen cap of the kind popular twenty years before.

"Somebody fell off the train?" asked another man.

"Yeah, that's what they say. Must have had too much to drink or something. Maybe he got up in the middle of the night to go to the john, thinking he was home, and walked the path until he fell right off."

"Ah, you're kidding. If anybody fell off, he'd be killed. Besides, how do they know where to look? If he fell off in the dark and no one saw him, you mean we have to wait here in the sun while they go back over the whole railroad and look for this guy? I don't believe it," said a stout man who was dressed in a business suit.

"Hot out, isn't it?"

"I could use some sleep. What do you say we hop on this train again and go back home?"

"Say, there's a lot of dust around here, isn't there?"

"Where?"

"There," and the stout boy tripped the skinny one and sent him down in a cloud of dust. Everybody laughed and the skinny boy got up coughing.

A truck was coming for them, up around the big frame buildings that looked like they might be office or administration buildings. They all looked new, probably erected since the start of the war in the rush to put an army on its feet.

It certainly is important that the truck driver knows what is in my note, Ira thought. *It may make a difference in my tent assignment.* Perhaps they had a special part of the camp reserved for the conscientious objectors. He had heard about such divisions in some camps.

He walked around to the driver's window.

"Hey, get on the truck, will you? Can't mess around when there's a thousand of you to be ready for roll call this afternoon."

"Excuse me."

"What's wrong?"

He took the note from his pocket and gave it to the driver. The driver looked at it. He began to laugh.

"Is it all right then?" said Ira. It irritated him to see the man laughing at his note. Did he think it wasn't serious?

"That's funny," the truck driver said. He dropped the note and it fell to the ground. He turned and looked back in his mirror. The men at the back were still standing and talking.

"Hey, what do you think this is? Get in the truck," the truck driver said. "Come on, get in." He gestured toward the back of the truck. "How many times you need to be told? You think this is a picnic or something?" The men began to crawl up onto the back of the truck. The truck driver put the truck in gear as Ira climbed over the back. The other

194

men watched him and noticed his black hat and Mennonite coat.

"What's with the clothes?" said one of the men. "You Jewish or something?"

"I'm Mennonite," said Ira, and he smiled a very little.

"Mennonite?" said the skinny boy. "What country's that from?"

"What country? Haha," said the stout boy.

"Well, how was I to know?"

"It's a — " Ira began and then he wasn't sure how to finish it. He had just assumed that people knew because they all did in his area. "It's a way of life," he said. "We're Christians."

"Oh, well, I'm Catholic myself," said the skinny boy. "Only way to get to heaven."

"It doesn't matter what you are here," said the stout boy, "or what you look like. They strip you and give you a uniform to put on and they cut everybody's hair the same and when they're done they give you a gun. Then you can't tell who's who, who's Catholic or who's Irish or who's rich or poor anymore."

"Whew. This dust! What do they think we are? Texas cowboys or something?"

"Me, I just want a good pancake or two," said the skinny boy.

The truck stopped again and an unsmiling, well-fed man in uniform looked into the back of the truck. "Everybody off," he said. Everybody scrambled off while he watched. "Line up in front of the tent." They lined up in front of the tent.

"Okay. So we're going to make soldiers out of you boys. Not girls — soldiers! There are no girls in this camp. If they do come, we have fun with them, right?" He looked into one man's eye.

"Right, sir." They all laughed, a little nervously.

"We're going to nail the Kaiser up against a tree someplace in Germany and let him rot. Right?"

"Right."

"Okay, I'm Sergeant Potts and when you address me, it's not 'right,' it's either 'right, sir' or 'yes, Sergeant.' Understand?"

"Yes, Sergeant."

"All right. We're not mean here, we're just tough because when you get to Germany the Hun won't change your diapers for you or get your bottle ready. You'll do it yourself. There won't be anybody there to make sure your rifle is in firing order when they come swarming up out of the trenches. You'll check on that yourself, too. There won't be anyone to kiss you good-night or make a clean bed for you. You'll learn to sleep anytime your head touches the ground. In other words, you're not boys anymore. You're men! You understand?

"Yes, sir."

It was getting hot and Ira's eyes kept falling shut. Sergeant Potts gestured. He was a short man, not more than three inches over five feet, but he had cultivated a special voice over the years to make up for the physical problem of shouting uphill over the heads of several hundred men. It was like a bark. He turned one direction and barked and then jerked the other direction and barked. Ira was reminded of pictures he had seen of Napoleon.

"You there with the funny coat — preacher, huh? — why didn't you answer?" Someone poked Ira with an elbow.

"I'm sorry."

"I said, 'Why didn't you answer me?'"

"I'm sorry. What was the question?"

"It wasn't a question. It was a comment. I said, 'We're not boys anymore, we're men.' Do you understand?"

"Yes."

"Not 'yes.' What's the answer, girls?"

"Yes, sir."

"Yes, sir," said Ira.

"All right, your tent's behind you. Take those cots and unfold them like this." He grabbed a man's cot and showed them, then folded it again and gave it back. "Put your gear *under* your bed. Not on top of or beside, but *under* your bed. The schedule is posted outside the tent with one important change for today. Roll call will be at two o'clock today and lunch at one. Everybody understand?"

"Yes, sir."

"Okay, on the double."

They ran into the tent under his terrible eyes and began to unfold their beds. Ira, however, didn't go. He took the paper from his pocket again.

"Well, Holy Coat. Get your ass moving."

"Excuse me, I — "

"What's wrong?"

Ira handed him the paper and the sergeant read over it, not once, but two times. Then he looked Ira straight in the eyes. He took hold of Ira's arm and led him to the tent door. He pushed him in with an easy tap, and Ira was suddenly sure that Potts, for all his rough exterior, was gentle inside.

"Men."

They stopped working on their beds and looked

up, easily, not at attention like old soldiers.

"I want you to know you have a girl in your tent. That's right, a son-of-a-bitch who won't fight. All right, Conchie, good luck to you in the Army."

He walked out and left Ira facing the seven others in the tent. They looked at him, and nobody said anything for a minute. The tall, skinny boy at the far end of the tent went back to making his bed. A boy with long, straight hair combed back looked up and said, "What did he say you are?"

The tent door flapped open and there was Sergeant Potts again. He poked his head through the door and looked at Ira. "Here, I don't want your paper. If you're smart, you'll drop that paper down the hole in the outhouse." The Sergeant left and the boys all went back to arranging their things.

After a bit the boy with the long, straight hair looked up and asked again, "Is it true you won't fight?"

Ira looked straight back into his eyes and nodded.

"Not even if I hit you?" The boy was wiry, but Ira was sure he could whip him. Ira was a farmer. The boy stood up and passed by Ira slowly. Suddenly he took hold of Ira's ear and twisted it around.

"Hey, cut it out, Rupe," A boy on the other side got up slowly from his bed and with one hand pushed Ira's tormentor over backward. "What have you got against him? Huh? If he doesn't want to fight for Uncle Woodrow, then I say he's just that much smarter than the rest of us. I don't want to fight, either. If I had my choice, I'd be home eating strawberries right now."

They all laughed and the confrontation was over.

Ira unfolded his bunk and sat down on it to root

through his bag for his Bible. Yes, it was there, but he didn't think it was wise to bring it out now. He closed the bag and wondered if he should show the paper to anyone else. Was it only rumor then, that the government recognized conscientious objectors? Would they force him to fight? No, he was sure they couldn't make him do that. They could take him to Germany and give him a gun but they couldn't force him to pull the trigger. Not in a hundred years.

Twenty minutes later a whistle blew outside. It was the sergeant again. He was mounted on a tall horse.

"Move," he shouted. "Everybody over to the examination hall on the double and peel down. We want to see what kind of bodies they sent us this time. See if you're good enough to fight for Uncle Woodrow. We'll find out if you're men or not. Let's go, on the double." He began to trot his horse alongside of them as they ran. "Jesus, you men are slow. What did you do before you came here? Is that the way you worked at home? No wonder companies go bankrupt with stiffs like you working for them. How many cows did you milk a day before the Army got you? Two? We'll teach you to squeeze teats all right. You'll squeeze that old trigger so often that you'll scorch those old cow teats, you'll squeeze so fast when you get back. If you get back. As slow as your rear ends move, you aren't going to get back. Let's go. Move." He clapped his hands and kept up a steady diatribe as he rode alongside.

"Hey, here we have a man now. Look at that chest," said Potts and he leaned out of the saddle to thump the man's chest with the butt of his riding whip as he rode alongside. "We'll have you heaving grenades. But what are we going to do with this little piece of pipe cleaner? Eh? That's it, a pipe cleaner. We'll wrap you up in cleaning rags and roll you around in the big guns a couple times to clean them out. How does that suit you? Move! Let's go, girls! Move!"

But when they got to the examination hall, they had to stand in line for half an hour anyway. Where was the sergeant now?

3

Ira was getting used to lines.

He imagined that he was standing in a line like the one he had seen in a *National Geographic* photo of hill tribesmen in Taiwan, and that instead of healthy men around him, there were women and children who had come for miles to see the wonderful doctor who in one minute knew what their problem was and prescribed a medicine from his big satchel beside the table.

Ahead of him a sergeant was standing before the doorway to a room into which an aide was throwing bags of clothes. It was already piled half full. Beyond the sergeant the men were all naked, except for their underpants, and it was amazing how much everyone looked alike without clothes on. Behind him the men wore their cultures and habits and hobbies and occupation. Mennonite clothes, fisherman's hats, Polish clothes, polished shoes, oxford shoes, scuffed shoes. Ahead of him they were only bodies. *We're in the Army,* he thought.

"Name. Residence."

"Undress! Put your clothes in the bag and leave them here." The others were undressing and he did too. But his letter of conscientious objection was in the shirt pocket and what would he wear if he had lost his civilian clothes? The aide stretched out his hand to take the clothes, but Ira held them back.

"Sir, I'm a conscientious objector. May I keep my clothes?"

"Give them here."

Ira hesitated.

"I said, 'Give them here.' You'll wear a uniform from now on."

The sergeant turned around.

"Let him pass." The men in the line looked back at him curiously and shuffled ahead.

There were fifteen or so doctors and specialists in the line ahead, each of them with a little bag of instruments on a small table behind him and each with an attendant dressed in uniform trousers and an open shirt.

The doctor with the stethoscope never looked at Ira, his eyes instead went right to his chest. He put the stethoscope against him and listened.

"Mark him." The attendant took a yellow piece of chalk from the table and marked a conspicuous X over Ira's heart. What did it mean? No one else had a mark. Were they going to exempt him? His heart murmured, he was sure of that. It made a trickling sound after each beat, like water dripping off a waterwheel as it went around. Pop said it was the rheumatic fever that did it to him.

The line moved on.

After that it was the throat specialist and then the man who checked your reflexes by knocking a hammer against the tendon in your knee. Ira sat down on the chair and crossed his legs for the test and then he was conscious of someone else there, talking to the examining doctor. He thought nothing of it until he noticed someone talking as he sat for the next doctor, too. It was Sergeant Potts. It was impossible to hear what he said to the doctors, but the rest of them only looked over Ira briefly and ordered him on. When he got to the end of the line, the last doctor reached out his hand and wiped the X off Ira's chest.

"You're in the Army, son," he said.

After all the inoculations and vaccinations, checkups on every hole in the body and questions about every disease mankind had ever had, blood samplings and a look at the teeth by the Army dentist, the men were given haircuts and sent to be outfitted in a little building that connected with the examination hall by a passageway.

Three clerks stood at a long window issuing smart brown uniforms, newly arrived from a Washington, D.C., factory. In front of the window a dozen or so men were trying on uniforms or measuring each other with tape measures if they didn't know their sizes. At the other side of the room by the door another officer was issuing hats, leggings, and shoes. It was all part of the conditioning. These were new men. They had come like sheep, been shorn of every trapping of the civilian world, and now, jacketed in Army clothes, they were new men. They no longer belonged to their families or their sweethearts, their churches or their companies. They belonged to the United States Army.

Ira felt it in his bones. To put on the uniform was the final step in the remaking. He had submitted to the haircut. Haircuts didn't make a soldier. Uniforms did. If he put on his sweaty civilian clothes, he was still a part of his people in Pennsylvania. If he put on the uniform — who would know what he was? He was confident as he came into the annex, even though his heart was pounding. They hadn't taken his clothes away yet, and he still held them in the bag in his right hand.

"Name."

"Ira Stoltzfus."

"Tent and company number."

"Company C, tent No. 7."

"Shirt size."

"Excuse me, but I cannot wear a uniform. I am a conscientious objector."

The little clerk looked up with startled eyes.

"But you must wear the uniform."

"I cannot."

"But it's government regulations. They'll court-martial you, sonny. Don't give me trouble, please."

"May I have permission to wear my regular clothes? I have them right here in the bag. Oh — " he remembered the conscientious objection papers and dug through the shirt pocket to find them. The clerk looked at the paper and nudged the other clerk.

In a minute the clerk issuing hats at the door came over to see what the trouble was and finally a third clerk appeared. The recruits in the room with Ira looked at him strangely. They were beginning to think of themselves as soldiers already — the smart uniforms gave them a glow of pride and identity. Did he think he was better than they were?

The hat clerk was first to speak. "I don't know. Your papers look genuine enough, but it doesn't say anything here about not wearing the uniform. Just because you wear a uniform doesn't mean you're going to be fighting. That's what this 'conscientious objection' means, isn't it? You won't fight?"

Ira nodded.

"But you're going to have to put a uniform on anyway. That's our job, outfitting you with a uniform. Everybody here — the officers, the soldiers, the sanitation crew, the quartermaster corps — wears a uniform. You can't live in this camp in civilian clothes. Once you get your outfit on you can go see Colonel Doolittle and see what he has to say about it. Okay?"

"I'm sorry. I can't wear a uniform either. Wearing a uniform is becoming a soldier, and I can't become a soldier. I'm a Christian."

The clerk got excited.

"Well, so am I. What do you think we are, a bunch of atheists or something? I don't know about this," he said. "We better take him to the officers right away. Jerry."

The window clerk named Jerry looked around at his clerks. He swallowed.

"Let's go," he said to Ira, and motioned him ahead to the outside door that went down to the ground. From there, the officers' quarters were only a few feet away across the grass and up another flight of steps.

"Can I put my regular clothes on?" said Ira.

The window clerk shook his head. "No."

He led Ira up the steps to the officers' headquarters. Ira was wearing nothing but a pair of summer briefs and carrying his clothes in a bag beside him. The clerk knocked, then opened the door and saluted.

There were three or four officers in the room,

smoking — Colonel Doolittle, Sergeant Potts, and several company officers. Their break lasted until the examinations were over and they were talking about the possibilities of getting into the action now going on in France when the clerk walked in, followed by Ira. The colonel leaped to his feet, although "leap" didn't quite describe what he did. He was a sixty-year-old man not used to getting up for anyone. Anyway, he was on his feet immediately, standing erect.

"Good God, man, what do you mean by bringing a man in like that?" Sergeant Potts opened his mouth and stared and the other men put down their cigarettes.

The clerk looked confused and he saluted again. He was only obeying orders.

"Well, don't stand there. Get a uniform on the man if we've got to see him" The colonel sat down. The clerk nodded and began to step backward toward the door. He pushed Ira out ahead of him and no sooner had the door shut than the clerk seemed to realize that was the very reason he had come to the officers' quarters. He knocked on the door again and went in again and saluted. Sergeant Potts had just began to explain things to the other officers.

"My company?" he said, "The only unconscious rejector in the whole blooming camp and he gets in my company. Do you know what I mean, colonel? He's a troublemaker, I can see that, and you get one of them in your company who won't do drills or something and you ruin the lot of them. Just one rotten apple, that's all it takes. . . ."

"Yes?" the colonel said, looking up. "Are you going to get a uniform on that man or aren't you?"

"But that's the trouble, sir. He refuses to wear the uniform."

"He refuses?"

"That's right. He's a conscientious objector, sir."

"Damned unconscious rejectors," said Potts under his breath.

"What's he got in that bag then?"

"His civvies, sir."

"Well, have him put them on."

"Yes, sir."

So Ira put on his trousers and shirt on the outside stairway, and he was embarrassed how sweated they were. *Maybe they'll think I'm not clean*, he thought. But he was glad it wasn't a uniform. The clerk led him in again. The colonel stood up and looked at the recruit who didn't even know how to salute.

"Well?" he said.

When they bring you before the authorities . . . the Holy Spirit will teach you in that very hour what you ought to say. The verse came to him like a sudden bird of peace, blown out of the storm. He felt calm again. What could they do to him? Was this the man to tell his story to?

"I am Ira Stoltzfus, and I'm a conscientious objector to war. I belong to the Mennonite Church and we think it's wrong to fight. The newspapers say President Wilson respects us and our position and won't force us to fight if it is against our conscience."

"So, you are a conscientious objector. How do I know you're telling me the truth? How do I know you're not just a coward, scared to fight?"

"No, it's not that I'm afraid to fight or die. 'Fear not them that kill the body, but fear them that kill the soul,' the Scripture says. The Bible also says,

'Thou shalt not kill' and 'Love thy neighbor as thyself.' How can I kill when the Bible tells me I'm not supposed to?"

"I see. In any case, you'll have to do noncombatant work if we find you're sincere. *If* we find you're sincere. Now what is noncombatant work? In a word, service in either the medical corps on the front, the quartermaster corps, or the engineering corps. You will drill just like anyone else and you will wear the uniform because we consider you a part of the Army. Do you have any questions?" The colonel was always conscious of his men. He stood if they stood, he only sat when they sat. Just now, he was standing.

"I can't work behind the lines either," Ira said, and he looked straight into the colonel's eyes. Not defiantly, but as if he were appealing. "The Bible says Saul of Tarsus was condemned, not because he threw stones at Stephen, but because he held the coats of the men who stoned him. So I cannot take any part in the war and I can't wear the uniform either because that is the symbol of the Army."

"I told you," said Sergeant Potts.

"Don't get me angry," the colonel said. "This isn't an argument. It's not even a discussion because I don't plan to discuss it. You'll put the uniform on and take part in the drills. We can't have some men walking around here in civilian clothes or everybody will want to. So I'm ordering you to put on a uniform. And I'd like to talk with you again at your leisure, Stoltzfus. You interest me. That's all." The clerk tugged at his arm, but Ira didn't move.

"I can't," Ira said.

Sergeant Potts jumped to his feet. "Look, I'll help

him with the uniform."

"Easy, Potts," said the colonel. "I don't want anybody getting hurt." He stood up again, and looked at Ira. "I'm sorry," he said, "but you'll have to wear the uniform." Then he walked out of the room.

No sooner were they outside than the sergeant turned to the clerks. "Take him to Room 48. We'll fix you up, conchie." Ira's mouth was dry. He hadn't had a drink since morning.

He must have waited two hours in the room. The shadows outside the windows grew long and stretched away from the building into the open field behind. Out there somewhere he could hear cicadas humming and away off a farmer was driving a herd of cows toward a small barn. From this window it was impossible to see any of the rest of the camp. At the beginning the clerk got up every five minutes and stepped to the doorway to look out. Then he would step back inside and look at Ira with a frown as though it were Ira's fault that the clerk was unable to go on with his work. After a while, a bugle sounded and the clerk looked at his pocket watch. Finally he gave up looking, and sat down in a chair, and went to sleep.

The room looked like an exercise gym of some sort, with weights and Indian clubs and charts showing the muscles of the body. There was one door and Ira wanted to walk right through it and out across the pasture to the little barn where the farmer was about to milk the cows. Who would ever know where he had gone? He got up. He was about to walk to the window when the door opened and Sergeant Potts came in with four or five corporals, one of whom was carrying Ira's suitcase.

Were they sending him home then? Or something worse? But no, another corporal had a new uniform draped over his arm.

"All right, Stoltzfus," the sergeant said. "I guess you thought we wouldn't come back, didn't you? We just went to check on your uniform and stopped for supper. They're keeping some food hot for you, but you're going to have to change clothes first. So you can start undressing anytime now. We have your suitcase and we're sending the whole pack back to Lancaster tomorrow." Ira looked at the sergeant and the men standing with him. The little clerk stood up and grinned and seemed about to say something, but he stopped, then looked at his pocket watch again.

"Let's go. Take them old things off, or we'll help you."

So it was not going to be a question of wearing a uniform or not wearing one, it was only going to be a question of how the uniform got on. He resolved he would not put the uniform on by himself. If he had to wear one, they'd have to put it on him.

Potts never stopped looking at Ira. He began to smile a little. Ira took off his shirt, and then his trousers, dropping them on the floor beside him. He looked at Potts again.

"Okay, keep your underwear and socks. Is there anything else you need out of the suitcase?"

Ira took out his toothbrush, comb, a supply of stationery, and some pills.

"Braintree." The corporal named Braintree knelt down and stuffed the trousers and shirt into the suitcase and closed it again. "Richardson." The corporal named Richardson laid the uniform on the chair beside Ira and stepped back again.

Ira looked at the sergeant.

"Well?"

"I can't wear the uniform because, to me, it's a sin."

Potts nodded and then looked at the corporals. "Okay, fellows."

On signal, two of them picked up the uniform trousers and began to pull them over Ira's legs, another corporal stuffed his arms into the sleeve of the shirt and buttoned it up, and another one got down on his hands and knees and began to pull on the leggings and combat shoes. They stood him up, not roughly, but efficiently, as though they were store clerks dressing a mannequin with new fall clothing. Finally they slipped his arms into a regulation coat, which amazingly seemed to fit, and buttoned it up crooked, with one button too many at the top and one buttonhole too many at the bottom. Someone put a hat on him, not a combat helmet, but a soft brim Army hat. One of the corporals unbuttoned his own collar buttons and snapped them onto Ira's suit.

"Here," he said. "It'll save you thirty cents." It was Ethan Allen tradition for the soldier to buy his own collar buttons and hatband. When they were finished, Sergeant Potts clicked his heels and brought up his chin.

"Attention!" Ira looked at him without malice, but he didn't salute. There was nothing to say. He was glad he hadn't compromised so far. Potts dropped his shoulders and walked around.

"So you don't even know how to salute. You don't know what respect is, you don't know how to

211

obey an order, you won't fight, and you can't even pull your own pants on. Good God, what can you do? Can you parade? Well, men, we're going to take him out and show the whole camp just how a yellow-belly looks so they can identify one if they see one again. Let's go."

The clerk stood up again.

"Excuse me, Sergeant," he said timidly, smiling.

"Yes."

"Can I go now?"

"All right. Just don't ever bring me another of these." Two corporals each took one of Ira's arms and they led him out of the building. There was no one on the grounds anymore. It was almost dusk and lights were on in the hall where they had taken the examinations. Up ahead somewhere a whistle blew and there was shouting — it appeared that the men were going back to the tents.

The whole of Company C was standing at attention in front of tents, not quite sure what was about **to happen. Was this another** part of the daily ritual? They had their hands at the side and legs together, but heads were gawking.

Sergeant Potts blew his whistle in Ira's ear and the talking stopped. A few heads even poked out of the tents of another company where the men were supposed to be polishing their shoes for the inspection first thing in the morning.

"Ladies and gentlemen," said Sergeant Potts, and the whole company burst out laughing. "Shh . . ." went the sergeant, and they got quiet. "You haven't proven to me yet that you're not girls. Just because you don't have any bumps on your chest doesn't mean you're not girls. I make that decision

212

when I see you looking like men. Big bellies, flat feet, pimple noses, protruding belly buttons, and humpy backs like so many camels. You guys call yourselves soldiers?" The men laughed self-consciously and straightened up. They were already beginning to think of themselves as soldiers. A day of being hollered at and a stiff uniform and hat did that to them. There was already a similarity among them that hadn't existed that morning. It was more than their uniforms. It was a feeling. It was a mixture of a feeling of awkwardness and not knowing quite what to do to avoid being hollered at and a little bit of pride thrown in — they belonged to a sort of corporation that was going places and doing things in this world.

"Now, what is the Army?" said the sergeant. He heard some of the men snickering. They had just noticed that the fly on Ira's pants was open. "We'll talk about him in a minute," said the sergeant. "The Army is a place for making men. Now occasionally, not very often, but once in a great while, we get someone in here who just refuses to be made into a man. He deserves a little special welcome, wouldn't you say? Well, here he is, folks, Private Stoltzfus. He's an unconscious rejector, he says. You know what that means? That means he won't fight. He's a YELLOW-BELLY." The sergeant was shouting. "We even had to dress him. Let's hear a cheer for Private Stoltzfus." He gave Ira a push and the crowd of men began to laugh and heckle. Most of them had never heard of an objector or rejector before, but if they couldn't even button their coats right and shut their flies, and if they wouldn't fight. . . . Somebody wolf whistled.

Ira walked slowly toward Tent Number 7, down at the far end of the gauntlet. His ear was ringing and booming from the sergeant's whistle. He looked ahead toward the mountains. A hawk was rising in the evening. How wonderful to be a hawk, he thought, rising and falling on the thermals along the mountainside. It must be cool up there. (The back of his shirt was sweated through.) The hawk began to rise and rise until it was only a tiny speck in the sky and suddenly the cheers and whistles turned to music! It seemed like a multitude of singers and their voices were coming from the other side of the mountain, there where red clouds were forming.

> *"This is my Father's world . . .*
> *And to my listening ear all nature sings*
> *And round me rings the music of the spheres."*

It was a beautiful hymn. He recognized it as one that he had heard at the singings, but he didn't know all the words.

> *"This is my Father's world.*
> *The birds their carols sing,*
> *In the rustling grass, I hear Him pass.*
> *He speaks to me everyday."*

Suddenly the music stopped and the hawk began to reappear, diving out of the top of the sky at a tremendous speed. It was going to hit the mountain. Yes, it would hit the mountain. . . .

The cheering faded and the last twenty men only stared at him. What was he smiling for anyway? Did he enjoy this or something?

214

"Hey, yellowbelly," Someone threw a pebble at him and it bounced off his hat. He didn't notice. It looked like he was going to walk out through the camp and on into Tennessee, but then he stopped.

At what seemed like the last possible moment the hawk angled and fell sideways and then it circled around and started to rise slowly once more, beginning all over again. He went inside the tent and sat down on the edge of the bed.

"Let me at him," someone said, and came running into the tent. It was Rupe with his fists bunched up to fight.

"Stay back, Rupe," said a soldier right behind him. "If he wants to make an ass out of himself, let him. Take a lesson. If you don't put on a uniform, they put one on for you. It's your deal." And he picked up a hand of cards and held them in front of Rupe's face. "They're yours."

"Anybody here who is afraid to fight the Huns is going to fight it out with me." The other five tent-mates had come in, but Rupe evaded their arms and ran around the other side of the bed to get a clear line of attack on Ira. "Come on, yellowbelly."

Someone stretched out a leg and tripped Rupe and he went down on all fours. He got up and brushed the dust off. "Okay, who did that? Huh?" It seemed to have taken the fight out of him, though, because he stopped and changed his tactics. "I don't want to sleep beside him," said Rupe. "Anybody want to trade beds? A yellowbelly, huh? My brother died in France to protect punks like you and this is how you show your appreciation?" He swore in another language and crawled into a bed first claimed by another man. He began to sort his cards.

The lights were controlled by some main office and they went out at ten. Ira got up and took off his uniform and folded it in the dark. He lay down on the hard mattress and imagined that he was back in Lancaster County. He could hear the crickets outside and if he squinted his eyes the tent flap looked like the window of his room. And Pop, was he sleeping over in his room? Would there be services tomorrow? And Mom? Did she work on the rug for their wedding today? Then he wondered if there would ever be a wedding. Because someplace deep in his bones he felt that he would never see them again. He didn't know what would happen, but he wasn't afraid. Only tired and sad. *I wish I would have kissed her goodbye when I left,* he thought.

4

The bugler woke the camp at 5:45.

Ira stumbled out of bed, half expecting to hear calves bawling in the barn. He felt below his bed for his clothes — that was where he always kept them, in a pile. Then it occurred to him that his clothes weren't there. They were lying at the foot of the bed and they were brown like everybody else's. His *only* clothes were a uniform coat and pants of the U.S. Army.

Should he put them on or stay here in the tent without dressing? There were two important things to remember in camp, his father had emphasized. One was to be faithful to his belief and the other was to be consistent in his faithfulness. The *Gospel Herald* carried stories of men who were behind bars in Leavenworth already because they hadn't been consistent — one time they obeyed an order, the next day they were sorry they had, and refused the same order. There would be no second chances here, he was sure. Had he already compromised, then, by wearing the uniform last night? Of course not. They had forced it on him. But suppose he put it on voluntarily this morning? Well, it had been forced on him by taking away his other clothes, hadn't it?

The skinny soldier, Rupe, looked at him from

across the room. He had been up since five, eager to get on with the show. He sat on the edge of his bed, grinning, with his uniform already on.

"Down with the bloody Huns!" he said to the men crawling out of their beds. They glared at him.

Ira put on his uniform. At 7:30 a whistle blew.

No one seemed to know quite what the whistle meant but everyone immediately associated it with Sergeant Potts. There he stood on the edge of the drill field holding up his hands for attention, watching them, unsmiling.

"Let's go!" he shouted. "Let's go, girls! Move your big fannies."

The men gathered on the drill field.

"Line up."

The whistle meant one thing to Ira. He was going to have to make some kind of a decision.

The sergeant walked back and forth several times, straightening up the lines. Finally he stopped and looked at them.

"How do you like the Army?" he said. Then he smiled and he had a truly beautiful smile. He stopped smiling. "That's okay. We don't expect you to like it. So, move when you hear that whistle. You're going to learn to run when the mess bell goes because if you don't you don't get any dinner — the beans get scarcer and scarcer the further down the pot gets. And you're going to learn to run to the drill field when my whistle goes because the men who don't will get a double portion of push ups. I'm not doing this to be nasty, although I can be nasty if the occasion calls for it. I'm looking out for your tails. If you learn to run here, you'll be dodging Germans second-nature over there. Furthermore, it costs us money and time to bury you, and the Army don't like to waste any more time and money than it has to.

"Okay, reach out to the man in front of you. Hand on his shoulder. Reach out to the man on your right. Hand on his shoulder. Now when I say, 'Attention,' this is what I want to see." He demonstrated. "I don't want to see any bellies. . ." he demonstrated." . . . or bowlegs . . ." he demonstrated, " . . . or Alice in Wonderland faces . . . or pigeon toes . . . or Adam's apples . . . I want to see *Chests!* At-ten-TION!"

"Now when I say 'salute,' I want to see the right hand, not the left. In case you don't know which your right hand is, it's the one on the side that the mess hall is. Anybody who puts up his left hand goes that direction for his dinner today." He gave a salute demonstration. "All right. Company . . . salute!" One or two men got halfway up with their left hands and hurriedly changed.

The sergeant looked back over the ranks.

"What's wrong with you?"

"I cannot salute."

"Why not? Aha, our little unconscious rejector friend. Come up here. Do we have any other 'yellow stripes'? If we do, show your colors now."

A very tall gangly boy raised his hand.

"Come up here!"

The tall boy came up and stood before the sergeant, his head and shoulders above the sergeant's head. The field of men laughed spontaneously at the odd combination. Potts seemed a little uneasy in front of the tall man. He stepped back to look at him.

"So what won't you do?"

"My minister said I can do some things in the Army but I can't carry a gun, sir."

"Do you see any guns here? Get back in line."

"All right, Stoltzfus, you haven't had enough? At least you have your uniform on today. You look good in a uniform and your hair cut, you know that? We could make a man out of you. What can you do?"

"I can't fight, or do anything that prepares me to fight. The Bible — "

"You can't fight? Well, if you can't fight, who do you think is going to stop the butchers of Europe? Huh? You want us to do it for you, eh? You want us to fight so you can stay home and read your Bible? You're a slacker, Stoltzfus. I'm sorry about that. I thought you might make a man. But you're not a man at all, are you? What do we do with the slacker, men?"

Ira looked at the mountaintop.

A few men offered suggestions, such as "throw him in the clink" or "give him a good whipping," but the majority said nothing.

"What do the rest of you think? I want to hear everybody's suggestions," said the sergeant and soon they were all hooting and shouting. "Okay, okay. Get back in line, Stoltzfus. You know how they feel now. My guess is your health will be better if you shape up."

"Next exercise is a march. I want you to march four steps forward, come to attention on command, and salute. Get those legs up. Ready, march! One, two, three, four. At-ten-tion! Salute! All right, turn around and we'll do the same thing going back. Ready, march! One, two, three. . . . Hold everything, men. Our yellow lollipop is acting up again. I want the boys in back of Stoltzfus to push him if he won't move and if he still won't go, kick him in the shins.

"Ready, march!"

Ira stood still and the men kicked him in the shins and pushed him. Each time after that it got successively worse, but he was resolved not to move. 'It's better not to obey any order than to obey one or two.' Pop's words were on his mind. After an hour or so, Sergeant Potts sent him back to his tent.

He got out his Bible and began to read the story of Joseph in Egypt. It seemed like it was his story. Alone in a strange land, the land of Georgia. But not really alone because there were 250 men with him, eager to reach Europe and do their part for the president. Was he a coward? If he wasn't, how could he convince them that he loved this land as much as any of them did, but he wouldn't fight for it?

Punishment for avoiding drills came swiftly. The next morning before breakfast two privates came to Ira's bed and, taking hold of his arms, led him to the mess hall. Was it coincidental that one private was Rupe? Inside the mess hall was a long serving line. The rest of the hall was filled with tables and chairs, enough to accommodate close to a thousand men. The two men led Ira to a spot near the middle of the hall.

"Sergeant Potts gave orders that you will stand at attention here until the rest of the men have eaten breakfast."

Then the two men sat down at the table right in front of him and began to eat their own breakfasts, keeping their eyes on Ira all the time. At seven the hall filled with men. They came off the line one by one and stared at Ira, not quite sure why he was there. The men in his own company, however, particularly those who had stood near him in the drill yesterday, recognized him.

"Why, it's our preacher."

"Hey, the preacher."

Shortly a pain started in his neck and he tilted his head to one side to relieve the pain. Rupe banged his glass on the table. "Straighten up," he said. The men in the dining hall watched him for a while and spoke to each other, guessing why he might be there. But soon they were all talking about other things. One man began to demonstrate how to skin a muskrat and he wasn't doing it quite right. Ira could see that easily. This helped to pass the time and take his mind off his neck, he found. The bugle sounded and the last of the men dashed off for the drill grounds and then he was alone with his two guards.

"All right, take your breakfast," said the other private, a red-haired man. It was cold by then, but it was lots better than standing at attention. They both disappeared for a while. When they returned he was finished with his breakfast and wondering if he should go back to his tent.

"Up on your feet, Stoltzfus," said Rupe. He blew a loud whistle. "Attention. We thought you needed a label." He put a cardboard sign on a string around Ira's neck. "*I'm a yellowbelly,*" it read. "All right, Get your chin in a little more and don't lean against that table. If you slouch again, I'm going to blow this whistle and if you don't straighten up, Blimey here hits you on the fingers with his bayonet. Show him how it feels."

"Put out your hand," said the redhead.

Ira refused. "I didn't do anything."

222

"Okay, okay." The private sat down again and took out a pack of cigarettes. They began to smoke. In no time, Rupe began to tell a story about a major he had heard of who was particularly good at "African Gold" — a euphemism for gambling with dice. "Why it almost seemed like he fixed them dice or something — he'd get doubles three or four times straight. Of course, he played on the sly." Rupe looked around nervously. "You know, I could stand a good game myself."

"Me, I don't play," said the other private.

"What do you mean you don't? I hear you're the company's top winner."

"Nah. It must have been someone else you heard about."

"You don't play at all?"

"Not but just a little, and I'm not good. Really, I'm not. Hey, blow your whistle." Ira's left shoulder had begun to itch and for a while he thought it would go away but it didn't. He leaned back against the table to scratch it. The whistle blew and Blimey got up with the bayonet. "All right, let's see your hand." Because Ira didn't move to put out his knuckles, the private reached down and took his wrist and brought the flat side of the bayonet down smartly on Ira's knuckles. He looked over Ira to make sure he was standing at attention again and then reached into his pocket. His eyes lit up.

"What do you know?"

"What?"

"I just found a set of dice in my pocket."

In no time they were squatting on the floor rolling dice and, for lack of money in their pockets, they used credit chips, little pieces of cardboard torn from the extra cardboard left over after making Ira's sign. Each chip represented a dollar. First Rupe and then the redhead rolled. The redhead's pile of chips grew steadily, and Rupe's pile went down. The redhead even outdid the legendary major in throwing doubles. Every once in a while Rupe would look up over his shoulder at Ira.

Ira, in the meantime, was now getting tired all over. His back ached, his legs ached, his neck seemed welded in one position. Several times, when both men were down on all fours looking at a throw, he gave all of his muscles a quick twist and went back into position. On one of those occasions, though, a wristbone cracked loudly and both men looked up.

"All right, put out your hand." They cracked his knuckles again. Finally the noon bugle blew and the men scooped up their chips and dice and sat back in their chairs as though they had been watching Ira all morning.

The soldiers were surprised to see Ira still there. With his sign, it was obvious why he was standing in the middle of the hall.

"Hey, how about a sermon?" said someone. They hooted and grinned.

"Son of a bitch," said someone else.

Then they were all gone again and once more Ira was alone with the two privates. They ordered him to eat his dinner quickly and then get back to attention again. They had barely gotten started in the afternoon crap game when Sergeant Potts walked in.

"What's going on here anyway? I sent you men to guard this man and you're down on the floor shooting dice. I could put you both in the guardhouse. I won't though. I give second chances to people I like.

224

Give me the dice." He turned to Ira and smiled. "Well, hello. Have a good dinner? Ready to do some drills by now? We're doing push ups, the perfect thing for an aching back." He grinned. "Of course, standing at attention is good for your posture, too. The only thing I don't like is your eyes. Those eyes should be straight ahead. Or would you rather drill?"

Yes, yes, I'd rather drill, his body was saying, but his head said, 'no,' and his head was still stronger.

"Thank you, but I can't serve in the Army no matter what the drill or job. That would make me a part of the Army. I'm not afraid of being killed, Sergeant, it's killing I'm afraid of."

"Why. . . . Then you can rot standing there," said Sergeant Potts and he stomped out. The two guards were less sympathetic now. They glared at Ira. It was his fault that they had to sit here with nothing to do, and it was his fault they'd been caught. He could have warned them Potts was coming.

"Why didn't you tell us he was coming, huh? Don't move your eyes either," said Rupe. The red-haired private passed him a cigarette, but he turned it down.

Rupe looked Stoltzfus over from top to bottom.

"I hate you," he said. "You won't fight. You won't work. You won't obey commands. What will you do? No, don't tell me. I don't want to hear. You want to say you will read your Bible, right? You want to say how good you are, but I don't care. I agree with Sergeant Potts. You can rot!"

A long time passed and the redhead had nearly finished his cigarette. It was quiet in the mess hall and even the sound of the dishes jingling in the back had stopped. There was only an occasional sound.

They were probably working on supper now. Outside the Sergeant's whistle blew again and he shouted.

"Crazy sergeant," said Rupe. "He'll kill us all with his exercises." He fished into his pocket for his wallet and brought out a picture. It was a young man in uniform and hat. He looked at it a bit and then smiled at the picture as though it were a living face. He showed it to the other soldier.

"Who's that?"

"My brother."

"Oh, yeah? He's in France?"

"Yes. He's in France. He'll always be in France." He held the picture up for Ira to see. "Look at him, will you? He's a hero. He got a medal from the Army and he's a hero. He's my brother, and he's a hero, and that's something you'll never be." Tears suddenly filled his eyes. "He'll always be in France because of people like you who won't fight. He's dead. Yeah, the Heinies killed him and this bastard loved the Heinies." He doubled up his fists and got up but the redhead pulled him down.

"Let him go. You hit him and we're both in the guardhouse. You can't hit a man with his uniform on."

"Then I'll take it off him. We have a score to settle, this yellow stripe and I."

"Sit down. You hit him and I call the sergeant."

"The sergeant would like to hit him, too," Rupe lunged for Ira but the redhead was faster again. He caught his coattails and Rupe sat down on a table.

"I'm warning you," said the redhead.

"How's come you're taking his part? Are you a conchie lover?"

"I'm for fair play. He ain't done nothing to you."

226

Rupe looked at the picture again, made the sign of the cross, and put the picture back into his wallet.

Ira had watched the whole affair. He hadn't even flinched when Rupe moved for him. If they were going to beat him, then they would beat him. The more Rupe talked, the more sympathy he felt for him. There was something about this immigrant boy and his simple country ways that seemed like his own home community. No, there was really nothing alike about them. They were from different traditions, different faiths, different views on the war. Yet he liked him and at the same time he was afraid of him. His eyes could be terribly cold but when he talked about his brother just now, they were wonderfully warm. He thought of Susanna's eyes. He closed his own eyes and imagined her hanging up the wash on a windy day like the one when he first went to see her. The whistle sounded.

"All right, we got you that time. Eyes straight ahead. Let me have that little knife and you take the whistle, Blimey. I'd like to give him a good rap.'"

Blimey shook his head though.

"Hold out your hand."

The bayonet cracked down on the knuckles and the pain paralyzed Ira's arm. How much longer could he stand? Perhaps he would just faint onto the floor. His nose was itchy again, and his mouth was dry. He tried to forget his nose and think about Susanna and the wash instead. But when he did, his eyes flickered involuntarily, and it brought another crack on the knuckles.

"Give me that knife, Blimey."

"You're doing fine on the whistle."

Rupe sat back in his chair and picked at his fingernails. A truck rumbled around the back of the mess hall and Rupe got up to go to the toilet.

When he was gone, Blimey got up and said, "At ease, brother."

Ira went on standing straight.

"Hey, don't you want to rest? At ease, man. Take a rest."

Ira sat down. His eyes closed and a second later, it seemed, Blimey was shaking him furiously.

"Get up, man." He pulled him up. "Attention."

Ira was hardly back in order when Rupe came in, chewing a piece of gum.

"You want to go to the toilet?"

"No thanks."

It was worse, not better, now that Ira had relaxed for a moment. He was terribly tired and he took another crack on the knuckles for closing his eyes. He looked at Rupe and his whistle.

"I'm going to pray for you, Rupe," he said.

Rupe stopped chewing. "You're not supposed to talk. Give him a rap, Blimey."

"Sergeant didn't say he couldn't talk. He did say don't speak to the conchie, but if he wants to talk to himself, that's okay. Let him talk. He'll dry up."

"Well, he wasn't talking to himself. He was talking to me."

"Ignore it."

Finally the two men went to sleep in their chairs, but Ira went on standing at attention. If that was what they wanted of him, he could do it.

The supper bugle sounded and the hall was full of men again. Then supper was over and once more Ira was free to get his meal. He sat down in the empty hall to eat while Blimey watched him from a tabletop.

"You're not such a bad chap," said Blimey. "How's come you're so stubborn? How's come you're afraid to fight — that's what makes Rupe mad, you know. Watch that boy. He's out to get you. You think Potts is tough. Well, he is, but he only gets mad when he wants to and when he wants to be nice, he's nice. But Rupe is a grenade. You bump the pin and off he goes. I know him from Pittsburgh."

"I like him," said Ira.

"Well, like I say — watch him."

Ira finished his peaches and looked at Blimey. Was it back to standing?

"Okay, you're free," said Blimey. Then he leaned over and grabbed Ira's arm. "Sorry for the rough time," he said, "but orders is orders." He shrugged his shoulders.

Ira walked across the drill grounds. A light rain was falling and it felt good. He stopped by the stables to look at the horses and reached in to rub one's nose.

"Hey, here's the preacher!"

He turned around. Five or six men had gathered in a loose half-circle around him. They were smiling.

"Hello," he said and turned back to the horse.

"Hey preacher, we want to talk to you." Ira turned around slowly again and rested his back against the wall.

"I'd rather talk tomorrow, if it's okay. I'm really tired."

"What do you think, fellows? We wanted to talk now, didn't we? I don't think we can wait until tomorrow."

"Hey, we have the preacher here," one of the others yelled to some other privates walking by.

The men were dressed in their new uniforms, their hands by their sides except for the middle one who seemed to be the spokesman. He hooked his thumbs in his belt loops and stood with his legs apart. He was still smiling.

"There's a question we have," said the spokesman. He had a deep Southern accent. "And it's too bad that other private — what's his name — "

"Rupe," said one of them.

"Rupe, right. It's too bad he's not here to hear your answer, but we'd like to know why it is you won't fight. That's really just your way of getting out of the war, isn't it? You're afraid."

He should have walked off because he was already so tired he could hardly see straight, but he wanted them to understand. It wasn't cowardice.

"I'm not afraid of dying," said Ira. "But I won't kill anyone else — it's wrong, the Bible plainly says it's wrong."

"The Bible, huh? And will the Bible chase the Huns back out of France and Belgium and Russia?"

"No. The way to defeat our enemies is not to fight them — it's to love them. The Bible says, 'Love your enemies, bless them that curse you,'"

"Love? Did you say love? You mean if we go to France and throw our arms around the Huns and love them, the war will end? Haha." The spokesman began to laugh. "Hey, this preacher says we should go to Germany and make love to the Huns and that will stop the war. Haha." The soldiers laughed. Several more had come.

"You know, you're a son of a bitch, that's what

you are. You don't believe a word you're saying. You know as well as we do that loving the Germans won't stop this war. You don't want to fight, that's all. You're a coward."

"Yeah," the men cheered.

"No it's not that I'm afraid. The Bible says, 'Thou shalt not kill.' Do you believe that?" He addressed his question to the spokesman.

"Sure. Thou shalt not kill. Unless someone else is killing first. Then you have to stop him."

"The Bible also says, 'An eye for an eye, a tooth for a tooth,'" said one of the soldiers, who looked like the product of a Sunday school somewhere.

"Then I say it's time we take out some eyes and teeth for all of the ones the Germans have taken," said the spokesman.

"Maybe we should start with the German-lovers," said a moustached boy and he rolled his eyes up in the air as though the idea had just struck him.

"Yeah!" the circle shouted. It was impossible to leave now. The stable was at Ira's back and at least a hundred men stood around him.

"I'd like to see if he really has a yellow belly like the sign said."

"Yeah!"

Someone stepped forward and pulled out Ira's shirt.

"It's pink!" he said, and dropped the shirt.

"Maybe it's a stripe down his back then."

"Hey, wait for me," shouted someone. It was Rupe, running across the lawn and pushing his way into the crowd. Ira felt like a cornered groundhog. He wasn't sure at all that he would be able to speak gently and convincingly to them as he wanted to. He was sweating.

"Aha, you got him. Good work." Rupe climbed up on an inverted tub. "What do you say we do with the coward?"

"Now wait a minute," the spokesman said. "Get down off that tub. We're not doing anything to him. We're just asking some questions. Right, men?"

"Right."

"I say string him up," said Rupe.

"Yeah!"

"Get off that tub. We're not stringing anybody up."

"Anybody have a rope?"

"Yeah!"

The spokesman reached up and pulled Rupe off the tub and jumped up himself. At that moment a gun sounded twice at the back of the crowd. The men turned around.

"All right, what's going on here?"

"We're going to string up the coward, colonel." It was Colonel Doolittle. He pushed his way through the crowd with a revolver in hand.

"Get down off that tub. Don't you men know there's a military law against taking justice into your own hands? I could have you all court-martialed. Now clear away. Get out. Come on. Were you the cause of all this, Thompson? I want to see you tomorrow."

"I just wanted to ask him some questions. It was that other private who suggested — " But Rupe was nowhere to be seen.

"Get moving. Hurry up. Stoltzfus, you're coming with me."

They went back across the drill grounds to the officer's quarters.

232

5

"Come in, come in," the colonel said, leading the way into his own tent. Another officer was sitting in the far corner, reading a magazine, his feet propped up on a hassock. The officer looked up and Ira nodded at him. The officer's face changed.

"Haven't you any manners?" he said. "When you meet a superior in the army, *you salute!* What's this nodding business?"

"I'm sorry," said Ira.

"He's just in," the colonel said. "Sit down." He indicated a canvas-bottomed chair beside the table and pulled out a similar one for himself. "Stoltzfus, is that right? Glad to meet you, Stoltzfus. You need a bit of whiskey or coffee to brace you up? I don't touch either of them myself, but we keep them on hand."

Ira shook his head.

"Well, they gave you a rough time," the colonel said, sitting down, but not really relaxing. He folded his hands on the table erect — not stiff, but still erect. He had an index finger missing, Ira noticed, but his other fingers looked powerful and chapped, like a man who has spent his life outdoors and not behind a desk. A cavalry sword hung point down over his head on the wall behind. "I'm sorry about that," the colonel said. "They're good boys, really. I've trained a lot of boys in my time, taken them off the farm and out of the city streets and given them spines and purpose. They'll come around, but they're new, you know. They don't understand you because they think you're a coward. But you're not, are you?"

Ira didn't answer for a moment and the colonel reached into his overcoat and took out a box of cigars. "Take one," he said. "They're good for your nerves. It's my one vice. No liquor, no coffee, no gambling, but when the day ends, a good cigar to relax me." Ira took one but he didn't light it. Cigars were for relaxing, as the colonel said, but there wouldn't be any relaxing here. He was on edge inside and cautious.

"So you won't drill and you won't work, they tell me," the colonel said. He looked at Ira. His eyes were not unkind.

"No," Ira said, "I can't do anything that would compromise my belief that war is wrong and fighting is wrong." He could trust the colonel to hear him, he was sure.

"I can maybe understand your point about drilling," the colonel said and he knocked some ashes into a tray on the floor, "but what's wrong with working? You're used to working. I can see that." He reached over and squeezed Ira's arm. "You don't expect to get off scot-free while everyone else does his duty."

"I want to work, colonel, but I can't work if my work contributes to the war. Maybe you think emptying garbage cans doesn't contribute, but if I empty the cans, another soldier is freed to drill."

"No, no," the colonel said. "Don't run this thing

of conscience into the ground. But I didn't bring you here to interrogate you. I want you to relax. Let me tell you about myself." The colonel laid down the cigar. "Are we bothering you, Lieutenant?" he said, looking around.

"No, sir."

"Well, let us know if we do. When I was your age —" the colonel said, turning back and his eyes twinkling. "When I was your age, I was a lieutenant for the Seventh Cavalry, riding a fine black horse that once belonged to a Cheyenne warrior whom I shot off it. A fine horse. We developed sort of a friendship, you know. She'd whinny when she saw me coming and sometimes we'd go for hours together, just like two good friends. We got to know each other's moods, I guess. I was a scout then with the cavalry — this was a few years after Custer's Massacre — but we were still chasing Indians. This time it was the Nez Perce, and they were tough little so-and-so's. They didn't come at you in whole armies, shrieking and waving their guns like the Cheyenne did. They were more clever. They'd fight in small squads and lead you into mountain traps. Guerrilla style, so to speak.

"So there I was, scouting out the territory one day and riding along a bluff over a river, when I heard a couple rifle shots. The next thing I knew I was rolling down the cliff toward the river and the horse was tumbling alongside of me. Those sneaky Nez Perce — that's what it was. I could hear them whooping and yelling some place up on top and I thought right then — this is the end. I was sure the horse was going to fall on top of me. She was just rolling over and over, slipping and clawing up the dirt, and about that time I hit the water. It wasn't a big drop, not more than thirty feet, and it slanted — about like that — so I wasn't hurt. Just bruised. Oh my, but I was bruised, but don't think that stopped me.

"I knew I had to look alive or that was the end for me, and as I came crawling out of the water, what do you think I saw? A black hole under the roots of a tree that hung over the water. I didn't stop to ask if there were rattlesnakes in it. No, I just crawled in and lay there. I mean I was scared. I thought that was the end. Pretty shortly I heard stones falling in the water and then a bucketful or two came down on my head from a hole overhead that connected with this same hole. I heard them splashing in the river looking for me — for my body, I guess — but they couldn't find me. I saw their legs go right past me in the shallows of the river — it was a deep river — and I noticed a lot of blood in the water. I guess that was my black mare's. After a half hour or so things got quiet, but I just lay there thinking. I thought really hard.

"You see, my father wasn't a religious man. He was a Civil War general. All rock on the outside, all honey inside. Don't misunderstand me. He wasn't sweet. No, a lot of people couldn't see past the rock, but inside he was just as gentle. . . . But he wasn't religious. No, he didn't have time for God.

"You see, Stoltzfus, the history of my family is the history of this country. It's the history of the U.S. Army. Some member or another of my family has participated in every war these United States have ever fought. I have a grandson in France right now and a son who's a major on his way over. We're a hand or a foot of this country, so to speak. We have invested in the future of the country. So it was only natural for me to get a commission with the Seventh Cavalry when I wasn't more than twenty-one. Is that what you are? Twenty-one or so? But I hadn't really thought about what life meant. I was out for the adventure, you see.

"Now my mother was different. She was the most loyal, warm, singlehearted Christian I have ever met. She didn't just get that way — no, I think it was during those years when my father was away from home with the Union Army and she was at home alone taking care of me — I was just a little pumpkin — that she grew deep in God. She would tell me about her secret conversations with God. But me, poof, what did I care about that sort of talk?

"Anyway, there I was under the roots of that tree and I started caring fast. After an hour or so I looked out of my hole and I would have bet my commission a Nez Perce was looking right back at me. He was sitting on the other side of the river with his feet in the water and chewing on a dried fish or something and behind him on the meadow it looked like there might have been two hundred more. Indians, I mean. What I didn't know until then I found out now. The reason why that little group that surprised me was so eager to shoot me down was because I was on the verge of discovering a war camp of theirs that we'd been looking for. I don't know what was wrong with that man's eyes that he didn't see me. It was miraculous that he didn't. I curled back into my hole fast, I'll tell you.

"That's when I started to pray. I set a record for praying, I'll bet, and I promised God if He'd get me out of there, I wouldn't forget Him. I waited until dark and wouldn't you know it was a perfectly moonlit night the whole night. I could see reflections on the river and occasionally someone would come down there, they used the river as a toilet, it seems. I lay there the whole next day and I was really thirsty by now. I didn't want to drink any of the water out of that river but I finally did, just a handful or so.

"The second night the moon was out again, even brighter than before, but a couple hours after sundown, wouldn't you know, it clouded over and started to rain. So I decided to make a try for it. The rain was making an awful clatter — it was a thunderstorm. I got into the river and started to float and maybe thirty minutes later the hard rain let up, but then the river started to rise. I got out and crawled into the weeds — the banks were much lower there — and I didn't see anyone, so I spent the rest of the night running in the direction I thought the camp was. And don't you know, I found it before morning.

"Now don't tell me God don't hear prayers. Close to morning I led our forces right to the Nez Perce camp and we surprised them and liquidated a good quarter of the camp in the first few minutes and that pretty well finished off the Nez Perce campaign for that year. They decorated me for that, but the one who should have got the decoration as far as I was concerned was God. He brought me out. Maybe you think He isn't concerned about the soldier and what happens to him, but He is. Praise the Lord!

"God is part of the heritage of this country, you see. We've been blessed by God. He gave the land to us from the Indians because of their savagery — I

238

could tell you tales that would ruin your supper. But what is our heritage? I'll tell you. It flows down from the Mayflower Compact, the Declaration of Independence, and our own Constitution. 'This nation under God,' as Lincoln said at Gettysburg. A people with a faith, a code to live by. It has been my good fortune, Stoltzfus, to train many young men over the years — to make men out of them. And I always like to begin as I am beginning now with you, by telling my own story and reminding them of their religious heritage. What is a nation without faith, without spiritual goals, without a sense of their mandate from God? Look at the horrors the German soldiers are committing in this war and you got your answer.

"So I guess what I want to tell you, Stoltzfus, is this. We want you We need high-caliber men of your type." The colonel put out his cigar. He was magnificent in the half-light of the tent, as straight and clean and purposeful as the sword that hung behind him. His hair was almost white. It was easy to imagine him leading charges up San Juan Hill or into Mexico after Pancho Villa, the bandit.

It was not easy to imagine contradicting him, but Ira felt that he was going to have to. He didn't know where to start, but if he kept quiet, wouldn't the colonel assume he agreed with everything? Wouldn't it be harder to speak the next time he was ordered here? *No*, he thought. *Let the man believe as he wants to. I know what I believe.* But a second later he was sure he would have to say something. Was it lack of respect for the old man? Insubordination! But if they were both children of God, there was no colonel or draftee, there was no old-timer or greenhorn, there were no wise and no foolish, were there?

If they were both children of God. . . .

"Tell me about yourself," the colonel said. He relaxed into his chair at last. "Did I bore you?"

"No." He fastened his big eyes on the colonel's face. Ira's eyes were like an unswerving force. The colonel looked back for a moment, then lifted his eyes to the wall behind Ira. "Colonel, maybe it's not right for me to judge, but I don't think it was God who saved you from the Indians and I don't think our country has a heritage from God. Yes, we always had Christians but America was never Christian. I'm only judging by the history books — I teach school and I've always been interested in history — we were the savages and the land thieves. There are awful stories. You can't be a child of God and do those things. I don't want to put down the good men. There were lots of good men, mostly good men who put our country together. I think, but even good men do things and say they do it for 'progress' that — "

The colonel's temperature was rising. His neck got red first and then his ears.

"Are you saying I'm not a Christian?" he said. "That's very serious — the Bible tells us not to judge — and furthermore I think I'm going to get angry."

"If we are brothers in Christ . . ." said Ira.

The colonel leaped to his feet and began to walk around behind the chair.

"It's your attitude that I don't like," he said, "and I've noticed it in all you conscientious objectors. The attitude that 'I'm right, he's wrong,' 'I have a corner on the truth, and anyone who sees God different can't be right.' I don't like that attitude. Not at all. I want to be sympathetic to your con-

240

science but don't make me think you're narrow-minded. A narrow-minded man has as much to succeed in this world as — that fly," he said, and he struck at it with a magazine. Ironically, the fly escaped. "Listen, Stoltzfus, I want to help you. You're a good man, I think. You could go a long way. But let me tell you what awaits you if you don't change your mind.

"You'll be disgraced and you may get hurt. I can't police the camp ground every time the men are free. It was luck that I happened to be going by there tonight. I'm glad I could help you. But these men have strong feelings and I don't want you to get hurt. You might get court-martialed, maybe life imprisonment or a sentence to be shot. Is that what you want? Do you want to be a social disgrace when you return to society? Or a man?"

"The Apostle Paul," said Ira, "was beaten five times, stoned, shipwrecked three times, often in danger, and he said — " He opened the Bible, that somehow he had managed to conceal in the bottom of a uniform pocket: " 'For the sake of Christ, then, I am content with weaknesses, insults, hardships, persecutions, and calamities, for when I am weak, then I am strong.' "

"The martyr, huh?" said the colonel. He was walking back and forth behind the chair. The lieutenant in the corner had stopped reading his magazine, although he continued to pretend to. He was prepared for a burst of artillery which might strike in any direction.

"What would happen if every boy in the country talked like you?" said the colonel. "What would happen to our country — have you ever thought of that? Tell me, what would you do if a big Hun came in your window at night with a pistol and threatened to violate your wife? If you see a man drowning and you let him alone, have you done your Christian duty? No, to let a drowning man alone is to kill him. To turn your back on a war-suffering Belgian is to kill him. Have you ever thought about things like that? A conscience is a fine thing but it's like water. Too much of it and a man drowns, too little and he dies of thirst."

Ira was silent.

"Make a bed for him, Lieutenant. He better spend the night here. When you're ready to work, Stoltzfus, we'll talk. If not, I'll let things take their course, and believe me, it's not a pleasant course. But it's your choice," said the colonel.

Then he turned and walked out of the tent.

6

By the end of six weeks, Ira was getting skinny from tension. It was the whistle. When the sergeant blew his whistle, it meant it was time for a decision. Was he going to sweep the floor or wasn't he? Would he carry out the garbage or wouldn't he? Was he going to drill or wasn't he going to drill? A dozen times a day he heard it, one time coming from the drill field, another time from the street just outside his tent, and the next time an inch behind his ear which left both ears ringing painfully. He jumped and flung his arms wide.

The sergeant was standing there laughing. He said something but Ira could only see his lips moving. He could not hear because of the ringing in his ears.

"I said you're getting nervous these days," said the sergeant. He put the whistle back into his breast pocket and walked away. It was true. Ira could hardly control the reaction that went through him when he heard the whistle. At first it was only surprise. But the pressure to make a right decision in a moment began to weigh on Ira's mind. The week before, a letter from home brought another story of an objector in Kansas who had been sentenced to Fort Leavenworth. Fifteen years for obeying an order one time and disobeying it the next.

He broke into cold sweat when the whistle blew. The muscles in the back of his neck got tight and his stomach drew itself together like a fist. He couldn't eat some days. The whistle had become a kind of Chinese water torture.

But the worst was yet to come — he began to fear Sergeant Potts. The sergeant only needed to walk into the room where Ira was and his body would act up. "Good morning, Sergeant," he said, and smiled, but drops of sweat began to run down his ribs.

One Saturday night the colonel came over to Ira in the mess hall. That in itself was unusual because he almost never ate at the same time as his men and, if he did, he didn't socialize. But on this particular night the hall was almost empty. *It usually is when I eat,* Ira thought, *because the other men line up to get in here and I wait,* but then, he didn't like eating with a whole tableful of men anyway. If he said anything, they all stopped talking and listened.

"What did the preacher say?" In a moment they were all talking at him — he grew tired of telling them why he wouldn't fight. It shouldn't be that way, he thought. After all, they had a right to know, didn't they? But whenever they asked, he felt the muscles in his throat getting tight, so he stopped eating at big tables. Strangely, he never minded answering that question to one man, but when there were twenty-five and he had to explain his beliefs loudly so the man at the far end could hear, it was different.

With the men of his own tent he had struck a truce. Several times the other seven petitioned Sergeant Potts to have him transferred. It wasn't that he gave them any trouble. Not at all. His cot was neat. He didn't argue or have any bad habits such as urinating in the grass behind the tent, which one or two of the men did. It was just that he was a silent question mark over all their good times — he was a question mark over their purpose for being here. The truce was unspoken. Outside the tent they pretended they didn't know him; inside the tent they treated him civilly.

So there he was, alone at one of the tables in a nearly empty hall, when the colonel walked over with a cup of coffee and a handful of cookies.

"Cookie, Stoltzfus?"

"Why, yes."

"You're looking skinnier every time I see you. Take a handful." He waited while Ira took a few more. "Care if I sit down?"

"No, no. Please."

"Hear from your mother lately?"

"I had a letter yesterday. They're cutting the tobacco."

"Is that unusual?"

"Well, it's early. It's been a good year, I guess. I wish I was there to help."

"You're tired of us, huh?"

Ira shrugged his shoulders and smiled. He hadn't smiled lately either. "It's been hard here — I wish I could do something helpful."

"You're looking thin. You been eating enough?"

"Oh, off and on."

"Look, you need some exercise. How about if I give you freedom of the camp tomorrow — Sunday? That means you can go anyplace you want to within the camp. Don't leave the camp area, though.

And don't talk to any farmers or town folks you might happen to see at the edge of camp. Are you interested?"

"Sure. Sure." He had an idea.

"You can comply with those few rules."

"Sure."

"Well, here's a pass. Good luck." The colonel gave him a wooden camp pass.

The idea played around in his head and tantalized him. Suppose there were other conscientious objectors in the camp? Every effort he had made so far to find them had resulted in nothing. He read over the little paper put out by Ethan Allen every Friday. He asked men who did delivery work over the whole camp. Finally he decided there were none or if there were, he would certainly never find them. After all, in a camp of 27,000 how could five or ten men be spotted? In addition, they probably all wore the uniform, either because they had had their other clothes taken or because they had finally conceded that the uniform was only a small compromise, as long as you didn't drill or do camp work. But he continued to hear rumors. Where would be the place to look for them? Why, the YMCAs, of course. But there were at least twenty YMCAs in the whole camp, and they were scattered over the whole area. He decided to get up early and spend the day looking. Sunday was a fine day, a day for visits from home or visits with fellow soldiers. A lot of the soldiers slept until dinner time and spent the afternoon backslapping and talking to old friends, or playing cards.

Ira got up, ate breakfast, and started off walking. The YMCA buildings were located in the center of each small camp within the larger camp. On the outside bulletin board of each building the head officer of the unit had posted a diagram of his camp area, marked off in companies with each company labeled. Was there a conscientious objector company someplace in the camp? He ran his finger up and down the diagram. Nothing. He walked on to the next camp. With his hat on, no one could guess that he was a conscientious objector. Why, it even felt good here in this new area to be walking along and no one staring at you. When he saw an officer coming once, he ducked off the road to avoid saluting him. There was nothing at the next camp either, nor the next.

At noon he came to the last YMCA in the camp. He looked over the map. In the bottom left-hand corner there was a small area labeled "Conscientious Objector Detachment," and roughly penciled in beside it, "Holy Hill." He looked up, saw a large old building like a barn not more than a block away, and began to run down the street. A woodpile stood almost against the street, blocking his view from the barn. He slowed down to a walk. It wouldn't be good to run up on them. He walked along the woodpile and suddenly he heard it.

Music! The most beautiful music in the world. Men's voices singing a cappella and in four parts that old hymn:

> *See from His head, His hands, His feet,*
> *Sorrow and love flow mingled down;*
> *Did e'er such love and sorrow meet;*
> *Or thorns compose so rich a crown?*

It filled him from bottom to top like a water

pitcher being slowly poured full from the coolest, freshest, purest spring in the world. He sat down on the ground behind the pile and buried his head in his sleeve. His shoulders shook, and the music continued to wash over him. He hadn't realized how thirsty he been—been. The memory of the last six weeks faded under the music.

When the music stopped, he got up. He walked around the corner of the woodpile and there they were, inside a stable with the men seated in a circle on the floor, looking out of three or four hymnals that they held in front of them. His impulse was to shout, but he didn't.

The men looked up at him and noticing he was only a private they ignored him and went on singing and then one of them took a Bible and began to talk about communion and what it meant. Ira sat down on the grass outside the door and propped his head with his hand to listen.

" . . . and the beautiful thing about communion," the leader was saying, "is that we do it as brothers, even though I never knew Rempel here before or Pyski either. We are brothers, even if it took a war to get us together.

"Now in my tradition, we look at communion as a symbol of Christ's blood and body that were broken up for us, so we only hold a service twice or so a year, but in your tradition, it's different, I think, Pyski."

"Every Sunday. We believe it is the high point of the mass, the celebration."

"Celebration. What a strange word," the leader said. "But I like it. When I was growing up in Philadelphia I always thought communion was such a solemn occasion, so we walked around quietly and I tried not to slurp when we drank the wine." They laughed. "And I was afraid my throat was making these sounds like a banty rooster when I swallowed the bread, and we were all very solemn, everybody in the church, and I think we completely missed Pyski's point, that communion is a celebration. We are one, praise God!"

"And the gates of the United States Army shall not prevail against us," said someone. They laughed again, but the leader held up his hand.

"Don't forget there are Christians there, too. It's not as if we are the only Christians. We are the most tested ones perhaps. But there are a good many people in this war who are asking if this is really a war to spread democracy. Be open to the soldier who approaches you honestly — they're not all out to collect our heads, you know." He looked out of the stable at Ira, who was still sitting there in the grass with his head in his hands.

"Do you want something?" one of the men called to Ira.

"I'm an objector, too," said Ira, but he didn't feel like one. He felt like an outsider. He was the only one wearing a uniform. All of them were in civilian clothes. Not one had compromised.

"Why the uniform?" said the man suspiciously. He was dressed in a pair of overalls of the same sort that Ira had worn on the farm. Good everyday overalls with a patch on one knee. A number of other objectors got up and crowded around, looking at him. Ira felt that they were brothers, but how could he convince them? Would they believe him if he said the uniform had been forced on him? He shook his head and walked away toward the woodpile.

"Brother." It was the one who had led the worship. He came from behind and put one hand on Ira's shoulder. He stood like that for a minute. "What's your name?"

"Ira Stoltzfus."

"You're an objector?"

"Yes."

"It must have been rough for you. Come back and tell us your story. Don't blame the men for their suspicions. We've been tricked several times and they're still sorting us out to see if we're genuine or not, but the men are all good men — take my word for it. Come on." He looked at Ira and suddenly smiled. "Guthrie — Willam Guthrie — I'm Quaker myself."

The men were gathering up the hymnals and Bibles, and another man was breaking out a Baby Swiss cheese he had received from home. The Quaker and the Mennonite walked back to the tent and Guthrie clapped his hand on Ira's shoulder and gave a tremendous catcall with his fingers in his teeth.

"Men, I think we ought to hear this man's story," said Guthrie. "He says he's an objector. If you have to go, go. But if not, why not stay and hear him out?"

"Give the man a chunk of that cheese, will you? Story's always riper when there's cheese," said an objector in a white undershirt, and he cut a big slice off. "How about coffee? With sugar? Without?" They got him a chair and when he had taken his first swallow of coffee, White Undershirt said, "Well?"

"Give him time, Pyski."

Ira suddenly felt overwhelmed by their warmth and he was sure he was among friends.

"I hardly know where to begin. . . ."

"Try the beginning."

"Okay." So he told his whole story. The men sat on the floor around him, drinking coffee and eating chunks of cheese and raisins and occasionally stopping him to ask a question.

"They actually pulled the uniform on you?"

"Yes."

"And took your civilian clothes away?"

"Right. They mailed them to my father, they said, the same evening."

"But I think that's against the law. I'm sure they can't take your civilian clothes away like that. You should write to the Secretary of War and report that."

Another time during the story — right after he had finished describing his punishments for refusing work — someone said, "Praise God."

"What do you mean, *praise God?*" said White Undershirt. "Look how he had to suffer."

"But look how God gave him strength."

When Ira was finally finished with his story, the men sat in silence until Guthrie said, "It moves an old conchie like me all over again." He laughed a little. A very skinny little man named Schnickerry, who looked as innocent as a field mouse, stared at the roof of the stable and began to squeak, "Praise God from whom all blessings flow, praise Him all creatures here below . . ." Everybody joined.

Ira laughed. It was good to be with brothers who understood you. For the first time in weeks Ira laughed. He felt warm all over, like when he used to crawl out of the tub at home on a Saturday night, all warm and relaxed from his hair to his heels.

White Undershirt was the first to speak after they

stopped singing. "Why don't you ask for a transfer? They'll let you come to Holy Hill, seeing's you know about us anyway. That's how some of us got here from the outside."

"It's three. You better get going," said someone else. "Guard usually pokes his head into our camp several times a day and we're not supposed to have visitors. We're considered prisoners, you know."

Ira got up, shook hands around the circle, and promised he'd see them soon again. "Why, if not before, I hope next Sunday." He wasn't nearly as confident about the situation as they seemed to be, though. There was still Sergeant Potts.

7

Ira had visitors.

"Mom! Susanna!" he shouted. He hadn't expected them, but there they stood under the gaslight, dressed in light summer shawls and black bonnets and carrying baskets. "I didn't know you were coming."

"I wrote. That's funny," his mother said. "You didn't get the letter?"

"They censor everything. It could be they weren't planning to let you come and changed their minds." He shook hands with his mother but out of propriety, Mennonite propriety, he only smiled at Susanna. Not now, while his mother was here.

"So how are you?"

"Oh, Ira, they make you wear the uniform, do they? You didn't put it on out of your own accord, did you? And you're looking awfully skinny. Susanna, would you get the basket? I wasn't going to bring anything because I thought you probably get enough to eat, but seeing you, I'm glad I did. It's just sandwiches. Here."

"I'm really not that hungry, Mom. Somehow my appetite — Is everything okay at home?"

"Well — " she looked at Susanna. "What should I say? We're getting along. Pop's getting better and we have the rationing now, you know. Oh, and Ruth had another baby — that's your Aunt Ruth."

"Was Pop sick?"

"Why, Ira, didn't I tell you? I'm sure I told you. Praise the Lord, he's better."

"I don't know what you're talking about."

"That's funny. I wrote about it."

"Maybe they censored the letter. I'm considered a prisoner, you know. I can't leave the camp or go anywhere within the camp, such as to another company, without permission and an armed guard. But what's this about Pop?"

"It's a long story," said his mother, "and I'm afraid if I get started, they're liable to come and ask us to leave before we hear about you first, so tell us about yourself, and then I'll tell you."

"Did they give you a time limit? I've never had visitors. I don't know how they operate."

"No, but we have to stay here under the light by the horse stable — the officer did say that — and we'll have to leave when your curfew comes. It's okay. We have a place to sleep in town, a good hotel. I interrupted you. I'm sorry."

"No, no," he said. "There's really nothing to say." He looked at Susanna and she smiled again. She had lost a little weight herself, he thought, and she seemed very quiet. "Was it a hard trip down? Did you come by train?"

"Yes," his mother said. "Lancaster to Chattanooga, and it was such a pretty ride. A lot of places they were harvesting, of course, and when we came into Tennessee we had our supper in the train's dining hall. A whole trout with all the trimmings. It must have been this long," she indicated about a foot, " — with the head and tail still on. It was cleaned, of course, but it was so good. Fried. What was I going to say? As we were eating there, we passed through a very poor section. Just shanties, practically, and mostly black people, some of them sitting out front and playing their guitars and it almost looked like another country. I told Susanna we just can't imagine. Half the world doesn't know how the other half lives. How did I get on that? We were asking how things are with you and you haven't told us a thing yet."

"I'm okay, Mom." They were sitting in a semi-circle of three chairs, with his mother seated between Ira and Susanna. The gaslight cast shadows across Susanna's face and he couldn't see her eyes. Further-more, he felt uncomfortable sitting right out here in the open where anyone passing by on the road into camp came within thirty feet of them. Other soldiers were allowed to take their families or visitors into the barracks. He was also wondering how things stood between him and Susanna.

"Oh," he suddenly smiled. "There *are* other objec-tors in the camp, I discovered. Sunday they gave me a pass to walk around — the colonel himself gave it to me — and I decided to check to satisfy my curiosity. So I went from YMCA to YMCA, checking down over their lists, and when I got to the last one, what do you suppose I found? Down in the lower left-hand corner it said, 'Conscientious Objectors De-tachment.'

"Well, I hurried over there and found them having a service, singing and talking — I hadn't heard hymns since I left home — and I just couldn't move. I felt so — I just could hardly hold myself together but after a while I walked around to the front of the building where they were all singing and sat down. They all thought I was a soldier, of course, because I was wearing the uniform and none of them were. They were suspicious of me. I could tell it, but you couldn't blame them. After all, how would you feel if a man in uniform came and sat down outside the door during our worship? But I told them my story and they all warmed up. They say it won't be long until I'm with them, too, and here all along I'd been thinking I was the only objector in the whole camp."

"I'm glad," his mother said, and she rubbed his hand. "It's rough, isn't it? I was afraid it would be like that. 'I will trust in the Lord and not be afraid.' I always remember that verse and then there's a little song I like. . . ."

"Don't sing it now," he said.

"Why not? There's nobody here."

"They're watching us, don't worry."

"But a little song. . . ."

"What's the story about Pop, now?" He glanced at Susanna, muffled in her shawl. It really was a bit cool, for September, anyway. He got up and moved his chair over beside hers. "You came all the way down to visit me," he said. "Why shouldn't I sit beside you?"

"Why don't I leave you two alone?" his mother said. "I know how it is."

"No, the story first," said Ira, and he moved his chair against Susanna's. "Are you cold?" he whispered. She shook her head. She pulled his hand under the shawl and curled her fingers around his hand. "You've been working hard," he said, feeling the calluses.

"And you haven't," she said, feeling his hands.

"Go ahead, Mom. He's okay, isn't he? I mean he didn't have an accident, did he?"

"You could call it an accident," she said, "but yes, he's okay again, except for what it did to his pride, maybe. You know Pop. Well, it was one evening just after supper. We were about to have the devotions and I heard something. Pop's ears are bad, you know. He didn't hear a thing, so I went to the window and looked out, and Pop asked me what I saw. But I didn't see nothing. You know how dark it gets there at night, especially under the apple trees. Well, about that time we hear a knock on the door and Pop gets up to answer it."

"Mom, must you tell a whole story? I mean, what happened? I don't want to sit here half the night to find out."

"Well, just a minute. The details are important because when Pop got to the door, he didn't see anyone at first until his eyes got used to the dark and then he heard someone saying, 'Reverend Stoltzfus, fine evening, isn't it?' Something like that. But he still couldn't see anyone. Then when his eyes adjusted he saw there were ten or fifteen men, I'm not sure how many, standing there in the dark with bags over their heads — so they couldn't be recognized, I guess — and one of them was carrying some papers. Well, Pop said, 'I don't believe I know who you are,' and the same man said, 'That isn't important. What is important is that we've been hearing you haven't been buying any Liberty Bonds and we were sure you just forgot, so we brought you some papers tonight so you can buy your share. Now how much would you like?' "

"Well, you know how Pop feels about Liberty

Bonds. He thinks they're wrong. So he told them so, that he wasn't going to give any money that would go for the war, but that he had been contributing to our church fund. We started a fund, you know — or didn't you know that? Has it been that long that you're gone? Yes, we started a fund to help with the relief effort for refugees, but they didn't know about that. One of the men hollered out that most of that relief money goes into the pockets of those who collect it, which isn't true, but Pop didn't say anything.

"Then this same man that spoke at the start said, 'Well, Brother Stoltzfus?' Now that was a funny thing to say, wasn't it? 'How much?' he said. Your father wouldn't buy any Liberty Bonds, and he told them so. Then they said, 'We didn't ask you whether you want to buy or not. We asked you how much do you want to buy? If you're going to be stubborn,' one of the other men said, 'why then we'll have to give you some buying medicine,' and then they showed him a great big rope they were carrying.

"Oh, I was afraid, Ira. I was standing in the kitchen with my back against the wall so they couldn't see me, but when I heard that, I ran into the living room and the next thing I knew there were men everywhere in the house, tearing open drawers in Pop's desk and scattering his papers around, going up and down the stairs, looking for money, I guess. Or things he'd written since he's a minister and I guess they took along about everything written in German that we had, too, because they wanted to see if we were spies or something since we spoke the dialect. And then a man grabbed me, and I screamed, and he slapped me — I don't know what would have happened but the leader told him not to touch me.

I ran outside after them because I was afraid what they'd do to Pop. Well, they had Pop's arms behind his back so he couldn't get away, and when he saw me, he said, 'Get back in the house!' but I couldn't. I just stood there.

"Then the leader started to ask Pop questions and Pop said afterward he recognized his voice right off. It was Pastor Rydell. He also recognized some of the other men, but I shouldn't tell you who they were — it will make you feel bad toward them — but they were all important people in town."

"What kind of questions did they ask him?"

"Well, they said, 'Are you a spy?' and when he said 'no' they said, 'Then why don't you support your own son in France?' Then they asked him how he would like it if we just let the German army run wild until they took over Europe and then came to America. 'What would you do?' They said. 'Who would protect your consciences? Not the Germans because they'd take away your children, take away your money, and string you up in a tree someplace.'

"Well, Pop said he didn't see that the Germans were any different than these men because they were demanding his money and they had taken one of our boys for a soldier and now they were threatening his life. He shouldn't have said that because it aggravated them. They started to carry him off in the dark, and I tried to follow, but someone turned around and hit me. I must have been unconscious a while, because when I woke up there wasn't any noise outside."

"Did they hurt you, Mom?" said Ira.

"No. I was sore the next day because I bumped my head when I fell down, but they didn't hurt me.

My feelings, that's all." She smiled. "Well, I ran across the field to your Uncle Eli's house and he came down with Aunt Lena and after a while another neighbor came down and we figured the best thing we could do right away was pray. So we began to pray — it must have been two in the morning by that time — and then we heard the back door open and it was your father. Oh, I was so glad to see him that — I guess I cried a little — and then we all started to sing a praise song. He was hardly even hurt — well, his neck skin was burned some because they put the rope around him and tried to hang him but the leader stopped them. He's not all bad you see. He wasn't drunk like some of the men were. But they cut off Pop's beard and all his hair, too. It was terrible — you'd hardly recognize him now. He won't go out in the public because of his looks, but we can praise God that's all they did. Hurt feelings are easier to fix than hurt bodies, I guess."

"That Rydell . . ." said Ira, and he smashed his hands together. "He calls himself a preacher and he does stuff like that."

"No, that's not the right attitude," said Mom. "It wasn't his idea, I'm sure. He tried to hold them back."

"Hold them back? He could have stopped them if he wanted to, but that kind of a man's no better than the Germans. He tells big atrocity stories, then he turns around and acts the same way. Some people I know make the Germans look pretty good in comparison. We have Sergeant Potts in this camp. Just like Rydell . . . out to make life miserable, that's what!"

"Now Ira — " she broke in, but he wasn't finished.

"Well, I hope God treats him like he treated me. When the Judgment Day comes, I wouldn't be surprised — "

"Don't say it, Ira. We're not to judge. God is to judge. Now stop it."

"It wouldn't surprise me if he goes to hell."

"Ira, that's enough. I wouldn't have told you the story if I'd known it would make you bitter."

"Bitter?" He shook his head. "You've never been out in the world."

"Do you feel this way about all the soldiers?" said Mom. "It's not right, Ira. 'Love your enemies, do good to them that persecute you, pray for them which despitefully use you.'"

"Nice words," said Ira. "But you know what, Mom. I heard music."

"Music?" said his mother.

"Music. During the worst of the persecution I heard music."

"Why Ira, it must be a miracle."

"A miracle?"

"Yes, it must be from God. Your father heard music."

"When?"

"When they took him down in the orchard to torment him. I was going to tell you. They had taken him to the orchard and as they put the rope around his neck, and cut his hair, he said he felt what they were doing to him, but then it didn't seem so important. Because he noticed the stars. It was a very black night — which is why they chose that night, I guess — and all the stars were out, and he noticed them when they pushed his head back. He kept his eyes on the stars and then he began to

261

hear beautiful music."

"What kind of music?"

"He didn't say. You know your father's not one for music with his bad ears — he hardly knows anything but the German songs — but he said he could hear it as plain as anything beside him. Beautiful music — it must have come from heaven — and when he took notice, he was lying on the grass where they left him and feeling awfully cold and wet. There was a big dew that night. He got up and, praise God, he wasn't hurt. Other than that scraping on his neck. And his pride, of course, which will heal."

"That's amazing," said Ira. "He heard music. I must not have imagined it. It must be real."

"All I can say is, it's a miracle," said Mother. Ira looked at her.

"How's Pop now? Has he seen any of those men since?"

"He's okay. I don't know if he's seen any of them since or not. You know how Pop is. There would have been a time when he couldn't forgive those men. He remembers and remembers. He remembers things I've forgotten long ago. But he's changed in the last few years. Even Mastie — he prays for him."

"For Mastie?" said Ira. "He won't come back."

"We can only pray," said Mom. "He sends us letters once in a while." She stood up and brushed the crumbs off her dress. "He's out of training, and I guess they're someplace in France now. He doesn't write much, only how they came to a village once that reminded him a lot of Susquehannock. There were ducks and farms and a little creek and I guess a lot of vineyards. They have them there for wine, I guess. He talked with a housewife and got permission to eat some of her gooseberries. He was always crazy over gooseberries, you know. He doesn't say much about the fighting and I guess that's a good thing. It's awful when you see the papers. Five thousand dead here, five thousand dead there, just like they were killing chickens." She looked down at her bag and got out some knitting. "I'm going to take a walk," she said. She was being considerate.

"Now, it's only us," said Susanna, with warm eyes.

"Yes," said Ira. "Give me some of those sandwiches, would you?" She got him a sandwich.

"It's good to hear your voice," she said. "The whole way down I was imagining, imagining us here, but for once my imagination is nothing like the real thing. It's more fun to pinch you than to dream about you," she said, and pinched him.

"Ouch."

"You'll recover. If I'm only nice to you, how long will you remember me? I know, you'll forget me as soon as your head touches the pillow and then you start to dream about someone else. It's wonderful, though, that music you have heard. Sometimes I wish I were a man so I would have to face the war instead of staying home and collecting peach seeds for gas masks. I shouldn't, should I, but when I think of those soldiers getting gas and suffocating, I remember the time I fell in the grain bin and nearly suffocated. When they got me out, my nose was full of grain. So I save my peach seeds. Is it wrong, do you think?

"But other times I'm glad I'm a woman. Women are more gentle, not so full of pride — don't you think? I'm just kidding you. I like to see you with your mother, Ira. She's a good woman, you know, everybody says so. Everybody says they don't know how she lives with your father, but she loves him. She's good for him, don't you think? You're like your father. Why do you look at me that way, Ira? Don't you think so? I'm sorry. I talk too much. Now you talk." She stopped. "Why do you look at me like that?"

She didn't say it harshly. No. But truthfully, he didn't know whether to trust her or not. Did he even know her anymore? Here she was, chattering away, but he wondered if she had any idea what his life in camp was like. He hadn't meant to say it, but he did.

"It's good to have you here, Susanna . . . but sometimes I think I like you more when you're away than when you're here. Oh, that's terrible. I didn't mean it to sound like I'm not glad you came. But it's true. . . . Yes, it's true." Their eyes crossed and he looked down.

"Oh," said Susanna. "That's a funny thing to say." After a bit, she continued. "You are like your mother said your father is. You remember and remember, don't you? Like an elephant. You never forget. You forgive, but you never forget. Oh, I didn't mean to say it like that. But you don't, do you? You know so much about not being a part of the war and you've suffered because of it, I know. You're a man who likes peace, aren't you, Ira? I like that about you. I like to hear you talk about that and about the war, because you talk sense. That's a good thing about you! But when you talked about the sergeant just now, I saw it, just like that, for the first time. You never forget, do you? You talk about it but — I don't mean to make you feel bad. I'm sorry, but you

264

never forgave me either, did you? For something. Will I ever know what? Why do you look at me like that?" She closed her eyes.

"This is a stupid conversation," said Ira. "We're together. Isn't that enough? I haven't seen you for so long, it seems I must be Rip Van Winkle coming out of the mountain valley. 'Yoohoo, where's my missus? Anybody see my missus?'"

"You don't like me, do you?" said Susanna. "You like me more when I'm away."

"Susanna! What's wrong with you anyway?"

"I don't know," she said. "I just feel uncomfortable."

"You're tired, that's all," he said. "I think it's about time you go to the hotel and get some sleep." His mouth began to feel funny, the way it always did when he talked under a strain. He wasn't sure why there was any strain. Didn't they know each other? His jaw hurt.

"Where's Mom?" he said, standing up and brushing his pants. He sat down again.

"Susanna," he said and looked at her. Of course he was glad she was here. How could he have ever let her under the impression he wasn't? Why was she always misunderstanding? Why did people's eyes always do that to him? He could tell by looking at them that they were afraid of him for some reason, and the more he tried to smooth things over the less they talked and the colder their eyes turned. A little muscle under the eye of the guest would begin to twitch and after a bit he felt a muscle beginning to twitch in his arm. Did they see it? Why didn't they trust him? Why didn't they see right into his heart and see that in there he liked them and had nothing but good intentions? So he waited for them to show one spark of warmth so that he could reciprocate with a spark of warmth. He waited and waited. He talked and talked. His jaw got sore and he covered his mouth with his hand. He wanted to hide his eyes to protect his soul inside from being seen. Why they could look right in through his eyes and see his naked soul scrambling in the dark, looking for a hiding place. He didn't understand his own feelings, and once they began to move they got stickier and stickier, and like a fly on fly paper, every move only glued him down a little more. He felt helpless — tired out and helpless.

He began to laugh.

"What's funny?" she said.

"I don't know," he said. He laughed harder and rubbed his eyes.

"Ira!" she said, and because it was funny to watch him laughing and laughing, even though she didn't know why, she began to laugh.

"There's nothing funny," he said.

"I know," she said, and they laughed some more. It was like the eucalyptus oil the quack sold at Red Dragon on Friday nights. Whatever was wrong with you, it fixed you up. He began to feel good.

The first of the soldiers returning from town came by.

"Hey, hey!" he said, looking at them. He was drunk. "Hey, you got a peach, did you? Oh, listen to her laugh. Hahahaha. Now that's a different looking peach. Not like a Georgia peach, haha. Not as soft as a Georgia peach. Here, have one." He threw a peach.

"What's a Georgia peach?" said Susanna, "Is it

what I think it is?"

"Sure," said Ira. "Here." He pulled the peach in half and stuck a half into her mouth. "Keep that for the boys with gas masks," he said, and dropped the seed into her hand. He bit into the other half. The juice ran down their chins. Oh, it was a good one. She smiled. "Don't make me laugh again," he said with his mouth full.

"Make you laugh? Who's making who laugh?"

But he did. He started to laugh again and choked a big piece of peach out onto the ground.

"Oh, for Pete's sake," she said.

He wiped his hands on a towel in the basket and gave it to her. "Is Mother around?" he said.

"No. I wonder where she is?" said Susanna.

"Well, all we can do is wait for her," he said and reaching over he kissed her. "Mmm, peaches," he said. He was feeling good.

"Ira." She threw her arms around him blindly.

Then it came out gently, bit by bit. All those things he had thought would be too painful to talk about. He felt good. He looked into her eyes without blinking. He wanted her to see right into him and see his naked soul inside reaching out its arms to her.

"It takes a long time to know someone, I guess," she said. "But you're not mad at me, are you?"

"I like you," he said, "real much."

"Am I like a peach?" she said.

"You're better than a Georgia peach," he said.

"And is there a long time?" she said.

"You ask such hard questions. I don't know."

"Do you want me to wait for you, Ira?"

"Who knows how many years it will be until the war ends? They're sending objectors to prison now," he said, "with long sentences. Isn't it enough we're together now? Let's enjoy it."

"Yes, Ira," she said. "Your mother is coming."

They stood up and Ira stretched his arms out and twisted his muscles. The bones cracked.

"Horrors!" she said. "Don't you do any work?"

"I'm glad you came," he said. "Kiss me once more before she can see us."

8

The following week Ira was transferred to the conscientious objector company.

He arrived in the colonel's car, driven by a chauffeur and guarded by a man with a rifle. He was no longer a rebellious soldier when he entered the conscientious objector company. He was now considered a prisoner of war. Two guards with rifles and bayonets saluted outside the conscientious objector camp when the car drove up. Ira got out of the car and smiled.

He went to the doorway and looked over the quarters. It was a Civil War horse stable. The conscientious objectors had been told to clean out the manure and wash down the floors but the good, rank smell of horses was still in the room. The stable was divided into stalls where individual horses had stood, and over each stall was the name of the horse that had been there: *Flight, Feather, Dun Dapple, Pretty Boy,* and so on.

Two men were discussing the Book of Revelation in Flighty's stall while over in Feather's, at the back of the building, a men's quartet was singing a hymn.

The big Quaker, Guthrie, saw Ira and jumped up. "I didn't notice you were here." He shook his hand. "Well, you see how we spend our days and nights here while the Army decides what it will do with us.

Look interesting?"

It looked like a bunkhouse in heaven to Ira, who was used to being pointed at whenever he entered a room. Here were a group of men in civilian clothes talking and singing and studying the Bible, the things he had missed most in the regular Army camp.

"What do you think?" said Guthrie. "Dun Dapple okay? She was a famous horse, they say. Won the Kentucky Derby in 1880 or thereabouts. Are they bringing a mattress for you?" One man was already lying in Dun Dapple's stall, playing a game of chess with himself, now moving with his left hand, now with his right. "This is Frymire," said Guthrie.

Ira shook his hand, but the men remained seated.

"Your name sounds Dutch."

"It is Dutch. Lebanon County," he said.

"Pennsylvania? What town?"

"Myerstown."

"Myerstown? I have relatives up there. You know where 501 comes into town and there's a butcher shop on the right? Yes? My uncle!" he said.

"Your uncle owns that butcher shop? The Amishman?"

"Yes."

"Are you Amish then? I wouldn't think an Amishman would wear a uniform."

"I'm Mennonite," said Ira, "and they put it on me."

"They sell good baloneys there," said Frymire. "You play chess?"

"No."

"Hmm. Too bad. I'll have to teach you. You sing?"

"Sing? Oh, some. But not what they're singing. I

270

don't know many of the popular hymns in English."

"Do you have any books with you?"

"The Bible."

"Nothing else?"

"No."

"You're up the creek then," said Frymire, and he looked up at Ira with blue eyes. His hair was long and curly and he didn't have a bit of tan. He looked very brilliant.

"Why?"

"Nothing to do. This is all we do every day. Sing some more, read some more, play another game of chess, or argue — if you like arguing. We die eventually of inactivity."

"But you don't have to drill? You don't have to wear the uniform? The officers leave you alone?"

"Oh, if you look at it that way, I guess we have it good. But I'm bored," said Frymire. "Anything's better than this. We could rot here and they wouldn't care."

Ira looked at Frymire silently.

"It's not right to waste your life either, is it?" said Frymire. "What if we have to live in this horse stable for five years? I've been here five weeks. What will we be like by the end of five years? Intellectually, bankrupt! There's no chance for study or a decent discussion here. Well, we always have the Bible boys over there, but I would go out of my head listening to them talk. Then there's the food racket — just wait. We're the last ones to be served and we're always served after the regular Army. They never make enough food for us, and we're all so hungry that when the gong sounds, you just grab what's in front of you on the table and eat it. So one man gets a meal of prunes, the next one gets a stomach of potatoes, and the next one beans or pears. If you're stupid enough to pass the dish around and wait for other dishes to come by, you'll go to bed hungry, I'll tell you. Well, it has its funny side, I guess. We get a balanced diet, as the officer in charge says. As a group, we get a balanced diet — individually, no. Tell me, what am I going to look like if I eat nothing but prunes for the next five years? I should be regular by then though, that's a consolation."

Ira said, "It's worse outside."

"You mean in the regular camp?"

"It's a lot worse."

"It couldn't be. At least you're busy out there."

"The pressure on you to give in is terrific." For the first time Ira began to think, though, that maybe he shouldn't have left the main Army camp for this enclave of objectors. Out there he knew who he was, and what he was up against. Every minute he was reminded of who he was and he wore his convictions like a crown of thorns that someone gave a sharp rap every now and then. But in here things appeared to be stagnant. There would be no constant reminders of who he was.

He sat down on a bunch of straw and got out his Bible.

"Are you hungry?" It was Guthrie again, carrying a bag of cookies. "We share everything in here — I do some kitchen work so I have access to the kitchen — I make cookies in the evenings sometimes.

"You work?" said Ira.

"Sure. Second Thessalonians 3:10," said Guthrie and winked. He waited for Ira to look it up. "For when we were with you, this we commanded you, that if any would not work, neither should he eat."

But, Ira thought, if one was not going to obey commands to drill and train as a soldier, then how could he obey commands to work in the kitchen which fed everyone, soldiers and nonsoldiers.

"Does it offend you if I do kitchen work?"

"You're not being consistent."

"Whether one's in the Army or out of the Army he eats. Right? And I've got to do something to keep my sanity. I can't sit around all day and write letters like some of the boys. Or read books like Frymire." He winked, but Frymire missed it. He was absorbed in the game of chess with himself. "I'd go out of my coconut. There are also an awful lot of boys out there," and he waved his arms to indicate the rest of the camp, "who have never met a conscientious objector and talked to him. They have all sorts of weird ideas about us. I think of them as a mission field."

"Oh," said Ira. He ate a cookie. "Maybe I should have stayed back in the regular camp. I had a mission field — I never thought of it that way though. What would Sergeant Potts be thinking of conscientious objectors if we had never met?"

"Probably like them better," said Guthrie, squatting.

"True."

"Aren't you bored?" said Guthrie.

"Bored? I wasn't in the regular camp, no. But Frymire says it's different here. What is there to do? The Army boys are bored with drills and they can't wait to get overseas. I can't wait to get back to the farm. Picking corn. They'll be picking corn soon. I never wanted to pick corn so bad in my life."

273

"What are you going to do when the war's over?"

"Go home, I guess," said Ira.

"After you've done your service. We still have to work, you know."

"We do?" Ira had been out of contact with the news so long that he didn't know of late developments.

"They're granting farm furloughs now, taking boys out of the camps and giving them farm work to do. Unless you'd rather spend twenty years or so in the cells of Fort Leavenworth."

"Well, I can't really say I'd like to."

"You don't think that when the war's finished, we're finished, do you? We've only been parasites here. We've been negative, and said 'no' at every turn of the road, but you can't be only negative. Jesus Christ was a positive man. He said 'yes,' many more times than He said 'no.' Check it out. But 'yes' to the right options. Let me make you an offer. How about going to France?" said Guthrie.

"France?" Ira felt a wave of suspicion. Was this man to be trusted? "You mean as a soldier? That's why I'm here, so I don't have to go to France."

"Don't get all worked up about it. I won't trick you. Sure, France. What do you think France is like, now that the Germans and the French have dug trenches through the vineyards and apple orchards and laid artillery down on the towns for four years? What do you suppose it's like?"

"Ruined, I suppose." He imagined trenches across his own beautiful county and artillery shells hitting the farmer's market or the schools and churches in Susquehannock.

"Ruined? It's like the face of the moon. Craters, dust, wire."

"How do you know?"

"I read reports from the Red Cross."

"So, what can we do about it? Go look at the craters, I guess."

"No, reconstruction, man. Listen, the Quakers are going to move into Verdun to rebuild houses and towns. They need men, dozens of men. They're going to need them for five or ten years, things are that bad."

"Are you going?"

"Sure."

"Could I — "

"There's a good chance. All we have to do now is wait for the Board of Inquiry to examine us and make up their minds if we're genuine or not. If you convince them, fine. If you don't, it's France for sure, with a uniform and a gun. Or maybe they'll be kind and let you stay in Ft. Leavenworth."

"Board of Inquiry?"

"They're on their way. The only problem is they have to examine 4,000 men to see if they're genuine — from one end of the country to the other. Who knows when they'll get to this end-of-the-tracks camp."

"What is it? The Board."

"You haven't heard about the Board? We'll be talking about it later this morning but — in a word — it's the Army's best bloodhounds, sent out to see who are the genuine conscientious objectors and who aren't. Have another cookie?" Guthrie smiled and walked away.

Ira leaned his head against the wooden wall of the stall. He would never have imagined that things could be so different not more than a quarter mile from his old tent.

The quartet had dissolved into a discussion of Thomas a Becket, a collie puppy and mascot of the conscientious objectors' unit who had been taken into custody over the weekend by the guards of the objectors and delivered to the machine gunners in the next camp. The gunners had court-martialed Becky, as the conscientious objectors called him, and sentenced him to death for his refusal to 'behave like a patriotic American and fight.' Interpreted, that meant the gunners were taking out on Becky their feelings toward the conscientious objectors. The guards, however refused to carry out the sentence and had instead furloughed Becky to a farm.

"Now what kind of a soldier is that?" said Schie, the tall skinny Lutheran boy who had a perpetual smile. Schie had come to his convictions on war completely by himself — 'just taking my Sunday school stories seriously,' he said. His preacher father back in Michigan kept writing him letters telling him not to 'disappoint your mother and I with this silly belief of yours.'

"Tell me if they won't kill a dog, would they be heroic enough to kill a Hun?" said Schnickerry, the Jehovah's Witness. "Of course, as they say, a dog is man's best friend. Would anyone want to kill his best friend? A Hun would be worse than a dog because he wouldn't even be a friend."

"What logic is that?" said Schie.

"Here's an easier question. 'There is a friend that sticketh closer than a brother,' " said Pyski, the Catholic boy from Pittsburgh, who carried scars from a beer bottle fight before he became a Christian. "Who is it?"

276

"Jesus," said Schnickerry.

"Wrong. A cootie!"

Schie slapped his knee. "Oh, that's too good. A cootie!"

"What do you think, Frymire?" said Schie, looking over toward Ira's stall. Frymire put his finger on his black queen as if not to forget where he was planning to move and cleared his throat. "What was the question?"

"Becky. Why did they furlough him to a farm instead of doing away with him like we all thought they would?"

"I think it shows the goodness of man's heart with which he is endowed by his Creator," said Frymire. "How can you kill someone when you have seen his face? That's the problem of this war — it's a war without faces. The artillery man, does he ever see the face of the men he's lobbing shells at? Of course not. He shoots from three miles off. The aeroplane pilot in his cockpit — does he ever see the face of the man he is tumbling with in the sky? Of course not. If they get close enough to see each other, why they both have their goggles on. It's easy to shoot at a pair of goggles.

"The generals — do they ever see the faces of the German soldiers? Aside from the dead ones, of course. No, they only see red and blue and green pins being moved back and forth on a board at the headquarters. The top general smokes his cigar — and I'm not knocking cigars, incidentally — and says, 'We'll advance to the river tomorrow,' so someone moves a red pin over a quarter of an inch on the board and the next evening three hundred men are dead because that pin moved a quarter of an inch.

"What about the average American citizen? Why, he never sees a face either. He reads a headline which some clever editor writes like *Allies Cut Through at the Marne, 10,000 Enemy Killed or Captured* and he says, 'Great! 10,000! Why at this rate the war will be over in a month.' But he never saw one enemy. He don't know the enemy looks exactly like he does. No, the only one who sees a face in this war is your ordinary foot soldier who goes running out after the artillery has lifted and here comes a German running at him with a bayonet and suddenly they're face-to-face." He hit his fist into his own head. "Smash, and it's over, and one of them is lying all torn up on the ground. Then the soldier sees that the man he has knocked down is in terrible pain. Why, he's in mortal agony. He can see it by the way the man clutches his side. He has seen the enemy's face and he knows now, as Schiller puts it, that all men are brothers. '*Alle Menschen werden Brüder.*' "

"I like that," said Schnickerry.

"Frymire, that's all very interesting, but what has that got to do with Becky?" said Schie.

"Why, everything in the world. Becket's not a man — he's a dog, right?"

"Right."

"But the guards couldn't kill him because they took one look into his face and they saw what an adorable pup he is. He probably wagged his tail. How can you shoot a dog when he's wagging his tail? It's too bad people don't have tails to wag. There wouldn't be any more shootings."

"Don't kid yourself," said Schie. "We'd find some way of depersonalizing tails."

"Furthermore," said Pyski, "it would just be one more part of your body that could salute an officer." He got down on his hands and knees and rested his hand on his back, just where a tail would normally be. "At-ten-TION!" He stuck his hand straight up in the air. Schie howled with laughter, and even Frymire smiled.

"So, anyway, they didn't shoot him. I'm glad of that," said Shnickerry, who really had a gentle heart.

"Would a dog go on to his eternal reward?" said Pyski.

"Look, let's not get into that." Frymire thought some conversations were too silly to be worth listening to. He went back to his chess game.

"Well, men," said Guthrie. He stood up and gave them one of his charismatic smiles. "It's ten o'clock." He put his fingers in his mouth and gave a tremendous wolf whistle.

"Bible study," said Frymire, upsetting his chess game. "Better go or they'll wonder about you."

9

The men walked out of the stable, and, by way of a path, they wound around the edge of the camp, across the railroad tracks, and up onto a high hill that overlooked the camp. The grass and wild flowers were high and the men sat right down in them and stuck flowers in their hair. Guthrie, it seemed, was again in charge. He took a Bible from his pocket and began to read from 2 Corinthians 11.

"I don't think there's a one of us here who doesn't see himself in that passage," he said. "Beatings, threats, taken advantage of. But it seems to me we should look at it again, now that it's definite the Board of Inquiry is coming to camp. What are they looking for? Sincerity, friends. Now I don't think there's any of us that's been beaten 200 times, or stoned, or shipwrecked, or imprisoned — yet, what do we have to *boast* about to the Board of Inquiry, to use Paul's word? And are our scars really marks of our sincerity or are they only marks of our bullheadedness?

"It hasn't been as bad in the last month or two. Some of you came directly into the Conscientious Objector Detachment without ever going through the regular camp. It's been easier for you. Are you holding to your convictions? Test yourself. Are you sure of your beliefs? Do you know why you believe that way? The Board of Inquiry men are sharp men, just like so many bloodhounds sniffing around to find a bad smell in your story and if they do — woof, woof. They'll either drag you off to the front or to the stockade at Fort Leavenworth and so fast you won't know what happened. Is it the Father in you, speaking in his still small voice through your conscience, who brought you here? Are you here because you've been whispered to, or are you here because everyone in your church has agreed that if you fight you'll be excommunicated? The bloodhounds will smell that one. I'm not saying we're all here for the same reasons, but what is yours? 'For the sake of Christ, then, I am content with weaknesses, insults, hardships, persecution, and calamities; for when I am weak, then I am strong. I have been a fool!'

"So I guess you could call this a morning for testimonies of scars. Does anyone want to boast of his scars?"

"No, no," said Schnickerry, "I don't think it's right. These are things between me and God. If I was persecuted, then it was for his sake."

"What did the soldiers do to you?"

"No, it's all past," said Schnickerry. "It's all past. One star in my heavenly crown for each scar on my body. . . ."

"I'm proud of mine," said Schie, and he jumped to his feet. "Look." He wiggled his jaw and there was a tremendous pop, and it slipped out of joint. Several of the men looked horrified. Just as easily, he popped it back in place again. "It was broken," he said. "The lieutenant we had before did that to me with a shovel.

"That's really all you can see anymore since the jaw healed up. They didn't like my attitude. They never did like my attitude. I went quietly about my business in camp for a while and just refused the orders and the officers said I was trying to hide something. So the next time a newspaperman stopped me, probably just picked me at random, I told him my views and they were printed on the front page of the Chattanooga paper, and then the officers accused me of looking for cheap notoriety. So you can't win, huh?

"Anyway, they decided to punish Berkshire and I for not drilling, so the officer in charge ordered us out to the toilets. Now the toilets weren't much back then, just ditches with a couple of inches of heavy oil on the bottom, and after a while they got full and then they'd dig a new ditch. Well, the sergeant ordered us out there to a full ditch and told us to climb in. So we did. Maybe you think we were foolish to climb in, but if we wouldn't have climbed in, they'd have thrown us in. The goo came up to our waists and it was terribly foul, and the sergeant said, "I'll give you one last chance to decide to drill with us. If you're willing, step out. If you're not willing, we'll drown you. We didn't step out, of course. 'All right, baptize the —' pardon me for saying it, 'baptize the son-of-a-bitches,' he said, and they took their shovels and baptized us. The soldiers didn't want to do it — of course not. They were decent men. Afterward one told me it was the hardest thing he ever did in his life. My friend was so humiliated that he cried but because I just stood there, and refused to lower my head, and went on looking our officer right in the eye, he told them to hit me with their shovels, so two of them did — one on each side of my face. It was broken for weeks but not once did I hate him for it (and I used to have the nickname 'Killer' when I was in grade school because I was good with my fists). Not once did I want to retaliate, praise God. For a long time after that when I went to bed at night, I'd pray for him."

"With his teeth wired together," said Pyski, "I remember it."

"Yes," said Schie, and he got silent.

" 'Blessed are you when men revile you and persecute you and say all manner of evil against you falsely for my sake,' " said Guthrie. "Next."

"But all that," said Schie quietly, "is nothing compared to letters from home from my own father asking me to please tell him what he'd done wrong, what he can do to make sure my younger brother don't object to fighting. And my father is a preacher!"

"Well," said Schnickerry, the Jehovah's Witness, "I wasn't going to, but if it can be a means of reassuring someone — I look for the return of our blessed Savior before this war is over. Before this war ends I think he will come back to take home his select and there will be a terrible battle on the fields of Armageddon. And then there will be a day of real peace when the lion and the lamb romp together on the French battlefield with the little French children. I know lots of you disagree with me, but isn't that sufficient reason not to fight? 'If my kingdom were of this world, then would my servants fight.' But Jesus' kingdom is not of this world. It is a kingdom with a dynasty to be seated on that Great White Throne very shortly. I am waiting, expecting that kingdom to be declared any moment. If I spend my time fighting, will I be ready? Will my heart be ready to sing for the great celebration on that inaugural day, or will my heart be filled with some battle cry or trench ballad, some song of death?

"I told that to the men in my tent when I first came and they didn't like to hear it. They stuck cotton in their ears, but I went on telling them the wonderful story. Well, they liked it less and less. You see, they didn't want to sing for the inauguration of the King. They liked victory rags and the trench tunes. Blood and action, I guess you could say. Most of them are dead now," said Schnickerry sadly. "May God bless them. But they left this to remember them by."

He bowed his head and showed them all a spot a half inch wide and two inches long where there was no hair. His hair had covered it earlier in the day.

"How did it happen?" said Guthrie.

"They shaved all my head but that strip. They put a stick in it and twisted it around until the skin peeled off. Father, forgive them."

Ira listened to it all with a sense of wonder. Why, he hadn't suffered at all! There were other stories. One man had gone on a hunger strike rather than leave his tent wearing an army uniform. They had forced tubes up his nose on the fifteenth day of his hunger strike and fed him. Another had scars all around his neck from being lifted up by a thick rope tied to a tree limb.

"Pyski," said Guthrie, "How did you get those scars on your knees. Show us."

"Well," said Pyski, and he grinned. "Those are my war wounds. When the war's over and people ask me what I did in the war, I'll just roll up my pant legs

284

and say, 'I was wounded at Camp Ethan Allen,' or if they wonder if I was decorated for my bravery, I'll say, 'Of course,' and show them those little scars."

"Well, tell us what happened."

"I fell," said Pyski. "I fell on the rocks, and cut them up."

"What were you doing on the rocks?"

"Running to keep from getting run over by the motorcycles."

"Motorcycles?" said Ira.

"Yeah, they wanted to check my abilities one day, so they double-timed me up and down the mountain in front of two motorcycles, for a couple hours."

"Oh, to check your abilities?"

"Yes. They saw I wouldn't drill, and I told them I wouldn't carry garbage, so they figured the only thing left was a little exercise."

"Oh."

"We're not complaining," said Guthrie. "God forbid that we should complain, but even Paul the apostle said he was foolish enough to brag sometimes about the things that were done to him to prevent him from preaching the gospel. But they didn't do a thing to me. Isn't it strange? I haven't a single 'war wound,' as Pyski calls them. It makes me jealous."

"He's a diplomat," said Schie, "that's why. He doesn't stand still and take it like some of us or argue like some of us others. He reasons with them and they like that."

The men sat in silence after the last man stopped speaking. After a while the quartet got up and sang the hymn they had practiced and someone prayed. Before they dismissed though, Guthrie held up his hand in silence.

285

"Thank you, men," he said. "Maybe that was a good thing for all to hear before the Board of Inquiry gets here. Do you know what you believe? You men who just came to the camp, think about that one. But a caution! Just because one suffers doesn't prove anything."

"What do you mean?" said Ira.

"It's nothing. That's what I mean."

"Then . . . you mean it's worth nothing? Our time in the camp?"

"Nothing! 'If I give my body away to be burned, but have not love, I gain nothing. . . . Faith, hope, love abide, but the greatest of these is love.' Love!" said Guthrie.

"Anybody else hungry?" said Pyski.

They all began to run down the steep neck of the hill. But Ira couldn't forget what he had heard. It was an intriguing thought. Love? Love for whom? Was there anybody he didn't love? Just the fact he was here in camp rather than on a battlefield, didn't that show his attitude? *I'm not like Mastie,* he thought, *off shooting people.*

IV. The Front

1

From the air an army on the move looks like a fantastic thing, beautifully planned, like a walking Great Wall of China. Over there the forest, there the rolling cow pastures and the river, and over there more cow pastures and forests and villages, while up the center like a squiggly line the army moves on for miles and miles and miles. But the closer you get to the ground the more everything looks like chaos and madness.

The Army was on its way to a new front to block the German lightning advances. On the right-hand side of that muddy trail were trucks, buses, ambulances, horse-drawn kitchen units, enormous artillery guns, and clean American faces — all moving up. On the left-hand side a weary French army was returning from the front. They were not young, healthy soldiers — most of them were old men, exhausted, dirty. Some of them were hardly out of high school, but they all looked like old men.

Traffic was jammed at the bottom of a hill where an artillery shell had just blasted a six-foot-deep hole in the road and a gang of German prisoners was dumping gravel in the hole while the two lines stared at each other.

"It looks like the war's over," said Churchill. "Like

it's all been fought." The fields alongside the column were nothing but shell holes filled with water and mosquitoes.

"Don't kid yourself."

"I wish I wouldn't have thrown away my cards," said Froggie. He had the cleanest set of pinochle cards in the whole company and they were all back on a garbage heap in the quiet sector they had just come from. "Did you see any Germans?" he shouted to a French veteran.

The veteran made a gesture of wringing a chicken's neck. Froggie nodded. "But who was the chicken?" he said out of the corner of his mouth.

The Americans were not as fresh as they looked. Mastie's regiment had been marching steadily for the last three days without sleep, and every time they got to a jam in the road like this one the men sat down on the mudbanks by the side of the road and fell asleep with their heads propped on their elbows. Many of the men had headaches from walking in the wake of the buses and trucks. Yesterday the lieutenant in charge of the company had fallen off his horse in a sleep and broken his nose. He had it bandaged today. When the call came to move ahead again, the men got up mechanically and looked around. Which direction had they been walking?

Were they going to the front this time? Why, they hadn't seen a hostile bullet yet. Nothing more than a few distant artillery shells. *War is a big bore, that's all*, Mastie decided. *So why don't they just let us sleep until there is some action?*

"Lieutenant says we're going to Paris," said Froggie.

"What will we do in Paris?" said Mastie.

"Defend it, stupid. Somebody's got to defend it against the advance."

"Then what are we marching north for — Paris is west."

"We'll make a turn at the river, that's what."

"What makes you so sure?"

"The lieutenant said."

"He doesn't know any better than we do where we're going."

"I can't hear you. The horns." The irritated bus drivers had started to honk their horns to add to the din of shouting that was already going on.

Mastie sat down on the bank and his eyelids fell as if they had been weighted with nickels. He woke when someone kicked his boots. The line was moving again. He got back in line, but even so he could hardly keep awake. The line kept moving along. A large town appeared ahead as they came to the top of a hill. The rumble of guns which had been faraway for the last two days, now sounded only a few miles beyond them and as evening came they began to see artillery shells flying overhead, cherry red with fiery tails.

The town was deserted.

It was like ghost ships he had read about as a boy, where the crew had boarded a strange vessel that seemed to be drifting toward them and found the ship in tip-top shape, the floors scrubbed, a bouquet of flowers and hot soup and toast on the captain's table downstairs, and his cigar, still wet from his mouth, lying on the ashtray and burning slowly.

Any moment he expected to see schoolchildren or some old man with a moustache stick his head out the window with an American flag in his hand, shouting, "*Voilà les Américains! Vivent les Américains!* (Here come the Americans!)

But no. Everything was silent. The line of returning French had cut away just before they came to the city limits. Now they began to pass trucks and buses stopped along the highway while soldiers jumped from them silently in the dark. No one spoke — only their boots squeaked, thousands and tens of thousands of boots. There were also cats. Every abandoned house seemed to have a cat in the doorway, yowling as the troops came up or following them along the tops of fences. The cats ran into the streets and rubbed themselves against the soldiers' legs until they were kicked away. They weren't even skinny.

The wagon carrying the company's machine guns had stopped and the driver tied his horse to a stairway that led into a church. The lieutenant began to pass out the guns and two by two the squads ran off up the dark streets. Still there was silence here. It was on the right that the noise was coming from, roar after roar. The sky was red over there, but here it was black, without stars.

Mastie was carrying his gun on his shoulder now and moving along a narrow street with his company. A thrill filled him. *We're here,* he told himself, and up ahead some place there were Germans. He hadn't seen any yet.

Running increased the tempo of his heart, but he had to run to keep from getting lost in the back streets. This group of a hundred or so, he belonged to them now.

"I'm dead," said someone behind him. It was Caloway, bouncing along with one hand holding the gun on his shoulder, the other hand holding his side.

"You're *what*?"

"Side stitches. I'm exhausted."

They were there. Where? Well, wherever they were going. The men had stopped in a huddle on a street corner, panting, while the lieutenant conferred with another officer in the dark whose face they couldn't see. But where was this? Where was the enemy? There where the sky was red, but now it seemed further away again. What was the hurry then? The men began to smoke. Finally the lieutenant signaled half of his men to follow him down a narrow path and into a row of pretty little cottages. Two by two they dropped off between the houses.

They were close to the river now. Mastie could smell the fishy smells that always seem to hang around rivers. The two of them were in a narrow alley between two houses — it seemed to be a small garden — and at the end of the alley he could see up across the roofs of several more houses to a large iron bridge, almost empty now except for the silhouettes against the sky of several men in American-style helmets who were pacing back and forth over it and other men who were looking at its stone supports.

"They're going to blow it up," said Froggie.

"Why?"

"That's the direction they'll come from, over there." He pointed in the direction of the red sky.

"There must be some of us over there, too, or there wouldn't be no fight. If we're retreating, we'll have to come across that bridge, right?"

"You're pretty smart."

"Mainly sleepy. So what did he say we do here?"

"Get a bead on the bridge and camouflage ourselves."

They worked for several hours, stacking up cartridges against the wall of the next house and tearing away some of the bushes that closed off the alley to make a hole for the gun. It was a warm summer night. There were still Americans on the bridge.

"I'm not sleepy anymore," said Mastie.

"Excitement, that's all," said Froggie. There didn't seem to be anything to do now but wait. It was quiet again. After a bit, he said, "You know, my heart's beating like an old motor. Feel it."

"Sure enough."

Another long silence and then Mastie said, "Mine's beating, too."

"I thought you don't get scared."

"Are you crazy?"

"Ooh, what's that?"

"Where, where?" Mastie strained his eyes toward the far shore.

"On my back. It's biting. Ooh."

"Oh, I thought you saw something."

"Look, is there something on my back?"

"How can I see?"

"Light a match."

"Light a match? Are you crazy?

"Well, slap my back then."

He slapped Froggie's back.

"Ah, that's better."

"I felt something crunch."

"Look, a bug. It was just a bug, but boy did it bite. You know what that is? It's a bedbug."

"Shh. . . ."

"A bedbug. No wonder the last guys got out of this town. It has bedbugs."

"I need a cigar," said Mastie. He lit one and took a deep breath. Something whistled overhead, hissed, and then exploded less than a hundred feet behind them. Mastie swallowed the smoke and dived onto the ground, but not before he saw Froggie's face in the second of light as the shell exploded. It was white and he had a very funny look in his eyes, as if he had just been punched unmercifully in his stomach. Dirt pattered like rain around them.

Mastie coughed into the dirt. The cigar smoke was terribly hot in his lungs. *Perhaps I'll die*, he thought. *Will they ship my body home?* There was another hiss and explosion. The fragments pattered against the houses this time and then the quiet of the night ended. Roar after roar shook the two houses between which they lay, and rattled their teeth. Mastie remembered lying in a hayfield in a thunderstorm once as a boy while the bolts cracked above and the rain nearly drowned him, afraid to move because he had heard that lightning struck the highest object and the field was on a hill. So he lay there thinking they would find him after a few days, while the ground turned muddy and ran down his pant leg.

What am I doing here? Mastie asked himself and shut his eyes in the dirt while the houses shook again. Dirt kept getting in his nose. He held the warm bright pictures of his home and Annie and green Pennsylvania fields to his chest for comfort and remembered the lieutenant saying most of the wounds in war are only superficial flesh wounds. Few men were hit directly by fragments or bullets. But even as he remembered that, he knew some of them would be hit.

Another explosion erupted close by and things began to fall all over him. He lay very still after they stopped and slowly moved his leg. It was okay. He wiggled his toes and then his fingers.

"Mastie!" he heard someone say and whoever it was began to tug at his legs. His mouth was full of dirt. He sneezed.

"He's okay! He's okay!"

"You hurt?" It was one of the company corporals.

"No." His uniform was torn but he felt perfectly healthy. "Where's Froggie?"

"Here."

The fat soldier was sitting beside the gun, eating a long, white radish that the explosion had thrown up. "Hello, care for a radish?" Froggie already had one cleaned for him, but Mastie noticed something as he took the radish. Froggie's hand was trembling.

It was dawn, and numerous soldiers were running on the opposite shore, hardly the length of a tobacco field away. Some of them already had started across the bridge and they were stopping to rest their guns on the bars of the bridge and fire back at the shore from which they had retreated. There were Germans back there — their helmets betrayed them — but there was also a mass of French hats in the scuffle. They were all fighting for control of the bridge.

The two were still waiting in the garden, their gun trained on the center of the bridge. The sky had cleared and the sun came up, round and red, and it was warm already before the sun was hardly up. A good day for harvesting, Mastie thought, and he wished that were what he was about to do. He wished he were harnessing the horses to the reaper and checking the knife before going out to the wheat

296

field. It was going to be a lovely day.

But no, they were still in the garden, watching the drama at the far bridge head. It was almost like looking at a painting — it didn't seem real. An intense scuffle was under way and a constant crackling of rifle fire. Now a man stood up on the railing, no bigger than a bedbug, and emptied his gun again and again, fearless of his own life. Then he threw his rifle up and his body began to somersault downward, arms and legs spread out as if he were flying. The water splashed a little and he was gone.

The bridge was alive with men, most of them French. They were running back across it, followed by squads of pursuing Germans, although only their helmets told who was who. The Germans were almost at the center of the bridge.

"Now!" said Froggie, but Mastie waited. The machine guns all along the riverbank began to cackle, and now he pulled his trigger finger firmly back. The belt of bullets began to move. They were too low, ricocheting off the iron girders on the bridge with whines. He turned the knob carefully and the figures on the bridge began to fall. They fell by the dozens, by the score, some of them leaping to get over the bridge side to safety and splashing in the water, but none of them were getting past the center of the bridge.

There was a plaque on the bridge at the center, and Mastie sighted the barrel of his gun just up from the plaque.

Another company was coming, and again they were all shot down before they passed the center. The river was bobbing with heads. Most of those who were still alive had lost their guns and were trying to swim back to the other shore, but those who had been hit bobbed under the surface once or twice and disappeared.

The Germans were trying a new tactic. Bunches of soldiers ran down to the water's edge and began to launch boats while more boats came floating downstream from a point just around the bend to pick up loads of infantrymen. The lieutenant came running through the garden. "Get your gun on the river," he shouted.

Mastie redirected the gun, this time on an imaginary line near the middle of the river. He pulled the trigger back again. In the center of the river a boat went down and masses of infantrymen, their guns in one hand, clutching at each other with the other while their boots filled up with water sank slowly and heroically out of sight. One boat had made it across, although only a handful of the men were left in it. Apparently another gun was covering them because none of them got onto the shore. More boats were launched and a new company of men started across the bridge.

"Don't they care for their lives?" said Froggie.

But Mastie was not listening. He sat fastened to the gun, his finger unmoving while the gun chattered. His heart was pumping away with excitement. All that mattered was those little figures in the water. Would they stop or wouldn't they? They stopped.

"Look how red the river is," said Mastie. They had stopped firing at last. "It must be the sun."

"Are you kidding?" said Froggie. He looked at Mastie, but Mastie's eyes were closed. His mouth was open. He had fallen asleep.

2

The company was in excellent spirits. They had held their first objective without a casualty. Within the company were many smaller squads, and their first fire was like the first baby of a young man and his wife. It had brought them together in a project that was separate from themselves, a new creation that took the utmost cooperation. In this case, the baby was a fallen town.

There were six in Mastie's unit. Bunched up and marching, the six of them had been together from the boat, although Sanders and Fahnestock tended to stick by themselves because they were from the same community in Alabama someplace.

"We should get a paper one of these days," said Churchill. "I mean, where are we? Who knows? We might be the furthest front point of the American line, just about to cross over into Germany for all any of us know."

"Do you think they'll tell us that in the newspapers?"

"Not necessarily, but it would be nice to know just roughly where we are." He looked up at the sky, the direction from which the papers always fell. It would be the "Paris Edition" of the *New York Times*, especially printed for the Army in Europe and dropped out of passing planes. But there weren't even any planes.

"What does it matter where we are?" said Froggie. "Wherever it is, we're going some more in the same direction. Now was this a town or the mason's supply yard?" They had come to an intersection in the road and a wooden plaque announced the town of Bois du Baussant, but was this a town? There were twenty-five or thirty mounds of brick and stone and in front of one or two a few singed flowers and onions were growing.

"Whoever lived here didn't leave a new address where the postman can reach him."

"Keep moving." It was their lieutenant.

They started up a winding road that seemed to lead eventually to a forest several miles away. Mastie noticed the condition of the hayfields. This one was ready to be cut. In that one the soil had been thrown up here and there by big shells, revealing shallow topsoil compared to Pennsylvania. But he didn't wish that he was back in Pennsylvania. The possibility never occurred to him. He was glad to be here. They were walking up to the forest. What would they find in it? He didn't know. He didn't even try to imagine. He was getting hungry because he hadn't eaten since early morning and a blister was forming on top of one toe, the result of getting a boot wet and having it shrink on his foot. What was he thinking about? Well, he wouldn't quite have been able to say if anyone had asked him. He was wondering where the farmers had gone who should be looking after their crops and whether those houses had been theirs at the crossroads? Beyond that he was thinking about his stomach and his blister and watching the box of cartridges rising and falling against Froggie's big behind ahead of him.

"Man, it's pretty," said Mastie, still looking at Froggie's behind.

"What?"

"The weather." It was — the skies were clear, the sun was out, and a little breeze was pushing the flowers. The flowers and the trees, they were the only things that hadn't turned refugee and fled the community.

Without thinking, the men raised their heads and looked at the sky. A plane was coming.

"Think he's bringing the paper?" said Churchill. "I really would like to see the paper. I mean, where are we?"

"What does it matter?" said Froggie again.

"If he drops it any place near us, you get it, Mastie. You're fast. There's going to be a hundred boys running after it." That's the way it always went. The paper, or maybe a handful of them, would start dropping out of the sky and it looked like it was coming right toward you, but by the time you got to it, there were a hundred boys waiting for it.

The plane came over the forest ahead and apparently didn't see the men right away because it didn't fly directly over them but seemed to be heading at an angle. It was going to cross their line.

The little thing looked like a bunch of orange crates pounded together, but there it was, floating along as gracefully as a butterfly over them, with two large black crosses painted on the undersides of its wings. Its shadow fell on the men and they looked up. Mastie thought he saw the goggles on the man's head.

"A black cross," said someone.

"Hey, a black cross! That's a Heinie," said Churchill. "I'm gonna nail him." He reached for his pistol.

"Nah, you can't hit him."

"Watch if I don't," He took out the pistol and held it at arm's length overhead and fired. There was a metallic ping. "I hit him. I hit him," yelled Churchill and began to load the pistol again. Suddenly the plane overhead swerved and a strange rat-tat-tat began. The grass seemed to come alive and hissed. Churchill dropped his pistol and ran for a tree.

"Every man for himself," yelled someone and jumped into a ditch. Mastie dropped his gun. He ran recklessly, throwing out his arms and legs, and crossed an old trench. He nearly bumped into an artillery wagon that was moving up, caught the horse's bridle and crawled under her neck, clinging to the neck with his eyes closed. He waited, expecting more bullets.

It was perfectly silent. He opened his eyes slowly and looked at the sky. He felt a hand on his collar. A large man was looking down at him.

"Let go of my horse," he said, and tightened his hand.

"Where's the plane?" said Mastie.

"What plane?"

"The Germans."

"What's that have to do with you holding my horse? We see planes every day," said the artillery man.

"He fired at us," said Mastie.

"So what? He's not going to stick around to get shot down. Let go of my horse."

The company was reforming on the road ahead and the heavy artillery, slow as it was, had already caught up with them. The lieutenant was angry and he went from man to man trying to find out who had fired the pistol at the plane. No one seemed to know. Mastie's squad was silent. They were all trembling. Their excellent spirits of twenty minutes ago had turned to fear of planes with machine guns, and fear was as contagious as good spirits.

"A plane never stands fire," said the lieutenant. "What kind of idiocy is this? Anybody who runs without an order in the future is going to be court-martialed and shot."

A messenger on horseback interrupted the lieutenant. The lieutenant read the message and frowned.

"March," he said. They entered the woods.

They walked through the woods a half hour or so, breathing the oxygen-sweet air. It was cool and smelled like moss. The squad was silent though — the German plane had done that to them. Churchill especially seemed under pressure. He was probably thinking of what *might* have happened. They came to a clearing and the lieutenant stopped and began to talk to his sergeants. They walked around the edge of the clearing and talked some more.

"I wish we had a paper," said Caloway, although he never read the papers. "Then we'd know where we are."

Froggie wandered off to the side a bit, probably to relieve himself. The men stood easily. Was something about to happen? Froggie came back with a double handful of something.

"Blackberries!" he said. His teeth were stained purple already from eating them. Mastie looked at the lieutenant up ahead and then at the little line of men behind them in the woods. It wasn't worth risking the lieutenant's wrath again. But Churchill immediately left the line. He brought back handfuls of blackberries. He was making restitution for his earlier mistake. The blackberries were sweet and full of juice.

The lieutenant turned around and waved.

"Move up." They moved forward another thousand feet to a spot where the woods opened up a bit into a natural meadow. On this side of the meadow there was a nursery of fir trees, planted perhaps by a French family who lived in the city, and almost a yard tall already. Beyond the open meadow the woods began again, thick and green. The men began to dig shallow trenches in the fir grove while the woods behind them began to crackle with men and horses. The artillery had caught up with them again and began to set up several hundred yards back in the woods. The lieutenant appeared among the fir trees, inspecting the row. They looked up at him casually.

"There's hostile cavalry up there someplace and running this way," he said. "How much I'm not sure. Everything's okay. We'll wait here. I don't want any man to fire his gun until I fire mine first. But when I fire, give them hell. Watch the woods. Any questions? No? You're hidden by the trees here, and they can't see you until they're so close that it's too late and by that time we have them. I have confidence in you."

The artillery began to fire behind in order to "soften up" the enemy a bit. Then they stopped. The men in the line waited.

"I need a smoke," said Caloway.

"Shh. . . ."

"We can whisper, can't we?"

The minutes stretched by and the men shifted positions in their trenches. Fifteen minutes. Thirty. Was he sure there was cavalry up there? Wouldn't it be all blown to bits by the artillery by now? Rest after the long morning hike would be good but this wasn't a rest at all. Everyone's eyes were on the far woods. An hour.

Mastie's mind began to wander. He was sitting up with his legs between the legs of the gun, his eye on Froggie's steel helmet halfway up the barrel of the machine gun. He looked at the other gunners on both sides of him, concealed in the long shallow trench. They were not alone. They were in this together, a squad connected to each other like Siamese twins. The tight feeling that Mastie had around his stomach was not his alone. It ran through invisible nerve filaments to every other member of his squad. A half year ago he hadn't known any of them and now his life depended on them. Their lives depended on him. Their faces were more familiar to him than anyone else he could remember just then. *My leg's going to sleep,* he thought.

"Mastie." The fat soldier was nudging his leg gently.

"What?"

"Look."

The meadow was still empty, and the woods? He didn't see anything.

"Where?"

"To the right."

He saw them, and then he thought he didn't. Their

gray uniforms and brown horses blended in with the tree trunks but it was their swords that betrayed them. Here and there they flashed dully and it was hardly more than the flash that a leaf makes when it turns over in the wind. Why the woods was full of them. Up and down. They began to move out in a long line against the edge of the woods and it appeared they were moving forward. Yes, they were moving forward because a space appeared between them and the woods now.

Mastie glanced back at the artillery. Had they seen? Yes, they had seen and were loading their rifles to defend themselves and the big guns. The horses were so close that shooting at them with the big guns meant risking hitting their own men hidden in the fir patch.

The horses began to gallop, massed together like wheat heads undulating before the wind. The ground began to vibrate and Mastie's hand moved down over his body involuntarily, feeling his neck and chest and legs as if to see if their flying, thundering hooves had touched him.

The lieutenant — was he aware? The lieutenant sat perfectly still behind his machine gun, looking out over the barrel a faint smile on his face. Was he daydreaming? Three hundred fifty yards away, then 300. Mastie swallowed and nudged the man beside him.

"Does he see them?" he whispered, meaning the lieutenant.

"I don't know. I hope."

The horses were so close now that they could hear them snorting clearly and Mastie thought he could see the faces of the men. They were intent, their eyes straight ahead. One hand held the reins while the other gripped their long swords. Two hundred yards and the riders suddenly swept their swords high over their heads. It was terribly beautiful. The sun glittered on the blades. Drops of cold sweat ran down along his ribs. He was sweating profusely. Surely now was the time to fire. A few moments from now and they would be cut to pieces. The ground was shaking violently and Mastie's finger fluttered on the trigger. He thought he would pull the trigger involuntarily and then he was afraid he wouldn't be able to pull it at all. His finger was sweating and slipping on the warm metal and he wanted to wipe it dry, but if he took his finger from the trigger perhaps it would be too late.

"Doesn't he see them?" whispered Froggie. He couldn't take his eyes from them now. One hundred and fifty yards. The horses seemed to grow in front of him. Then all together the horsemen yelled — a yell that turned the blood to ice water and made goose-pimples rise on his arms and scalp. Their faces were distorted, their mouths wide open, and their teeth like so many more sword blades ready to strike. The horses' mouths were open and contorted. It was all over. They had been tricked into lying here to wait. A hundred and thirty. Froggie's body pressed against his, his muscles tight. "Fire, fire," whispered Froggie intensely. His eye was fixed on a tall rider who wore a row of medals on his chest.

"Then a rattle began — a terrible rattle like the rattle of a rattlesnake spitting venom, and the entire line was a row of rattlesnakes striking. Venom hit the horses and their horsemen and the front row of horses went down, their riders tumbling over and over while the great mass of horses came on, leaping over the backs of the fallen and then, hit in midair by the line of rattlesnakes, falling themselves.

"Fire, fire!" shouted the lieutenant. "Fire harder."

Mastie hardly heard him. His finger was stiff on the trigger and he clung to his marvelous machine gun. It was performing a miracle. The unstoppable horsemen and their razor-sharp swords were falling. Their yells had turned to cries and now they were the ones who waited and struggled in fear for it all to end.

A horse came over the top, his rider dragging by one stirrup, and the bullets failed to get him. He leaped the line of guns and ran on in panic through the woods until the men in the artillery unit shot him down.

That beautiful mass of horses and men was down. The ones that weren't hit were caught in the bodies of the others and the horses reared wildly and neighed while their riders waved useless swords in the air or struck their horses on the flanks with the flat side.

"Keep firing," shouted the lieutenant. Here and there, especially in the rear, horsemen had broken loose and were running away, some on foot, a number still on their horses but leaning down along the far side, Indian fashion, to keep the horse's body between them and the bullets while they galloped for freedom. A group of doughboys ran after them with their rifles and the artillery soon began to chase them with its big shells.

The guns opened little red holes all over the pile of horses and men. They lay in every imaginable position, dying. Ten minutes ago they had been the pride of their country — young, powerful, and beautiful. In minutes they had been butchered and laid out to dry in the sun.

"Cease firing."

The men jumped up out of the little fir trees and Froggie threw his arms around Mastie and slapped his back.

"Bravo, bravo," shouted Froggie. "You were wonderful." He was laughing now that it was over and his teeth were still stained purple by the blackberries he had eaten.

All along the line the men were shouting and raising their fists triumphantly as they saw their friends coming out of the ditches.

"Were you scared, Caloway?"

"Who me? No more than you."

"How's come your pants are wet?"

Sure enough, the soldier had wet his pants. He was shaking all over and laughing. The men laughed at him.

"It's horse steaks tonight, boys. Tenderloin or T-bone?"

"I just wish I could have had one of those horses alive. Some beauties, eh?"

"Congratulations!" It was the commander of the artillery.

"Some bloody mess, eh?" said the lieutenant, shaking the commander's hand. "But it was either us or them."

"And I'm damn glad it was them," said the commander, and he chuckled.

3

How can a man shoot his enemy and then rush up with bandages to cover the wound? First it amazed Mastie, and then it only seemed natural.

The doughboys went to the assistance of the men they had shot down. Great numbers of the horses and men lay silent in the positions in which they had fallen, their wounds like a row of red ribbons pinned on their chests or backs. Other men heaved deeply once or twice and fell forward on their faces. But a number of the men and horses were still alive and struggling to get to their feet. The pile must have covered an acre. The cries of the men and horses were terrible. It seemed as though the ground itself was crying out.

Mastie found a tall man near the edge lying face up on the grass, his right leg completely out of sight under his horse. Mastie stood over the man, his revolver in his left hand. The man shook his head. "No, no," he said in English. Behind them a revolver cracked. They were killing a mangled horse. The man's face became desperate and he shook his head, repeating again and again. "No, no, no. . . ." Mastie reached down with one hand, but the man repeated again. "No, no." It was the revolver he was afraid of. Mastie put it back into his side pocket,
310

and the man immediately became more quiet and began to smile. He pointed to the wedding ring on his finger and began to talk in German.

"*Meine Frau*," he said and then gesturing with his hand began to talk about his children. It didn't seem at all strange to Mastie that thanks to his Pennsylvania Dutch background he could get the gist of what the man was saying.

"I won't hurt you. I understand," he said in Dutch.

"Thank you, thank you," the man said in English and he smiled again. He was thin-faced and blond-haired, maybe in his early thirties, and he had dark rings under his eyes as though he hadn't slept for several days. He was very pale. Probably from pain. The horse was not dead. It had been hit several times in the chest and once in the front leg and every half-minute or so it would make another effort to get up, pawing with its one foreleg and rolling its eyes around and then, puffing, it would fall back again and stretch out its neck. Each time it moved, the German groaned and tears filled his eyes. It must be painful, Mastie thought. He called Sanders. If the horse died, the problem would be compounded. They found a tree limb and shoved it under the horse's body the next time it moved to get up. That prevented the horse from falling back on the leg, but it wasn't far enough to get the leg out. For one thing, the foot was still in the stirrup and lying almost completely under the horse. They needed more help. Another man came and they tried putting a second limb under the horse, but now the horse wouldn't move at all. It appeared to be dying.

"You stay here by the man," said Mastie. "Let me try something." Years of working with horses had taught him that their mouths were more tender than anyplace else. He went to the horse's head and caught hold of the reins. "Now when I pull, you shove the stick under as far as it will go and, Caloway, I want you to get the man's foot out of the stirrup." He gave the reins a violent pull to the left and sure enough the horse made a tremendous effort to get up, lashing with his feet. He got up. "Watch out he doesn't fall back on you." The horse leaped out over the body of another horse and rider, threw his head up and ran down the mountainside.

"He won't go far," said Mastie.

The German had passed out, either from the effort or the relief on his leg. His foot was crushed and it appeared that several leg bones were broken, too, but other than that he was untouched. The medics came up to make a temporary splint for him and in no time they had him on his feet, hobbling with a makeshift crutch.

Most of the prisoners were already being herded back to the main American lines which weren't over two miles away. They took the prisoner to the lieutenant, who was examining another prisoner who had been left behind, in fact almost buried alive with the other dead, because he appeared dead also. A bullet had plowed a long red line along the top of his head and left him unconscious. He was lucky. He came back to life in time to flutter his eyelids and escape being buried alive. He couldn't have been more than sixteen — his face was hairless — but he had ridden his horse as well as the rest of them.

"Mastie? Froggie? One of you take these men back to the lines."

"I'll do it." The fat soldier got up off the ground

where he had been sitting. "Mastie needs rest." He looked at the two men. "Germans, huh? Lucky they weren't shot. So they get to die in a prisoner of war camp. How lucky can you get? Why don't we help this one out of his misery, lieutenant, let him pray and then. . . . He looks bad."

"He'll make it. Lose his leg maybe, but he'll make it," said the lieutenant. "Take them back."

Froggie took out his revolver and nudged the two men toward the trail.

"You're okay," said Mastie in Dutch. "He'll take you to camp." The man with the crushed foot clasped Mastie's hand between his.

"Thank you, thank you," he said and laughed. He was happy to be alive. He reached into his shirt and pulled out a long necklace chain with a locket on the end and opened it. Inside was a picture of a pretty woman with her hair in pompadours and signed, "*In Liebe, Ilse.*" He made a gesture of hugging some-one. "*Meine Frau,*" he said. "Thank you, thank you." He dropped the necklace over Mastie's head, waved gaily, and then hobbled down the trail ahead of the boy prisoner and Froggie.

Mastie turned back to the battle scene. He didn't watch the burial detail collecting bodies. Instead he walked up to a horse that was still pawing the ground, her neck arched magnificently but her backbone was broken.

"Look at all the good horses we killed," he said to a member of the burial detail. "Look at this bay. It's a shame, huh, but her back's broken. A horse like that would bring $300 in New Holland. Shoot her, would you? I can't."

"Where's New Holland?" said the soldier.

"New Holland? Why, in Pennsylvania," said Mastie. "Look at that neck, would you? What an arch!"

The burial detail finished in the woods and they returned with the Army chaplain who had come up to say a benediction over the bodies of the three hundred and fifty slain horsemen. No one bothered to bury the horses. It would have taken two days to dig a hole big enough. The wounded ones were shot to put them out of their misery.

Magically, it seemed, the kitchen appeared in the woods with their supper and the men of the artillery came running up. Mastie was sent on an errand back to the field telephone before eating and right in the middle of delivering the message he heard shots in the woods.

"What's that?" said the telephone operator.

"Snipers?" said Mastie.

"Couldn't be a raiding party, could it? Not coming from that direction." They peered through the woods, but it was getting dark. After twenty minutes or so, a man came up through the woods, walking. It was Froggie.

"Did you hear the shots?" said Mastie.

"Mine," said Froggie, and he shrugged his shoulders.

"What was it?"

"Those Huns."

"You shot the prisoners?" said Mastie, hardly believing.

"They tried to get away," said Froggie. "I had to."

"How could they run away? They were both wounded. The old man had a crushed foot. Where could he go? Tell me."

"Who knows? What are you so excited about?" said

the fat soldier and he came over and put his hand on Mastie's shoulder.

"Don't buddy-buddy me," said Mastie. "Anybody who can shoot two defenseless prisoners in cold blood ain't my buddy. The Germans may be murderers, but so are you. Defenseless! A sixteen-year-old boy and a man with a crushed foot. Where could they run, tell me that? You're a murderer! If you get your blood up, you kill anything, don't you? You'd shoot your own family, wouldn't you, if you had to? Or Maria."

Froggie suddenly came alive.

"Take it back, take it back," he said, and caught Mastie by the collar with one hand. "Don't mention her in the same breath with the Huns, you hear? Take it back."

Mastie twisted away again. He was quicker than the fat soldier.

"Take it back," said Froggie, and he ducked for Mastie's legs. Mastie raised one knee and Froggie bumped into it. He got up and spit. His mouth was bleeding.

"Cut it out," said the telephone operator.

"I want to say one thing first," said Froggie. "He says I'm so bad, but what do I do? I kill two men. Maybe they tried to get away, maybe they didn't. But he kills a hundred. Two hundred maybe. I saw him. Oh, but he is a fine gunner. When Mastie shoots the gun, everything goes down. He is a perfect shot. Everywhere we go, horses tumble this way and that, men fall upside down, rightside up, on their heads, on their bellies, under their horses, over their horses, on the bridge, off the bridge, maybe they drown, maybe they just fall overboard after they're shot. Maybe he gets them in the head, maybe he gets them in the heart, but he gets them. Tell me, how many did you kill? How many? And I killed two because I am only the ammunition carrier. So you think I am the bad boy? Well, there's the kitchen bell. I'm going for my potatoes and meat. Think about it."

Mastie found them along the trail where they had fallen. Their feet were almost on the trail and they had been shot in the back. He sat down and buried his head in his hands. He saw them again in his mind, riding toward him with their terrible bright swords over their heads and whooping so that it seemed his backbone would peel loose and curl up and his fingers turn to jelly, the ground moving beneath him like jello and then the gun, firing away quietly and confidently while the terrible army melted away before his eyes like Little Black Sambo's tigers turning to butter. How many had he killed? Two? Twenty? A hundred? Three hundred? He opened his eyes and looked into the smiling face of the horseman with the crushed foot, holding out his locket and pointing at the picture. "*Meine Frau, meine Frau,*" he said, and laughed happily.

What if it had been me, he thought. *What if they had swept over us and captured us and I had shown them my picture of Annie. Would they understand who she was? Mastie Stoltzfus, missing in action. Would she cry for me?* "Annie!" he said. He was sure now that he would never see her again. He tore off the German woman's necklace and put it into the soldier's pocket.

The chaplain and several soldiers came to look for him after an hour, and the chaplain sat down beside him on a stone while the other soldiers stood back out

316

of sight. If they had to take him back forcibly, they had to be ready for that, too, the chaplain explained. The chaplain put his arm around Mastie's shoulder.

"It's Chaplain Harlan," he said. "Are you ready to go back now?"

"I can't," said Mastie. He shook his head. "I can't."

"What's wrong?" said the chaplain. "Tell me about it."

"I killed hundreds of men," said Mastie.

"Today?" the chaplain said.

"Yes, today. You said a prayer over them, but it didn't do no good. They're in hell, like I'll be in hell when my turn comes. My Pop was right. He told me the truth." He kept shaking his head.

"Stoltzfus, you're too hard on yourself," said the chaplain. "War and murder are two different things. Murder, the Lord says, is wrong. 'Love thy neighbor as thyself,' the Scriptures say, and again, 'Thou shalt not kill.' But the Bible also tells us in Romans, 'Let love be genuine: hate what is evil, hold fast to what is good,' and in Romans 13, 'But if you do wrong, be afraid, for he [that is the government] does not bear the sword in vain, he is the servant of God to execute his wrath on the evildoer.'"

"Then it is right to kill them?" said Mastie. "Jesus would do it?"

"Stoltzfus," the chaplain said, and he gripped the boy's hard shoulder. "I could not do the work I am doing until I could see Jesus himself sighting down a gun barrel and running a bayonet through an enemy's body."

"You lie!" said Mastie. "He wouldn't."

"No, Stoltzfus, I also shrank from associating Jesus

with the gun and I tried to put into his hands the sword which he himself allows in the New Testament. But then I reflected that the sword, which we no longer use, was in his day the most terrible weapon of mutilation and destruction. One night shortly after I joined our boys I had a dream in which I saw heaven open and I saw the Son of God. He wasn't mounted on a white horse or dressed in white garments sprinkled with blood as John, the Revelator, pictures him. He wasn't carrying a sharp sword with which to smite the nations.

"Rather, through clouds of gas and smoke I saw him dressed in our olive drab, stained with blood and mud, and in his hands he held a rifle. He didn't ask any man to go where he wouldn't go. He didn't lead his men up to the painful and bloody job which climaxes the big battle and then disappear just when the disagreeable deed had to be done — and I know how disagreeable it is. It goes against the grain, yes. — No, he stood right there in the center of the line at the very front in the thickest of the fight and I heard him say quiet words to assure the hearts of his company: 'Lo, I am with you always, even unto the end.' It's that Christ, Christ the judge of evil men, whom we are teaching the enemy to fear."

"I don't believe it," said Mastie. "I don't believe a word of it. Who says they're all evil men? Some are innocent."

"Innocent!" exploded the chaplain. "Haven't you read the papers, man? Everywhere they go, they murder civilians like so many grasshoppers, rape the women, and shoot the prisoners."

"We shoot prisoners. Look. Look. Two hours ago, they were prisoners."

"Maybe they tried to run. . . ."

"With a crushed foot?" said Mastie, pointing at the bandaged leg of the dead prisoner.

"I believe God is speaking to you through this experience," said the chaplain.

"God!" said Mastie, and suddenly he laughed. "God! Haha!"

"Why are you laughing?"

"God!" said Mastie, and he laughed again.

4

The next day they dug in on the edge of an oats field that ran for a quarter of a mile or so between two stretches of woods, the one behind, where they had defeated the cavalry charge, and the one ahead, where the main body of the retreating German infantry could be seen, digging in trenches that ran for a mile or so in length along their edge of the oats field. The oats were ripe and unharvested. Flocks of starlings occasionally flew in to help themselves, but no other living creature dared to stick his head up in that quarter mile section of no-man's-land. For three days the artillery of both sides pounded each other until it seemed there couldn't possibly be anything left on either side. Raiding parties from both sides were caught and shot up in the oats field. On the evening of the third day, though, for some reason buried in the heads of the American commanders, the artillery was ordered to stop firing, and within a half hour the German artillery stopped. The quiet was unbelievable. It couldn't last . . . but it did somehow, for one hour, then two.

Froggie was the first one to break the silence in the machine gunners' shallow trench.

"I'm taking a bath," he said, and climbed out. "If I'm going to die, then I die clean. I hate body smells."

The men waited — would a sniper with glasses in a tree take a potshot at him? Nothing happened, though — no one ordered him back in. He stripped to his shorts and dropped his clothes beside a large shell hole that was filled to overflowing with water, even clean water, because a little stream ran in and out of it. He waved at several artillery men who were back a hundred yards or so in the woods and dipped his helmet into the shell hole. He dumped the water down over his back and shrieked, "Ooh, mama!" It was cold. He threw his hands over his head and did an imitation of a belly dance, his great stomach flopping up and down in rhythm. Then he switched to a piece of Italian opera, and his tenor carried the whole way along the trench. "*O sole mio. . . .*" He held his hands together on his naked belly and rolled his eyes around in his skull. For all the world he looked like one of those fat singing cherubs carved here and there in the great music halls of the world.

"All I need now is a little juice to drown the microbes in my stomach. Anyone, come on, help a fellow out. Is that all you appreciate the special feature of the evening . . . one, two, three, mama!" and he did the belly dance again. "It needs water." He dipped a helmet full of cold water again and pulled it down on his curly black head, "Mama!" The water ran out from under the helmet and down across his dancing body. He looked ridiculous. Someone started to clap.

"Give us the opera again." They weren't watching the enemy line anymore. They were turned around watching the Manhattan boy, but there wasn't much danger of a surprise. There were plenty of artillery men and officers with binoculars constantly watching the other line. A dozen or so men came out of their trenches, although they did leave their guns in ready-to-fire positions so that with a jump and a grab they could repel the first raiding party to venture out of the oats.

Froggie had gotten a bottle from somewhere. Someone had risked his career to bring along a bottle. Risk? That was a strange word. How could one risk anything more when his life was already only a quarter of a mile or so from destruction?

Froggie took a swallow and it did to his inside what the mountain water had done to his outside. It burned the whole way down. "Hot mama! and welcome to the club. Would you like a swallow, would you? Only if you first take a drink of this down your back. Come on, give those cooties some air. I baptize you in the name of the . . ." and he gave the soldier three flings of water, one for each member of the Trinity.

"Ooooh. . . ." The soldier squealed.

Mastie joined another group outside the trench. They were sitting on the ground with their clothes spread out in front of them, jerking their fingers through the seams of their uniforms in search of lice. When they found one, they dropped him into a can that was suspended over a candle.

"*Brothers . . . my own ridiculous brothers!*" It was Froggie, dressed only in his soaked shorts and Army helmet, singing out his greeting. He grinned at them as he dropped his hand dramatically over the tin can. "Only one lice to die for my country," he said sadly.

"One?" said Churchill incredulously. "Why they just love that fat body with all its mountains and val-

322

leys and forests of hair. I'll bet Froggie's even got a special breed of lice. Here look . . ." and he reached above Froggie's ear and held his fingers up to the light of the setting sun. "Look at it, would you? Hey! It's wearing a gas mask! And it's got a helmet and a private's stripes and a little machine gun! It's a shame to kill it, don't you think? But then, it has a lot of brothers — ridiculous brothers — left in the world, so . . ." He dropped the louse, real or imaginary, into the tin.

Froggie didn't seem to mind the insult. He tipped Mastie's helmet down over his eyes and sat down beside him.

"Cut it out."

"What's wrong with you? Don't you love me anymore?" He put a big arm around Mastie. "Am I really such a bore?"

"Cut it out."

"What's wrong with him?"

"He's been a grouch the last couple days," said Churchill. "You didn't notice?"

"Is it me?" said Froggie.

"Yes, it's you, doughnut," said Churchill.

"Well, what's wrong? I can't read minds, unless it's still that cavalry officer. . . ."

"I won't forget him," said Mastie. "It wasn't right."

"Well, who said it was right? Is this a confession box or something? I thought it was a war."

"So, now we can shoot anyone — it's a war. I'm sick of you, so I'm going to shoot you. Just like this." He pointed his imaginary machine gun at Froggie and shouted, "Ba-ba-ba-ba-ba-bum!"

"Is this man okay?" said Froggie.

"Cut it out," said Mastie.

"Okay, I'm sorry I did it to them. Now what?"

"Don't say you're sorry. It's not your fault. It's the whole business. I shot more than you did."

"What's wrong?" said Churchill.

"I shot some prisoners," said Froggie.

"So what? It happens."

"Well, he didn't like it. He took a liking to the one, I guess, because the man showed him his wife's picture."

"Still a Heinie, wasn't he?" said Churchill.

"You're soft, Mastie," said Froggie. "Sure it's people we're shooting. What did you think — we're on a pheasant hunt or something? Who took my bottle? Who took my bottle?"

Caloway grinned sheepishly and brought it out from under his uniform shirt.

"Drowning your cooties in it, are you?"

"No, I just thought — "

"You wanted a drink. Okay, take one. Hurry up." Caloway uncorked the bottle and tipped it to his mouth. Froggie reached across the fire and tipped the bottom of the bottle to the sky so that the cheap red wine filled Caloway's mouth and ran down his chin and into his nose. He came up sputtering and coughing. "Good stuff, huh? And now, I take a sip." He gurgled once and the last quarter of the bottle ran down his throat. He threw the bottle into the crater and began to sing.

"Oh, Marie, Oh Marie, you're the stars and planets to me . . ." and as he sang he put his arm around Caloway and tenderly touched his forehead, then patted his cheeks.

"Oh, Marie, Marie, may I kiss you? What nice red lips you have, Marie. What, you won't let me kiss you?

Nasty girl. What beautiful ears you have, Marie."
Everyone laughed because Caloway had cauliflower
ears, "And your neck — what a nice neck, so nice
and white and clean." And that was strange because
Caloway's hadn't been washed for three weeks, just as
nobody else's had. "And what nice — Marie! What's
wrong? You've lost them! Marie, Marie, what will we
ever do? How can I love a girl without — Brothers,
I don't want to embarrass such a nice girl by
mentioning it in public like this, in front of all
these people, and especially in front of all those
people over there with binoculars, but Marie just
isn't all here. One ringy-dingy, two ringy-dingies
missing."

For the last two days Caloway had been living in
turmoil. The lieutenant had ordered him to another
squad that was having personality clashes, effective as
soon as a lull in the fighting came. Caloway was
crushed. He had pleaded with the lieutenant
with tears in his eyes to let him stay in this squad.
These were his friends, the only ones he had in
the company. The rest of the squad took up his cause
and not more than ten minutes ago, word had come
from the lieutenant. He was not being transferred.
Caloway was overjoyed. So it was good to be embarrassed — he was one of them again.

"I always carry Maria with me, see!" said Froggie,
and he jingled a locket that was on a chain sewed
fast to his shorts. "And when the whizzbangs are going overhead I just reach down and pull up Maria
like this, and open her up, and there she is. . . ."

"A curl!"

"Sure, oh, she has fine black curls, and she is like
— Brothers, I am going to have to have another

bottle to sharpen up my memory of Maria."

Of course they wanted to hear about Maria. It was no problem to run down and buy another bottle off the same fellow who had brought the first one. Where did he get them anyway? The soldier didn't want to tell, but he did reveal where he had found the chocolate bars he sold Sanders, the Alabama boy, for black-market prices. A German cavalry officer had carried them in his uniform pocket the whole way to his death under the machine gun fire, and it didn't hurt the candy a bit to have a bullet hole through it and a bit of blood dried on the outside paper. "Chocolate don't melt or get moldy under gunfire. It's still all right, you know. In that respect, it's superior to human life, eh?" said the soldier to persuade Sanders to pay his price.

The sun had set and it got dark but a moon came up with a skyful of stars. It was going to be a beautiful day tomorrow.

"Here's your bottle, Froggie."

"Aha, now as I was saying, aaah, mama! Is that good! Mastie, take a drop — it'll revive you. Where were we? Ah, yes, Maria. I don't know if I want to tell you about Maria."

"Hey, give that bottle back then," said Sanders, grabbing for it.

"No, you don't. No, you don't. Why should I tell you about her? You'll want her then."

"No, we won't," said Caloway.

"Okay then," said Froggie, "Now Maria isn't one of these little French girls. She's big, something to put your arms around. . . ."

"Mastie." There was a voice at his shoulder. The light from the fire they had built showed it

326

was Churchill.

"What's wrong?"

"I have a premonition, Mastie, and it scares me. I have to tell someone."

"You have what?"

"A premonition — a feeling."

"Oh."

"Listen, I haven't told anybody this before. But we're jumping off tomorrow, you know. You didn't know? Yes, I got it confidentially from the lieutenant, but there will be an announcement a little later. I thought you'd heard."

"We're advancing? Into those guns?"

"They won't get you, Mastie. You don't have the look. And they won't get me either. I know it. I can feel it. I have a mystical power, Mastie, that I can't explain. Nothing will hit me as long as I keep that power. It comes from an absolute belief in the power of mind over matter. I can go through barrage, I can go through machine gun fire, because my will can turn aside explosive shells and machine gun bullets. You don't believe it, do you? But it's true. What are bullets compared to the mind of a man who is in touch with the great Universal Spirit of this world, as I am?"

"You're crazy."

"Maybe so, but it works. I found it out in college when I would concentrate on someone very intensely and in a few minutes he would come over and speak to me, every time. Then I found that by concentrating when I was on the soccer field, not laughing and talking foolish like a lot of players do, I could make the soccer ball come in my direction. Sure, someone kicked it, but he kicked it in my direction, even a player of the opposite team when he didn't want to.

"But it worries me because I can also tell by looking into a man's eyes and by watching his actions
which man will be killed tomorrow. And it's Caloway,
Mastie, I can see it written all over him. He's going
to be killed."

"Shh. . . ."

"It worries me. I mean, I'm sorry now that I
have that ability, even though I know I won't be
hit. You're smart . . . tell me what I should do."

"I don't know."

Churchill became silent.

" . . . Maria . . ." said Froggie. "So what if
she's big, and we'll get the best Catholic priest to
marry us. Very religious like. She's *very* religious,
Maria is, and then we'll get ourselves a little sec-
ond-story apartment in the Bronx and on Sunday
nights we'll sit on the porch, me and Maria . . . the
kids down in the yard eating a watermelon maybe.
Oh, yes, we'll have lots of kids. A cellar full of kids
because I love them and it's fun making them. What
are you laughing about, Caloway? Laugh, laugh,
that's all you do tonight. Well, we'll sit on that
porch eating tamales and tortillas and big, burping
enchiladas and little weensy hot peppers that make
you cry. Yes, brothers," he said in a solemn voice
like the voice of that priest himself.

"O, give me a home where the buffalo roam," Froggie sang melodiously. It had to come out of
that flabby chest somewhere because he didn't
have any clothes that could have produced the music.
His voice rose, "Home, home on the range, where
the skies are not cloudy all day. . . ." Then the men
around the fire joined him, singing away and scour-

ing their clothers with their fingers. The men down the trench started singing and now Froggie stood up and let his voice roll on the chorus. They clapped when the song ended.

"More, more," and suddenly they grew silent. Who was that? It came out of the woods on the far side of the oats field, a little faint for having gone a quarter of a mile, but it was "Home on the Range" all right. In German. The whole German trench was singing. The American trench clapped wildly and the men stood up and were unafraid now. A good volley of artillery fire would have blown the line apart. They sang "My Bonnie Lies over the Ocean" and the Germans responded again. It was like a game, back and forth for an hour, antiphonally: "Swanee River, "Silent Night" (even though it was five months from Christmas). Sometimes the chorus across the field didn't know the song and then they would wait until it was finished and begin a song of their own.

A shot rang out and everybody jumped. They grabbed their clothes and dived for the trench. Was that really an enemy soldier in the oats or was it a young lieutenant who wanted the boys to get back in the trench and get some sleep so they would be ready to advance at 5:30 with their guns firing and their eyes open? In any case, that was a signal to the light artillery behind to open fire again.

The holiday was over. The war was on.

5

Very early in the morning the big guns boomed and practically lifted Mastie out of his trench. He was lying on the dirt, wrapped up in an Army blanket that had once been green. There was no going back to sleep. The lieutenant was shouting at them, but even his voice was almost drowned by the big guns. You had to stand beside a man to talk to him.

On all sides, men of the machine gun company were getting up — it wasn't hard because they had slept with their clothes and shoes on. There was nothing to say. It was morning again.

But to Churchill, even a morning on the front was a miracle. He was dancing about, polishing off his gun barrel, and whistling some forgotten symphony. "Today we get 'em," he said, and pounded his fist into his palm. Mastie was glad they weren't on the same gun. He wasn't sure he could tolerate Churchill.

"This round for the Kaiser himself," Their guns were hardly fifteen feet apart on the wall of the trench. "What day is it?" said Churchill cheerfully.

"Friday."

"No, it can't be, because it was Friday when we came through the city. It hasn't been two weeks, has it?"

330

"Then it must be Tuesday."

"Maybe it's Tuesday, and that would make it July, wouldn't it? We're in July, aren't we? My birthday's in July, you know."

"I don't know. Give me part of that bread, and don't eat it all yourself." They had lost all sense of time.

"Commence firing," the lieutenant shouted, and the row of machine guns began to sputter. What were they shooting at? Mastie wondered. It was hard to tell. There was no enemy in sight since the oats field ahead of them blocked out their view of everything, but there were enemy guns over there. He could hear the heavy shells whistling overhead. Furthermore, a fog lay across the middle of the field.

He didn't know the day, he didn't know where they were — oh, roughly northeast France, but was the other side of the oats field Germany? — he didn't know what he was firing at, except that the lieutenant had told him to fire. The roar of the guns was too great to hear anything else by now. Ahead of the machine gun trench, the infantry was crouched in their trench with the machine gun bullets flying several feet over their heads. They were waiting for the jump off.

Froggie pointed across the oats field. Germans! They were coming out of the fog with their guns ready. The infantry got down in their trenches and took aim. The enemy fell into the oats field. Was it a fake? Had they dropped down to crawl through the oats until they suddenly burst into the American trench to jab them one by one with their bayonets? There was no time to think about it. Another line of Germans appeared through the fog, running at them and this time the machine guns came down to catch them. They vanished like so much fog.

The big guns stopped and the machine guns stopped. The soldiers in the front trench got up out of their trench and began to run into the oats field. The sun had just come up and it shot through the clouds of fog and touched helmets and bayonets here and there, and then the fog swallowed up their legs.

"Beautiful!" said someone. Mastie turned around to see who was talking. It was Churchill. Tears were running down his face.

"What wrong with you?"

"It's beautiful. It's just like a painting." But the enemy had caught sight of the American charge because their guns began to go off.

"Forward," shouted the lieutenant, and the machine gunners came out of their trenches and began to run. The oats brushed against Mastie's legs. He couldn't help but notice the grain was ripe. It was ready to harvest and where was the farmer? "Take cover." Ahead of them in the grass lay the first row of Americans, their guns aimed toward the woods on the other side of the field.

Froggie dropped and, because Mastie was carrying the gun and running a little slower as they came over the brow of the little hill, he saw the big artillery shell coming, whistling some symphony of its own, right at Sanders and Fahnestock. He yelled and then it hit. There was a red puff and bits of clothing and flesh were sticking all over his arms. His own shirt was torn off his back by a fragment and his pouch of food with the little box of strawberries was completely blown away. Mastie dropped into the oats. His whole body was trembling.

"Sanders and Fahnestock," he said. "They got Sanders and Fahnestock — a shell," and he motioned with his hands to show how big the shell was while he set up his own gun in a frenzy. They began to fire into the woods, but between rounds they could hear someone crying over on the left.

"Must be Caloway," said Mastie, but he didn't want to believe it. "Maybe he's hit. I'm going to see." He crawled through the oats on his hands and knees and the nearer he got the more evidence of the end of Sanders and Fahnestock he found. Parts of them were scattered all over the last five feet and there was Caloway, lying in the oats on his stomach.

"Caloway, it's me."

"Come here," said Caloway, reaching out one hand to Mastie and pulling on his shoulder sleeve. "I'm hit," he said. "Here." He rolled over and showed the red hole where a tiny fragment had gone right through his stomach.

"You'll be okay," said Mastie. He pulled off the boy's shirt and tore a long strip to wrap around his stomach. The fragment had not come out. It was in there someplace — they'd have to operate to get it.

"No more fried chicken for a while," said Caloway and he laughed a little in spite of his pain. "You won't leave me here, will you?" His face was full of fear.

"We'll get you back to a hospital in short order. We have them pinned down in the woods now and when I get a chance I'll take you back. Does it hurt? Is that too tight?"

"It doesn't hurt," said Caloway. "It seems like a

small wound, doesn't it?"

"You'll be okay," said Mastie.

"Sanders and Fahnestock," said Caloway, and his eyes were full of knowledge. Mastie nodded.

"I'll give you my strawberries," he said, and reached back to take the little container off his back, only to discover that it had been blown off, clean away, along with his pack and a great section of his shirt. "Good God!" he said, and felt the hole with amazement. He ran his hands up and down his back, but no, there wasn't a scratch. "Look at that — they got my strawberries and the shirt off my back." He laughed. "My guardian angel," he said and pointed at the sky. "Well, my water's still intact." He handed the canteen to Caloway who rolled over weakly and took it with one hand and emptied it.

"It's hot," said Caloway. His clothes were soaked with sweat. The fog had cleared and the sun was shining down brightly on the oats field, but Mastie was shivering. He rubbed his hands to get warm. He kept hearing artillery shells and ducking. He patted the boy's shoulder and began to crawl back through the oats field.

"Thank you," shouted Caloway. "Thank you. You'll come back?" Then he was quiet again.

The artillery from the German lines stopped.

"Here they come," said Froggie. Line after line of Germans began to come out of the woods. The American line fired gamely, then leaped to their feet. The lieutenant was calling a retreat.

"Take the gun," said Mastie. He ran for Caloway, picked him up and carried him across both shoulders. Retreating soldiers passed him on both sides, and one of them shouted.

334

"Put him down! Put him down!"

He dropped the wounded soldier in the oats and began to run a zigzag path back through the oats, while the air buzzed around him. He was the last man into the trenches.

"I thought they had you," said Froggie.

The Germans now held the top of the hill and were lying in the oats where five minutes before Mastie and his buddies had been. Occasionally a spiked helmet flashed. In the evening they still held over half of the field in spite of two or three American charges. The Germans had brought up machine guns and it was impossible to charge. Someplace between here and there, Caloway lay among the wounded.

Night came, a beautiful night with a skyful of stars and a warm breeze. But the breeze brought the cries of the wounded. All night long they groaned and Mastie couldn't sleep. He was about to drowse off when another particularly loud moan came, hardly more than a hundred feet in front of their trenches. Then he heard Caloway. He was sure it was Caloway because he was calling, "Mastie . . . Churchill . . . Mastie . . . Churchill!"

He woke Churchill.

"I hear Caloway. Do you want to risk it?"

They crawled out across the field on their hands and knees. Occasional shells were still flying overhead. Someone was awake over there. But he couldn't remember where he had dropped the boy, and in the dark it was difficult to judge distance. He came to numerous wounded soldiers, each time crawling almost on top of the man before he saw him. He emptied his canteen giving drinks. Churchill was directly behind him — they almost had to hold onto each other to keep from getting separated. Finally they decided to separate and cover more territory.

"Help!" It was Caloway, he was sure, about a hundred feet to the left. He began to crawl in that direction.

"Caloway!"

He put his hand down on someone and the man moved and gasped.

"*Kamerad. Bitte!*" It was a German soldier.

"Would you like some water?" Mastie said in Dutch. He gave the man a few sips and crawled on. Had he accidentally moved behind the German lines? He stuck his head up. He could see the top of the hill over there and that was where they were. A machine gun began to fire. A gunner had seen his helmet against the light-colored oats. He ducked and ripe heads of oats tinkled on his helmet and fell down inside his collar. They had a bead on him. He began to crawl rapidly and the gun followed him, shooting the heads off the oats behind him. He lay still and after a while the gun stopped.

Now he had no idea where he was going and he wouldn't risk sticking his head up again. How could he get back? The stars, of course. He turned over on his back and looked up for the Big Dipper and North Star. What if the stars were different in France? No, there they were. Knowing the sun had come up in the morning over the German lines, they were east, or to the right of the North Star. The opposite direction, or west, must therefore be his lines. He began to crawl and finally he heard English voices ahead.

"Don't shoot. It's Stoltzfus." He called out.

Churchill and Froggie were there to welcome him. Froggie slapped his back.

"I thought they had you," he said.

"No sign of Caloway?"

"No sign."

Almost at that moment they heard him again, calling. This time Mastie was sure he knew where he was if he crawled straight for that spot. He crawled out again but in another hour he was back. No luck. Morning was breaking.

For ten days they faced each other across the oats field and for the first three nights Mastie and several buddies crawled out looking for Caloway. At first they heard him strong and clear someplace, mocking their rescue efforts by the way he seemed to jump around. Only a few hundred feet separated them. If it were light, they could all link hands and find him in five minutes. But when it was light, no soldier would have risked it.

Caloway's calls became weaker and weaker, and now it was hard to tell if it was the wind or a voice. The field began to stink. When the wind blew the smell into their trench, some soldiers put on gas masks, it was so bad.

The voices had stopped calling from the oats field.

6

They made a splendid advance.

On the morning of the eleventh day the artillery threw enough shells just over their heads and into the enemy lines to sizzle up that little oats field and tract of woods. When the infantry went out at nine they found no one there, only a field covered with the dead of both sides like so many decaying black leaves. The German line had left during the night.

The men were hardened. They advanced all day through artillery shells and past hundreds of bodies in the woods as unconcerned as if they were a high school hiking club. All they were conscious of was that they were tired, hungry, and dirty after four weeks on the move.

In the evening they came to a narrow farming valley with a village at the head of it. The villagers ignored them as they marched through. They were French but had been behind German lines for four years. They had learned to cope. When the soldiers came through, they didn't so much as turn their heads, though they knew they were Americans. Soldiers were soldiers, and war was occurring around them, but they went on farming. A mile or two ahead the retreating army was burning villages and the smoke could be seen plainly. They were only happy their village hadn't been important enough to burn. They looked at the Americans as if to say, What are you soldiers about to do?

Mastie let his eyes run in wonder over the town.

In ten minutes they had passed through it. On the far side they came to a farm and the lieutenant went to the door to ask permission to stay there. The people were not home, although the house looked recently occupied. The men at the barn were already busy. Five or ten of them went into the pasture with their rifles and began to shoot the cows, at first picking only the healthy looking heifers that would be most tender, but as more and more men arrived and began to build fires in the meadow to roast huge steaks over, they went on shooting more until the entire herd of fifty or sixty cows was shot and roasting on knives, sticks, and bayonets over the fires. There was a shortage of good wood, so several men broke down grain sheds for fuel and when the artillery arrived they fed the grain and hay to their horses.

The lieutenant could have stopped the whole thing at the beginning, but it was soon out of his control. Apparently he figured it better to pay the farmer afterward than to deprive his men — they hadn't eaten decently in two weeks.

The ducks and chickens were more difficult. They flew noisily from fence post to fence post but there were soon more men than posts. They grabbed the birds one by one and wrung their necks, hardly taking time to pull the feathers off before they put the birds over the fire.

The house was declared off limits and the lieutenant had placed armed guards around the porches, but after a while a cry went up for salt and there wasn't any because the kitchens were still back in the woods with the main body of the artillery, so the lieutenant gave one man permission to search the house for salt. He found some, and he also located a huge crock of pickles, which he brought out, carrying the bag of salt in his teeth.

About that time a spring wagon with a man and two women came in the lane. It was the farmer and his family. The farmer stopped the horses and stood up in the wagon, his mouth wide open. He began to shake his head and shout angrily. A crowd of soldiers came up. He sat down again and burst into tears. His daughter screamed. No one was harming her — it was simply that forty men who hadn't seen a girl in weeks were staring at her, drooling over her as though she were the last piece of bread on earth.

The lieutenant ordered the men back. He reached up to the man and put his hand on his knee and shook it. The man shook his head.

"We will pay," the lieutenant said. He reached into his pocket and took out a wad of franc notes and pressed them on the man. "It's only a start, I want you to know," he said, "but my men are hungry. What was I to do? It's your country we're defending, you know." The woman and her daughter began to weep and hold onto each other.

The farmer could not understand English, nor could he understand the lieutenant's combination of French and English. He looked up fiercely. He picked up his whip and started beating the horse. The horse wheeled around and the soldiers scattered. He went out the lane, leaving the lieutenant standing there with a handful of franc notes. The lieutenant shrugged his shoulders and went to the house.

The men kept throwing wood on the fires and then one by one they fell asleep in the meadow and barn, their stomach full, their clothes and shoes still on.

The lieutenant slept in the house with the armed guards to make sure that it wasn't pillaged. He was determined to save the house.

In the morning the men were free to move about as they wished after they had dug a few positions around the front of the farm. It appeared that the German army was on the run — two or three miles away pillars of smoke and fire rose over little towns, marking their retreat. They were destroying supplies and food that they didn't want to let fall into American hands. In command of one of the highest points of the countryside, the lieutenant ordered his men to rest, before continuing the chase.

The soldiers found the pond behind the farm house. It looked as if it might have been used to irrigate, because a canal ran away from it toward the fields. The pond was covered with algae, but what did that matter? The man who discovered it gave a big shout and everybody came running. They peeled off their clothes and left them in piles on the bank. The water was full of naked white and brown bodies, oblivious of the guns not more than a mile and a half away.

Oh, it was glorious. The pond was so full of men that the water spilled over the edges like a bathtub with a fat man in it. Mastie was swimming about up to his ears in water with a veil of algae on his head. His hair hadn't been cut for weeks. It was long again. He began to laugh and laugh.

"What are you laughing at, Stoltzfus?"

"So nice. So nice," he said and sank right out of sight. A moment later he came bobbing to the surface shooting water out of his mouth like a gargoyle. He hadn't seen his whole body for a month. Was the scar still there below his ribs where the cow had gored him? Did he still have a belly button? The dirt refused to come off his toenails — they were stained black. Three feet away Churchill stood, completely naked, pouring water over himself with his helmet and singing at the same time. Why, he even wore his glasses in the water.

"Asperges me, Domine, hyssopo, et mundabor, lavabis me, et super nivem deabor."

"What was that?"

" 'Thou shalt sprinkle me with hyssop, O Lord, and I shall be cleansed. Thou shalt wash me and I shall be made whiter than snow.' Only it isn't true, I've scrubbed myself with this piece of soap three times now and I can't get clean." He poured another hatful of water over himself.

The next time Mastie went down, he felt a big hand over his nose as he came up. He spluttered.

"Shh. . . ." It was Froggie. "What we need now is girls."

"Girls?"

"Sh. . . . I know where there are two just waiting for some American boys. Yesterday when I saw them they said, Come.' Well? You interested? I've done you some dirt, that's all this is — *dirt*, but now let me do something nice for you and introduce you to a girl. Caresses . . ." he touched Mastie's shoulder. "Flowers . . ." and he pretended to smell one. "A

342

little laughter and then the bed. Not hard ground but a bed. . . . How do you like that? Let's go. Too bad there's only two. Churchill will just have to go on with his bath."

They got out of the water and their clothes were dry already from the wind and sun.

"Where are you going?" said Churchill.

"Back to bed," said Froggie.

"What's wrong with you? We get a free day and you spend it sleeping."

"I don't know if I'll be able to sleep," said Froggie, and he yawned mightily and pulled on his shirt. "He won't be following us," he said when they got back in the meadow. They cut off two large pieces of meat from one of the cows that was lying on the ground like an open butcher shop, one of the few remaining after last night's feast, and it surely wouldn't be left by tonight. Nothing edible, anyway. They were only taking their share.

"I don't know," said Mastie. "I don't want to catch some disease."

"No danger at this house," said Froggie.

They cut across the field and into town and only now did they begin to see the damage that had been done in town. The people who saw them ducked back into their houses, and most of them were old people who were not useful to war in any form. They were simply living out the war, hoping to hold on to their homes.

They went down a narrow alley and into a sunny garden behind. A woman was standing in the garden under a flowering tree, peeling peaches, it seemed. She must have been middle-aged. She certainly wasn't pretty, although she may once have been. Her sleeves were rolled up. Froggie touched her arm. She turned and held the pan of peaches between them. She opened her mouth to scream.

Froggie held up his hands and closed his eyes. We won't hurt you, his action implied. He opened his eyes and gestured — he was embracing a girl and giving a present. He held back his arm to Mastie and Mastie lay the meat, wrapped in a clean shirt, in his hands. Froggie unwrapped the meat and it looked beautiful, red and marbled with fat. At least the cows weren't suffering from the war. The woman pointed her finger at herself and looked up questioningly. Froggie nodded. The woman began to laugh.

"Lise, Lise," she shouted, never taking her eyes from the meat. The second-floor window of the house flew open and Lise looked out. She looked like the first woman's older sister — she had once been fat but hunger and hard work had obviously reduced her — although she was still heavy. The first woman said something in rapid French and Lise began to laugh and laugh. She pointed to herself incredulously. But she was looking at the meat, too. The younger sister washed her hands at the pump and led them into the house and up a narrow stairs.

"They're old," said Mastie.

"But willing," said Froggie, "and clean. If you close your eyes, all women are the same." The two women laughed again over their good fortune when they unwrapped the meat. The younger sister ran and got a pot and hung it over a wood fireplace that had been burning when they came in. Apparently there was a lot of wood around. Lise got out two dishes and set them on the table. She looked at Froggie.

344

"*T'as faim?*" (Are you hungry?) she said, and gestured toward her stomach. He nodded his head. She got out two more plates, but Froggie held up his hands.

"Just a minute. We didn't come just to eat. What about this?" He signified a kiss and took off his shirt.

"Yes, yes," the younger sister said in English and she kissed Mastie on the forehead. She held up one forefinger and went through the motions of eating, then she held up two fingers and gestured a kiss. She blushed. Froggie interpreted it:

"First the stomach, then the bed. Okay."

The younger sister, whose name appeared to be Annette, now sat down on Mastie's lap and held his hand.

"Alan," she said and spoke rapidly to her sister, pointing at Mastie's nose and face. Mastie wasn't really comfortable. He was mostly hungry, but now he felt a new desire.

Annette got off his lap. She wasn't pretty — no, not at all. They were old women, that's what they were, the husks left behind while the rest of the village had gone until the war ended.

But the meat was delicious. The women ate it with a tremendous gusto, cutting off huge pieces. Probably neither of them had eaten meat in years. The cows that were left were all used for milk to feed the old people of the village and now that the cows were butchered, what would they eat? It was a problem for the parliaments and prime minister to figure out. Either the soldiers or the people ate — there wasn't enough for both. Nothing stopped the sisters though. Between the two of them they ate one piece and a quarter of the second, swallowing it along with tumblers of red wine that had been made locally.

Froggie held the red wine up to the light.

"Beautiful, eh? What are we doing, so many moles in the dirt when there are still some beautiful things left." He put his arm around Lise's shoulders and she smiled at him with a mouthful of meat. She laughed again and put her finger to her lips incredulously. Her broad shoulders shook. "Maria," said Froggie. "How do you like my Maria? Well, maybe she's a little tough but she has the same general shape, wouldn't you say? A little stretched here and there." Froggie filled his glass again.

"Life!" he shouted, and the sun shone through it and mirrored a big patch of red on the floor.

Suddenly the house shook and rumbled and Froggie's hand dropped. The wine spilled down over the front of his white undershirt and spread like so much blood. Annette laughed but the two men were out of their seats instantly and running for the beds in the other room. The women laughed again. Mastie looked out from under the bed.

"Come on, do you want to be killed or something?"

Annette threw her hands up.

"*Je m'en fiche de la mort*" (I don't give a damn if I die), she said.

Were they under artillery attack? Had the Germans begun a counteroffensive then? Or was it only another threatening shot from the retreating lines? Annette came into the room and helped him out from under the bed. He put his arms around her and she patted his face.

"Alan," she said. She hiccuped. Froggie and the other woman passed them and went out.

346

She was old and out of shape, but what did he care if she was the leftovers. She was alive, she was a woman, she was laughing, and the bed was right behind them spread with a real white sheet. The wine was already warming him. He seized her with as much enthusiasm as a drowning man seizes a life preserver.

After a long time, evening came. When he opened his eyes Annette was leaning over him like his mother, seated on the chair beside him. She smiled and seemed a little embarrassed. She was dressed again.

"Pour quel genre de femme me prends-tu, Alan?" (Do you think I'm a bad woman, Alan?) she said.

"I wish you'd speak English," said Mastie. "Or Dutch." He meant the Pennsylvania dialect. *"Kanscht du deitsch schvetza?"* (Can you speak German?)

"Tea," said Annette and she went back to the kitchen and came in with a cup of tea that was still almost boiling.

I should be getting back, Mastie thought. The sun was apparently down or almost so because the light was fading. Annette watched him drink the tea and then began a little song.

> *"Plaisir d'amour . . .*
> *ne dure qu'un moment*
> *Chagrin d'amour*
> *dure toute la vie."*

> (The joy of love
> Is but a moment or two.
> The pain of parting will linger
> Your whole life through.)

"Very nice," said Mastie. She reminded him more of his mother all the time, and now he was lonely. He hadn't felt a bit of emotion the whole time with her, nothing that even vaguely touched his heart. Yet, he did feel good. He was relaxed like a man who had soaked for an hour in a hot tub, but nothing had growled in his stomach like even a look from Annie could start. He almost wished she would ask him for some money because he would feel free to go then. But instead she was smiling at him and saying "Alan" in a warm soft voice. He didn't look at her.

Then it hit him again. He was terribly lonely. She had come just close enough to him to remind him — how he didn't know — of his own mother. And Annie. And people back home. He didn't want to think of them here, in her bed. Maybe she was a good woman, only a little lonely, but this was all a part of war, just an interlude in the fighting. It had nothing to do with *life*, as one lived it in Pennsylvania.

But when he gave her back the cup her face was strikingly like his mother's. "Mom," he said without thinking. He almost expected her to answer. She got up, bent over, and kissed him. He thought of home again. He wanted to hear soft voices, and children's voices. Yes! Children's voices — how long had it been since he heard any? He wanted to get his hands down in rich dirt and plant tobacco seeds and watch them coming up. He wanted to put on clean overalls, and walk barefooted. Most of all, he wanted to be home — and then it struck him again, the anachronism of thinking of home while he sat on this bed.

He got out of bed and went to the kitchen.

Froggie was standing by the table, dressed only

in his undershorts and finishing off the bottle of wine. He set it down with a bang.

"I don't know where you been, Mastie, but I've been to Paradise and back. No difference, huh? They're all constructed the same, you know. Baby, I'm happy...." He shook his big stomach.

"Let's go," said Mastie. They went downstairs and Annette threw her arms around Mastie.

"Good-bye, Alan," she said.

"You know, you must visit me in Manhattan, Mastie," said Froggie, when they got outside. "Maria will cook you a big feast. Tortillas, huh? How about that? Do you like tortillas? You don't? Ah, come on. They're better than all that stuff you eat."

"I never ate one. How do I know?"

"Okay, when you come, we'll fix you tortillas. And hot sauce. Then we'll sit on the porch and watch our kids playing down below and tell the women how we chased lots of Germans off this old ball. You and me will have rum, while Maria and — what's her name?"

"I don't know."

"Sure you do. The one you get letters from."

"Oh, Annie."

"You're going to marry her, right?"

"I don't know. Who says we'll ever get out of here?"

"Oh, we'll get out of here. Look at that, will you?" They passed a hundred-year-old oak tree that had been flipped up in the air like a coin and was standing on its head with its roots supported by another tree.

It was dark when they got to the camp.

"Everyone else wants something," said Froggie,

seemingly not connecting his comment with anything else they had talked about. "They want me to sing for them — okay, so I sing. They want me to laugh for them — so I laugh. They want me to entertain them — so they can forget all the nasty stuff we have to do. The women want meat — okay, okay." He looked at Mastie. "Do you understand?"

"Not really."

"But you don't want anything, do you?" said Froggie. "With you and me it's different. So you see, it's very important, Mastie. Very important. Are you and me square now?" Mastie looked at him and grinned.

"We're square." They shook hands. Then they both broke out laughing.

7

Toward morning it began to drizzle, which disgusted Mastie. He needed the sleep, he told himself, if they were going to move out in the morning. He threw the raincoat over himself and watched the drops collecting on it. Froggie was there on the other side of the tree, less protected from the rain by its leaves than he was. He moved a little closer to the tree trunk and leaned on his elbow to look at Froggie.

How long had he known him? Hardly eight months. Was it eight months since he tripped over him in the haymow in Lyoncourt? *Yet I know him better than I know my own brother,* he thought. *He is Froggie the trolley conductor and he is in love with Maria.*

Rain was trickling down the fat soldier's face — he knew every inch of that face from seeing it by the side of the barrel as he sighted — and every time a drop reached his nose he involuntarily brushed his hand against his nose. Finally he rolled over and began to breathe deeply and regularly. *I love him,* Mastie thought. *I love him as much as I ever loved a girl.* They were in this together. It was sort of a battlefield marriage, 'till death do us part,' and the gun was their terrible war baby. He reached over and spread his raincoat over Froggie. There was no more sleeping anymore this morning. He sat up and leaned against the tree. He dozed off again.

He awoke. Someplace someone was crying, but when he listened, he couldn't hear it anymore. It sounded like it was coming from the woods. Who was sleeping over there? He heard a single shot, like a revolver, and then another shot. Was it from the outposts who had been posted in the woods and told to "die as loudly as possible" in case of an attack, although no attack was expected?

"Froggie! *We're under attack!*"

He threw off the blanket and scrambled for the gun. The whole valley below was crisscrossed with creeping German soldiers barely visible in the drizzle and faint light of morning. Was the woods on the left full of them too? A volley of shorts went off behind him. Someone else had seen the approaching enemy. Suddenly the camp was alive and Froggie and Mastie were working feverishly on the machine gun in the hole behind the great tree.

"Mother of God!" said Froggie.

A bolt of lightning shot across the sky and then thunder. The rain began to advance in ranks up the valley. They could see it coming, faster than the soldiers with the prickles on the top of their helmets could run.

The machine gun began to stutter and now on the right and left other guns began to go off. The first row of German soldiers below fell in confusion, but the rows after them never lost a stride. The machine guns were only buying time for the men behind, where all was confusion. The lieutenant was dispatching hundreds of infantry men around the house and barn on all sides. It was ideal for defense. But was it too late? Men kept running across the barnyard to their posts, and bumping into other men running from the barn to their positions in the house.

The rain, roaring as loud as the guns themselves, swept up the hill and in a few minutes began to run in streams down the men's backs, off their noses, and in rivers across the barnyard. Red rivers. The oncoming soldiers dropped halfway up the hill and fired into the bewildered American camp. The men were not protected by a trench and hardly awake. They fell in the barnyard or rolled backward down the raise toward the pond.

The German line split in front and began to go out around the hill to avoid the fire of the machine guns on top. They were moving in squads. The machine guns were exacting a high price for the hill, but could they be outflanked? A volley of hand grenades fell on the hill and the house. There was a loud poof — the house caught fire and at the same moment a machine gunner stood up with a terrible cry and began to stagger along the top of the hill toward Mastie's emplacement.

"Get down! Get down!" But the soldier wandered on, his hands to his eyes. "My glasses!" he mumbled. "I can't see without my glasses. What a headache!" It was Churchill, the grenade fragments had shattered his thick glasses and pushed the pieces into his eyes. He wandered down the hill toward the pond and stumbled.

The rain was in the hole up to their ankles and the bank had turned to mud. A suicide squad charged out of the woods, bayonets fixed, their eyes on the machine gun.

"Turn the gun!" The gun caught the squad halfway between the woods and the tree, and the bullets tossed them into the pond. But the squad was spread out. The last two men splashed through the puddles and as Mastie turned the gun on the one, the other brought his bayonet down on Froggie, who was half-kneeling, half-rising in anticipation. Froggie fell back and the enemy, a tall powerful man with a moustache, tried to pull his bayonet out again, but it was stuck in Froggie's great stomach.

Mastie leaped up and threw his arms around the man and attempted to trip him. The man resisted. They were both bare-handed. It was a matter of raw strength alone. Mastie slipped in the mud. They were both on the ground now, each struggling to get his legs in a pincers around the other's waist, each struggling not to let himself get caught, and clawing with his hands on the other's wet shirt. Who would be fortunate? That was all that held them between death and life, wasn't it? Fortune? Under which of them was the ground more slippery? Who had stronger legs? Who had slept better the night before? Who had eaten or not eaten in the last three days?

Mastie broke loose and leaped to his feet, his shirt open in the front and mud dripping from his hair. He was breathing in wild pants and he felt like he was going to vomit. Not now! No, not now. The light of the burning house behind reflected red on the other man's face and there were bits of foam on his lips. *He is as tired as I am*, Mastie told himself. They stood facing each other, panting, but he couldn't bear to look at the other man's eyes. Eyes had a way of hypnotizing — no — he must watch his feet. It was the feet that would move first.

Then they were at it again, recklessly now, scratching and biting and kicking. They wrapped their arms around each other and stood locked like lovers, panting, unable to move. You or me, will it be you? Me — never! The rain poured over them. Suppose we decided to quit? No, no . . . no quitting.

The man broke the lull. He worked his body behind Mastie's and brought his arm around his neck in a hammerlock. It was all up. Mastie could think only of his throat and his arms dropped. The dagger. Of course, the dagger. He was choking. With a superhuman effort, he pushed the blade backward, with his left hand and hit it with his right. The arms around his shoulder went limp and dropped away. The man fell. It had gone through his heart.

Mastie went down on his knees, gasping for air. He vomited and his body shook.

Froggie was lying on his side by the gun. He had pulled the bayonet out, slicing his hands and now he lay there with a great red spot covering the entire front of his shirt. His eyes were glazed. He smiled.

"You pray, I can't," he said.

"You'll be okay," said Mastie.

"No, don't say it. It's all over. I know it."

"You'll be okay," said Mastie, but he knew it wasn't true as his hands tore open the front of the soaked shirt. The wound was high and ragged. It had gone through Froggie's stomach, two inches wide.

"I killed that son-of-a-bitch," Mastie said.

"Oh my — " said Froggie.

"I'll show him to you," said Mastie and he ran back to where the enemy lay and pulled the dagger from his chest. Tears and rain were running down his face and he could hardly see.

"Oh my — " said Froggie again.

Mastie cut off the head and carried it like a lantern back to Froggie. "There, see him!" he was shouting. The spiked helmet had fallen off. Mastie went back and got it and set it on the head. "He paid for hurting you, Froggie. I made him pay for it."

Disregarding the fighting Mastie went down on his hands and knees and said, "See, it's only a small wound. You'll get back to see her." Froggie's open eyes stopped him. He was dead.

He spread the only clean thing in sight, a handful of leaves, over the fat soldier's face. Then he jumped up. A round of fire from a hiding soldier caught him in the leg. He went down on all fours again, not sure where he was hit, but he couldn't stand up, he was sure of that.

Then he rolled over on his back and lay there while dozens of feet ran by him. The Americans had taken the offensive. The rain ran down his face like tears — thousands and thousands of tears. It seemed as though the ground had washed away beneath him and he was falling and falling and the red lights of the burning house were the outposts of hell and the cheering soldiers running by him were cheering devils who had come to welcome him.

"Don't leave me here!" he shouted. "Don't leave me here!"

He was lost. Lost! He envied Froggie, lying in silence. He envied his silence. He envied him because for Froggie the problem was solved.

"Don't leave me here alone!"

The cheering devils were not about to leave him. He could hear them running to greet him and chuckling over him. He tried to pray, but there were no prayers in him.

V. Ira, Fall of '18

1

Army life for Ira had become a trial by stagnation. The men in the Conscientious Objector Detachment were waiting for the Board of Inquiry to come and judge them sincere or insincere. But there were 4,000 objectors all across America and the Board was traveling by train.

In the meantime, the men had nothing to do but play checkers, cook for themselves, sweep their horse stable, and hold long discussions about most anything — what was going to happen to them here, the Judgment Day, the Sermon on the Mount, how to catch muskrats. . . . If you could keep your eyes off the guards with loaded guns who stood at the entrance to the Detachment and marched on both sides of the objectors wherever they went, you might even think it was a holiday party, Ira thought. But even parties get boring when they last thirty days.

Ira was bored. *Am I wasting my life?* he wondered. *No one has questioned my beliefs for a month, and isn't that part of why I came here? To be faithful to what I believe?*

The last week in September, though, the Board came. The men were marched out of their quarters to a large lawn below the division headquarters. It was a sunny day. Pyski cracked jokes and everyone

359

laughed, but really they were all tense. Would they be judged sincere or insincere? Would they be given long prison sentences or furloughed to France or a farm? The men stood around on the grass, under the sharp eyes of the guards, and talked. The Board was taking its time with each objector.

On the stroke of noon, the major who was conducting the interviews came out on the porch and held up his hand for attention. "Gather around me in a circle here on the lawn. The interviews are taking longer than we thought but we promised you a chance to air any grievances you might have."

The guards were standing at attention now and, as soon as the major mentioned a circle, they began to herd the men toward the major. One guard stood in front of the major with a loaded gun across his knees as if to protect the major from a possible attack. The objectors were almost all dressed in civilian clothes, generally baggy and rumpled because they didn't have an iron in their quarters. About half of them were thin and undernourished, but still they smiled and moved easily, not stiffly like soldiers.

"I don't come as a friend," the major said, when they were resettled. "I don't believe in your ideas. But I don't come as an enemy either. I'm here to interpret the law and to answer questions if anyone has any." The men were silent, close together in a semicircle around the major with the guards a foot or so behind them. It was a little hard to think of questions. "It will take several weeks for us to evaluate your interviews," said the major. "In the meanwhile I expect you to abide by the guidelines set down by the president, which are that you will be excused from drills, military work, and wearing the uniform, but you are expected to keep yourselves and your surroundings clean."

"Question?"

"Yes." Schie stepped out of the semicircle so the major could see his face, but the armed guard by the major's side indicated he should stop. The major didn't appear quite happy with the rigid look of things, and he turned around and said, "Must we have all the formality, colonel? I'd rather have the men relax so we can have a discussion."

For the first time Ira noticed the man standing on the porch, a familiar looking man. Why, it was the colonel, the same colonel who had saved him from the mob two months ago and taken him to his tent for a lecture. He was dressed in a riding outfit and when the major called to him he stopped walking on the porch and rested his riding whip on his shoulder.

"All right, major," he said. "Cowpers, you're dismissed." The armed guard stepped away like machinery and left the major alone, facing Schie. "Is that better, major?" The colonel didn't seem to be in a good mood — he paced while he talked to the major.

"I'd rather have the men sit down."

"I don't think we can afford that, major. A lot of our soldiers are walking around over the dinner hour. I'd rather they didn't see the objectors sitting at ease before an officer."

"Okay," the major gave in. He nodded to Schnie. "Go ahead."

The colonel resumed walking. It appeared that the objectors bothered him, for as he walked, he looked hard at them, then down at the floor with his chin in one hand and his riding whip tucked under his other arm, then back at the objectors again.

Schie looked up at the major. "What exactly are our surroundings and quarters?" he said. "We've been ordered to cut the grass around the camp, major, and I consider that military work. The president himself said we will be exempted from military work."

"Correct. But you will not be the one to draw the line and say, 'This is military and this isn't.' That's exactly up to your commanding officer, which will be Colonel Doolittle as of today, I believe. At my request, he's been appointed and ordered to pay more attention to you than you were given in the past."

(So that was why the colonel was there, pacing on the porch.)

"But before we go any further, let's get one thing straight. Whatever you do, you are aiding this war, so don't think you can avoid it. It's a total war, every farmer, every industry, every garbage collector is contributing to it just as much as the soldier is. When you die you're helping the war because that means one less mouth to feed, so let's forget about whether you are contributing to the war or not. You are."

"I'm not," said Schie. "I am willing to keep the quarters where I live clean, but nothing else."

"You are being picky," said the major. The Army is already making a concession to you by allowing you not to drill as a common soldier. I wouldn't press my luck too far by trying to interpret the president's ruling by yourself and then taking some rash stand."

"On the other hand," said Schie, "the Army is not making any concession to us. It's we who are making the concession by even coming to camp. We are free men, responsible to God alone. The fact that a group of old officers called the Army suddenly decided it needs us to fight a war we don't believe in isn't our fault. If they want to make war so bad, why don't they go fight themselves?"

"I'm not interested in philosophical discussions of the war and whether it's right or wong," said the major. "We're in the war — you're in it — and the question right now is what you are responsible to do during the war. The president has set up generous guidelines and he expects the officers to follow them. And what I am saying is this — nonmilitary work is whatever your commanding officer decides to call nonmilitary. You might want to think that through."

"Think?" said Pyski. "I thought we weren't supposed to think."

"Don't get cocky," the major said. "If the colonel decides your quarters extend for ten miles and he wants his front lawn mowed, you'll mow his front lawn. I think that's the end of that question."

Schie sat back in a huff.

Why argue? Ira thought. If one did want to argue about the war, who should he argue with? Who had decided that there was going to be a war anyway? Certainly not the Board of Inquiry — they were only sent around to see whether the objectors were sincere or not. Nor Secretary Baker, either — he was only prosecuting the war as the president told him to.

Well, then, the president — surely he was the one who had decided the country was going to war. Perhaps letters and protests should be written to him, but he was constantly getting letters and protests, and also letters of commendation. Who would he believe, the many people who told him he was right in fighting the war, or the minority who told him war was wrong? Anyway, the president had fought this out in his conscience a long time ago. He had held off fighting as long as was humanly possible, but finally *the conditions* demanded that he enter the war — the American people looking at Europe and her condition demanded that America enter the war. So then it was *the condition* of the world that was to blame.

How could you sit down and have a reasonable discussion with the world about its condition? For one thing, a sick man is rarely in a mood for discussion. For another thing, the world was made up of many sick men and how could you get around to all of them and tell them it was time for healing? In most cases, the sick men didn't realize they were sick. They thought they were doing the right thing for their own countries. They sang patriotic songs and went off to war to shoot each other in the name of changing the other's sick condition.

Maybe there was only one hope left — the people. The American people. The condition of the world was always bad, but if one could somehow tell the American people that the best way to respond to bad conditions was not to fire 75 mm shells and grenades into it, but to heal the bad conditions! So you go to the nearest soldier and tell him that. When you're in an army camp of 27,000, he's representative of the people, isn't he? And he looks you in the eye and says, "What? Are you crazy in the head or something? We're fighting a war and I'm trying to get some sleep right now. I ain't got time to sit around and talk. Go spout off to the sergeant if you have to talk with somebody."

So there you were back at the beginning again. Ira

had gone the whole circle in his mind at least a half dozen times since his first day in camp. It only frustrated him. Should he just give up on everybody else and make sure he wasn't contributing to the war effort himself? God understood. If nobody else did, okay. That was how he finally made up his mind. For that reason he followed Schie's question carefully. It made a big difference whether 'Keep yourself and your surroundings clean' meant cleaning up the former horse stable where ten boys slept or cleaning up the entire camp so the soldiers could have more time for bayonet practice. But argue about it? No. He hadn't done that since he came into the objectors' detachment.

The major looked over this group. "Are there any other questions?"

"What about farm furloughs?" said someone.

"All right," the major said. "Furloughs. We're considering them. The nation must be fed, of course, but I'd rather not make a statement today on where we're at with furloughs. There's a good possibility they'll be granted. When you come before the Board of Inquiry this afternoon, tell us what you're willing to do if you're judged sincere. If you're ready to do hospital work or bridge construction in the rear of the war zone, say so. In a few cases, we're recommending men for reconstruction work in France under the Quakers. Does that answer your question?"

Schnickerry put up his hand. "What about beatings, major? Is it right to beat someone who in good faith can't obey an order?"

"There will be no beatings," the major said. "The colonel and I have discussed it and there won't be any beatings if we can help it. God knows we don't want any martyrs on our hands. There are enough of you guys already without starting a stampede of sympathy. Report any mistreatment you might get. Any other questions? If not, you're dismissed until one o'clock."

The answers were unsatisfactory in Ira's mind. He didn't know any more than before — and it looked like more of the same stagnant life for a long time yet. The only bright spot was the possibility of reconstruction work in France. It interested him.

2

Colonel Doolittle was waiting for them back at the conscientious objector quarters. He was carrying a riding whip and sitting astride a horse that was held by a private. He was short, maybe five-six or so, and had a bit bigger paunch than the Army usually allowed. But then he wasn't a combat officer anymore; he was strictly a training officer. He looked royal, certainly not the shrewd, questioning old man that he had appeared to be when Ira first met him. The conscientious objectors came as usual, flanked on all sides by guards with guns. The colonel leaned over and said something to the private, then straightened and pushed himself up a bit in the saddle by extending his legs in the stirrups. He smiled. He wore his forty years in the Army well.

When the conscientious objectors came within ten feet of the colonel the guard shouted. "Company, Halt! Attention! Salute!"

The ragtag group of conscientious objectors in their civilian clothes (with the exception of Ira who was still wearing his uniform because his clothes hadn't arrived from home) stopped and jostled into each other. On the command for attention they straightened up, but on the call for "Salute" they merely smiled at the colonel. Big, beautiful, genuine smiles — not at all what the colonel was expecting. The six guards stood erect, their hands quivering in a stiff salute.

The colonel opened his mouth and looked over the detachment. His eyes went back and forth over it and suddenly he whipped his hand into a salute. The conscientious objectors relaxed, still smiling, silent. The colonel closed his mouth and looked at the guards. "Don't you teach your men to salute?"

"No, sir."

"Then, I will." The colonel got down off his horse and waited until it had been led away. The guards glanced at each other without moving their faces. They didn't envy the conscientious objectors behind them at this moment. The colonel scraped the ground with his toe. He took a long time. When he looked up, he seemed to have made up his mind.

"Men — " he stopped, and ran his eyes over them. "Men, we're going to spend the afternoon cleaning up and this evening we'll call a general council to talk about where we go from here. You're in the Army and I expect you to act like Army men. I understand very well that you don't want to fight. Okay. You don't want to wear uniforms. Okay. But we're still going to behave like a disciplined group of men in the service of our country. Okay? I want you three men," he pointed at Schnickerry, a Mennonite boy named Rempel, and Frymire," to clean those latrines across the street. I'd be afraid to sit down in one for fear I'd catch crabs. Understand?"

The latrines across the street were not a part of the Conscientious Objectors Detachment. They belonged to a different detachment, and up until now those grounds had been off limits for the conscientious objectors. Schnickerry raised his hand.

"Yes?"

"I'm sorry, colonel, but I cannot help clean up the latrines over there. They belong to an Army detachment, and it is against my conscience to — "

"Against your conscience?" said the colonel incredulously.

"Yes."

"Well, I don't give a damn about your conscience. Will you work or won't you?"

"No, I will not."

"Take him to the guardhouse."

A guard took Schnickerry firmly by the wrist and led him out. Then, with his gun and bayonet leveled, and Schnickerry out in front, he said, "March!" and the two went walking away. The colonel looked back at the men, expecting to see fear in their eyes. There was no fear.

"Let that be a lesson," said the colonel. "Anybody who doesn't obey a reasonable command goes to the guardhouse, and I'm going to ask that that boy be put on bread and water for the next week, Stanley."

The boy who had led the horse away appeared around the corner of the stable. "Yes, sir."

"I want you to bring the notebooks from the saddlebags."

Stanley brought them and the colonel opened up a notebook and began to read the president's definition of noncombatant service. When he was finished, he looked up.

"Probably some of you do not understand what it means to disobey an order. I want you to understand that refusal to obey the order of an officer may be punished by death or by any other punishment as the court-martial decides. I am not making that up. That's the 64th Article of War as declared by Congress."

The colonel looked over the men again and pointed to Ira, Pyski, and an Amish boy. "I want you men to pour several loads of clay on the floor of my quarters and on the floors of those latrines, and the rest of you — What is it?" Ira's hand was raised.

"I'm sorry, but I cannot do this work, it violates my belief —"

"Damn it," roared the colonel. "I'm not asking you what your beliefs are. Can you get that straight? This is not a Sunday school. It's an Army camp, and I'm asking you to do some elementary work to improve the health of this place. Do you all want to die of syphilis? Worms? Tuberculosis?"

"I'm sorry, but I can't either," said the Amish boy.

"Nor me," said Pyski.

The colonel stared at them. Guthrie, who had been pretty much silent today, asked the guards for permission to step out of rank, and approached the colonel.

"Colonel, we don't dispute your authority. We respect you," he said. Guthrie had a way of being diplomatic and cooling feelings. "We don't want to disobey you or any of the Articles of War, but we can't compromise our belief that if we do anything for the Army we have contributed as much as the soldier. The Division Commander himself told one of our men that sanitary service is as important as military service, and without it, it would be impossible to go on with the war."

The colonel breathed in deeply and then, impulsively, he bent forward and lashed at Guthrie with his riding whip. It cut a long red line along his cheek.

"Silence! At ease," he said to the guards. The colonel folded his arms and looked at the sky, composing himself, maybe. When he spoke, it was gently, not like an angry man at all.

"Men, I've spent forty years with the Army. I'm proud of it. I'm proud of our country. I've made men out of a lot of boys and it takes a lot of discipline on the part of both of us. I'm not here to throw my weight around. I'm here in the interests of America, the United States Army, and of you men. You're going to have to obey some orders, that's all there is to it, whether you like it or not. Take my word for it, it's for your own good. I've made men for forty years and I'm determined not to fail now. I'm not asking you to fight. I'm just asking you to clean up in your own camp, which is all that the president's ruling asks of you. I want those of you who are going to obey me to remain here where you are, and those of you who will not obey me — think about the punishment for disobedience! — to step to the left."

He covered his eyes with his gloved hand. When he looked, they were all standing to the left of the guards. The colonel's eyes were terrible. "Take them away," he shouted. "I don't want to see them again. Take 'em out. Get out! Out!" He waved his whip wildly. The guards marched the whole group away to the guardhouse and then something happened to the colonel that had never before happened in all of his forty years of service. Two big tears fell from his eyes. Stanley, the horse private, looked around in amazement. The colonel was crying because he had no men.

3

The commanding officer of Camp Ethan Allen had ordered a massive cleanup. A general was on his way from Washington to review the division and there was a good possibility they would be sent to France immediately, where the big drive on the Meuse-Argonne was underway. The commanding officer was thorough. Not only were the troops to be as immaculate and regular as a roll of new pennies — he wanted the grounds to look the same. Why not give some of the work to the conscientious objectors?

Colonel Doolittle immediately ordered the conscientious objectors released from the guardhouse and put to work on the cleanup. As it came out afterward, the colonel had two reasons for bringing them out. One, he was doing his part toward making the division the brightest and best, and two, he had decided to force a showdown with the objectors. The colonel did not like to physically abuse men — forty years had taught him that did not change their hearts and he stood a chance of making a martyr or two. And he disapproved of the way the conscientious objectors in this camp had been treated before he was assigned to them.

But he did believe in fear. Fear had a wonderful way of changing men's minds about most anything, according to the colonel. In this case, it wouldn't be fear of pain but a fear of a prison sentence that he would put to use. All that was necessary was to send the conscientious objectors out on a work project and have one or two of them refuse again to obey orders (and he was sure they would refuse). Then let another officer witness as the first officer asked them once more, very clearly, yes or no, if they would obey. If the answer was "no" — it was sure to be — the objector would then be charged with disobeying an officer, punishable by years of imprisonment or death. If one or two of the men were court-martialed, wouldn't that put a fear into the others that nothing else, even the guardhouse, had done up until now? The colonel had determined to break their resistance — for one thing they had made him look ridiculous. The colonel took it very personally.

Sergeant Potts was briefed and told to take his own company and the objectors for the afternoon. The objectors came out of the guardhouse looking a little worm-eaten and worn from a week on bread and water, but otherwise they were in good spirits. Several of them started to sing.

The colonel had ordered marigolds from a local greenhouse, trays and trays of the pretty little flowers already in bloom. The men lined up around the trays, the majority of them regular soldiers, and it was hard to know which was more curious to the regulars — the marigolds or the conscientious objectors who were all together in a group by a stone wall singing the old spiritual "Swing Low, Sweet Chariot."

Potts came up leading another group back from a warehouse, with shovels, spades, and sprinkling cans. He was dressed in a new uniform. It was apparent that he wouldn't be planting marigolds himself.

Ira hadn't seen Potts for two months, but as soon as he saw him, he felt his organs freezing. He stopped singing and moved several feet back so he wouldn't be the first one that the sergeant saw. Potts held up his hands for silence.

"We're going to plant some posies around the commanding officer's house and when we finish here, we'll plant them around the headquarters. Now I'm going to take one crew of men and show you all how it's done. I want seven of you." He pointed out several soldiers and then turned to the objectors. At that moment Guthrie bent over to tie his shoelace and Ira saw Sergeant Potts looking right at him.

"Well, well, what do we have here?" said Potts. "Our yellowstriped friends and my little canary himself, Stoltzfus! Something's been missing, just been a little boring around here since I lost you," said Potts, and he smiled. He was in an excellent mood. He began to pass out shovels and sprinkling cans and also spades to the men and finally he gestured a flower tray to Ira and a soldier. Potts explained how and where the flowers were to be planted and then he lifted his whistle and blew it.

"Commence working!"

The men by the house began to dig a narrow trench.

"Flowers!"

The soldier picked up his end and looked at Ira. "I'm sorry," said Ira. "I can't do it."

The soldier looked back at his buddies, who were enjoying the fine weather. Planting flowers was almost as good as a holiday to them, certainly better than drilling. "Somebody take his place," said the soldier to several of the men who were only watching while the sergeant got his first crew underway. Nobody moved to replace Ira though. Several of them grinned. The soldier got disgusted.

"Sergeant!"

But the sergeant was busy overseeing the spadework.

"Look, either you pick up that or I'll plant this in you," the soldier said, waving his spade.

"I'm sorry," said Ira. "I can't do it." Planting flowers? What was wrong with that? he asked himself. But in the next breath he found himself saying, 'no' he wasn't going to obey a military order. Didn't they know that by now? Was planting flowers as innocent as it looked? A general was coming to review the division and if he liked what he saw he would send them off to France on the next ship. Maybe flowers would influence his decision, who knew? In any case, this was not a case of keeping his quarters clean, he was sure of that. All this went through Ira's head in a moment as he watched the other soldier with the spade in his hand. Fortunately the soldier was frightened enough by the thought of a court-martial that he didn't put the spade through Ira.

"What's going on here?" The sergeant came over and looked at Ira. "What's wrong with you, Stoltzfus? Your conscience extends to flowers, too, does it?" Potts laughed. "Next thing you know you'll have a conscience against breathing, like the holy men in India who wear those masks to strain out the gnats. Can't swallow them. They're vegetarians."

The men chuckled. Potts was in a good humor, that was plain, and when that happened, he sometimes ordered a special dinner for the whole company.

"Get me a belt."

Someone took off his belt and gave it to the sergeant, who used it to tie Ira's hands to the tray.

"Okay, move." He blew his whistle again. The soldiers were all interested in what was going on now. Even the first planting crew — the ground was ready and they had nothing else to do but look. The man at the back of the tray began to push so Ira had to move, but he made no effort to go in the direction of the waiting flower crew. The lawn away from the commanding officer's house sloped downhill, so in a minute Ira had been pushed right across the hill and against the wall of the division headquarters. The soldiers began to laugh. During the whole incident Potts stood with his hands on his hips.

"Look, he'll lose his temper," said the soldier, "He'll lose his temper and then we all suffer."

"I'm sorry," said Ira and he looked at the soldier without blinking, "but I can't obey a military order."

"Son of a bitch!" said the soldier.

Sergeant Potts looked around and lost his jovial mood in the same moment. He untied the box of marigolds from Ira's wrists and ordered two men from the other half of the unit to bring back the other empty tray and take the full one back and begin working on it. He now tied the empty tray to Ira's wrists and told two soldiers to begin piling stones from a construction pile onto Ira's end of the tray. It was terribly heavy. The belts chafed Ira's wrists.

"Okay, take him for a walk," said Potts. The tray was piled high with stones. The soldier began to walk.

"Sergeant, I can't do it," said the soldier.

"What do you mean, you *can't?* If I say you can, you can."

"I'm doing all the work. I'm pulling him. He ain't doing a thing."

"Okay, put them down," said Potts. "Untie him." They had wasted a good thirty minutes and the bulk of his men still weren't working. "Corporal," he said, "Take over the flower detail. We're going to settle this little matter right now. Hey, lieutenant!"

A lieutenant had been standing outside the headquarters building watching the drama unfold. He came over to the flower detail. "He won't obey me," said Sergeant Potts. The lieutenant turned to Ira, "I command you to assist with the flowers. Will you assist, yes or no?"

"I'm sorry," said Ira.

"I don't care how you feel. I want to know, yes or no, will you plant flowers?"

Ira looked at Potts. Although he didn't know it, the carefully constructed net was closing on him. "No," he said.

The lieutenant saluted Sergeant Potts and walked off.

"Okay, Stoltzfus," said Potts, "that took care of the legal end but you and I aren't finished. We're going to the bathhouse. Come on."

Ira followed him across the lawn, past the marigold plants, and down around the back of the mess hall to the large bathhouse. They went inside.

"Stand over there against the wall." The sergeant went around to each of the doors and locked them. He came back and stood two feet from Ira. "Take off your collar buttons and hatband."

Ira's heart began to pump faster. As long as a man wore his collar buttons and hatband, he was in complete uniform and no officer could strike him. Without them. . . . He took them off.

"Give them here." The sergeant lay them on the floor behind him."

"You and I have had this rendezvous coming a long time, Stoltzfus. I asked you to plant flowers and you didn't. I don't know why. Flowers have nothing to do with war, if it's war you're against. I could have you court-martialed, do you know that? Huh? Do you know that?"

Ira nodded.

"Will you plant flowers? Yes or no."

"No."

The sergeant's reaction was so sudden it nearly knocked Ira down. He slapped Ira with his open hand, then with the other hand. Ira gasped.

"Come on, get mad," said Potts. "Don't you ever get mad? That's what I hate about you objectors, you're so good. You never said a bad word in your life, did you? You never got a girl in trouble. You never got mad either, did you? You can't fight. You can't work. Are you human? That's what I want to know. You have any blood in you or is it all lemonade, huh?" Do you think there's a woman alive that would look twice at a ball-less animal like you?"

He reached into his pocket and smiled, never releasing his hold on the lapels of Ira's uniform with his one muscular fist. It was the whistle. The sergeant put it in his mouth.

"You won't answer me, will you?" he said with the whistle in his mouth. It bubbled a little as he talked. "You're above thinking of stuff like that. You think about angels and the birdies, right. And heaven, where the trumpet shall sound, huh!" and he leaned forward and blew the whistle against Ira's ear until his face turned bright red. Then he grabbed the ear and began to knock Ira's head against the stud that stuck out of the wall.

There was no music — only a tremendous ringing in Ira's ears like a seashell and the 'plop' of fists hitting him and salty blood in his mouth and lights like acrobatic lightning bugs in his head. He could think of nothing but how to make it stop. For the first time he hated the sergeant. It was, as the sergeant said, you or me. Me. No, no, not me. The sergeant wrung his nose and suddenly Ira's fists came up. One, two, he drove them into the sergeant's stomach. The sergeant's hands stopped halfway in the air, his face went white, and he fell down backwards onto the floor.

Ira leaned back against the wall. He shut his eyes — they were swelling and he could hardly see — his face was hot. He was sweating and gulping air to catch the breath that had nearly been knocked out of him. When he opened his eyes, the sergeant was still on the floor with his hands clutching his stomach. *What have I done? An officer — An officer — I've hit an officer. . . . I didn't mean to do it.*

He knelt on the floor and put his arms around the sergeant's broad shoulders and began to lift him up. "Are you okay?" he said and the sergeant's eyes came open. He set him against a pole in the bathhouse and dashed a cup of cold water in his face.

This time the sergeant's eyes snapped wide open. He stood up painfully and looked at Ira. "You son of a bitch," he said, and then smiled a little. "You're strong, anyway."

"I'm sorry, sir."

"Don't apologize like a woman. You'll make a soldier all right. You've proved that."

4

Ira woke up about midnight. His whole body was as hot as if he had lain in the sun until he had burnt red. He moved his tongue slowly around in his mouth, running over torn edges of skin and a wobbly tooth. He spit a mouthful of blood.

He called Guthrie for some medicine, but no one answered. Where was he anyway? It couldn't be the objectors' stable. All he could make out in the blackness was that he was lying on a cot and across from him there was another cot, empty.

He sat up, but the buzzing that started in his head changed his mind. He lay down again.

Where am I? Why, it must be the solitary cell, the "hole" as they called it. And the marks all over his head, they were mementos of Sergeant Potts. Thinking of Sergeant Potts, he struck his head with his fist in grief and immediately regretted it. There wasn't a single place from his collar up that didn't have some ache or cut.

He was about to look around the room for some water when he heard a noise outside. One man was shouting at another one. Then he heard keys, and the form of a man appeared in the door. The door opened and banged shut again. Something flopped on the floor beside his bed. Ira lay silent in fear. Suppose it was a drunken soldier — the man had appeared to have a uniform on. Who knew what sort of weapons he carried in his pockets? The man didn't appear in the mood for hurting anyone, though. He simply lay on the floor and groaned.

"Get up," said Ira. "There's a bed for you."

The man groaned again, but a moment later one hand grabbed hold of Ira's bed. The man slowly pulled himself into a sitting position and then flopped back on the floor.

"Sinners!" he said. He sat up again.

"Can I help you?"

"A better question is, Can I help you? You're the one who needs help," said the man. He finally got his elbows onto the bed, and heaving, he fell onto it. "Sorry, no medicine, though."

Ira lay on the cot with the pillow rolled under his neck to keep from touching any of his sore spots. His eyes were getting used to the tiny bit of light in the cell and what he saw was a man much like himself, young, but not in uniform. Instead he was wearing a farmer's overalls with suspenders, a work shirt with the sleeves rolled up, and a light straw hat — as a matter of fact, he looked like a Mennonite boy and there was something about his face that was enormously familiar. He was sure he had met the man hundreds of times, but he couldn't place him.

"So how are you feeling?" said the Mennonite boy on the other bed. "It's been a pretty hard night, I'll bet."

"You speak Dutch!" said Ira but he said it in English from force of habit. He reached across to shake the young man's hand. The Mennonite man looked at him, and there was something piercing about his eyes, something a little unsettling. Then he shook hands. Ira began to smile but cut himself short — it even hurt to smile.

"I have to admire you for holding out on him so long," the Mennonite said. "You held out longer than I would have."

"On who?"

"Who? Why, Sergeant Potts, of course. Anybody could see he was getting to you, that he had a grudge against you, and he was out for blood."

"You know about it then — I mean, the whole story?" said Ira, and he held his breath. If the story had gotten out to the camp . . . "I don't know why I did it."

"You don't have to worry. The whole camp doesn't know," the Mennonite said, "and I can keep a secret. Do you have any water in here? I could stand a drink."

"But how did you find out?"

"It wasn't hard," said the Mennonite. "Where's the water?" He seemed to be recuperating fast because he got out of bed now and padded across the room in search of it. That was a sure sign that he was a plain Mennonite. No one else went barefoot in October. It was one of Ira's own habits — he hated shoes. Back on the farm he sometimes went for weeks without wearing shoes except on Sundays. "Here it is," said the boy. "And something else, too — soup, I believe. Your supper, probably." He brought the soup bowl and glass of water back.

"Eat the soup," said Ira. "Or is it cold already?"

"No, it's still a little warm. Bean soup, I believe." He sat down on the bed across from Ira again and leaned over with the soup bowl. "Here," he said. It was the first time they had looked each other squarely in the eyes. A chill ran up Ira's back.

"I know you!" he said. "Something's wrong with me. I'm seeing things." The young man on the other bed was Ira's exact twin. The only difference was that the man he saw on the other bed looked healthier and windburned as if he had spent a summer reaping wheat and plowing. "I'm seeing things!" said Ira, and he set down the soup and jumped up. His head started buzzing again and he really expected that when he looked over, the man would be gone. He wasn't though. "I must be going out of my mind," Ira said, and he sat down and put his head in his hands. He was surprised the second time — this time it was the shape of his own face that surprised him. It was extended painfully in all directions and tight like a balloon — his eyes had puffed out until they weren't really in their sockets anymore. The hollows in his cheeks had swollen out and merged with a huge nose. In fact, his face felt like a tomato that had been lying in the sun.

"Pat a little water on your eyes. It might make them feel better," said the Mennonite boy.

"How is it possible that you're speaking to me?" Ira said. "Or am I dreaming all of this?"

"Not at all," the Mennonite boy said. "It just takes a little basic geography to figure it out. Take the moon, for example. The moon has its light side, which is lit by the sun."

"And its dark side," said Ira.

"Exactly. Now if the moon has two sides to it, why should you be surprised to find that you have two sides?"

"Which side of me are you, though?"

"Well, frankly, the dark side," said the Mennonite, looking at Ira. For the first time Ira noticed something that he hated about himself. The boy's eyes stared suspiciously at him, as if he were afraid Ira was about to discover who he really was. "I thought we might talk a little about what happened today. In many ways, you know, I was proud of you today," the boy said. "The way you bore up under the sergeant's slapping, well, all I could think of when I saw it — "

"You saw it? Then — "

"Why not? I was there. Of course I was there. Think of me as your other side, Ira. You can't spend only the head of a nickel, can you? You have to spend the tail side, too."

"But I didn't mean to do it. It just happened so suddenly," said Ira. "I didn't hate the sergeant, believe me."

"Save your strength," the Mennonite said. "Let me do the talking. Of course, you didn't. Your conduct has been exemplary up until now. He could see that. That's what got him. He couldn't stand to see a good man."

"I didn't get mad until . . . did I get mad?" said Ira. "I guess I did. All at once I hated him . . . yes, I did. I hated him . . . and I had never felt that way before — it was when he blew the whistle, I think. He said I wasn't a man and accused me of only thinking of angels, which isn't true. Then he blew the whistle and something popped — "

"Of course," said the man, and turned up his hands amiably. "It was only natural."

"Then you don't think I was wrong?"

"You handled it like a martyr," said the Mennonite. "It wasn't until the last moment that —"

"All of a sudden I hated him," said Ira, walking around the room," and I hit him . . . oh, I told you . . . I wasn't going to tell anyone." He regretted it immediately.

"I knew it anyway," said the man quietly.

"I hit the sergeant," said Ira, walking about. It occurred to him, then, that someone might be listening outside, and he tiptoed along the wall until he came to the door. It was not a barred door, but a solid wooden one several inches thick, to judge by the hole in the center where a small shelf had been cut out. This was where the Mennonite had apparently found the soup. He tried to look out, but he couldn't get close without bumping his nose painfully.

"There's no one there," said the Mennonite.

"How do you know?"

"Because it's one o'clock. Everyone's asleep."

Ira bumped back across the room.

"Don't tell anyone about it," he said.

"Trust me. Maybe you need a cigar to relax you," said the man. "I mean, there's no point in our being stiff around each other or keeping secrets. I know you, you know me."

"No thank you," said Ira.

"Well, I'll have one anyway." He took out a big cigar, lit it, and leaned back against the wall to blow out a stream of smoke. "Are you sure you don't want one?"

"No."

"Where were we?" said the Mennonite boy. "I think you were talking about people finding out what you did. Trust me. It's between you and me." He clapped one hand over his mouth and the other against the back of his neck.

"But God knows," said Ira. "How does he judge me? Did Jesus retaliate when he suffered? No, Jesus said, 'Blessed are ye when men shall revile you and persecute you. . . .' "

"Yes," said the visitor. "Yes," he nodded his head thoughtfully. "In many ways his suffering parallels yours."

"I have often thought of it!" said Ira with excitement. "Yes, I have often thought, if he could suffer like that, then why not me? What is my suffering compared to his? He died and he was completely innocent. What a painful death. One of our preachers investigated it and he says it must be one of the most terrible ways to die — crucifixion. But he suffered. How he suffered. . . ."

"You come from a tradition of martyrs, you know," said the Mennonite. "The Anabaptists . . . ah, weren't they burning examples? No pun intended." He smiled good-naturedly. "Fiery examples of good men who suffered for nothing, even went to the stake singing — it strains our imagination — and for what, for what. For their great beliefs. I used to love to read of the martyrs as a boy. Stephen stoned, Michael Sattler tortured — would I be that strong? Would I cry out or bear it radiantly like they did? You bore it radiantly as long as you could, you know."

"But I didn't," said Ira. "I didn't bear my pain at all. Do you know what it means to hit an officer of the Army? A court-martial and a long sentence, possibly death."

"He wasn't an officer, if you want to be technical

about it," the Mennonite said. "He was a noncommissioned officer, but in any case — "

"In any case I hit him," said Ira, and he walked back to the door and turned around to see the image of himself sitting on the bed of the prison cell. Talking was bringing his emotions up. "I wasn't going to tell anyone — because I'm ashamed of myself. I got down on my knees beside him, like this, and I said I was sorry."

The Mennonite on the bed nodded. "The Apostle Peter cut off the high priest's servant's ear, the Bible says, so you can see what sort of company you're in there. Martyrs are human, of course they are. But it's little things like that — Peter's cutting off the ear, your hitting the officer — that show the real mettle of the martyr. You're not a weakling or namby-pamby sort of fellow, not a coward at all like the sergeant wants to think you are. 'Lemonade instead of blood,' huh? It takes guts to be a conscientious objector. You're a man with guts and a lot of courage."

"No, no," said Ira, and tears welled up in his eyes and ran painfully down across his cheeks, like drops of hot wax. "I couldn't stand fast. I am not a man of their caliber. When it came to the test, I couldn't take it. I didn't suffer in silence. I hit him." More tears. "I'm not good at all. What could I do without the Lord's help? And the prayers of my mother and father and the church back home — what could I do without them?" The feelings had been corked up inside him like one of those immovable antique ships in a bottle, but now he had touched the right button and like a collapsible ship, out came his pain and doubts.

"Why didn't the Lord come to me?" Ira said. He

was still kneeling by the door. "Everytime before he came like music — I know it sounds strange — but it was like music in my ears. It was wonderful music and I was able to hold up. 'A miracle, that's what it must be,' my mother says. A miracle from God, like the singing which our grandfathers did as they were taken out to die. They never noticed their pain. But this time, no music. Did he forget me, do you think?"

"We can only conclude — " the visitor began. He stopped and started again. "Was the music you heard from God, or was it the kind of thing that often happens to people under stress, when they think about anything else to get their mind off the present? It's common, you know. Ask anyone on the dentist's chair what he's thinking about and you can bet it isn't his teeth. It's his wife or what he's going to do tonight, or the dentist's face — anything but his teeth. What you call a miracle can be explained by psychologists. I'm a schoolteacher like yourself. I'm interested in such stuff. But if it was a miracle, Ira, then we can only conclude that God abandoned you later, at the moment when you needed him the most.

"Why would he abandon you?" he continued. "Well, as the Scriptures themselves say, 'Who that was innocent ever perished? Were the upright ever cut off? Let's face it. You did hit a man, and I can't imagine that God is happy about that. You made the break, not him. You hated the sergeant — you said it yourself."

"True," said Ira. "It's true. I did it."

"But it was only natural to hate him — wasn't it? — when you consider all that you've been through for the last three months. Only God doesn't think that way, if I can be so presumptuous as to guess what's going on in that mind. He expects his people to be full of love, joy, and peace all the time.

"Am I making sense?" the Mennonite said. "I'm trying to make it clear that what you did wasn't wrong — it was only natural, even for a Christian it was natural — and there is a way out that I want to tell you about. But you must be tired."

"Not really," Ira said. He stood up slowly and leaned against the door of the cell. His eyes followed every move the man on the bed made.

"Why don't you eat the soup anyway?"

"Where did you come from?" said Ira. "Are you a dream? Or a devil? Are you a devil?" The thought frightened him.

"Do you think I have horns under my hat?" said the boy, grinning. He took off his hat and pulled out a comb. "You'd think they'd snag if they were there, wouldn't they?" He ran the comb back through his long hair. "No, don't make me out to be a bad guy. Think of me as a part of yourself. I know how you're feeling. Right now you're hungry and you better get some food in that stomach of yours."

Ira sat down on his bed, facing the door rather than the Mennonite, and ate a mouthful of the soup. It was bean soup all right, but cold and there weren't any beans in it, only the cold skins of several kidney beans. It was horrible. He spit it back into the bowl.

"Pretty bad, huh? I get the feeling they don't care if the objectors die on their hands."

"If you're part of me," said Ira, "why haven't I met you before?"

"I'm like a good Mennonite child — I don't assert myself. I only come when I'm needed and I sensed that you needed me tonight. It was going to be a long night and who knows what will be in store for you in the morning? You've been hurt — I'm good at handling affairs during a time of emergency like that. What I'd like to talk about," the boy said, picking at one of his toenails with his comb, "is what you're going to do next. I'll go on with my suggestion if you're up to it." He looked at Ira. "Okay?"

"What do you mean, 'What I'm going to do next?' "

"All right, let's look into Sergeant Potts' head. 'You'll make a good soldier,' he said when you hit him. Do you remember? That was what he was working on all along, to get you angry, of course, so you would make just that kind of a slip. As far as he's concerned, your testimony is finished, washed up. He has you right where he wants you, in his soup pot, and he's ready to fill the stove up with wood. He'll push for a court-martial, probably, and that could mean execution or life imprisonment — *if* he even decides to wait for the law to take its course before he gets his revenge."

The visitor leaned forward on the bed now, his bare feet on the rung of Ira's bed, speaking intensely and gesturing with his hands. "But he doesn't have the lid on his soup pot — no, he doesn't — and you can jump out, if you want to. Aha! You see, the Articles of War strike both ways. He hit you first, didn't he? Your face answers for that. It's painful, I'd say. Right? Now that would be enough to get him demoted or at least transferred far from this camp if it came out in court. If nothing else, it would invalidate his case against you. So what if you did punch him. He beat you first — the court will listen to that."

390

"I asked the sergeant's forgiveness," said Ira. "I said I was sorry. If I turned around and cut him down at the trial —"

"Forgiveness. Haha." The Mennonite laughed heartily like a farm boy. "What is forgiveness? It certainly won't save your neck from the rope. The sergeant doesn't care about your forgiveness anyway. What are feelings to him? No, you've been inconsistent according to the law. Your best course is to take the initiative and use the law against the sergeant."

"'If we confess our sins . . .'" said Ira, "'he is faithful and just to forgive us our sin.' What does that mean? I don't hate the sergeant anymore. No I don't. He is a weak man, a lonely man. I see that for the first time."

"He's a bigot, a real bigot, who's out to get you, that's what he is. He'll discredit your beliefs in court and cast doubts on the sincerity of all the objectors. He'll make trouble because he feels inferior to you, that's what."

"Let God be the judge," said Ira. "I think I love him."

"He'll hurt you again before he's through," said the Mennonite. "Why do you argue? Don't you want my help? Aren't you glad I came?"

"Who are you really, anyway?" said Ira.

"You still want to make me out to be a villain or a devil, don't you? But I'm only the other side of you. Granted, the dark side, but I'm able to see things in a different light. I only wanted to help you."

"I've made up my mind," said Ira, and his eyes were like a moral force, combating the Mennonite on the other bed. "I was wrong. I'm sorry."

"Then suffer, martyr!" said the Mennonite and he got up off the bed and started walking toward the door. Ira heard boots on the stairs. Someone was coming.

" 'Fear not those who destroy the body, but fear him who destroys the soul,' " he said to himself. He looked up suddenly. "Are you the one — "

There was a sound of keys and someone was at his door. The door swung open.

"You'll need me yet," said the Mennonite and he slipped out. The door came shut behind him and banged loudly.

"Jesus, Jesus . . ." said Ira. Something strange happened then. He felt light and good. The pain in his face seemed almost gone and he wanted to sing. Powerful trapped forces inside him were breaking loose, like a volcano about to throw up hot rocks. "Yes, I forgive him . . ." said Ira, touching his swollen eyes. Then he began to sing. He didn't hum — he sang at the top of his lungs.

5

Very early in the morning — it was still dark — someone shouted into Ira's cell and then came in and shook him by the shoulder. Ira blinked. He had hardly slept.

"Let's go." the man said. It was a soldier.

Ira got up — he didn't need time to put on his clothes because he still had them on. He'd slept in them all night and by now they were wrinkly and splotched with dried blood. He looked like a rumpled bed sheet ready for the laundry. But in spite of all this he felt wonderful.

The soldier held the door open, then closed it behind him. They walked up a long stairway to the outside door. Apparently "the hole" really was a subsurface cellar. Ira's face still hurt although the swelling had gone down, but it was as though he had just won a tremendous spiritual victory — he felt lighthearted.

The outside door was open. They pushed through and came out into the cool, snappy morning. There were stars overhead. It felt like it was going to frost by sunrise.

"Aha, good morning, Stoltzfus!" said a dark figure.

"Sergeant Potts!" At that moment Ira was overwhelmed by the feelings that had been going through him all night. He ran up and seized the sergeant's hand. The sergeant was surprised. He apparently thought it was an attack and pulled loose.

"Get him, men!"

Ira was immediately surrounded and someone forced his hands together in the front and handcuffed them. The men were carrying rifles.

"I'm sorry, sergeant. Forgive me," said Ira over their heads. "Forgive me."

"Did he hit you?" said one of the soldiers with his rifle leveled, apparently mistaking what he saw for a blow.

"No," said Potts, and his usual composure seemed a little shaken. "No, just fawning on me, that's all. They're all that way — these objectors. So, Private Stoltzfus, we have the pleasure again, don't we? I only regret it has to be such a sad occasion. The law, lieutenant."

A lieutenant unfolded a piece of paper and began to read.

"The 64th Article of War: Any person subject to military law, who, on any pretense whatever strikes his superior officer, or draws or lifts up any weapon or offers any violence against him, being in the execution of his office, or willfully disobeys any lawful command of his superior officer, shall suffer death or such other punishment as a court-martial may direct."

Sergeant Potts looked sober.

"You witnessed him violate an article of war, lieutenant?"

"Yes."

394

"Okay. The verdict, please."

"The decision of the court-martial reads as follows: Private Stoltzfus is guilty of refusing to obey an order by his superior officer. He shall be shot by musketry at sunrise."

"Shot by musketry at sunrise," said Sergeant Potts in an emotional voice. "It's a pity."

Ira stood still.

Shot! Some sixth sense had told him this was it even before the sergeant began to read, but hearing it came like an injection of a powerful drug. It took him by surprise, slowly. First his ears knew it, then his mouth and it opened, then his hands and they dropped open, and finally his legs. They turned as weak as asparagus plants.

He never questioned the legality of what they were doing or asked to see the paper that the lieutenant held in his hand. Even the fact that he hadn't heard anything about a court-martial or been called before it didn't seem strange. Nothing seemed strange. It seemed like the natural climax to all the strange things that were happening to him. He felt at peace within himself.

"Let's go! We can't mess around," said Potts, looking at the sky.

"Normally we give the prisoner a chance to write a letter or two to his family," the lieutenant said. "Do you want paper to write? We'll wait ten minutes."

Ira nodded, and the lieutenant motioned to one of the soldiers who came forward with a pen, small tablet, and several envelopes.

"Make it snappy," he said.

Ira took the sheet of paper and wrote on it:

Dear Pop and Mom,

I have just been informed that I am to be shot. . . .

He crossed it out and began a new sheet.

Pop and Mom,
I am going to be with the Lord,
  Your Son,
  Ira. October 6, 1918.

He wrote a similar note and addressed it to Susanna.

"Okay," said the lieutenant. He took the notes, folded them, and gave them to Sergeant Potts who put them in his coat pocket. "Let's go." They started across the lawn toward the railroad tracks and the high hill beyond. It was the same hill where the objectors had held their services numerous times. On the top of the hill, looking down over the camp, they stopped. The camp was dark except for a few lights on the street. Rising time was still an hour away. The grass was tall here, almost up to the knees. A rabbit ran away through the grass and then another one. The sky had just begun to lighten a bit and the bright stars were fading. October 6, 1918. Why . . . it was his birthday!

"Take off the handcuffs," said the lieutenant. "Okay, Sergeant Potts."

"My pleasure," said the sergeant. He strode up to Ira and stood not more than a foot away from him. "Well, Stoltzfus, as Macbeth himself said it, 'Out, out brief candle,' eh? You broke a law, but so what? I forget quickly, you'll find. Look. I have the power to

396

offer you your life and reproof [he meant reprieve] right now if you give your word you'll obey all orders as a soldier from now on. If you can't promise me that. . . . Men! Show the prisoner your guns." The four soldiers broke open their guns and even in the pale light of the hill the cartridges showed clearly.

"Ready."

The four men dropped down onto one knee.

"Aim."

They pointed their guns at the sky.

"Fire."

The four guns cracked and then cracked again as they echoed off a faraway hill. The empty cartridges fell to the ground, and each of the men took from his pocket another cartridge, loaded it, and closed the gun. Potts looked at Ira.

"Those are yours, Stoltzfus. Anything to say?"

"I'm sorry I hit you, Sergeant Potts. I asked God's forgiveness and I want to ask yours."

Sergeant Potts turned his hands' palms upward. "Forgiveness? Ha! In the Army? I don't care what you say you did. What's done's done. Here you get two choices — punishment or reward. I offer you the reward of no punishment if you start obeying orders. What do you say?"

Ira stood silently in the grass with his hands together in front of him. The stars had all gone out and the sky changed from black to a deep purple lightening over at the rim of the mountain to blue. He was getting cold.

"All right, Sergeant," said the lieutenant. Sergeant Potts stepped back. "Handcuff the prisoner and take positions. You have fifteen minutes to change your mind, Private Stoltzfus."

The privates handcuffed his hands together in front, then went down on their knees in position in front of him with one hand on the muzzles of their rifles and the barrels pointing toward the sky. Several of them began to smoke and Ira noticed that the one man's hand trembled as he lit the cigarette. The lieutenant and Sergeant Potts stood together on the right-hand side. The lieutenant took out his pocket watch and looked at it and put it back into his pocket again. Their backs were to the camp.

He stood facing the valley with the camp sprawled out below. The examination hall where he had gone the first day, the officers' quarters, the row of tents and, yes, he could even see the tent where he had been. Sometime today the men in that tent would read the notice of his execution. He ran his eyes around the perimeter of the camp. Things looked different from up here and he really didn't know the camp too well. He couldn't find the objectors' stable and now a wall of fog was coming up on the south side of camp from the river and moving in over the camp. It would be another foggy morning and they wouldn't be able to see the drill master. The fog covered up the camp and only the railroad was left, running north out of the fog like funny things always do in dreams.

That railroad ran back to Lancaster. . . .

"Ten minutes left. . . ."

Maybe this morning they were starting the cider-making back home . . . Mom and Pop. . . . Someplace off at the other end of the railroad they were just waking up to milk their cows and the sky was growing light over them, too. Susanna. . . . She came and stood before his eyes bigger than life and smiled on him. How gracefully she moved and what was

398

that she had in her hand? Why, a dandelion chain. She threw her arms wide open around him and the dandelion chain fell someplace. Who cared? Susanna on the lawn with a picnic lunch spread out, asking him why he didn't sit down and eat. Susanna by the horse telling him not to say "good-bye." Susanna catching up her little nephew and holding him tight against her telling him he was "a good little onion" and she was going to eat him. Susanna taking a letter from the mailbox, his letter, and opening it and reading it and. . . .

October 6, 1918. It was his twenty-second birthday.

"Five minutes . . ." the lieutenant said. "Blindfold the prisoner. . . ."

They blindfolded him and for a minute he thought he was going to fall. An early morning breeze blew his hair and made the grass shake. A mourning dove was hooting on the backside of the hill.

Music! It broke over him like a red sun bursting over the mountain and throwing its first warm flickers on the houses on the hilltops. Softly first, then like the mountainside at Atglen on that one Sunday every summer when they held the big singing. It seemed like the whole hillside and its rocks were singing and he knew God was smiling on him again.

> . . . *Hearts unfold like flowers before thee,*
> *Hail thee as the sun of love.*
> *Melt the clouds of sin and sadness,*
> *Drive the dark of doubt away.*
> *Giver of immortal gladness*
> *Fill us with the light of day!*

The soldiers out there on the other side of the

blindfold seemed insignificant and powerless before such power and light.

> *Mortals join the mighty chorus*
> *Which the morning stars began.*
> *Father love is reigning o'er us,*
> *Brother love binds man to man. . . .*
> *Joyful music lifts us sunward*
> *In the triumph song of life!*

"Time's up." There was a pause while the lieutenant looked at the sergeant, then at the prisoner. The prisoner was singing.

"Time's up!" he shouted. Another pause. The prisoner was still singing.

"Ready." The soldiers threw away their cigarette butts, dropped back into position and cocked their rifles. "Aim." This time, not at the sky, but at the left shirt pocket of the prisoner. "Fire!"

There was absolute silence.

Not a bird, not a song, not a gun, not a breath. Silence.

The men still knelt in position. The lieutenant's arm still hung with his index finger extended as he had given the signal. Sergeant Potts still stood with his cigarette burning in his mouth, his arms crossed, and his legs apart. The prisoner still stood with the blindfold on his eyes. A minute passed. Two minutes. Then the lieutenant walked over to the prisoner and untied the blindfold.

"We don't want to kill you."

The prisoner's legs buckled and he fell among the long grass.

6

"Good, God, what happened to you?" said Pyski. They crowded around as Ira came into the large cell room.

"Did Sergeant Potts do that to you?"

"Get the man some tea and let him catch his breath." Someone brought up a pot of lukewarm tea and poured him a cup'

"My brothers . . ." said Ira, and he shook their hands all around. Tears welled up in his eyes. "It's good to be back!" he said.

Guthrie put a big arm around his shoulders and hugged him. "You're a good man, Ira. . . . So we suffer, we suffer but even when we are called to suffer we do that joyfully."

Why, Guthrie had never been maltreated, Ira remembered. He was the diplomatic one who could always talk his way out of bad situations. Is he envious of my experience?

"Let's have the story," said Pyski. "No more checker games tonight —we have a story. Give the man some more tea, would you? What a greedy bunch of people."

So Ira told them the story, beginning with the beating and the morning on the hill.

"Were you afraid?" said Schnickerry.

"No."

"You were sure they wouldn't shoot?"

"I don't know. But I stopped thinking about them. I completely forgot about them."

"You forgot?" said Schie.

"Yes, I forgot."

"How could you forget when it could have been the last fifteen minutes of your life? I mean, what did you think about? Didn't you think about telling the sergeant you would back down and start taking orders?"

"Good grief, Pyski. Take it easy, would you?" said someone.

"No, it's okay," said Ira. Should he tell them? "It was like. . . ." Their faces were in the dark and he couldn't see any of them. Perhaps that made it easier. Who knew, maybe one of them would have the same experience someday. He decided to tell.

"It was like. . . . I heard music. First I thought of my family and then I heard music, coming from . . . I don't know where."

"What kind of music?"

"A hymn, 'Joyful, Joyful We Adore Thee.' It seemed like there was chorus or a whole mountainside of people singing. You haven't been to Atglen, I'm sure, but once a year they do it out there on the hillside — thousands and thousands of young people get together and sing and it seems like the whole mountain is singing. That's what I heard. Then someone said, 'Fire!' — I heard them say that — and I thought I heard them fire. It seemed like my body fell behind and I was being transported through the sky to heaven. I saw the kingdom far off, growing closer and glowing like a whole city at sunrise, and it looked wavy like when you see a fish on the bottom of a stream, you

402

know? Next thing I heard voices and there were the soldiers standing over me throwing water on my face and I told them to stop. And then I knew I was on a cot in the 'hole.' "

"Music!" said Schnickerry. "And a vision."

"Oh no, Schnickerry's going to be after you now," said Pyski.

"Schnickerry sees visions, too," explained Frymire.

"Amazing!" said Schnickerry, sucking in his breath and looking thoughtfully at the ceiling. "But why was the vision broken off before he *reached* heaven? Why didn't God reveal himself. Perhaps it was not a dream from God, but a dream from the devil."

"Schnickerry!" Schnickerry's eyes came back to the room.

"You are one of God's elect, I believe. You are one of the 144,000," said Schnickerry. "One of those chosen to share with Jesus the thousand-year reign on the earth when the lion and the lamb — "

"Be careful, Ira. He's very persuasive," said Guthrie. "If you don't watch out, you'll go home a Witness and not a Mennonite."

But Ira didn't tell them everything. He couldn't tell them he had hit Potts. The further he went in the story, the more he found himself skirting that part and also leaping over the strange conversations in the solitary cell of the guardhouse. He stopped talking and Guthrie looked at him strangely. He wanted to tell the story, but then again he didn't.

"Is that all?" said Guthrie. Did Guthrie sense he was holding something back?

"A threatened execution — that's the first time they've tried that," said someone.

"We followed your example, Ira," said Schnickerry.

"Not of us planted marigolds and Brother Potts brought us — "

"Brother Potts!"

"Positive thinking," said Schnickerry. "I'm praying for him, aren't you? Anyway, he brought us all back to the guardhouse and told us he had put you out of the way. We weren't sure what that meant."

"Well, we're not afraid of court-martials and imprisonment either," said Schie. "We took torture — why can't we take court-martials, too? The whole thing's a scheme, you see, to make us break. The colonel thinks he can change our minds before the Board of Inquiry reaches its decisions and makes it too late for him to make soldiers of us."

"Don't be afraid, Ira," said Schnickerry. "We're behind you. We'll go with you, if necessary."

"Thank you," said Ira. "But with me, where?"

"Why, to prison, if they send you."

Did they know he had hit the sergeant then? Ira stretched out and closed his eyes. A man's voice at his ear awoke him.

"Ira, are you sleeping?" It was Guthrie. It had to be late, he thought, because everyone else was sleeping.

"No."

"Everything okay?"

"Yes." He was noncommittal.

"Did you know they're going to court-martial you, Ira?' It's obvious." Guthrie sat down on his heel beside the bed.

"Court-martial?"

"Yes. Potts didn't threaten you with it? That was the whole purpose of that scene with the flowers the other day."

"Again?" said Ira, sitting up. "They're going to court-martial me again?"

"Truthfully," said Guthrie, "I think that first court-martial was a figment of the sergeant's imagination. He made it up.

"He did!"

"Sure, to scare you. There was no court-martial."

"He's a lonely man," said Ira.

"The next court-martial will be real," said Guthrie.

"What will they try me for?"

"Why, the 64th Article, of course. Disobedience of an officer's orders."

"Court-martial!" said Ira. No one was ever found innocent in the Army court trials. Not in this war anyway. They didn't want to kill him; he saw that now. They wanted to totally discredit him.

"That's the way it is," said Guthrie, and he sat down on the edge of the bed and crossed his legs. "They'll always get you on technicalities, not because of what you believe. What could they care about your beliefs? What they want is to get you into uniform and carrying a gun as soon as they can so they'll get you for something tiny like refusing to take out the commander's garbage or refusing to plant marigolds. That's the way it always works, and people outside hear the story and they say, 'Look at those conscientious objectors. They won't do a lousy thing. All they do is sit on their behinds. They won't even take out the garbage they make.' And they'll try you for that someday. Marigolds, garbage, what's the difference? I saw a man court-martialed for refusing to put on a uniform and word got out that he wouldn't dress himself, so they sent him to prison, when in fact it was the uniform he objected to, not to dressing, and the uniform in turn stood for the Army in his mind, and belonging to the Army was a violation of his belief that you should love your enemies!

"So when the time comes, Ira — and it's going to come, have no doubts about it — when the time comes that you're put on trial or brought before the division commander for a little misdemeanor, then seize the opportunity and tell your story from the beginning."

"So what if they don't understand why I believe this way," said Ira. "God understands. I'm doing it for him."

"Okay," said Guthrie. "You're an idealist. I'll tell you one thing — don't be snobbish about what you know. The whispers that your conscience hears from God — there are lots of people in this country just waiting to hear the truth, just waiting to see one man who takes his beliefs seriously. 'Love your enemies and pray for them who persecute you' — sure, sure. They all believe it. Even the devils believe and tremble that someone might start doing it, but I could probably count on my two hands the number of people who practice it. It's a free country, believe anything you want, just don't practice it or we may be forced to lynch you.

"God won't be hurt if you share your story with the Army brass. Make sure there's a reporter near-by. Then tell your story. As for the little misdemeanor that caught you, don't worry about that. If they want to lock you up they will, but at least you've done your witness."

"Mmm." But Ira was thinking, *Do I have a story? Will anyone believe me when they hear what I did to Sergeant Potts?*

"Everything okay?" said Guthrie again and Ira felt the story so close that it rattled against his teeth. He wanted to tell everything. Guthrie was waiting.

"No," he said.

"What's wrong?"

"They won't get me on a technicality because there's lots of big stuff to get me on. I hit the sergeant, Guthrie."

"No!"

"Yes, I did," and the story was out. He told him the whole thing from beginning to end, watching Guthrie's eyes, then occasionally looking at the floor and scraping it with his shoe. When he got to the part of the Mennonite boy who had visited him, Guthrie looked at him. "The devil, that's who it was."

"But why did he look like me then?"

"He's sly, Ira. He's terribly sly. He came to you with a beautiful story of who he was. Modern psychology, huh? 'I'm just the dark side of your personality. . . .' Don't let him fool you, Ira."

When Ira came to the part about the singing on the mountaintop, Guthrie smacked his hands together and looked around to make sure he hadn't woken anybody.

"It's beautiful, Ira, yes . . . it's like the music was a confirmation from God that — "

" 'Anybody who ever sits on a dentist's chair uses the same trick,' the man in my cell said."

"Psychology has the answer again, huh. But don't let that shake you, Ira. It's real, of course, it's real. The devil walks to and fro on this earth. Why shouldn't God also be walking to and fro and making himself known? Why should the devil have all the fun?"

"I feel good," said Ira. "I'm glad I told you the whole thing."

"Listen, you have to sleep," said Guthrie. He reached out his hand and squeezed Ira's. "God bless you," he said, and stood up. "Oh, my leg's asleep." He hopped off toward the dark corner of the room, slapping his leg and hopping around cots.

Ira laughed to himself. He had the same good feeling that he had had the night he spent in the "hole" — a feeling that great trapped forces were moving around inside of him. He fell asleep.

When Ira awoke, Guthrie was standing beside him again, laying a pale yellow telegram on the cot. A telegram? He had never before seen a telegram, let alone read one. He tore it open and when he read it, whatever structure was left of him after six months in camp, collapsed.

"Your mother passed away this morning. Influenza. Please come home. Pop."

The men were all helpful. One of them called the guard and told him. Guthrie sat beside him and put his big hairy arm around his shoulders.

"Could we sing for you?" said Schnickerry. He was almost apologetic, almost sorry he had to break into Ira's thoughts.

Schnickerry began to sing in his mouselike voice, "Nearer my God to thee. . . ." It was the same song that they had sung in the conscientious objector barracks every evening for the last month. The guard outside came running up and rattled the door of the cell.

"No!" he shouted.

But Schnickerry didn't stop. Other voices joined him.

"E'en though it be a cross. . . ."

Ira's skin tingled. The beautiful hymn ran around the heavy timbers, across the cement floor, and out through the spaces in the door.

Someone began to sing *"Gott ist die Liebe"* then, without even thinking that it was a German song. Why, they could be thrown in jail for singing a German song in the middle of a war with Germany. But they were in jail! Well, the guardhouse anyway. Who could prevent them from singing? They were like schoolboys on a school trip, singing song after song. The guard gave up shouting. After all, there wasn't anything in the regulations against singing, was there? He was only bound to enforce the regulations.

Ira sat with his head in his hands. For the first time in the whole war it struck him that he was fortunate. He had never experienced anything like this before. Ten men were singing songs to comfort him. How strange — in the middle of an Army camp, in the jail, 500 miles from home, the Christians were carrying out one of their oldest traditions, comforting those in mourning.

On the third day a funeral notice came and the camp authorities must have believed by now it was not just a bluff for Ira to get a vacation. They granted him a pass for one week.

7

By morning Ira's train was in Virginia, speeding northward. It all seemed so strange to him, those people wandering around on the train in ordinary clothes. They appeared so fat, most of them, and relaxed. Why, they sprawled in their seats and laughed, and some of them shouted from one end of the train to the other. And girls! Two schoolgirls sat opposite him, grade school, maybe, and chattered away about a school play that they were both in. Every once in a while they would just look at each other and burst into laughter. When he got tired of observing people, he looked at the scenery. They were in the outskirts of Washington, D.C., now and row after row of brick tenement houses went by, and after that several miles of quiet countryside with a river. The railroad tracks seemed to be singing. It almost made him forget why he was going home.

"Next stop, Susquehannock," the conductor said, poking his head into the nearly empty car.

The train slowed and jolted.

Ira jumped down with his little bundle of clothes intact. There was no chance that anyone had come for him, was there? He didn't see anyone in the small crowd. They had probably given up on him since he hadn't replied to either telegram. If he was coming home, why he'd certainly be home by now, only an hour or so before the funeral. In fact, it had probably begun already.

Ira had been in Acey's store many times, but he didn't recall that the clerks had ever paid that much attention to him before. No sooner had he entered the door than their heads all popped up and Acey himself, a dark-haired, dark-complected clerk of immigrant background, came front. He clapped his hands and smiled.

"Well, Soldier Boy, back for a holiday, eh? Or you're just passing through?" He grinned broadly. "Not back from France yet, I hope — there's a lot of mopping up to do over there, eh?"

Ira smiled politely. "I want dress pants and a shirt," he said.

The man went through his piles of clothes and they found something suitable. Ira paid. "Can I put them on here?" he said.

"Ah, wear the uniform," the clerk said. "It's a good uniform. Your parents will be proud of you. You remind me of my son." He shook his head and sniffed. "He died at Montfaucon. Only 22. Wear the uniform, believe me, it'll make your papa proud."

Ira shook his head. "He won't be proud," he said. "We're Mennonite."

"Oh," said the clerk. He looked over at Ira slowly, without recognizing him. "Oh." He showed him to the dressing room. When Ira came out, the clerk paid no attention to him, but busied himself at the cash register.

"Thank you," Ira said, but the clerk was busy. He went out.

He walked slowly down the long dipping road

toward home and let his eyes run across the valley and up the other side. The harvest was over. The wooden barns were full of tobacco, the stone barns full of hay, and the empty tobacco fields rolled away from the river as gently as an Amishman's hat does toward the brim. A flock of geese hissed at him as he came across the river. He had never seen the driveway so full of carriages before. They were parked all over the lawn and their horses were tied to the fence and apple trees. The ground was covered with apples which had fallen, probably in a strong wind, and the horses tied by the tree were eating them. They looked at him. He opened the door without knocking and went in.

The house was full of people, most of them wearing black, and there were smells of supper cooking. He had never seen so many people in the house before either. They turned as he came in, silently, almost like a silent movie, and then his father came out of the living room and the people opened a way for him to pass. His father came up and laid his hands on Ira's shoulders. His face was thin and his eyes were red. Ira had never seen him that way before.

"We were hoping you'd come," said Pop, and he turned and walked back through the crowd of people. Ira followed. He felt conspicuous in his new clothes but he was glad he wasn't wearing the uniform. The living room was also full of people, but it was too dark to tell how many. The shades were drawn and only a small oil lamp burned at the desk, beside the coffin.

He wanted to look at his mother, but not now, not with all these people. His father motioned him to an empty chair by the coffin and then sat down himself.

There were several other chairs on the other side of the coffin and everyone else in the room was standing. He looked across at the other chairs. It was the minister, Ben K. Stoltzfus, and his aunt, Lena, his father's sister. The minister nodded to him and he nodded back. Then the service began.

When the service was over, the pallbearers, six of Ira's strong young cousins, all of them too young to be drafted yet, lifted the coffin and carried it out to the hearse-carriage. Ira and his father went out first, got into his father's carriage and followed the hearse up the road. It was the same road down which he had walked an hour before. Behind them, the line of buggies and a few cars stretched for more than a mile.

"We knew you would come," Pop said. They were moving slowly, and Ira held the reins. His father sat erect with the blanket over his knees. It was cool.

"They wouldn't let me go until I got the funeral notice," said Ira.

"Oh."

"Was Mother sick long?"

"No. It was quick — the influenza. Your Susanna's been awful sick, you know."

"Susanna has?"

He hadn't looked at Pop closely, but now he realized his beard was short — six inches shorter than he usually wore it. It was growing back again, but they had really trimmed it for him — the vigilantes had. Was his hair short, too? He couldn't quite tell when Pop had his hat on and he hadn't noticed when they were back at the house.

Pop started coughing.

"Are you okay?" Ira said.

"Just my sinuses. Still acting up on me."

"You've suffered a lot, haven't you, Pop," Ira said, and then he added, "Pop, is it true you had a vision that night when they took you down in the orchard. Is it true?"

His father nodded, but kept his eye straight ahead on the horse's back.

"Have you had any since?"

"Ira," his father turned and looked at him. "I've had them all my life. I never told your mother until that night, but I've had them before. I had one the night she died."

"You did? What was it like?"

"I couldn't describe it. Wonderful. Wonderful. It could only be from God. There was sweet singing — "

"Singing?"

"Yes, like the sound of angels, and I thought, yes, it's that angel band welcoming home your mother."

"What were they singing?"

"I don't know. It was some song I'd never heard before. More beautiful than any earthly tune." His father didn't know the English songs that they used at singings, Ira knew. He was only used to the old German ones and a number of more popular English hymns. Pop often led them himself.

"I had a vision in camp," said Ira.

"It's hard in the camp?"

"It's not easy, Pop."

His father chuckled. "Then it's hard. Hard is the opposite of easy, ain't it?"

They were nearing the cemetery.

"How long can you stay home?"

"I have a week's leave, which means with two days for travel each way, I have three days here."

414

"Then you'll have to leave Thursday or so."

"Yes." He looked at his father. "I wish I could stay longer and help. It's rough, huh — Mastie's leaving and now Mom and no one to help you with the crops."

"I'm still smoking cigars — that's about all that hasn't changed," said his father. "And even the cigars are getting hard to find because of the war. Mastie — " and he turned his palms upward. "We haven't heard from him in half a year, but we keep praying. We keep praying, son, I want you to know that." He hit his fist forcefully on the buggy seat. "We keep praying!" He blew his nose.

They were not the first ones at the cemetery, though. A shiny black Model T was by the roadside and a man in a dark hat and suit that covered a lightly protruding stomach was standing by the open grave, his arms folded. He started to walk toward them.

"Pop, who's that?" said Ira, as he tied up the horse.

His father didn't look at him when he answered.

"It's Pastor Rydell of the Immanuel Bible Church," he said.

8

Everybody came back from the cemetery for supper and the house was full again. Ira's Aunt Lena was in charge of the meal — she shouted orders to a crew of young girls running great bowls of food out to the barn which had been cleaned up so well you could almost eat mashed potatoes off the floor if you had to. Tables were set up on the second floor between the two haymows at both ends and all the farm equipment had been pulled out into a harvested wheat field for a few days. In all of the preparations, Pop had hardly moved a finger, except for a strategy session on the day after Mom's death. Aunt Lena had simply taken over the kitchen and Uncle Ike and his boys had gone ahead with the milking — in addition to milking their own cows, of course.

("You just take care of Emma," Aunt Lena had said, so Pop built her coffin himself, down in the basement. He worked on it all of two days and half of the next, and pounding in the nails and sandpapering the roughbox seemed to work away his grief.)

Aunt Lena was passing food to her runners at an almost unbelievable pace.

"Lena, you mean you did all this yourself?" said Jonas B.'s Mary, and she stood with her hands on her hips watching the food go by. "I'll bet even Emma didn't know her stove could cook so much."

"Well, it wasn't all me," said Lena. "Anna Ruth made the pumpkin pies — 59 of them, and one of Emma's cousins brought the red beet pickles and pickled eggs, and I had a lot of helpers. Like your Annie here. What would I do without her?"

"Are you talking about me?" said Annie, swinging around toward her mother and Aunt Lena with a stirring spoon in her hand.

"I said I don't know what I'd do without your help," said Lena.

"Oh, Aunt Lena. . . ." Two tears rolled down Annie's face. It wasn't that Lena really was her aunt, not at all. Aunt Lena was an aunt to a lot of people who were not related to her. "Aunt Lena, he isn't coming."

"He's not. Oh, that's too bad, Annie." Lena reached into her pocket for a handkerchief. She reached out and brushed Annie's cheeks. "It wouldn't do for the cook to be crying," she said.

"Annie, you take the honey out now. We're about finished here." She handed her a kettle containing five sections of fine comb honey that Red Isaac had robbed from his bees a month ago. Annie was hardly halfway across the sun porch though when Magdalena said, "She looks so hard these days. Aren't you feeding her enough, Mary?" Annie stopped on the sun porch.

"It's not that, Lena. It's that boy. She can't get him out of her mind."

"A new one?"

"No, Mastie."

"Well, nothing wrong with that, I suppose."

"No? He doesn't want to marry her, Lena, but she

can't see that. She's got her hopes up again because he sent her another letter, from the hospital this time. I guess you knew he was in the hospital. Well, of course, being his aunt. She was thinking he might come home for the funeral, I guess. I mean, she's so out of touch with things as they are — he won't come home, *never*, I could see that when he left. He had the wild look. But try to tell her that. Try to convince her to stop wasting her time and tears and sleep over him — you can't. Well, what do you think — do you think he'll come back?''

Annie stood perfectly still against the wall of the sun porch. A group of girls was coming. She got down on her hands and knees as if she were searching for something.

"I don't know," said Lena. "That remains to be seen, of course."

"You don't need to hedge with me, Lena. We've known each other for years. How can one discourage the girl from thinking about him? I don't want her to end up an old maid. The way I look at his letters, he's just like most men when they get hungry or lonely or along about dark — they start thinking about a girl. The rest of the time they couldn't care less. And that's all that boy wants — but if he can find it someplace else, so he don't have to come back to the church, then he will." Annie opened her mouth in horror and stood up.

"You mark my word," her mother said, "he won't come back. I'm not saying he'll be killed, or injured, God forbid, but when a boy separates and goes worldly and disobeys his father and mother in the way he has, then they don't come back."

The girls on the walk stopped talking when they

418

saw Annie, one or two smiled, and as soon as they were past and in the kitchen they began to whisper again. Annie opened the door and ran to the barn with the honey. She set the honey on the table and began to set it out on small white plates. When she turned around, she almost stepped on Aunt Lena's toes.

"Aunt Lena!"

"What is it?"

"Is Mastie coming back?"

Aunt Lena looked at Annie and pursed her lips. "I don't know," she said. "But. . . . Well, they usually don't, it's true, but Mastie's an unusual boy."

"Do you think so?"

"He always was impulsive — you know that. One day he just up and walked off and enlisted. Some day he'll just walk right back and surprise us."

"Do you think so?"

"Sure, he will," said Aunt Lena. *But I really don't think so,* her eyes said.

"You don't believe so, do you?" Annie said. "But I do, Aunt Lena. He promised me he's coming."

"Are we ready to begin?" said Uncle Ike. He was standing on a hay bale to look over the crowd, which was standing in groups near the table. "Is Isaac coming? Is your pop coming, Ira?"

Ira was sitting by the head of the first big table. "Is he coming?" said Uncle Ike. "If not, I guess we'd better begin." He stretched out his hand for silence and prayed. Then the food began to move and the sight of it loosened people's tongues.

Then Pop walked in, followed closely by the tall man named Rydell. They sat down together at the head of the table. Rydell seemed to sense he was being watched but it seemed he didn't mind. "Church he preaches at holds 500," someone said in explaining to the man beside him who Rydell was.

"My son, Ira," said Pop in English and he motioned toward Ira. By now, Ira was in a set of his own plain clothes, but his hair was cut short, like an Army boy's.

"We've met before, I believe," said Rydell, leaning over the table to shake his hand. His face was scarred, from smallpox perhaps, and he wasn't in the least handsome, but he had a bold grin that made people feel at home. "The train station at your send-off, maybe. How's the camp. You're still in camp?"

"Yes."

"Eats okay, are they?"

"They're okay."

"I was sorry to hear about your mother," said Rydell gently. Ira nodded.

Rydell suddenly reached over and put his hand on top of Ira's. "God bless you," he said, but Ira couldn't look up. He was afraid his eyes would show what he was really feeling. Suspicion. Resentment. What right did this man have to come to his home? It was a trick, he was sure of it. He was aware now of all the ways there were to trick people. The officers used them all the time on the conscientious objectors in camp. This man had led the vigilante squad against his father, hadn't he? He took his hand out from under Rydell's and picked up a dish of potatoes. A potato jumped off the spoon onto the floor and he reached down to pick it up. Noticing where his father's legs were he reached past Rydell with his foot and tapped his father's leg three times with his foot.

His father put a forkful of ham into his mouth and looked at Ira. He blinked his eyes like an old turtle. What was he thinking? Didn't he see through Rydell?

Rydell looked down the long table at the rows of Amish and Mennonites eating and talking.

"This is amazing," he said. "What a wonderful custom. What a good way to show that they identify with you in your hour of trouble."

"Our people always stand by each other," said Pop. "But sometimes only out of habit. The war is teaching us again that it's all we have."

Rydell reached into his pocket and got out a handkerchief and wiped his forehead. "Mr. Stoltzfus," he said, lowering his voice, "I really came to tell you how sorry I am about that night — "

Pop looked at his fingernails.

"I don't know," said Rydell. "I just didn't realize before — but I've been watching you ever since then. You're not a slacker at all," he said.

Pop went on looking at his fingernails.

"Can you forgive me?" said Rydell, and suddenly that big rough face was full of misery. An actor, Ira told himself. He's an actor.

Pop looked up with a little smile.

"Sure," he said. He reached over and clasped Rydell's hand with both of his. He held Rydell's hand much longer than an ordinary handshake, and he looked into the other man's eyes all the while, neither coldly nor warmly but with deep feeling. Some of the folks down the table a bit who weren't talking looked at them curiously.

"Oh . . . I feel a lot better," said Rydell, and he loosened his collar button. "I've been thinking about this for the last two months. I couldn't even preach last Sunday, would you believe," and he laughed heartily, gaily. "I felt like a hypocrite. I still don't agree with you on the war, don't get me wrong, but you're entitled to your belief. Right? It took a Mennonite farmer to teach me that. I'm sorry. I didn't mean that like it sounded. I mean I had to learn that lesson from a man like yourself, and I always thought you were so different, I guess. Behind the times, maybe, if I were to be truthful about my feelings. But you're not. You're way out ahead. You were the Christian that night in the orchard, I was the heathen. I better stop before I put my foot in my mouth again, eh?" He grinned.

"I knew that was why you came," said Pop.

"You did? Amazing," said Rydell.

"No," said Pop. "Very human. I only wish Emma had been here to witness this. I'm glad Ira — Ira — " He looked toward Ira, but somehow Ira had slipped away. He was down at the other end of the table where Aunt Lena had buttonholed him. She crushed his fingers in a strong handshake.

"Ira, it's so good to see you. I often think of you down there in the camp and I think, isn't it wonderful we have boys with convictions like that? We're all behind you, Ira. You've met, haven't you?" she said, looking back at Annie. "Why, of course, of course."

"Hello, Annie."

She smiled at him. She was dressed in a deep blue dress with a blue cape, so immaculate that it looked like she had stepped out of a quilt. She wasn't pretty at all. No, Susanna had her beat there, but something deep and warm came through her smile. All at once he was lonely for the home community and he wanted to stay.

"I'm sorry about your mother," she said, and in the next breath her real thoughts came out. "Mastie didn't come."

"No, he didn't," said Ira.

"I was sure he'd come," said Annie.

"Here, have a pickle," said Magdalena, turning around and presenting the tray. "Come, don't be so serious, Annie. When I was young — ach, we were always laughing like a bunch of I don't know what. But when I think of it, we didn't have any reason not to laugh. We didn't have a war to pull us apart like you folks have."

"It's Ira's mother's funeral," said Annie.

"Yes, that's so. Be strong, Ira," she said. "For I know that all things work together for good for them that love the Lord." Ira nodded.

"There are so many sick," said Aunt Lena, shaking her head. "Funerals, funerals, funerals, it's like the night that the angel of death passed over Egypt.

"How is camp?" said Aunt Magdalena, changing the subject.

"It's hard," said Ira.

"I thought so. Is the food okay? You're looking thin."

"It's nothing like this."

"No, I wouldn't suppose so. Nothing like a good get-together for putting your body back in running order. It is a sad occasion, of course it is, but with friends, even death loses some of its sting."

Ira thought of the men singing in the guardhouse on the morning of his mother's death. "Yes," he said. "It's true." He started to walk toward the haymow, full of hay that he hadn't helped make.

"Ira, I thought you might want to know — "

He turned around. Annie was standing right behind him. She didn't lower her voice at all because the people at the table were making so much noise that she didn't need to.

" — about Susanna," said Annie. "It was really close, the doctors said. But she's over the worst now. We're taking good care of her."

"Can I go see her?"

"Really, you shouldn't. The place where she works is quarantined and I haven't even seen her for a week. Her employer lady calls out the window to Mom and tells her how things are."

"Look, I'll get Pop's rig. Can you show me where she works?"

"You can't see her."

"Why not? I'll look in the window and say 'hello.' I came the whole way from Georgia."

"She's upstairs and they can't move her. And you can't go inside. Really, it's dangerous. People are coming down with it everywhere."

"You say she was close?"

"She was close, yes. We had a special prayer meeting for her and in the morning her high fever left. She opened her eyes for the first time in twelve hours. Isn't it wonderful?" Annie looked at him and for the first time he saw how she had caught Mastie. Her eyes were full of trust. "If he could heal your friend, don't you think he can bring mine home again?" she said.

"Mastie? He won't come back."

"How do you know?" She was reading every thought that flickered across his eyes, and he knew it.

"I know Mastie, that's how. When he makes up his

424

mind on something, he doesn't change it."

"Shame on you," she said. "You're his own brother and you say things like that. You don't want him to come back." She was upset.

"Well, you asked me what I thought."

"Well, let me tell you something, Mr. Stoltzfus. My sister's not so keen on you anymore either." Annie whirled around and walked away swiftly. He was immediately sorry he had offended her but he was too cut by her remark to run after her and say so.

"Hey, Ira." Uncle Ike slapped his behind. "It's not good for you to stand around by yourself."

"Just looking at the hay," said Ira.

"Good hay, huh? That's the good weather that we had last summer. Listen, come over and join the conversation. They're all wondering about you, how it's going in camp. They want to hear your stories." Uncle Ike squeezed Ira's elbow. "Or aren't you in the feel for it today? You know, she was really a good woman, your mother was. I knew her since she was a little girl and we used to laugh at how she sat in with the big people and every once in a while her pop would turn to her and say, 'Now what do you think, Emmy?' And she'd say something that really seemed wise to us other children and we got a big laugh out of that. But the way it turned out, that was all just training for living with your father, and advising him. Your father's under a lot of pressure, you know. He's got the church load and the farm load and neither of you boys to help him. Well, anyway, what do you say for some stories, Ira?" He reached out and snapped one of Ira's suspenders. "How do some people stand to go around in belts anyway?"

Ira shook his head. "I don't feel like telling stories."

"Well, it's up to you. Everything okay?"

"What I want to know is, what's the biggest Mennonite-hater in the county doing with my father?"

"Ahh . . ." said Uncle Ike. He rolled his eyes up into his skull. "You better ask Pop that question."

9

The day after Mom's funeral, Ira milked the cows
for the first time in three months. He brought one
pailful into the house. The house was quiet and dark
and he thought no one was home until he opened the
door. There was Pop, sitting in the rocker with his
back to the almost dark window.

"Come in," he said from the rocker.

Ira pushed the door open and closed it behind him.
He set the milk on the table.

"I thought no one was home," he said.

"No place else to go," said Pop, and he began to
rock slowly in the chair. Ira sat down at the table
and the clock struck overhead. He hadn't noticed
the quiet before but now he realized it as one of the
effects of his mother's going. The house was terribly
quiet. The guests were all gone, even Uncle Ike and
Aunt Magdalena were gone.

"Pop, I just have one question. Why did you ask
that preacher to Mom's funeral?"

"Ben K.?"

"No, Rydell."

"I didn't ask him. He came of his own free will."

"Then why did you ask him to the supper and
eat with him? That man is down on the Mennonites
and the conscientious objectors. If he had his way,

we'd all be strung up or have our hair cut with cow clippers."

"I can't chase a man away from my table."

"You don't have to invite him in the beginning. That's the man who led the gang against you, isn't it? He preaches war to his people every Sunday and sells war bonds during the week. I know his kind, Pop. We have them in the camp and they're all soft words and nice manners but they're out to get you. I tried to tell you at the table. Didn't you feel my foot? He was there to spy on us for sure."

"I invited him," said the old man simply.

"Yes, I know you did. Why?"

"Ira, I haven't been around in this world for sixty years for nothing. Maybe I learned something, maybe I didn't. That's neither here nor there. But when a man comes with a broken heart to ask forgiveness, I never turn him away."

"He wasn't for real."

"How do you know he wasn't for real? I know him better than you do."

"No, you don't, Pop. You don't know his kind. You haven't been around in the world, so you think you can trust everyone and believe what they say because that's the way it is among us, but that's not the way it is in the world. Some men look at you so honest-like and say such nice things at the camp but you can bet on it they have another motive. And when you're not looking, it comes out. Rydell is that kind. He's a politician, that's what he is."

"No," said Pop. "I don't like to say this, but you're wrong." He leaned forward in his chair now with his one finger up in the air to make his point, his face black against the window behind him. "Pastor Rydell is a sincere man. Yes he is. He loves his people just like we love ours. The problem is, he's sincere and wrong in this case. Now that's putting it strong, but think about it. He sees this war as a good one — to save democracy as the president says. So naturally he tried to help the cause of the war — he talks war bonds, he talks against the 'slackers,' he preaches against the Kaiser — but he is sincere. He's no politician. Someday maybe he will change his mind about the war, Lord help him.

"Now, to back up a little, why did he come to your mother's funeral? He didn't know her. Why, because he wanted to see me. I saw that right away. If he wanted to spy, he'd send some boy over on a bicycle. But he came like a man and shook my hand and I could see in his eye — listen to me, Ira — I could see in his eye he had something to say and it wasn't easy to say it. I forgave him, of course I did. Remember the parable of Jesus and the high-up man who forgives his servant a big debt but the servant turns around and grabs another fellow by the throat because the man owes the servant a little debt? Sure you know that story. Then the high-up man throws the man with the big debt into prison. 'So will my heavenly Father do to every one of you, if you do not forgive your brother from your heart.'

"Don't you think that came to me easy, Ira. Everything we learn wears a price tag. Light the lamp, would you? No point in ruining our eyes yet."

Ira put the milk away and lit the lamp. It cast crazy shadows from their heads into the corners of the room.

"I lost your mother," said Pop. "That's what it took."

"I don't know what you mean," Ira said.

"That's what it took — that's what I mean."

"Took for what?"

"Took to tell me to forgive. Ira, you don't see the whole picture yet. You just see your side of it but the whole picture — "

"Is this a riddle or something?"

"I'm talking about your brother, that's what I'm talking about," said Pop.

"Mastie."

"You don't have any other brothers, do you?" said Pop. "Your brother and I didn't part with good feelings. That's saying it plain. I didn't want to see him go, no! but he walked out of here without a word of good-bye to me or your mother and that hurt. Oh, it hurt. You don't know what it's like to have sons yet, Ira, but when you do, then you'll find out what it's like to be hurt. 'Love them while they're in your lap because when they grow up, they'll tramp all over your heart,' like they say. But it wasn't all his fault, you see. We were both to blame. Did I cut him off too quick? Does he understand why I did it? You see why I don't get any sleep."

"I don't see what all this has to do with Mom's passing," said Ira.

"Everything!" said Pop vehemently. "Forgiveness, don't you see? It's hard to forgive Brother Rydell, but not so hard. But my own son — is that what God is trying to tell me?"

"People's passings don't always mean something," Ira said. "It was the influenza." An old worm of jealousy began to stir restlessly in his stomach. He had always thought that the old man catered to Mastie and loved him more because Mastie was brash and impulsive and laughed easily, unlike himself.

"Sure, sure, it was the influenza. But don't fool yourself. Nothing happens that don't mean something. Did God have to take your mother?"

"She did so many kind things," Ira said.

"She was beautiful, Ira!" Tears began to run down the old man's weathered and hairy cheeks. "She was beautiful, son, and I mean that." He put his head between his hands.

"When I worked with the threshers last summer," Ira said, "She would save back supper for me every night and sometimes she would even fall asleep there on the sofa before I got home, but she would always get up to set it out on the table for me. I told her to go on to bed, if I'm late, but she said she never had anything else to do at that hour of the night."

"Oh," said Pop. He nodded his head.

"And her eyes. She knew they were bad and I guess most people would have been afraid. I would have been afraid I'd lose my eyes, anyway, if they were as bad as hers, but she kept saying that verse every time, 'I will trust and not be afraid.'"

"Yes," said the old man, "yes. She was a real gemstone, that's what she was. I knew that the first time I saw her. There was just something outstanding about her. The way she carried herself and the way she had of smoothing things over. Her father was a bishop, you know, and a lot of people would come to him with their troubles. He'd tell her all about the people he counseled — although she was still a girl in her teens — that's how much he valued her advice. Then he'd say, "Now, what do you think I should have told them?" And she'd tell him. No hem-hawing with her. A bishop handles a lot of tough ones, the discontents who want to leave the church, rebellious boys who won't listen to anyone, and sometimes he'd come down like *that!*" The old man slammed his fist on the table. "Then your mother would come along and help smooth things over." He waved his hands gently. "And after a while the problem was solved."

Ira suspected the old man of no longer talking about her and her father. Why that was the way the old man himself operated, coming down hard, and if it hadn't been for his mother's presence there wouldn't be a church anymore. There wouldn't be a family. But the old man was too proud to admit that probably. He talked about her and her father instead.

"And she could pray," said Pop. He took off his reading glasses and began to polish them on his shirt. He was breathing noisily. "I can't pray anymore," he said in a whisper. "No, I can't." He sat with his head in his hands and the rocker was still. "I just can't."

"What's wrong?" Ira said at last.

"I can't tell you."

"The other conscientious objectors sang for me when Mother died," said Ira, changing the subject.

"They did?"

"Yes, they did."

"That's good," said Pop. He put his glasses on and took them right back off again. "It's terrible not to be able to pray," he said.

"Why can't you?"

"I can't tell you, Ira. I can't tell you."

"How do you expect me to understand then?"

"I'll say this. The powers of evil are much stronger than we can ever know."

432

"Is this another riddle?"

"The power of devils." said Pop.

"Devils?"

"Yes, devils."

"You believe in them?"

"Believe in them? Oh, they're all around us, as real as this rocking chair, as real as the food we eat. They keep us from praying."

"How do you know?"

"I just know," the old man said. "I can't tell you everything." He stopped and seemed to want to go on but something was holding him back. Was he afraid that even speaking thoughts was making them true? "I saw them."

"You saw them? Devils?" Ira could hardly believe it. It sounded like his own experience and he would have said so if it had been Mom in the chair instead of Pop. But he and Pop never talked about such things. If they did, it was Pop lecturing and him nodding. So he didn't say it.

"Yes," said the old man, "they tried to keep me from praying and they succeeded. And it's devils that are keeping your brother from coming home. Pray, Ira, pray. And trust. That is our only hope." He got up and walked to the doorway. "I must check on Mollie," he said. "She's due to calve tonight."

10

Ira was taken directly to the guardhouse when he arrived back in camp and told that his court-martial was to begin the following Wednesday, which was still four days away. In the meanwhile he could collect his thoughts, ask for legal counsel, or hunt bedbugs, as far as the camp authorities were concerned. As for his friends, they had all been released and sent back to their regular quarters.

Ira declined the legal counsel. He had an idea: Guthrie had said the trial was the moment to tell his story. He asked for a tablet of paper and sat down on the cot where he slept and began to write out his speech carefully. He worked on it as hard as he had ever worked on a lesson for his schoolchildren, referring back and forth in his old Bible, jotting down ideas and questions, and finally going back and writing out his whole speech in longhand. At the top of each sheet was a question or a statement underlined in red.

On the morning of the trial he woke up confident and self-assured. Today was the day he would lay everything out before the court. In a sense, he thought, it was like a bull's heart, still beating, that he had seen as a teenager when they butchered.

He was going to operate on his own heart and lay

open the tissue, the protective fat — the tradition that had wrapped around him to protect him and supply him with everything that he needed to grow up. Then the veins and arteries leading to and from the heart — the questions that had been thrown at him in camp and the answers that his heart supplied. Finally, the heart itself — the great belief which was humming like a sump pump, carrying lifeblood to every corner of his being.

If a man sees your heart pumping away inside you, can he possibly have any doubts that you're alive? It wasn't just a matter of not planting marigolds — of course it wasn't — it was a whole belief that he wanted the court to see.

A soldier with a loaded gun and bayonet brought Ira into the courtroom. Well, it was really only a makeshift courtroom, just another meeting room in the division headquarters with a flag in one corner. But it was a courtroom today. A semicircle of Army officers acting as the court or jury, sat on the right side, spiffy in their clean uniforms — a few majors, a few captains, several lieutenants. There may have been twelve of them. They looked up a few at a time as Ira came in and then they went back to whatever they had been doing. One or two were reading the newspaper, a third was yawning and trying to balance his head on his hand, while several others were laughing and blowing cigarette smoke at each other.

In the center behind a table was the judge, or judge advocate as they called him, and on the left several familiar faces — Colonel Doolittle, who was handling the prosecution, the lieutenant who had accompanied Ira to the hill that morning of his birthday, and Sergeant Potts. The colonel was erect and wide-awake. He nodded to Ira when he came in. That was in contrast to Sergeant Potts who looked tired out and not at all his usual self. There were bags under his eyes. He didn't look healthy at all. He didn't look up when Ira came in.

The court had been in session since 9:00, and in the first two hours they had tried four objectors from another camp in an average of thirty minutes apiece. Guilty of refusing to obey an order to burn camp trash — probably 30 years at Leavenworth, although they hadn't started sentencing yet. Guilty of refusing to wear the uniform — 30 years probably. Guilty of inconsistency in obeying orders — 50 years probably. Another man guilty of the same. What was there to distinguish this case from the last one? A captain who was due in Chattanooga for an evening ball looked at his watch.

The soldier led Ira to the center of the floor where he stood, not at attention, in the plain vest and dark pants he had brought along from home. He had shaved and felt in full possession of his thoughts, even though the guardhouse had taken fifteen pounds from him over the last several weeks. He was eager to tell his story. The charges were read, witness called to the stand to substantiate them, and then the judge advocate turned to his prisoner.

"Do you have anything to say for yourself, Stoltzfus?"

Ira nodded. He reviewed the whole room. In the ten minutes since the trial had opened an officer had gone to sleep. The officer nearest him was looking at the comic strips, chuckling silently, and pointing one out every once in a while to the man next to him. In contrast to them, the colonel had his eyes fixed on Ira. Ira saw in a moment that the colonel was his one hope. *He is a reasonable man, not one who is easily persuaded to change his mind but a man who tolerates other ideas.* He decided to concentrate all his efforts on making his beliefs clear to the colonel. He realized the colonel represented the prosecution assigned to convict him and send him off to prison. But it made no difference. He was sure that none of them were sympathetic toward him as the trial opened.

He dropped his eyes to the floor and began simply.

"Friends, I am a member of the Mennonite Church — "

He looked up at the colonel. Throughout the entire speech he continued that pattern, looking first at the floor to concentrate his thoughts, then at the colonel as he spoke. Did the colonel understand? Was it clear beyond a doubt? He disregarded the written statement which stuck out of one pocket and relied on his memory.

"I don't know what you know about the Mennonite Church but it forbids us to go to war. So far in this trial we have talked about what I did do and didn't do, and nothing about what I believe. I would like to tell you *why* I didn't plant marigolds for the lieutenant.

"Perhaps you think my church or one of its ministers told me I shouldn't become a soldier, but this is not so. It was my own choice. When I was baptized I made a vow to God and his church that I would remain true, and since we are forbidden to kill both by the Bible and our church, I have been obedient to that. No one has brainwashed me. My own brother decided he wanted to fight and went to France.

"Let me tell you about the Mennonite people. We take the Bible literally. If it says, 'Thou shalt not kill,' as it does, and 'They that take the sword shall perish with the sword,' and 'Love thy neighbor as thyself,' as it does, then we must live that way. If it says, 'The head of every woman shall be covered when she prays;' as it does, then our women cover their heads with a veiling. Maybe you've seen them. If the Bible says, 'Do not be conformed to this world but transformed,' as it does, then we live different, we dress different, we think different than worldly people because of that.

"Because we live by the Bible, some people find us painful to live with. So we have to suffer. But suffering is not so bad — is it? — because the Bible also says, 'Blessed are ye when men shall revile you and persecute you for my sake, for so persecuted they the prophets. . . .' Yes, they also persecuted our forefathers, the Anabaptists, in Europe four hundred years ago. They died rather than give up their faith. I have read a book which says they died rejoicing, singing. The higher the fire rose in which they were tied, the more they sang."

One or two members of the jury began to listen out of a sense of curiosity but Ira didn't notice them. He looked confidently at the colonel. He was more sure of himself now. The colonel looked back, unblinking. Not one muscle in his old faced moved.

"Colonel Doolittle, we were chased all over Europe for our beliefs until we settled down in Switzerland. We became farmers and minded our own business. But after a hundred and fifty years things got rough again. My grandfathers refused to serve in the army. Not the Swiss army, but the army of the countries

438

who used Swiss soldiers to fight their wars.

The noblemen — I like history, Colonel Doolittle, and I have checked into this story — the nobles of Switzerland conscripted men and were paid by the armies of other countries. They used the money to build their own estates. Our ministers, of course, taught our people it was wrong to go and consequently there was a price on their heads. Some were hanged, some were thrown in prison, some ended up as galley slaves. But we refused to leave Switzerland because it was our home.

"One day, however, a representative of William Penn's government in Pennsylvania contacted us and offered us free land there and the right to believe the way we wanted to. So we loaded everything we had on barges and floated all the way to Holland, and from there we caught ships to Pennsylvania. I'm being very brief. . . ."

"You're not being brief," said the judge. "I wish you would."

"So we settled in Pennsylvania and became farmers again. The U.S. Constitution, when it was written, promised not to interfere with our beliefs. 'Congress shall make no law regarding the establishment or practice of religion. . . .' The First Amendment. The *first*, colonel, that's how important they thought it was. But if the United States and this court now decide to disregard this law, then we have no choice except to suffer again.

"Now I want to talk about myself and why I refused to plant marigolds. Yes, I'm guilty. I don't deny it. Why did I refuse? I like to plant flowers, you know. When this war is over, I will plant a garden of flowers for you, or anyone, if you wish. So why did

I refuse such an innocent order? Is it such an important thing — planting flowers? Of course not. But in this case, planting flowers was a military order and I have decided not to obey military orders because that means I support the war and disobey our Lord's commandment, 'Thou shalt not kill,' You say, that isn't killing — planting flowers — but Saul didn't throw any stones. He only held the coats of the men who killed Stephen, but the Bible says, 'He consented to Stephen's death.' You see, I couldn't consent to the military's right to exist because I know why the Army was created. It was created to kill men."

The colonel's face suddenly came to life.

"Objection! Objection!" he said. The judge advocate opened his eyes.

"Yes?"

"This testimony is getting ridiculous. The prisoner says the Army was created to kill men. That is incorrect, I think you will find, if you look at President Wilson's speech when he ordered mobilization. I have it right here," the colonel said, and he fumbled for his bifocals, put them on, and began to read

"It is not an army that we must shape and train for war, it is a nation. . . . It is a new thing in our history and a landmark in our progress. It is a new manner of accepting and vitalizing our duty. . . .'" The colonel's voice began to rise dramatically. " ' . . . to give ourselves with thoughtful devotion to the common purpose of us all. . . . It is nothing less than the day upon which the manhood of the country shall step forward in one solid rank . . .' This is it, gentlemen. Listen carefully. Here's the reason, '. . . in defense of the ideals to which this nation is consecrated."

"Objection overruled," said the judge advocate. "Go ahead, Stoltzfus."

"Captain!" The colonel stood up.

"I'm sorry, colonel. You'll have your chance to speak. Let the prisoner finish."

The colonel sat down and propped his chin on his hand. Ira continued.

"But looking at the order another way, colonel," he said, "why were we to plant flowers? So the camp would be beautiful and the general who came to see it would be impressed. But if he was impressed by our camp, might he not order our division to France sooner? So it does have something to do with killing. Even planting flowers, yes."

One of the members of the jury looked curiously at Ira and commented to the officer beside him. The officer looked up from his newspaper and nodded. Ira took his Bible from his pocket. The pages were loose and falling out so that he had to hold them as he flipped back and forth.

"What does the Bible say about killing? 'Thou shalt not kill' is perhaps the first reference against it, and in the New Testament Jesus told His disciples, 'Love your enemies, pray for them which despitefully use you.' The very first Christians had a motto, 'Jesus is Lord,' and I believe so, too. What shall I do then when the president of my country tells me to do something which the King of my country —" he indicated which country he meant by a gesture toward the ceiling, "tells me not to do. Whom shall I obey? Whom shall I disobey?"

"He's crazy," one of the captains said aloud. "How much of this religious twaddle must we listen to?"

"Maybe I'm crazy," said Ira, fixing his eyes on the captain, "but not a coward. I'm not afraid of death as some people accuse us conscientious objectors. I have scars to show for my five months in this camp. Would you like to see them? My scars are nothing compared to those of some of my friends." Sergeant Potts became restless and crossed his legs, then ran his hand through his hair so that it stuck up in rooster tails.

"The Bible tells us not to fear those who will kill our bodies but to fear only the ones who could kill our souls forever. Don't think that I want to die. I don't want to be a martyr — I love living. I have a girlfriend whom I might someday marry, and who is teaching my pupils now that I'm not. But let me ask you frankly, wouldn't I be a hypocrite if I backed down on my belief just because I am threatened with punishment? You would call me a hypocrite, wouldn't you?"

The court member broke Ira's gaze and moved uneasily in his seat. He picked up his newspaper, then in a moment he dropped it and started listening again.

"But I am ready to suffer — after all Jesus suffered, didn't he? First in the Garden of Gethsemane and then on Calvary.

"A long time ago, colonel, you asked me what the results would be if we all talked like this and refused to fight. What would happen to us? Would we become another state of Germany? At the time I couldn't answer you. You also asked me what I would do if a maniac came into my house to kill my beloved. [Ira used the word unselfconsciously.] We are not married, but supposing we got married and that happened, what would I do? Do you remember
442

asking me those questions? I couldn't answer you then. But I've had a lot of time to think since. I do thank you for that. The guardhouse tends to clear out one's mind.

"Colonel, I am a schoolteacher, as I said, as I teach a little geometry and a little history. Let me give you a geometry problem then."

"Stoltzfus, is this relevant?" the judge said.

"I mean to answer the question, 'What would I do if someone attacked my wife with a gun?'"

"Proceed."

"In geometry," Ira said, "we set up a theory and then line up proofs so that in the end where there was only a vague idea, the answer becomes clear. When you asked me the question, 'What would I do if my wife were attacked?' meaning that I would be there, perhaps in bed at night, it seemed there were only two possible answers. *Yes*, I would try to kill the maniac, a bad man, which would leave us safe but him dead, or *no*, I would not defend myself which means he would harm my wife, or maybe both of us would be left dead, or badly hurt. The meaning of *yes* is: I should be a soldier because I am willing to defend. The meaning of *no* is: I am a fool and a coward because I let myself be killed when I might have saved myself. But some questions cannot be answered with yes or no.

"Let us look at the possibilities just as we would look at a problem of what the shape of a triangle is when we only know two sides. Perhaps you thought there was only one choice when someone attacks you? Really, there are five."

"First a tragedy. My wife and I might be killed because of my foolishness. In your mind this would be the worst thing that could happen. God would not want such an evil to happen, would he?''

The court members looked at the prisoner.

"What sort of court is this anyway?" The man with the newspaper whispered. "Is he guilty or not guilty? Isn't that what we're here to find out? Well, what's that have to do with someone breaking into your house?" But out of curiosity at this man in his unusual clothes, and what he was saying, the other men didn't answer.

"Second, we might be martyrs," said Ira. "This means that sometimes dying is a good thing. Yes, Christians believe this. By dying, a martyr may make a greater contribution to this world than if he went on living. Why, history is full of such examples. A Christian died at the hands of an unbeliever and became a greater witness to the power of love. Nor are Christians the only ones who have martyrs. Ethan Allen was a martyr, some say, because the British executed him as an American spy. History is popping with such examples!

"Third, might there not be another way than killing the wild man? Could I trick him? Or persuade him? Or step in front of him so my wife could escape even if I was shot? I have no idea what the other way would be now. No doubt my mind would be thinking fast. . . ."

"Thinking?" said a court member, "Ha, ha, scrambling!" The other members laughed. They were all awake and several of them were leaning forward at their desks to listen to the 'geometry problem.' Even Sergeant Potts had come out of his lethargy to look at Ira over his hand, which covered his mouth and nose.

"The fourth possibility, colonel, is a miracle. First Corinthians 10:13 says, 'There hath no temptation taken you but such as is common to man. But God is able, who will not suffer you to be tempted above that ye are able but will with the temptation also make a way of escape.' What does that mean? 'A way of escape?' Colonel, I am also puzzled. But if our life is in God's hands, as we Christians believe, then he will know what to do. Didn't he send plagues on the Egyptians until they cursed their Jewish slaves and Pharaoh sent them out of the country? Doesn't he count the hairs as they fall off your head? So it says.

"If I could tell you now what miracle would save me from the madman's gun, then it couldn't be called a miracle, could it? Might the gun jam? Or the man be astonished to hear me welcome him to my house? Or something fall on my porch and frighten him? Or I be shot at but the bullets go wide and pass through my clothing? You see how silly it is to think what the miracle might be. The miracle is greater than anything you or I can think of.

"Finally, I might try to kill the man, and if I succeeded the police and court would probably clear me because I shot him in self-defense. Maybe they would call me a hero in our community. But this choice is not as simple as it looks. Suppose I miss him. Or wound him? Then what? The chances are great that I won't kill him, you know. He has surprised us. We are asleep, not prepared for an attack anyway. So he has the first move. He may be a better shot or fighter than I am. In that case we may have double tragedy. He is a cornered groundhog. And a groundhog, sir, will do anything to save itself. Maybe he hadn't planned to kill anyone when he came. Maybe he kills my whole family now — who knows what passes through such a man's mind? So you see, the answer is more than yes or no.

"So what? Tragedy is terrible, but double tragedy is worse, wouldn't you agree? But more important — if I try to kill the man, I make the three good possibilities of martyrdom, another way, and a miracle impossible. I say I trust God but this proves I do not trust him. The coins say, 'In God we trust,' but if I defend myself is it God or the gun that I trust? So I renounce killing because I don't want a double tragedy and I want to leave the door open for the three good possibilities."

Ira looked at the floor again, composing himself. He felt completely collected. The web of his geometry had snared them.

"Now, you see, we are ready for the other question that you asked me, colonel. *What if everyone believed like I do?* Would our country be destroyed? Would we become another state of Germany? I don't know. God looks out for us. He looked out for the children of Israel when they were taken into captivity. Would the maniacs take over the world forever?

"No, I am sure they wouldn't. Germany, maybe, is a maniac. But the maniacs will eventually fly apart like a lopsided planet. They are too lopsided to go on spinning. That's how it is in history. Nero went crazy and burned down Rome. Napoleon . . . well!

"It's the good people that we're to fear, Colonel Doolittle. It's the good ones who don't know that they are wrong and set out to save something and end up destroying it. They kill people in order to bring democracy to them. They killed the Indians be-

446

cause they thought God gave the American settlers a mandate to do so."

"Objection!" shouted the colonel, leaping to his feet again. "What does this have to do with the case? Are we trying the whole war? All of American history? There has been so much irrelevant material introduced here...."

The judge advocate shook his head.

"Objection overruled," he said, but the colonel refused to sit down. He stayed on his feet, staring at Ira.

"They destroy a country in order to save it," said Ira, "because they don't know that the Christian way is not to stop evil or kill it — because that makes you just as evil — but to suffer with evil." He smiled with excitement. "We will suffer as Jesus suffered. I thought of it when I was ridiculed and hit in camp. I am tasking a little of the cup he drank from! Suffering. Those are his peace terms for the world.

"So I don't know what I would do if a maniac attacked. But I know what I should do. I should pray for a miracle and pray that I don't do something evil. Then I let my King make the decision. He cares! That's the miracle. That's why we pray. Why pray if you don't think he can do it? Do you believe in prayer, colonel? I know you do." He was finished.

One of the jury members clapped. Then the room got silent. "Is that all?" said the judge advocate.

Ira nodded. He wanted to sit down.

"You may sit down. Colonel Doolittle."

"Private Stoltzfus, an amazing speech," said the colonel, folding his arms. "I didn't know you had it in you. So he is not unintelligent, gentlemen. You can see that by his answers to the questions I asked him on another occasion and by his reply to the charges against him. In fact, he is so intelligent that I could only marvel at the wrong choices he has made ever since he got to our camp and now I see some of the mind behind it. But let me ask one question to satisfy my curiosity. You talk eloquently about your beliefs and conscience against defending yourself. Now I want to know if you live up to what you talk. Have you ever defended yourself?"

Ira sat in silence, his eyes on the colonel.

"Have you ever hit a man?" The judge advocate looked at the colonel.

"Do you want him to answer that question?"

The colonel held up his hand as if to stop the judge and looked at Ira again.

"When was the last time you hit a man?" he said. He went back and stood by his table and nodded to the judge.

"Answer the question," said the judge.

Ira's eyes were still fixed upon the colonel. "Three weeks ago," he said in a small voice. It was an electric shock. The court began to talk among themselves and the judge advocate's mouth fell open. Sergeant Potts covered his mouth with his hand and looked at his shoes. The colonel walked to the center of the room again, smiling confidently.

"Three weeks!" he said, "Incredible. We have spent the last two hours listening to this man tell us why he won't fight or won't be a part of 'the military which is created to kill,' as he put it, and now he tells us he hit a man three weeks ago."

"I told him I was sorry," said Ira. "I —"

"Sorry!" the colonel exploded. "Miracles, confessions, 'I'm sorry' — what is this? A court or a Catholic mass?"

448

The court chuckled.

"Colonel." The judge looked at him severely.

"Three weeks ago," said the colonel. "That would be in this camp, wouldn't it? Would you like to tell us who you hit? Was it a soldier?"

Ira stood up slowly.

The judge advocate smacked his gavel on the table.

"Do you know the implications of what you are asking, colonel? If this is true, colonel — "

"True?" said the colonel. "He just said so himself."

"This could mean new charges, Private Stoltzfus," said the judge. "If you wish, we'll all take a recess and you can consult a lawyer. Which of your officers in camp was asked to advise the boy?"

Ira looked across the room at Sergeant Potts. The sergeant sat with his hand still over his mouth, his eyes on Ira. Sweat stood on his forehead.

"I hit an officer, sir," said Ira. "It was Sergeant Potts. I apologized to him and I want to tell him again that I didn't do it out of hate. Something snapped in me and before I knew it — "

The room was absolutely breathless. Leaves could be heard blowing on the lawn outside.

The colonel sat down.

"I have nothing more to say."

"I'm sorry," said Ira, looking at Potts. Potts covered his face with both hands and breathed heavily. Ira sat down.

"I would like to call Sergeant Potts to the witness stand," said the colonel. Potts made no move to get up, however.

"Sergeant Potts." The judge looked at him.

Potts shook his head.

"Come to the witness stand, Sergeant Potts."

Potts got up slowly then, walked to the Bible beside the court stenographer, and repeated the oath after him. He went back to the center of the room.

"Sergeant Potts," the colonel said. He was in perfect control of himself, not a trace of sarcasm, not a hint that he had known about the incident for a week already. He stood behind his chair, as stiff as a salute, his forty years in the Army sitting well on him. They gave his face a kind of Greek nobility.

"Sergeant Potts, would you tell us about the incident that Private Stoltzfus just referred to?"

The sergeant never took his eyes from the floor.

"The story is not true," he said.

"What?"

"It's not true. He never hit me."

"You're speaking under oath, sergeant — I want to remind you — an oath made on the Bible. Do you deny that he hit you?"

"I deny it."

The judge advocate looked at the colonel.

"In that case, colonel, there is no point in going any farther. The private's statement was not made under oath and the sergeant's was, so we will have to take his word for it unless you have other witnesses. If this were true it would prejudice Stoltzfus' case of course, because he has declared he would never fight, but we can't try him for hitting a noncommissioned officer if there is no *corpus delicti*, no body of evidence, so to speak. A man can't just walk into a police station and say, 'I killed a man and threw his body overboard into the Atlantic Ocean,' and then be held for murder. There has to be some evidence to prove that a man actually died. Even if he swore he did it that wouldn't be enough, and the man in this case who was supposed to have been hit swears he hasn't been, so we don't have a dead body, so to speak, and until you have further witnesses we will drop this accusation." He looked at the colonel.

The colonel looked at him and then dropped his head.

"I want to comment tomorrow," he said.

"Court dismissed," said the judge advocate, "until tomorrow morning."

He smacked his gavel on the table and looked at his watch. He was also going to the ball in Chattanooga.

11

Ira was depressed. He looked at his shoes the whole way back to the guardhouse. He was having doubts about the testimony he had given. He was not at all relaxed and confident like he had been in the morning. His story had been blown apart. But why? Not because the thoughts were not well-presented, but because the Potts story had come out at the end to upset the whole speech and send it whirling right back at his head like a badly thrown boomerang. It was enough to convince them that he wasn't sincere, that he was a fighter.

But at the same time, he was wondering what to make of the strange behavior of the sergeant. What went on in that man's head anyway? Something was happening, he was sure of that — first his moody looks in the courtroom and then his strange testimony. For what? It was a perfect opportunity for the sergeant to send Ira to the prison at Fort Leavenworth for years and years — even that would be a light sentence for hitting a superior in wartime — and he had turned it down. He had deliberately lied and saved Ira's life by doing it. Was the sergeant afraid that the story of his own mistreating of soldiers would come out? That was it. Ira was sure of it.

The guard opened the barred door of the guardhouse. There was a shout from the inside.

"Ira Stoltzfus!" The whole objectors' unit was inside, grinning at him.

"We're back, Ira. We couldn't let you rot in this place all by yourself. How's the trial going? You were sentenced?"

Ira shook his head. "We're not finished yet."

"Schnickerry's been court-martialed and sent to Leavenworth, poor thing. Thirty years of hard labor for not planting flowers around the headquarters. I don't want to spoil your hopes, Ira, but look at it this way. Schnickerry's trial only lasted twenty-one minutes. Thirty years in twenty-one minutes, huh? That's justice?"

"And we've all been granted farm furloughs," said someone.

"Except me," said Guthrie. "It's France for me."

They were all a little whiter, a little thinner for their time in the guardhouse and the influenza, which had passed swiftly through the camp.

"How's come you're back here again?" said Ira. "They told me you were released from the guardhouse."

"Aha, you haven't reckoned with our friend the colonel," said Pyski. "To begin with, he liked our singing."

Dinner was being served through the slot on the door, and the men picked up their bowls and sat down around the cell.

"The good life, huh?" said Pyski, and he made big eyes as he found a piece of chicken in his soup. "So, as I was saying, he liked our singing and that was our downfall. He sentenced us to do some more of it in the guardhouse."

"The rest of the story," said Schie, "or should I say 'the interpretation of the story' is this: after you left we continued to sing every day and usually we didn't really feel like singing until it got dark, so as you can imagine, there were some ill-feelings."

"Not everybody likes whippoorwills, you see," said Pyski.

"Right. Some people prefer silence. Such as officers. But the colonel took a real liking to our singing."

"Colonel Doolittle?" said Ira.

"Himself. As we found out, he not only has a long history in the U.S. Cavalry, but also a beautiful voice. Anyway, one day after we were back in our quarters he ordered us out on the drill field — it was a windy day, leaves falling down all over the place — and we figured it was just going to be another bad occasion with him ordering us to do some work that we couldn't. He takes a special interest in us objectors, you know."

"Unfortunately," said Pyski, through a mouthful of soup.

"But when we got to the field, he told us to line up, basses on one side, tenors on the other, and then he got out of his pocket one of those things — "

"A tuning fork," said Frymire, who as usual was only following the conversation with one ear, while he concentrated on a game of solitaire checkers that he was playing on the floor while he ate.

"Right, a tuning fork. Then he looked at us and said, 'I hear you can sing. Is it true?' Then he led right off into 'O beautiful for spacious skies' and he had a beautiful voice."

"Like one of those operas," said Pyski.

"We sang along and sounded pretty good," said Schie.

" 'Excellent! Excellent!' " said Pyski, imitating the colonel's dignified but fervent way of talking and shaking a finger to make a point." 'With a little rehearsal and some snappy suits we could go on tour. Cheer up the boys. How would you like that, eh! I knew you men were good for something. What was wrong with you, eh? Eh?' " Pyski pointed at Frymire. " 'You didn't open your mouth the whole time. Name. Name!' "

Frymire looked up. He didn't see anything so funny about it all, even if everybody was choking on their soup. "So I told him it was hopeless to teach me. I can't sing."

"Not all birds sing, you see," said Pyski. "He's a woodpecker."

"So the next song on the colonel's list," continued Schie, was 'Over there.' You know it? 'Send the word to beware that the Yanks are coming,' and we refused to sing it because as Pyski said, 'We're not going over there.' And that really ended the singing for the day. The colonel got hot and sent us all back here again. As I see it, the colonel thought he could instill a little of the war fever in us by singing."

"The colonel?" said Ira.

"Who else are we talking about? What's so surprising about the colonel? He's very predictable, I think," said Schie. "Anyway, as you can imagine, we turned this old cell into a church when we got back here. We sang until we thought our lungs would pop."

"Why not a song right now," said Guthrie, "in honor of our coming together again. Maybe the last time. Who knows? When's the rest of your trial, Ira?"

"Tomorrow morning."

Somebody started a song. Ira sang along half-heartedly. He couldn't shake his thoughts of the trial and the feeling that it was going to end badly. Not so much that he would get a sentence — he had been sure of that from the beginning — but that his beliefs would be totally discredited by the things which had come out. The more he thought about it, the more depressed he became and as he looked around for something to blame it on, Sergeant Potts came to mind. *The colonel can squash me and bring me a heavy sentence*, he thought. *I trusted him to hear my story and understand it but he never accepted my beliefs one bit. His sole ambition is to make a soldier of me, even though he is more gentlemanly about it than Sergeant Potts. But the colonel could never discredit me. Sergeant Potts discredited me. He trapped me into hitting him. And since I hit him, even if it won't be proven in court, my record can never be clear. What good was my time in camp?"*

No, he couldn't sing at all. The forces inside him were settling back in place again like rocks after an earthquake tremor.

The rattling of the cell door caught his attention. It was Sergeant Potts, leading a young man Ira had never seen before.

"Brought you a buddy," said Potts. He locked the door again and looked at them. "How is everything?"

How is everything? That question from Potts? What did he care how they were when he had been instrumental in getting them locked up in the beginning?

"Fine, fine," said Guthrie, walking up to the cell door. "We've been singing, talking a bit."

"Hello, Stoltzfus," said Potts, and he put his hand through the barred door. Someone slapped Ira on the back.

"He wants to welcome you back." Ira got up, somewhat dumbfounded. He shook the sergeant's hand.

"Singing, huh?" said the sergeant. He seemed a little nervous, and the bags under his eyes were quite distinct. He laughed. "I'd think you could sing a song or two for me, seeing's I brought you a buddy."

"Sure, sure," said Guthrie.

Potts wanted to be sung to? What sort of a trick was this?

" 'Nearer, My God to Thee,' " said Guthrie turning around. The men sang the whole song, from beginning to end, while Sergeant Potts stood at the door, his face completely immobile, watching them.

What is going on? Ira wondered. He was sure it wasn't good.

They stopped singing.

"Please sing another one," said Potts.

They sang "When I Survey the Wondrous Cross." Then Ira noticed a curious thing. Tears were rolling down the sergeant's face and he was making no attempt to stop them. Only the eyes blinked in that stiff mask. Ira looked at Potts curiously. *If it hadn't been for you,* he thought, *I would be on trial innocent. Like Joan of Arc, or Jesus, or one of the Anabaptists.*

"Thank you, boys," said Potts, and he wheeled around, his keys banging against his side pistol.

The prisoners looked at each other in astonishment.

12

The atmosphere of the court on the following morning was in sharp contrast to the day before. No one was sleeping or talking and the court looked up with marked interest when Ira was led in by his armed guard again. Sergeant Potts was physically in worse shape than he had been the day before. His hair was tousled right from the start and his uniform looked like he had slept in it overnight. He looked up with bloodshot eyes when Ira came in and watched him sit down. He seemed to be trying to get Ira's attention, gesturing toward the hall, but Ira couldn't understand what the gesture meant.

"Do you want to talk to me?" he said in an inaudible whisper. The sergeant nodded eagerly, almost happily, and without saying when he wanted to talk, he looked down at his desk again and put his hand over his mouth, exactly like he had done the day before. It was 9:10, and the colonel still hadn't made his appearance. The judge advocate looked at his watch and lit up a large cigar.

At 9:15, the door opened. It was the colonel. He strode in with dignity, and nodded to the judge advocate, the court, and finally to Ira. He dropped a handful of notes on his table, and still standing, looked up.

"You ready?" the judge advocate said.

"Yes."

"All right. We will begin. Colonel Doolittle, for the prosecution, will present any comments he might have on the prisoner's testimony yesterday and what sentence he will ask if the prisoner is found guilty by the court. Colonel." He put out his big cigar and sat back in his chair to watch what kind of approach the colonel would take.

The colonel stood up.

"Gentlemen," he said, "I think we were all impressed by the prisoner's speech yesterday. I certainly was. No one can say he is a stupid man, though he only has a tenth-grade education. But we were also startled by his inconsistency. He hit an officer, he says (although in reality an NCO) which seems to blow the crux of his beliefs — the idea that self-defense is wrong — all to hell, to use a colloquialism. We have also seen the NCO he said he hit deny that he was hit, thereby throwing this piece of damaging evidence out of court, legally, but leaving real doubts about the prisoner's character. If he didn't hit him, then why did he say that he did?

"But today I want to take a different tack. I would like you to notice with me the prisoner's extraordinary speech, and if you review it carefully you will see as I did an amazing thread, running like a red hem, you might say, along the bottom of his whole argument. Let us look at several of the phrases he used."

The colonel motioned to a member of the court and together they rolled a movable blackboard to a spot behind the colonel's desk. The colonel unscrewed both ends of the board and turned it over.

On the other side were written five phrases, one above the other:

1. *The King of my Country.*
2. *He talks of miracles.*
3. *Some questions cannot be answered with "yes" or "no."*
4. *He asks us to love our enemy.*
5. *The good people of the world will destroy it.*

He gave them a moment to look at the writing and then turned to face the court.

"What about the first phrase, 'The King of my Country'? You'll remember the prisoner made a gesture to indicate a heavenly King up there and of course he contrasted him with the president of our country. The prisoner did not pretend to say he is not guilty of the charges — he admits to them. But then he appeals to a loftier law, a law that he feels is higher than the law of our country — the law of his Country with a capital 'c', or God's kingdom — as if it were a nation to which he belonged.

"I would like to take up the challenge that he has thrown. Legally we have seen enough evidence to convict him of breaking the 64th Article of War — disobeying an officer. But let's look at his challenge.

"Is he a citizen of this other Country [he gestured skyward] or is he a citizen of our country? It would seem logical that if we could decide which country he really belonged to we would know which law he should obey. I would like to remind the prisoner of something about himself. This country of the United States of America blesssed the marriage of his parents. Without this country's blessing and license

460

he would be an illegitimate child. She gave him an education through tenth grade so that he could stand here yesterday and talk to us of geometry, history, and ethics. What price should a country charge for the education she gives a child? She protected his family with her laws and gave them some of her most valuable land, the bottoms of Pennsylvania. She gave them her culture and language so that the prisoner could stand here and talk to us in the English language. Is that a small gift? She gave him a place in the democracy where his vote counts equally with anyone else's and all she asks in return is that he submit if the majority votes against the way he thinks.

"How does he receive this gift? Gratefully? No, viciously! 'I will not fight. I will not submit to the will of the majority because I belong to a greater Country.' What has that Country given him? Life, his soul. The same things that any dog or rabbit anywhere in the world has. That is the difference between life and a happy life. A happy life demands that a country take these raw gifts which God gives every animal and direct them toward a purpose.

"What is a country but its goals and purposes? What are the goals of America? Progress. Democracy. Patriotism is love of the country and love of her national goals, the love of her laws, even if one doesn't agree with all of them. Is it possible that 2,800,000 boys in this war (most of them Christians) who have decided to fight are wrong and three or four thousand men, some of them outright atheists, although I would not include the prisoner in that group, are right? That simply defies the imagination. It's about as likely that a pear will fall back up into the tree. The chances that two million are wrong and four thousand right must be a molecule over zero. Are there any mathematicians here?

"What is your conscientious objector, then? Is he *un*intelligent? No, he is not. Army IQ tests have shown he is above average in intelligence. He is a man who sees the world through religious glasses. The Bible, he says, is his only authority. How is it then that a man who seems so intelligent could be so misled? Fanaticism, narrow-mindedness, nearsightedness, that's it. Like the ancient Pharisees he takes a few Scriptures and blows them way out of proportion while ignoring others completely. He sees 'Thou shalt not kill' but doesn't see 'Let every person be subject to the governing authorities. For there is no authority except from God!'

"It is my own opinion that if the prisoner had been in heaven when God drove the devil and his angels out and down into hell, his conscience would have prevented him from helping to chase the devil out."

The jury chuckled.

"My conclusion, gentlemen, is that the consientious objector is unable to see his own country because of his fanatical devotion to God, who — if the objector would care to hear it — tells him to be obedient to his country.

"What about the second phrase, then? 'He talks of miracles.' Let us think for a moment about the prisoner. What kind of a man is he? He is from a rural background, a farmer, and out of a long line of farmers going back hundreds of years. He can hardly be said to be part of the twentieth century. Look at his clothes. He is a fanatic. Look at his eyes. How

462

intense they are. When they hook you, they hardly let go. Like most of his people, the church is the center of his world. He has hardly learned to think critically about issues because again he appeals to his God and the 'brotherhood' as they call it in Mennonite circles.

"Yes, he is in intelligent! He compared himself yesterday with Christ, which is typical of the fanatic, to connect himself to some great hero, living or dead, and in camp he was able to suffer at times — of course there is some suffering in the camps, a lot of name calling — because he thought of himself as suffering like Jesus suffered. He is not a slacker or a coward, but a martyr type.

"Now what does that remind you of, gentlemen? Miracles, martyrs, fanatics? Why, the Middle Ages, of course. What we often call the Dark Ages. The medieval mind believed in devils and spirits and miracles. People did not look to law to defend them or the doctors to cure them in those days. They called on God for a miracle or exorcised devils from their bodies. It's not hard to imagine how this idea has survived until today, even though the majority of our people would laugh at such suggestions. These people — I'm referring to these religious communities the objectors are from — and have isolated themselves, stuck together, passed the ideas of the Middle Ages onto their children — through their blood practically. This is the sort of mind that believes in miracles.

"For myself, I find the miracles of the Bible hard to believe literally, although I won't deny flatly such things may have taken place. I am a Christian, but I won't get into a theological debate with you, gentlemen. Miracles are a record of how strongly people believe. God *could*, of course, send angels and raise men from the dead if he wanted to, but he doesn't in this age. No, he depends on us to take care of our world, to use the brains and bodies he has given us.

"I might sum up this discussion on miracles with a quote from the Bible, although I'm not as good at chapter and verse as the prisoner. 'God helps those that help themselves.'

"What about the third point then? 'Some questions cannot be answered with *yes* or *no*.' The prisoner gives the example of his wife being attacked. Should he defend her or not? He says we cannot answer this with 'yes' or 'no,' and then he proceeds to give us a bundle of mental chess games and geometry problems. This world isn't a geometry problem, unfortunately. It's hard facts. Kill or be killed. Forty years in the Army has taught me that much.

"Perhaps the prisoner is one of those people who believe there are no answers — that each situation must be judged for itself. But tell me, if a robbery is in progress, is a law officer supposed to let it go on because the robbery may be neither bad nor good but might ultimately work out to the glory of God if he lets the robber get away? That is the kind of fuzzy thinking the prisoner expects us to believe.

"The law cannot operate in such a cloudy atmosphere. Something is either right or it's wrong — yes or no. If the vast majority says 'yes,' then we allow it. If the majority says 'no,' then we forbid it. So we fight a war that must be fought but we do not allow robbery. One extends democratic freedoms; the other leads to chaos. The beauty of our law system is its

464

ability to create order in a country.

"One of the amazing things about these conscientious objectors is their refusal to accept facts as facts. One of them — not the prisoner — was talking to me and I asked him about the war. Didn't he think Germany had committed atrocities against the German and Belgian people? And he said, 'Perhaps. That's what the papers say.' It seems unbelievable to me that he had any doubts, so I said, "Well, what about the *Lusitania?* You know that the innocent merchant ship *Lusitania* was torpedoed, don't you?' and he said, 'Well, that's what the papers say. I didn't see it, but I might take the papers' say for it.'

"The conscientious objector questions simple facts. He questions law, he questions the decisions of the majority, he questions progress. There he sits, in his Mennonite clothes, substituting in his mind the ideas of miracles, religious facts, confession — he actually asked his Army superior to forgive him for committing *criminal assault*. How can you run a country like that?

"Fourth, he asks us to 'love the enemy' or 'suffer with evil' like Jesus, I believe he said. On the surface this sounds fine. It's a lovely ideal, but can it apply in the twentieth century?

When Jesus said those words — it was Jesus you quoted, wasn't it?" he said, looking at Ira. "When Jesus said, 'Love your enemy,' what was the situation like? The enemies of the Jews were the Romans. Granted, they weren't very friendly, but did they rape the Jew's wife and cut off her breasts? Pardon me for speaking so frankly in court, gentlemen. Did the Roman bayonet thousands of old Jewish men?

Did the Roman launch a savage attack aimed at destroying the country of Israel? No. There was hatred, but nothing like that.

"There comes a time when deeds done are so terrible and the people who did them so hell-bent in destroying that they cannot be forgiven. They cannot be 'suffered with' anymore. They have committed the unpardonable sin, complete disrespect for human life. The comparison of the Jew-and-Roman situation with modern Germany is pitiful. History is being made. There is no comparison to the present. Nowhere in history.

"By the way, when we look carefully we find the prisoner's own church doesn't suffer with evil. When a man does wrong they excommunicate him and make him suffer. Is that right, Private Stoltzfus?"

Ira nodded and opened his mouth to speak but the colonel went on.

"No, I find this point one of the weakest of all his arguments. Finally, then. . . ."

"Colonel . . ." It was the judge advocate.

"Yes?"

"Is all of this relevant? Does it have anything to do with the charges?"

"I'll get to that in a minute, sir."

But he didn't have to worry, he wasn't boring the court. They were following the case he was building, sometimes nodding their heads, sometimes looking at him with questions scrawled on their faces, and then brightening as he touched a new point. But where was he leading? You couldn't convict a man just by analyzing him.

The colonel pointed to the last item on the blackboard. "The good people will destroy the world."

"This is the most incredible statement of all," the colonel said. "I couldn't believe what I was hearing. But when I looked at it carefully it fitted into everything else that the prisoner had said. I see no point in debating it. If it were true there would be no point in any of us living anymore. 'The maniacs will fly apart . . . it's the good people who . . . destroy a country in order to save it.' There is nothing in history that substantiates that, and it simply proves again how disconnected the prisoner is from the modern world.

"But if it were true — I say *if* — then we could take that idea and turn it on the prisoner himself. In all respects he is a good man — morally, that is. He almost said between the lines of his speech that none of us are Christians like he is, that he has a corner on the truth. But here is a case of a good man, maybe three or four thousand good men, conscientious objectors, who by their mile-wide consciences and refusal to support the national goals might destroy that country."

One of the court members began to clap and shortly several of the others joined him. The colonel stopped and took a drink of water. He opened another folder, looked at it for a few seconds and began again. He walked back and forth behind his desk, stopping to put one hand on his hip and look at the jury. Walking, stopping, handsome as an heirloom portrait, commanding as a cavalry officer about to lead a charge, methodical as a termite intent on completing the job he has begun of bringing the house down.

"In summary, what do you see when you look at those five ideas from the prisoner's speech: 'The King of my Country,' 'He talks of miracles,' 'Some questions cannot be answered with *yes* or *no*,' 'He asks us to love the enemy,' and 'The good people of the world will destroy it'?"

The court waited for him to tell them.

"What do I see? I see a sixteenth-century mind where the Renaissance has not yet begun. Is he intelligent? Yes, but so were men in the sixteenth-century. He and his people have frozen back there, even their clothes. Look, they have not yet discovered buttons, but still use hooks and eyes. If there has been no progress for four hundred years, what must our judgment be?

"Is this the state of our democracy? We are fighting for democracy in Europe, yet it is in such disarray here. Would you like your children to be influenced by such ideas — should his own brothers and sisters be kept locked up in that sort of darkness? No. We can't even try his ideas in this court. They're not a part of the age of progress and democracy, just as the Mennonite or conscientious objector isn't. They're frozen in the Dark Ages, the age of religion and miracles.

"We should simply relegate them to the museum, along with the saber-toothed tiger and the crossbow. You can't run a country on miracles and forgiveness and loyalty to the kingdom of God. It must be run with an eye to progress, democracy, and technological advance.

"I could ask the court to consider the fact that, by his own testimony, he contradicted himself by admitting he hit a man when his whole belief and life is based on opposition to fighting. But I will leave that matter out for the moment. I only ask you to consider the charges of disobedience to a superior, an act which grew out of a conscience, mind, and life that are irrelevant to our present age.

"I suggest we confine him to the past. The prison, where all human relics go. I ask the jury for the ultimate penalty for this man." He turned and pointed an arm stiff from shoulder to fingertip at Ira. "Obviously he is guilty and I want life imprisonment." The colonel sat down and the court began to talk among themselves immediately.

The judge advocate brought down the gavel. "The prisoner is dismissed while the court considers its verdict."

The guard led Ira out into the hall. He had no doubt how they would rule. Would it be life imprisonment then? *Life?* For refusing to plant flowers?

A man suddenly separated himself from the wall of the hall and came toward them. The guard turned with his rifle and bayonet ready, then lowered the rifle respectfully. It was Sergeant Potts. He reached and grasped Ira's hand in both of his. He shook it. "Thank you for everything. Thank you," he said. He seemed nervous, but he broke into a big smile and embraced Ira with one free arm, and went on shaking and smiling. "Forgive me," he said.

But Ira was silent. Was another trap about to spring on him?

The sergeant was exuberant. He went on shaking Ira's hand and smiling. Neither of them said a word.

Ira smiled faintly. He was ready for anything.

"All right, step ahead," the guard said, putting a hand on each of their shoulders and gently pushing them apart.

The sergeant waved. He was still smiling.

When the sentence came a day later it was mild: twenty-five years in Ft. Leavenworth.

But Ira was gloomy. He was sure he had been discredited.

VI. Susquehannock, 1919

1

Dear Annie,

Don't be shocked. It's just me again.

I guess you heard about my wound by now. They have us all laid out here in a makeshift hospital. It used to be a church before the war, I think. A lot of colored glass windows and arches and steeples and such like, although I haven't seen the outside of the building — they brought us in on stretchers.

Anyway, the church was hit by a bomb back in the beginning of the war and one whole side is blown out, so we get plenty of fresh air. That's good because there are some awful smells here. I just can't describe them. There must be 500 men here lying all around me.

They did an operation. It wasn't nothing to get excited about. I was afraid before the doctor did it because he has a reputation for amputations. If you even have a black-and-blue toe, he amputates, some of the men told me. I had about ten bullets in my leg — he showed them to me after the operation. They were flat and curled a little like lily pads. I am lucky to be alive. So now they have my leg up in the air, all wrapped up in white so you can't see it and pulleys attached to keep it up. You don't have

473

to worry about him amputating though.

From here they take us to a place in southern France where they have mineral springs, hot ones, that is, and they do massages. But that's a long way off for me. So I just lay here on my back and look at the ceiling, which seems to be about a mile up. Every once in a while we hear pigeons cooing up there and everybody gets mad because they crap on us but there's no way to get them out, I guess. They were here before we were.

Anyway, here I lay with nothing to think about except my wounds and when will they feed us next and who will be my nurse. If you're lucky, you get an American and you can talk to her. If you're unlucky, you get a French lady and all you can do is smile. I think I'm going to go out of my gourd if I have to lie here with nothing to do too much longer.

I got your letters. There was a whole pile of them waiting for me when I got to the hospital. See, we hardly got any the whole time we were on the push, so I got three months' worth all in one day. I read them front to back, starting in June or whatever and going to September. I must have read them three or four times.

It was awfully good to hear from you. I don't know why you did it. I guess I didn't write to you for a half a year or so, did I? You're awfully good. I know you're much too good for me. I've done some terrible things. I know you could never want me back.

All I know is I'm going to be here an awful long time. But don't worry about them taking my leg or anything. If you even want to think about me anymore.

Yours truly,
Mastie

Dear Mastie,

A greeting in our Savior's wonderful name.

Sometimes there is nothing more encouraging than a letter. On Thursday night I came home late from the Federoffs and our house was dark. No one was waiting for me and I was tired. I was really lonesome. I put on some water for tea and sat down in my room to knit a little on the sweater, but before I had done three stitches I saw the letter there on the stand beside the picture of you and me at the Red Dragon.

I opened it quickly to read it but before long I found I couldn't read. All the words were a blur and were swimming. It was because my eyes were full of tears. Pretty soon they began to run down my cheeks. I wanted to cry because I was lonely and helpless and my heart was full of joy and happiness. You may think that I'm a real *Brutzbuppy*, crying like that, but I couldn't help it. Only you could write to me like that. All I can say is, Thank you very much, Mastie.

I can't help but think you're getting what you deserved, but still I feel sorry for you. I hope the wound heals quick. I am so glad that you are not on the front anymore because it was not good for you. One hears awful things about the front. Every once in a while when I got to town I picked up the papers and read the big story and always there was something about the war — so many captured, so many killed — and it made me pray that you were safe and not near the place they were writing about. But I guess that's the way it will always be in this world — wars and rumors of wars.

We're all concerned about you. All of the ones who know you ask me about you. Your name was in the paper after that battle and we got a copy. I just want you to know I'm praying for you. That's all we can do, I guess.

Don't worry about my waiting for you, Mastie. I never think of that anymore. I used to think about other boys, especially right after you left and things were bad, but now I don't mind waiting at all. Your letter was a big help.

I must close, wishing you a "good night."

Love,

Annie

October 25

Dear Annie,

It's all very nice of you back home to think about me and pray, like you said, but I don't think it will do any good. I want you to read this letter and then burn it before anybody else sees it.

Mom's passing away was a big shock. Of course, you know why I couldn't come home, laid up like this. I'm not sure I would have anyway. When I think about it, maybe I caused it. She used to worry about me.

I really couldn't face Pop. I never told you this, but he as good as told me I'm going to hell when I left, and I'm sure he thinks so by now, after those newspaper reports. As long as Mom was still alive, I thought I might come back, but now I don't want to. You can see why.

Anyway, there I was lying on my back as usual. I was really feeling low. I was looking up at the steeples. Then I heard this old, familiar voice say, "Hey, Pennsylvania!" Now the only people who called me that were the boys in my unit and I thought

476

they were all killed, but who do you think it was? Old Churchill, the man on the other machine gun. It was a nurse that got us together, neither of us knew the other was still alive. It was really thrilling to see him as you can imagine — the first person I knew in two months. So I went to shake with him — I can move around in the bed as long as I don't move the leg — but he wouldn't shake.

Now that's funny, I thought, so I said, "Don't you shake anymore?" and he said, "I can't see your hand, I lost my eyes, Pennsylvania." A grenade did it on that big counterattack. It broke his glasses into his eyes. He never had good eyes, but now he has no eyes. So there we were. He lost his eyes, I lost — I don't know what all I lost yet. But right then, it was Mom I lost. So I told him to sit down and he did, on the edge of the bed and pretty soon we were back in the old groove, talking all sorts of things.

I wanted them to let him move over to my side of the church. There's an empty bed next to mine since last week. But they wouldn't let him. Rules, they said. All the leg people have to stay together because the pulleys are too hard to move around.

The truth is, Annie, I'm lost. Maybe you don't understand what I mean — I'm not sure I do — but I think I really am going to hell. I have these dreams. When you lay on your back looking up in the air all the time like I do, what else are you going to do? Eat and think. And have dreams. I can't talk to the guy beside me because he sleeps or groans most of the time. He has the gangrene, nurse says. The guy on the other side went crazy not so long ago and they took him away on a special cart.

I was going to tell you this dream. That's why I want you to burn the letter. I don't want anybody else to know it. But it keeps coming back, the same dream. I'll just be sleeping and then I feel myself falling. After a bit I see red lights getting close and then I hear someone laughing and when I look I see devils. I mean a whole field full of them. They're waiting for me to come down so they can catch me like a baseball. They're calling my name.

Then I see an iron fence all around the field, with spikes on top. On every spike there's a head. Just a head, and it's wearing a German helmet. It starts to wink at me and come toward me. Hundreds and hundreds of heads. I think I know what it means.

Then I hear horses coming and the heads move away and up out of the fire — this whole field is just like waves of fire — anyway, there are horses coming up, and their manes are flames of fire and the people on their backs are full of holes. They're holding swords and calling my name. They keep coming closer and closer — I think they're going to run over me, and I can see the horses' teeth at my throat.

I try to roll out of the way and just when it looks like they'll squash me, it's over. I wake up and my shirt is wringing wet. I'm coughing to get air and there's two or three nurses there looking at me. I don't know what it means, but I'm lost — I'm sure of that.

I guess that's why I'm sure I won't be coming back. I had to tell you this. Don't write and tell me you're sorry for me — I won't feel any better. Please burn this letter.

Yours truly,
Mastie

Dear Mastie,

A greeting in our Savior's name.

I hardly know what to write after your last letter but I know you are not lost if you come back. I don't mean to come back here, but to come back to God. I know he still wants you, just as I do. He wants you to come back. I'm praying that he will bring you back, even if you don't come back to me. Oh, that is hard to write, but I mean it. I want you to come back to me, but even if you don't it's important that you come back to God, the Father. Also to your earthly father. You must ask them to forgive you.

The important thing I want to tell you, Mastie, happened at your mother's funeral. I didn't see this, but one who was sitting close to your father at the supper table reported it to me. You know how the gang of men roughhoused your father one night last summer and he was sure he recognized one or two of the men. One of them, he thought, was Pastor Rydell of the Immanuel Bible Church. Do you know who sat down at the supper table beside your father? Pastor Rydell!

Everybody was surprised because we knew how he's been acting, talking every Saturday down at the bank for war bonds, and we thought, too, he was in on the raid when they nailed the American flag on our church doors. But your father talked to him and after a while this individual heard Mr. Rydell tell your father he was sorry for that night and he wondered if your father would forgive him, and your father said, "Sure," and Mr. Rydell got up from the table all smiles and shook your father's hand and thanked your Aunt Magdalena for the supper.

Oh, I don't know, Mastie, but if he forgave a man he hardly knows for that awful trick, won't he forgive his own son? I'm sure he will. It isn't true that your father has a hard heart. He misses your mom awful much.

By now you are probably all right and I hope my letter doesn't bring back the sad day of the news and make you feel worse. If so, I'm sorry. I remember that you often told me you have a big shoulder for me to put my head on. Well, I have a shoulder for you, too. I just hope you're not terribly discouraged.

I like to believe that now there is another one above looking down on you and watching you. I wrote a little poem for you on the back of this letter.

The flu has been bad — so many people caught it. People are starting to say the flu killed more than the war did. I volunteered for nurse duties a day a week, and that plus the Federoffs plus the farm work for my pop just did me in every night. I was grouchy so much and then I couldn't eat. Finally I went to the doctor and he said I have an ulcer — too much worrying and running around, he said. So I quit the hospital. Now I'm drinking two quarts of milk every day to heal the ulcer!

Finally I wanted to say, Mastie, that I know you did terrible things. I forgive you, however. Everyone tells me that you won't come back, but I was always sure that you would. You promised you would. The only other person who still thinks like I do is Uncle Solly. You know how he is, and some people who don't know any better make fun of him, but it's funny how he always knows a person's feelings. Last night he was eating an apple dumpling and all of a sudden he looked up and said, "Is Mastie coming tonight?" And my father said, "No, he's gone." "He'll come back," Uncle Solly said and my father said, "No, he won't." Oh, it hurt me to hear them say it, but after supper Solly came up to me and said, "He's coming, Annie. I can hear his buggy," and I just laughed, but he kept saying "Pretty soon, Annie, pretty soon." When he went up the stairs to bed, he was still talking about you to himself. "Well, Uncle Solly must go to bed," he said, "because Mastie is coming," so I said, "How do you know?" He got real loud. "I just know," he said.

We got a good crop of corn.

Good night,
Annie

November 25

Dear Annie,

I guess the big news is I got a medal. Maybe they already made a splash about it in the papers back there. This big general I'd only seen a time or two before came in a couple days after the Armistice. It was the commander of our division. Well, he had colonels and lieutenants and captains and photographers flying around like turkey buzzards. There was a regular parade. He decorated some other fellows first and finally got to me.

He asked me how I got wounded, so I told him, and then he opened up this little box and took out a medal. I had sheets up around my neck and I wasn't wearing a shirt, so they pinned the medal fast to the pillow and everybody clapped, including

481

the nurses. I'll read you what the citation says:

"For extraordinary heroism in action. In the face of a direct charge of enemy infantry Mastie Stoltzfus succeeded in mounting a machine gun and holding off the enemy assault, including an attack by a suicide squad. Although seriously wounded in this gallant act, he remained by his gun until an American counterattack was possible."

Well, when the general left, Churchill came over again and sat down. The first thing he noticed was the medal. He jagged his finger on it. So I told him who had just been there and he started cussing and after a bit we saw tears coming out from under his dark glasses. He called it a blood medal and wanted to take it and throw it down the toilet but I convinced him not to. How would that look if someone came up and asked to see it and I told them it was down the toilet? Anyway, I promised him I'd drop it over to the fishes before we get home.

There's a new nurse on duty here, a big fat one with yellow hair. Her name is Christiana. She's a Catholic, or a Sister, I guess they call them. For some reason, she likes me. Not in the girlfriend sense — I mean she's fifty or so — but she comes by an awful lot. Well, at first I liked her because she listened to me, so I told her just about *everything*. She tends my skin grafts and that takes a lot of time.

Then one day she asked me if I'd ever noticed the picture of Jesus, and I said, No, I hadn't. Well, it is a great big one, bigger than two men on top of each other, of him standing in the middle of a lot of clouds, and he is looking over toward our corner. I don't know how I missed seeing it before. Then she started talking religious stuff and asking me what I'd do if I died and such stuff. I got mad. I told her to get out.

She smiled at me. That did it. I made as if I had a machine gun and wiped out that smirk. Then I really was shamefaced and I said I was sorry and all. You see where I've gotten to?

I want to forget everything, Annie. I want to go back to the way things used to be with you and me. Only even better than that. I can only count on you and God to help me forget everything.

Yours truly,
Mastie

P.S. Do you have a Testament in the German words? I would like one both in German and English if you get them.

December 16

Dear Mastie

First a greeting in the name of the Prince of Peace.

I wish you were here now. We've started stripping tobacco and you could help us. See how lazy I am getting! That wasn't the real reason though. It's because I remember you every time I go down into the stripping room and fire up the stove. Remember that day you met me down there in the winter and we were eating hoarhound lozengers and you called me a big hoarhound drop? I often think about those days.

How happy we were for a while and yet in another way we weren't happy because we didn't live like God wants us to and I never prayed in those days. I believe we are going through this long separation and you had those terrible experiences because we didn't obey God as we should have. He is punishing us. If we had to go through it all again and I knew what was coming, I'm not sure I would be able to do it. But when I'm lonely, I pray and pray. I never tell anybody these things.

After you first left I used to just hope that you would suffer enough loneliness and troubles that you would be ready to come back (and I believe you are, even though you didn't say so yet) to face God and your father again. No, I didn't want you to get hurt. I hoped that you wouldn't be hurt, but I asked God too to let you suffer. Does it sound like two opposites? I do hope that you will come home and live a better life, whether you come back to me or not.

Isn't it wonderful that a big picture of Jesus is hanging over you? It isn't an accident, I'm sure. I don't think that nurse Christiana is an accident either. Maybe she was sent to help you get things straight again. She sounds like a good person to me. As for forgetting everything that has happened and going back to the way things were before, I don't know if that's possible. It's hard for us to forget. We can forgive but we can't forget. Only God forgives and forgets.

I hope I didn't make you mad by this letter. But this is the way I have been thinking.

Love,
Annie

P.S. I guess you haven't heard the news of Ira since your pop's not writing. He's been sent to prison for 25 years. We could hardly believe it but he wrote and said it's not strange. Some of his friends got longer imprisonment, and for what? Not because he wouldn't fight but because he wouldn't plant marigolds, Susanna was saying. I don't understand it. You know what marigolds are, don't you?

I don't understand Ira, either. When he was home for the funeral he was stiff and grouchy. But he and your mother were always close. I'm sure it was a shock to him.

I'm worried about Susanna. Why is everyone in such awful pickles? I thought for a long time that it was only me and everyone else seemed to go on living as they always had, the young folks getting married and having children and starting farms. But now Susanna's confused, too. She says she can't wait 25 years — I guess they had been thinking of marriage, but since he was sent to prison she's gone to the singings with several other boys.

December 26

Merry Christmas, Annie,

While you're eating your mom's fruitcake and duck, think about hungry Mastie over here on a hospital bed. Well, it's not so bad. We had a good dinner.

After dinner I thought I heard music and when I stuck my head up, who do you think I saw? Christiana, the big fat one, leading a whole bunch of little French kids. They were all singing these Christmas carols but we couldn't understand a one. They sang them through their noses — well, you know how French is. But the last one was "Away in a Manger" in English.

Something funny happened to me last night after they left. You remember that picture of Jesus

I talked about? It looked at me! I'm not joking, it looked at me, and it started to talk. I think I was probably dreaming. But if it was a dream, for the first time it wasn't that horrible one. Something really wonderful is happening to me. I can't describe it just now. I'll tell you sometime soon.

The war is over and boys are leaving all over, some from our hospital. I don't know yet when I'll be shipped out or to those hot springs, but it won't be long anymore. I've made up my mind though. I want you to marry me, Annie. Would you consider such a bum as me?

> Yours truly,
> *Mastie*

April 13, 1919

Dear Mastie,

In answer to your letters of late, I'm not sure what to think. Things just aren't settled yet. You must do some preparing before you come, Mastie. I hardly know how to say it, but if we're to get married at all you must get right with your father and the church, I think. Now I've said it and I wasn't going to.

But I don't want to run away to get married. I know how you feel about your pop, being afraid of him and all that, and I know how you think our community feels, but is it true? I don't think so. Where would we go if we ran away? To Indiana? If we go to another community, we would hardly know anyone, even in another Mennonite community. I think it's our community you must ask to forgive you. I think your pop is also much softer these days. Everybody says so. Just as our Heavenly Father forgives you, so I am praying our earthly pop will. As for myself, I have long ago forgiven you.

I guess I'm just like a child before Christmas. I can hardly wait for you to come, but we must wait, mustn't we? In the meantime, shall I tell you what I do? I think about you, Mastie.

I went to market this morning real early, mainly to take eggs and pickled things for sale, since there's no vegetables from the truck patch yet. I drove the back way as usual down around Esch's cornfields (he just plowed them) and over the covered bridge — the same way we used to come home when you were here. Every time I go that way I think of you. So I can say I have thought of you in every season, especially in the early mornings.

When you got the ship it was winter and it was always dark when I started. The Eschs had their barn lights on to do the milking and it was often snowy, so I wore my thick shawl and thought how we used to wrap it around us on cold nights riding home. Then in the spring, like now, it would be light already when I left, just getting light, and how good it felt to be out of winter clothes. Amos Esch was plowing some mornings (he always was one for starting early) and he always had a wave for me. The robins used to like to eat the worms he plowed up. I'd always see my first robin there. And soon we'd start having sugar peas and lettuce for market.

When summer came I usually got to Esch's about in time to see the sun pop up over their barn, big and fat, and then I'd think how it just came from France. I think I love summer mornings the best because there's always such a promise in them, don't you think? The mill meadow used to be just white

487

with all these spider webs. I guess even the spiders have to get up early and work.

But the time I thought of you the most was in the fall. I don't know why. Maybe it was because you were last here in the fall and we'd go out to a singing or something on a snappy night and you liked to see Apple Boy making those steam clouds when it got cold. I guess my heart was broken in the fall, too, and that is why I remember it, especially that night you came to my house at midnight. The morning after you left I cried the whole way to market because there was no one out there that early to see my red eyes. And I cried again when you were wounded and sent me that first letter but this time I was crying with happiness, I guess. I carried your letter in the bottom of my market basket for a week and when no one was looking I'd pull it out and read it. It's awfully creased now but I still keep it. I loved you every season, and what season will be here when I see you again?

Now you know how silly your Annie is, always thinking about you. And praying, too. We can say now that in *weeks*, you'll be home, can't we? Maybe six or seven weeks, but still it's *weeks*, and not years as it was when you left. If I had it to do over I'm not sure that I would have the faith to pray, not knowing if I could ever see you again or not.

Will you still know how to farm after fighting?

Love,
Annie

P.S. It's all over between Ira and Susanna. Do you know Abram Glick? Probably not. He's from our district, not yours. He's been taking her out lately.

Dear Annie,

Your letters usually perk me up but that last one got me down, plus I was already down on account of Churchill.

I spend hours and hours in these dumb mineral baths. We soak with the stinky water up around our noses. Then we get out and get massaged. Actually I like the pools. It's the massage I hate. When you sit in the pool, it's so hot that you think your body is going to dissolve. No kidding, it feels like you only have a head left. It's weird. All the while you smell the orange blossoms outside the windows, when the windows are open. Maybe heaven is like the hot springs. And white sheets to sleep on!

But the massages — oh! They hurt so bad I bite my tongue or sometimes suck lemons and just yell to keep from feeling my legs.

Now I'll tell you the sad story of Churchill and you'll see why I'm down. One morning when I was in the pool he wandered in and was feeling his way with his feet, all the while saying stuff to himself like, "And why did we come here? Why, to thank Harold the Conqueror, to be sure," and after a bit he pretended to be shooting a bow and he said, "An arrow for King William's eye," and he started to laugh. Then he went to work scratching his head. I don't know where his nurse was. He started pointing at the ceiling of the pool house and saying, "A Heinie plane — you can tell them by the black crosses," which is true, by the way, and a little later he said, "No, that's not a Heinie plane, stupid, that's a tossed salad." Before anyone could catch him, he took off his clothes and crawled out the window.

So you see why I'm depressed when my last friend here goes crazy. I was really down.

What I want to know is, who am I marrying? You or the Mennonite Church? Or my father? If I'm not marrying them, then why should I bother with them? If you and God can forgive, that's enough.

The transport I am going on will leave here June 5. I should be home two weeks after that. I will send you a postcard telling you exactly when I'll arive in Lancaster. Let's meet at Acey's Emporium. We'll go someplace and get married and then get a train for Indiana. Don't forget your clothes and things. Does that suit?

Yours,
Mastie

May 18

Dear Mastie,

I will meet you at Acey's but I can't run away with you to get married. Please believe me. They will welcome you back.

Love,
Annie

June 6

Dear Annie,

I have changed my mind.

Last night I met Christiana, the nurse, at the harbor where we were supposed to leave yesterday. Postponed again. Crazy ships. Nothing goes on time anymore. I let her read your last letters. She says you are right.

I decided to come home. It will all depend on Pop, but I am going to tell him I'm sorry. I'm going to tell him everything. If he still thinks I'm going to hell, as he did the last time, then I'll leave again, but I've tried, haven't I? That's what you want, isn't it? You say he'll take me back, Annie. I'm going on your word. I am reading my Testament in the English words regularly to pass the time.

The waiting is killing me. They treat us like the war is still on — we have to wear uniforms and report for inspection. I wish I could jump into this letter and come home. The censors would probably take me out. I can't wait to see you.

Yours truly,
Mastie

2

Mastie was sentimental.

The road that cut off from the highway dipped and then dipped again and dipped once more to the creek at the bottom. It was a dirt road, and how often he had walked it with dry dust squirting up between his toes like mud. He wanted to throw his combat boots in the cornfield and walk home barefooted, but no, he thought, that wouldn't do — it just wouldn't do. Not with his leg like it was. So he kicked stones with his shoes but he didn't laugh and run like he used to when he kicked stones. He didn't feel like laughing.

He looked over the bank of the road. The road did have banks here, and they had been cut by his father years and years ago. He looked over the bank and saw his uncle's farm there on the other side of the tomato field. It looked like a painting. The barn was white with stone walls on both ends and a silo and windmill sticking up above the roof. Over there was the house with the *grossdawdi* house attached and someplace out of sight was a duck pond. He could see the backs of the steers around it though. There must have been a hundred of them. Uncle Eli was getting rich, no doubt, from the war. He had a new Model T in the driveway.

What would it look like blown up, he wondered? Huh? What would it look like after two days of shelling and a counterattack coming down across the tomato patch? He could imagine the barn with its doors hanging cockeyed on their hinges and the roof torn off by artillery, one whole wall reduced to a pile of stones which soldiers were piling up again as a barricade. On the top of the silo a machine gunner would cover the hillside until he was shot out and in the pasture every one of those fat steers would be on its back side with its legs sticking straight out, bloated, dead, and concealing gunners. The house would be burning and the whole valley crackling with gunfire. This road would be all dust, kicked up by soldiers scampering toward the hilltop.

But it wasn't blown up. The valley was perfectly quiet except for someone's calf. It was a habit of his, a bad habit. He couldn't see anything anymore without picturing it blown apart, but it was like his other bad habits. Wishing them away wouldn't get rid of them. He had too many scars. He wasn't going to hide them. None of them.

He was coming back and they would either take him as he was or not take him at all. He had no illusions. He was sure they wouldn't take him — even if he didn't tell them everything. Anybody who read the newspapers could tell them. He had been decorated for doing those things. Where was that medal by now? He smiled wryly. He hoped some fish had swallowed it and died. If it hadn't then it was lying down there among the sea anemones and starfish. God had forgiven him, but even God forgave more quickly than the man called by his name on earth, Father.

He had memorized the speech he was going to give. He went over it again as he limped along, and he knew he looked like a tramp with three days' growth of beard, unwashed since Newport News, and white and pale from nine months in the hospitals. They'd know him. If they had forgotten his face, they'd know his voice. Soldiers don't speak Dutch, only Pennsylvania Dutchmen do.

"Father. . . ." He never called him Father. It was always "Pop." "Well, I'm back, Father. All those things you heard about me in the papers are true — I've done terrible things . . . to you and Mom, too. But I'm sorry about it all. . . ."

There wasn't anything else to say. After that it would all be up to Pop. Mastie didn't have any illusions or hopes about Pop. It was better to go expecting nothing and be surprised if there was something than to go expecting something and then have him tell you to get out and look past you as if he didn't know you.

If the worst came, he still had Annie, didn't he? Well, he hadn't seen her yet, but he was sure of her. His dreams, maybe, would disturb her. And his leg. But he was counting on her. They could go to Indiana and start up a little dairy farm out there if Pop told him to go to hell. He had said it before, and there wasn't nearly as good a reason to say it then as there was now. But this waiting and not knowing, this last five hundred yards, it was working on him. He was breaking into a cold sweat.

Meetings are painful. If it were all over with. If it were three hours from now and he *knew!* His heart was thumping in a strange way, and now his hands began to sweat.

494

He was almost at the creek. Were there still brook trout under the bridge, if you let a hook down between the boards? The bridge had a huge poster plastered on it. "Kill the Hun — Kill his hope" and underneath a picture of a hundred dollar bond and a bayonet.

On the other side of the bridge in that big stone house somewhere his father was maybe sitting down to dinner. Or was he out cultivating his corn? Mastie looked across the creek to where the road began to rise up the other side.

No! There he was.

He saw his father at the far end of the bridge, running. Why, he was an old man now. His beard had white in it. His running was like the shuffling of a crab. He stopped at the edge of the bridge as Mastie came across. He threw up his arms as if for a benediction and breathed in loud gasps.

"Mastie!" The old man's arms circled him and clutched and clutched. His beard was wet against Mastie's cheek. "Oh, my son, my son." He was weeping.

Something strange happened then. Mastie began to cry, too, and he had never cried before in front of his father.

The old man's arms gradually relaxed. He looked into Mastie's eyes and kissed him, not once, but twice. "Let's go," he said, and turned around toward home, his hand on Mastie's arm.

"No."

The old man stopped.

"I can't, I can't, Father. There's terrible things — "

"You're not coming up to the house?"

"Too terrible. . . . You couldn't forgive me if

you knew everything. . . ."

"Mastie, we're all waiting for you. Now come. . . . Your mother . . ." Pop began to walk. "She wanted so much to see you come home. She prayed and prayed and before she went she prayed 'Oh, my, oh, my' over and over again, and I knew she was thinking of you. She was too good for me, I guess, and God took her away. But he gave you back. The corn — isn't the corn good this year? And the tobacco is so high and it's only June. And the cows, they're giving milk something tremendous this spring. Will the Army take you again?"

"It's over, Pop. I've been discharged."

"You have? Well, thank God. It was terrible while it lasted. Haha, even Teddy hasn't forgotten you. Look at him wag his tail." His laughter didn't boom like it used to do. "Is your leg sore that you limp like that?"

Someone opened up the window on the second floor and threw out a quilt to air and at the same time stuck her head out with her waist-long hair hanging down like Rapunzel's. Aunt Magdalena had just washed her hair. "Mastie's home!" she said, and drew in her head.

"Come in," said Pop.

"Not like this." He was wearing his uniform, of course, unwashed for three days.

"Well, we won't have you undressing in the front lawn. What did they teach you in the Army?" The old man pushed the boy in ahead of him.

"Mastie's home," said Pop.

Mastie's home. How good it sounded to him. The house still smelled like a cool water cistern and peaches.

496

"Sit down," said Pop. "Mastie's home," he said, going into the next room.

Mastie sat down on the chair awkwardly. He wasn't used to walking distances on this leg yet. The table shook and a little pitcher of milk on the other end fell off and broke on the floor.

Mastie leaped under the table and hung onto the leg. "What was that? What was that?" he said. "Don't let me go to sleep, Sister." He looked around the room, clinging to the leg. "Wake me if you see me dozing. I see terrible things in my dreams. Frightful things. I see puddles of blood and a body. I see a man without a head walking with his head under his arm, and there's a German helmet on it. I see him every night. It's queer, ain't it, Sister? Could you put something in my milk to make me sleep? *Please!*" He changed to a falsetto voice. "It's nerves, you know, Mastie." He changed back. "I didn't know I had a nerve in my body before." He went to the falsetto again. "Can't you sleep?" "No, my heart keeps pumping and pumping. May I smoke? Sister! There he is again. He's coming to me . . . Sister! . . ." He was panting.

Aunt Magdalena looked around fearfully.

Then Mastie let go of the table leg and lay down on the floor. "Jesus. . . . Jesus," he said.

"Isaac!" said Magdalena, holding her head as if she were about to faint.

Pop got down on the floor beside Mastie and put his hands on his shoulders. "You're home, Mastie. Everything's okay."

"Jesus, Jesus," said Mastie, and after a long silence he sat up and looked at them. He smiled helplessly. "I'm sorry," he said. "I have dreams . . ."

and he gestured wordlessly with his hands to show how frightening they were.

"It was rough, wasn't it?" said Pop. "Lena, get him a cup of tea."

"Terrible things . . ." said Mastie. "I've done terrible things." He stood up with difficulty on his one good leg and sat back on the chair. "Tell me to leave, Pop, and I will."

"Don't be ridiculous," said Pop. "Are you okay, now? I think you should take a bath and we have some new clothes for you. . . . Do you feel up to it? Would you like to lay down on the summer porch?"

"I'm okay," said Mastie. He began to strip in the center of the kitchen, first the hat, then the uniform shirt, the shoes, the stockings. . . .

"Your foot," said Aunt Lena. "I didn't know. . . ."

"Yes," said Mastie, and peeled off his pants, showing the leg which was real down to three inches above the knee and then a beautiful leather and steel one with buckles that had taken him three months of massaging and exercises to learn to walk on.

"War," said the old man bitterly, between his teeth.

"Let's get these clothes on and then you can take your bath.

"Can you take a bath?" he said, gesturing toward Mastie's leg. There was an uncomfortable silence.

"I can do anything with it," He unbuckled it and began to skip around the room. They watched him curiously. Suddenly Pop laughed. Then Aunt Lena laughed. Uncle Eli laughed.

"Lena, bring the clothes. Lena had them made up," explained Pop. "We measured from your old clothes, but we didn't know you were so skinny. We'll put something on your ribs. Lena's in charge of the supper." Lena winked.

It was a tailor-made set of clothes — black trousers, a white shirt with a pin for the collar, a black vest, contrasting white suspenders, a coat with a Mennonite collar, and a light straw dress hat. He stepped into them. "All good except for the hair," said Lena and she rubbed his short hair behind and shook her head.

"And this," said Pop and he brought a gold-cased pocket watch with a long golden chain.

"Yours?" said Mastie.

"Mine," said Pop, and he gave him the beautiful pocket watch.

"Get a mirror, Eli. Lena, you have marked what you're going to mark? Get it over with. This boy wants a bath." Lena got down on her knees and began to take in the cloth a bit at Mastie's waist and pin it where it needed to be taken in.

The face in the mirror wasn't a healthy Mennonite face — it was peaked and whiskered and there was something in the eyes that said, *Can I trust you?* and then a moment later, *I want to trust you.* He smiled at himself and put on the hat. He rubbed his short hair on top and looked at his father and shook his head. "Terrible, huh?" He began to laugh and laugh and Lena looked frightened. Now what? He leaned against her and hugged her. "Beautiful," he said, referring to his clothes. She smiled.

"Okay, the bath," said Pop and he wrinkled his nose. "How long has it been? Food, Lena, food! Is it cooking yet?"

When the bath was done, Mastie sat in his new clothes in the parlor. He felt clean and good. He sat down in a new chair and in a moment Pop came in.

"Tell me about it," Pop said.

Mastie looked around the room. It had a familiar feel to it. He felt warm. For some reason he remembered a Sunday when he was a small boy sitting on his father's lap in the carriage, a blanket over them, while it rained and rained three feet away.

"I was in the hospital already when I woke up," Mastie said. His father nodded. He was sitting on the rocking chair opposite with his bearded chin propped on his hand. "You see, it was smashed hopelessly — there wasn't any way they could have fixed it."

"Did you have good doctors?"

"Sure, they were good, but they had hundreds of patients. Each one of them. Anyway, here I was with my left leg up in the air — you know the pulley contraptions that they have — traction, that's it. I was in traction with a big sandbag on the end to hold the leg up. I didn't know it, but I already didn't have the leg."

"They didn't ask you about taking off the leg?"

"How could they, Pop? I was unconscious."

"They should have waited. If you could have told them you were a farmer and needed that leg — "

"No, Pop. There's an awful lot of gangrene in those hospitals. It smells terrible. They couldn't wait. I don't know if I'd have made it at all if it hadn't been for Christiana. She was a nurse — a Catholic nurse, but don't let that scare you. She was the most beautiful lady — I mean her character. She wasn't nothing to look at. For one thing she was fat, but she had a heart in her. . . . Anyway, there

I was with one and a half legs and I was dreaming about the men I'd killed."

"Killed?" said Pop.

"Hundreds of them."

"Mastie!"

"I told you I did terrible things," said Mastie and he shook his head. "I'm a killer." He looked at his father. "If you want me to stop, I will, but the good part of my story's still coming."

"Thou shalt not kill," said Pop in a soft voice. "Lord, forgive us."

"Yes, he does!" said Mastie and he jumped up. "It makes me want to shout! I was just like Saint Paul on the road to Damascus. I had my eyes opened." He sat down again. "Did I tell you about Christiana? Yes, I guess I did. Well, she was praying for me, you see. I was having nightmares and I'd wake up trembling all over and she'd be there holding my hand. She didn't even know me. And it wasn't nothing romantic, Pop. She was fifty."

"No, no," said Pop, shaking his head to indicate that the romantic idea hadn't even entered his head.

"Well, there was a picture in this room. Let me tell you how the hospital was. I mean — it wasn't a hospital — it was a church with one side blowed off and the stained glass in smithereens from the bombs. It made a dandy hospital. Anyway, there was a picture, a picture as big as you and me standing on top of each other, hanging on the end wall — but I had never seen it before. I wasn't looking for pictures. All I was looking for was my meals or someone to talk to, but Christiana, bless her heart, she sat me up in bed on this particular night and she pointed out the picture to me. I said, 'Who's that?' I couldn't figure it out right away — you know how paintings are. And she said, 'That's Jesus.' Wasn't that something?

"I got to noticing this picture in the daylight. I didn't have anything else to do. They didn't have any books. The men on both sides of me were too sick to talk. And it was his eyes that struck me. They weren't happy eyes. No. They weren't miserable eyes either. They was what you might say . . . asking eyes. I didn't think anything about it right then."

Pop wasn't rocking on his chair. He was only listening.

"It was getting toward Christmas, Pop. I couldn't make up my mind if I was coming back or not because I knew what you said."

"What's that?"

"About going to hell. I knew it was true."

"I never said that, Mastie. I never said you were going to hell."

"I knew I did terrible things."

"Now I want it straight," said Pop, raising his finger. "I never said you were going to hell and you know it."

"I don't want to argue, Pop. I thought you said so."

"No. No!"

"Anyway, it was Christmastime."

"Yes, go on with the story."

"And I didn't know about coming home. But Annie kept writing."

"Thank the Lord for Annie," said Pop. "Thank him for her, Mastie. She's a genuine diamone stone."

"One night I had the nightmare again, and when I woke up I heard singing. I heard children singing, and I thought, "It's all over now. I'm dead. But

502

why are children singing happy songs if I'm dead? Where I'm going there won't be no happy songs.' Then I noticed Jesus looked at me. Yes, those eyes were looking right at me — I could see it like I see you now — and those eyes were asking and asking — "

"What were they asking?" said Pop.

"They were asking, 'Who are you running away from?' and I said, 'I don't know.' Then he said, 'It's me. *Why?*' And I said, 'I've done awful things — I don't want to die,' and he said, 'You can be forgiven. Here. Here, touch me.' Then I reached out to him and I could feel the dips in his hand where the nails had been stuck through and the dip in his side that the spear put there, and I said, 'Jesus! Jesus!'

"The next thing I was lying half out of my bed, with my leg still up in traction, and I was sweating and sweating and Sister Christiana came up and I said, 'Did you hear him?' And right away she seemed to know who I meant because she turned around and looked at Jesus. It was that real, Pop! I said to her, 'Christiana, I want to be baptized.' And the next morning she brought in a Catholic priest and he baptized me. Was it wrong, Pop?"

"Praise God!" The old man said.

"I'm a different man, Pop," said Mastie. "I mean I'm the same but I'm different. I'm clean."

"Praise God!" The old man said again.

"After that I wanted to come home to Annie. But she said she wouldn't go away with me to marry. She just kept working at me and working at me and finally I said, 'Okay, I'll come back and meet you, Pop.' And she was right."

Pop was visibly moved by the story. He began to sing in his cracked, off-key voice the hymn, "Praise

God from Whom all Blessings Flow." Then he got up and shook Mastie's hand.

"We're going to celebrate," he said. "Now you go get some sleep."

3

In less than two hours, Pop had told his friends.
"Good news! Good news! My boy's home!" The
horse was breathing hard and its sides were wet
and steaming. He drove the buggy back through
Susquehannock on his way home. In the post office
window two men were standing with their hands on
their hips, making a business deal in front of the
public telephone.

Five hundred feet beyond the window, Pop got an
idea. He wheeled the horse around in the road and
drove back to the post office. The two men looked
at him as he came in. They nodded respectfully.
The war was over, after all.

"Horse looks lathered up," said the clerk.

"My boy's home," said Pop.

"Oh," said the clerk.

"Home from France," said Pop.

"Oh, it was the one in France," said the clerk.
"The one that got the medal. There's a fine boy."
He shook his head and grinned. "Fine boy, Ike."

"I want to use the telephone," Pop said. "Call
Kansas for me."

"Kansas?"

"Ft. Leavenworth."

The clerk looked at him and reached for the telephone. He spoke to the operator. Then he looked back at Pop.

"The prison?" he said.

"Yes."

It took a while for the call to go through. In the meantime, the clerk went on sorting the pile of mail in front of him. Pop took off his hat and wiped the sweat off his bald spot. He set his hat on again. The clerk looked up.

"That your other boy?" he said.

"Yes."

The clerk lit a cigar. "There won't be any amnesty," he said, "Not for those boys. Your average American wouldn't stand for it. He don't forget. Two hundred and fifty thousand casualties! Two hundred and fifty thousand! You see what I mean." He smiled and shrugged his shoulder. There was nothing in the way he smiled that betrayed his membership in the War Bonds vigilantes. The operator rang and the clerk answered. "She has Leavenworth," he said. "Who was it you wanted?"

"My boy, Ira," said Pop. "Ira Stoltzfus."

There was another long wait. The prison officers were reluctant. The clerk looked up at Pop again.

"You know how it is. I mean, it is a prison." He looked at the telephone suddenly. "Hello, hello. He's here, Ike."

Pop smiled. The clerk turned the mouthpiece around for him.

"Hello. Hello. Ira?"

"Are you the prisoner's father?" A voice said at the other end.

"Yes."

"Okay."

506

"Hello," a voice said.

"I want to speak to my son, Ira."

"Pop!"

"Is that you, Ira?"

"It's expensive, isn't it, Pop?"

"How are you?"

Silence.

"Ira?"

"Not so good," Ira said.

Pop switched to Dutch. "*Smacht nichts aus.* [It doesn't matter.) It won't be long, Ira. They're talking about amnesty in the papers."

A voice interrupted the conversation. "All right, speak in English or we'll cut you off. What's wrong, English ain't good enough for you?"

"We have to speak in English," Ira said.

"Yes. I have good news," Pop said. "Mastie's home! *Lobe Gott!*" (Thank God!)

"Mmm." There was a long interval of static over the line. Pop shook the earpiece at his end.

"What do you have? Static?" The clerk said.

"Hello. Hello." Pop raised his voice . "Hello." The static stopped. "Ira, hello. Can you hear me?"

"Yes."

"Did you hear what I said? Mastie's home!"

"Mmm."

"I wish you were here with us. I wish you could see him. He's lost — " Pop could hardly say it. "He's lost a leg. A leg, Ira. What can a farmer do with one leg? But he's good on the wooden one they gave him. Are you still there?"

"I know what soldiers are like," Ira said.

"He's not a soldier anymore."

"Oh, yeah? Why did he come home? Tell me

that? He's back for money, that's what, Pop."

"No."

"He won't stay around long. Did you think he came back to stay? Not Mastie. Maybe he came for Annie — well, if I was her, I'd be careful. Soldiers I knew in camp carried all kinds of diseases I would hate to mention."

"Ira!"

"We put him out of church."

"Who asked to have him put out? I did. Then who has the right to decide if he's worthy to come back? I do."

"Has he made a church confession?" said Ira. "Is he sorry for all the things he did? Do you think we'll ever know the half of them?"

"No, no, no!" said the old man. He was getting angry. "I wish you could hear him talk."

"War stories, huh? They're pretty exciting for us nonresistants, huh?"

"They aren't war stories." Pop switched back to Dutch unconsciously. "God has found him, Ira. You should hear him talk. I'd give — I'd give my right arm if your mother could be here today to hear him. Maybe she saw from heaven. Yes, I'm sure she did. She was rejoicing with me."

"So now what?" said Ira. "He'll go join Rydell's church where you can be a Christian and a soldier. Bloody Christians, huh?"

"Ira! Stop. I forbid it. Don't talk."

"Okay, so I'll. . . ."

"Don't talk. You listen to me. What did your time in camp do to you? It made you a scoffer. It made you unforgiving."

"I'm surprised you mention *me*," said Ira. "You

always take his side. He was your favorite. It was Mom and me, and you and Mastie."

"No!" said Pop. "There were never favorites. Listen, I want to tell you something. You did the right thing — yes you did — and he went wrong. But he came home, Ira. What about Moses and David and Abraham in the Bible? What kind of men do you think they were? It doesn't say anywhere that they were good men. You're a man. You know what that story about Bathsheba means. But the Bible says David is in heaven. Why? Because he was a good man? No! Because he loved the Lord God and was sorry for what he did. Sure, he was punished. His little babies died. And don't you think your brother hasn't been punished for what he did. Don't think it. But we forgive a boy when he's sorry," Pop said. And now his voice pleaded, "If you can't forgive him, then I want to know, have you ever been forgiven? Do you know what it feels like?"

Ira was quiet on the other end.

"Do you?" said Pop. "Our Lord said, 'He who has been forgiven much, forgives much, and he who has only been forgiven a little, only forgives a little.' That's the Bible — that isn't your father speaking. How do you think I learned that? Ira, Ira . . . it came hard. Your mother passed away — was that God's way of telling me to forgive my son in France? How could I preach about love and not practice it? Do you see? The Bible calls such people tinkling cymbals. 'Though I speak with the tongues of men and of angels and have not charity' — meaning love — 'it profiteth me nothing. I am become a tinkling cymbal.' Do you see, son?"

Something clicked on the phone. "It's about time

I go," said Ira. "They chain us to the cell here. We have to stand all day."

A voice interrupted on the other. "I told you no foreign languages."

"Ira . . ." Pop said. The connection was broken. Pop hung the earpiece up. He dropped his hat on the counter and stared vacantly at the clerk. "Tinkling cymbals . . ." he said.

The clerk looked at him curiously. Pop took out his wallet and paid.

4

"Guests!" said Aunt Lena from the kitchen.

"Guests?" said Mastie.

"Guests." While he slept, huge bowls of food had filled the table. Pots were cooking on the stove. Outside in the yard young men were tying their horses fast to the trees and barnyard fence, or parking their Model-Ts carefully. All of them were dressed in their Sunday best.

"You'd think we'd been expecting you, huh, Mastie?" said Lena. "But we weren't really. We didn't know whether you were coming today or tomorrow."

"Is this a party?"

"They want to meet you, Mastie."

The guests began to come in, dozens of them. Some of them were boys Mastie had known for years, bringing their new wives, and there was the bishop's son with his wife and baby.

"Benjie!"

To Mastie's amazement, Benjie was wearing a new Mennonite coat. The defiant cocky look he had always had was somehow suppressed.

"Glad to have you back," said Benjie. They shook hands. "Lost a lot of weight, didn't you? Didn't they feed you in the Army? Yeah, this is our little one," he said. His wife smiled shyly and opened the blankets up enough for Mastie to see a red yawning face. Mastie shook his head.

"Look at that," he said.

"Make you jealous?" said Benjie, and they all laughed.

"Farming?" said Mastie. They were both awkward.

"Annie's here," said Aunt Lena at the kitchen door.

"Where?"

"On the back porch."

"Excuse me." He walked through the house, trying not to limp. On the way a cousin stopped him.

"Mastie." They shook hands. He walked through the dining room and out through the screen door. She was sitting on the back porch with her parents. They all three rose when he opened the door. There was an awkward silence. Her father extended his hand.

"Mastie," he said. Mastie stepped forward to shake his hand and immediately he felt her eyes go to his leg. Her mother shook his hand and nodded politely.

Annie extended her hand to him. It was rough and suntanned. They had been planting tobacco for several weeks already. "Mastie," she said. They shook hands and he looked at her. Her face was also suntanned already. Something turned over in his stomach. She breathed in sharply and bit her lip. She was going to cry.

"Well, let's go in," said her father to Mastie. "Why don't you folks go first?"

Annie walked past him into the house. He followed, and as soon as they were in the dining room he caught up with her and wrapped his arms around her from behind. She turned and her body felt wonderful against him. Her eyes said, *Yes.*

"Well!" said Mrs. Beiler. "Right in public. Jonas, really...."

Not now, Annie's eyes said.

"Annie," said Mrs. Beiler. He let her go.

Benjie and his wife were standing on the sun porch, looking at the potted plants. "Well..." said Benjie, looking at Annie.

"Annie!" His wife said. They hugged each other. They were old friends, and immediately Benjie's wife began to talk about the baby.

"How's old Sol?" said Mastie, meaning Benjie's brother Sol. He couldn't take his eyes off Annie.

"Who knows?"

"He ain't around anymore?"

"Run off and never come back."

"Is that right — you got no idea where he is? What about Glickie?" He slapped his hands together. "Old Glickie. Me and him used to race our teams down Route 49. Remember the time we rubbed hubcaps? Aye yai yai."

"Glickie's dead," said the bishop's son.

"Glickie's dead?"

"Yep. Ran away to the Army like you did and got gassed. Mustard gas, is that what it's called?"

"No!"

"Yep. And little Ezra. You remember little Ezra with the clubfoot? Ezra got spiritual." Annie was kissing the baby.

"Ezra got spiritual?"

"Yep. Got spiritual in the objectors' camp, I guess, and joined the Pentecostals. Now everytime you see him he has to tell you his testimony."

"Things have been happening to me too," Mastie said.

"They sure have," Benjie said. "We all read about you in the paper."

"Not that," Mastie said. "Jesus." He grinned.

Benjie looked over his face silently. "Oh," he said. He nodded his head and turned to join his wife, "I think we're holding up the line," he said. They walked away into the kitchen.

"Don't you ever ask me to write you another letter or I'll spank you," said Mastie. Annie was standing by the window screen of the sun porch, looking at him.

"I won't. I don't need letters anymore."

"Will you need help with the tobacco this year? I got to get some work."

"You're staying on the farm? I'm glad, Mastie."

"What's wrong? Who's tired of farm life? It's the best. When you see other ways, then you see it's the best."

"I'll be a cream puff when you start keeping me out late at nights again. I'll just fall asleep for you."

"I don't mind if you're asleep with me."

"Mastie." She slapped his hand. She was losing her stiffness gradually.

And here was Bishop Moses and the deacon. They held out their hands and shook with Mastie. They nodded to Annie. The bishop looked at Mastie's hair as they went into the kitchen.

"How long will it be until your hair grows out?" said Annie. The conversation hopped from stone to stone. There was too much to say to know where to begin. But Annie didn't say everything she thought.

She was thinking, how skinny he looked, and his
eyes, why they flickered back and forth like that,
hardly still for a second. They were not quiet steady
eyes like her father's, for example. He seemed ill
at ease here, and that was strange. It was his own
house. His voice also sounded tired. How bad was his
leg? There was one good thing though. When he
smiled, it was a smile to melt her. She thought his
smile had gotten better over the years and as
they stood there on the sun porch, meeting the
guests, she lived from smile to smile. Now it was
gone and there were only the jerking eyes in the
skinny white face, and suddenly, he smiled again!

"I just want to kiss you to pieces," he whispered,
but it was almost out loud. "Schnoogli-boogli," he
added. She turned red and looked around as if to see
if anyone had heard.

Mastie didn't say everything he was thinking
either. He was thinking that she seemed innocent and
quaint. What had she seen of life in comparison with
the French girls who had been through the war? Her
eyes were placid and trusting. They gazed on him
with such trust that it frightened him — didn't she
know he was a killer? But she was also more self-
confident and not about to fall apart, even if he
walked out the door and never came back. That was
a change. He wasn't sure he liked it.

Pop came in.

"Pop, what is this anyway?" said Mastie.

"Well, who do we have here?" said Pop, and he
pinched Annie's cheek. She laughed.

"Pop, what is this?"

"What does it look like?"

"A party."

"Okay, then it's a party."

"It looks more like a wedding."

"Good as a wedding to me," said Pop. He put his arm around Mastie. "I've waited a long time, son." He looked at Annie and winked. Then he laughed. "But all my boys are the same to me, Mastie, I want them all home. I never had favorites. No, no! Don't you ever think it. Now come on in and be friendly when you get tired of each other." He went into the kitchen. It was getting dark.

The guests had begun eating.

Pop walked to the open window and looked out across the lawn. A rosebush was down there in the dark, smelling sweet. The house cast its light out across the lawn and lit up a few horses. Beyond that, everything was dark. For a moment it seemed to Pop that his lighted house was like the Mennonite community and happy sounds were coming from its windows. His boy was home! But Pop wasn't as happy as he had thought he would be. Out there somewhere beyond the light and the sound of their voices was Ira. Beyond their reach. He didn't even have an Annie to pull him back. Out there somewhere the devil and God were gambling for his son.

He turned around and walked to the living room.

"Hey, Mastie, you still play the mouth organ?" said Benjie, the bishop's boy. "Here, catch!" He threw him one. Pop held up his hand.

"Now the order of the program is this," said Pop. "We're glad you're all here." And he opened his arms up wide as if to welcome them. "Maybe it's wrong to be proud, but I'm proud. There he sits, my boy, and I didn't know if I'd see him again. But we're glad he's back. Welcome back, Mastie."

516

The old man's voice trembled and now his sinuses began to act up. He cleared his throat once and then again. "Excuse me. It's an allergy," he said. "Tobacco dust, that's what does it." He cleared his throat again. "I want to give you a special welcome back, Mastie." He began to clap and looked around at everybody else for a little support. They set down their soup dishes and clapped with him.

"Now the order of the program is this," repeated Pop. He cleared his throat again, "Food — you found the food all right, but there's more chicken corn soup. Aunt Leah?"

"There's another bucketful," said Leah, standing up and looking over the crowd to see if anyone wanted some.

"There's more corn soup," said Pop. "The next item on the program is a story from Mastie and then we'll have a little music."

"Yahoo!" shouted someone in the sort of voice one uses to cough the week out of his lungs on a Saturday night. Everybody laughed.

"But first the story," said Pop.

"A story?" Mastie said.

"Sure, did you think you were getting this meal for free? Nothing's free anymore, not since rationing." The people laughed. They knew what he was talking about.

"What kind of a story?"

"Any kind you want to tell us," said Pop and he grinned. Something about Pop's face made Mastie want to laugh. Pop's face turned sober. "One thing first that I want you all to know. *It's an artificial leg*. Pull up your pants leg and show them,

517

Mastie. Okay, gawk now and get it over with."

Mastie pulled up his pant leg.

"I knew it," Annie said. "I knew it." She clutched his arm. Mastie rolled down his pant leg and stood up.

"I really only have one story," he said. Then he grinned and Annie noticed it again. Over the years his smile had definitely gotten better.

THE AUTHOR

Kenneth Reed describes himself as "a Christian of the Mennonite *Freundschaft*, a little over six feet, age 29, graduated from Lancaster Mennonite High and Eastern Mennonite College, formerly an English teacher in Asahikawa, Japan, and an editor at Mennonite Publishing House, unmarried, and a tax-paying resident of Paradise, Pennsylvania."